THE WRITER'S
CHAPBOOK

ALSO BY GEORGE PLIMPTON

The Rabbit's Umbrella (for children)

Out of My League

Writers at Work, Volumes I–VIII (ed.)

Paper Lion

The Bogey Man

The American Literary Anthology, Volumes I–III (ed.)

American Journey: The Times of Robert F. Kennedy (with Jean Stein)

Pierre's Book (ed.)

Mad Ducks and Bears

One for the Record

One More July

Shadow Box

Sports (with Neil Leiffer)

A Sports Bestiary (with Arnold Roth)

Edie: An American Biography (with Jean Stein)

D.V. (with Christopher Hemphill)

Fireworks: A History and Celebration

Open Net

The Curious Case of Sidd Finch

The Writer's
Chapbook

A COMPENDIUM OF FACT, OPINION, WIT, AND
ADVICE FROM THE 20TH CENTURY'S
PREEMINENT WRITERS

Edited from *The Paris Review* interviews
and with an Introduction by

George Plimpton

VIKING

VIKING

Published by the Penguin Group
Viking Penguin, a division of Penguin Books USA Inc.,
40 West 23rd Street, New York, New York 10010, U.S.A.
Penguin Books Ltd, 27 Wrights Lane,
London W8 5TZ, England
Penguin Books Australia Ltd, Ringwood,
Victoria, Australia
Penguin Books Canada Ltd, 2801 John Street,
Markham, Ontario, Canada L3R 1B4
Penguin Books (N.Z.) Ltd, 182–190 Wairau Road,
Auckland 10, New Zealand

Penguin Books Ltd, Registered Offices:
Harmondsworth, Middlesex, England

First published in 1989 by Viking Penguin,
a division of Penguin Books USA Inc.

This collection is derived from interviews first
published in *The Paris Review*, some of which also
appeared in the *Writers at Work* series edited by
Mr. Plimpton and published by Viking Penguin.

Library of Congress Cataloging in Publication Data
The Writer's chapbook / edited by George Plimpton ; introduction by
George Plimpton.
p.   cm.

1. Authors—20th century—Interviews.   2. Authorship.
I. Plimpton, George.
PN453.W7   1989
810'.9'005—dc19
[B]   88-40277

Printed in the United States of America
Set in Perpetua
Designed by Ann Gold

In gratitude to
E. M. Forster
and to both interviewers
and interviewed

I don't know exactly how it's done. I let it alone
a good deal.   —*Saul Bellow*

A writer is somebody for whom writing is more
difficult than it is for other people.
                              —*Thomas Mann*

There are three rules for writing the novel.
Unfortunately, no one knows what they are.
                              —*Somerset Maugham*

READER: Miss Moore, your poetry is very difficult
  to read.
MARIANNE MOORE: It is very difficult to write.

NOTE

Following, in alphabetical order, are the names of the interviewers, with their subjects in parentheses. In many cases, the authors were interviewed by more than one person.

Zoltan Abadi-Nagy (William Gaddis, Walker Percy), Nelson W. Aldrich, Jr. (James Jones), Alston Anderson (Nelson Algren), Gene Andrewski (Lawrence Durrell), Franklin Ashley (James Dickey), Jeffrey Bailey (Paul Bowles), James Baker (John Fowles), Michael Barbar (Kingsley Amis, Anthony Powell), Lawrence Bensky (Harold Pinter), Ted Berrigan (Jack Kerouac), Sven Birkerts (Joseph Brodsky), William Brandon, trans. (Blaise Cendrars), Elizabeth Pell Broadwell (Erskine Caldwell), Peter Buckman (Robert Graves), Edwina Burress (P. L. Travers), John Burrows (Joyce Cary), Chris Busa (Stanley Kunitz), William Cahill (John Hall Wheelock), Marion Capron (Dorothy Parker), Olga Carlisle (Arthur Miller), Alfred Chester (Ralph Ellison), Ronald Christ (Jorge Luis Borges, Pablo Neruda), Gerald Clarke (Allen Ginsberg, Gore Vidal, P. G. Wodehouse), William Cole (S. J. Perelman), Carvel Collins (Georges Simenon), Frank Crowther (E. B. White), John Cullinan (Anthony Burgess), J. Darribehaude (Louis-Ferdinand Céline), Jonathan Dee (John Hersey), Benjamin DeMott (Archibald MacLeish), Carolyn Doty (Jessamyn West), Jordan Elgrably (James Baldwin, Edmund White), H. McCloy Ellison (Richard Wilbur), Ralph Ellison (Robert Penn Warren), Duncan Fallowell (Arthur Koestler), Harold Fender (Isaac Bashevis Singer), Jim Fergus (Jim Harrison), Paul Fergusson (John Gardner), William Fifield (Jean Cocteau, Robert Graves), William Flannagan (Edward Albee), Edwin Frank (Robert Fitzgerald), Ray Frazer (Aldous Huxley), B. Frechtman, trans. (Simone de Beauvoir), Thomas Frick (J. G. Ballard, Doris Lessing), John S. Friedman (Elie Wiesel), Blair Fuller (Françoise Sagan), P. N. Furbank (E. M. Forster),

NOTE

Madelein Gobeil (Simone de Beauvoir), Herbert Gold (Vladimir Nabokov), Richard H. Goldstone (Thornton Wilder), Annette Grant (John Cheever), Sinda Gregory (Thomas McGuane), Jerry Griswold (P. L. Travers), J. Guenot (Louis-Ferdinand Céline), Rita Guibert (Pablo Neruda), Shusha Guppy (Eugène Ionesco, Rosamond Lehmann, Edna O'Brien, Alain Robbe-Grillet, Tom Stoppard, Marguerite Yourcenar), Allan Gurganus (Hortense Calisher), Donald Hall (T. S. Eliot, Marianne Moore, Ezra Pound), Alex Hamilton (Joyce Cary), Ron Hansen (John Irving), Gordon Lloyd Harper (Saul Bellow), F. J. H. Haskell (E. M. Forster), Rosemary Herbert (John Mortimer), Fayette Hickox (J. P. Donleavy), E. Clay High (Derek Walcott, Richard Wilbur), Pati Hill (Truman Capote), Edward Hirsch (William Meredith, W. S. Merwin), Ronald Wesley Hoag (Erskine Caldwell), Anne Hollander (Lillian Hellman), Vilma Howard (Ralph Ellison), Jannika Hurwitt (Nadine Gordimer, Peter Levi), Julian Jebb (Evelyn Waugh), Edmund Keeley (George Seferis), Barbara Kevles (Anne Sexton), Conrad Knickerbocker (William Burroughs), Stanley Koehler (William Carlos Williams), Linda Kuehl (Joan Didion, Eudora Welty), Rocco Landesman (Jerzy Kosinski), Thomas LeClair (William Gass, Stanley Elkin), Hermione Lee (Philip Roth), John leMarchand, trans. (François Mauriac), Alfred MacAdam (Gillermo Cabrera Infante, Carlos Fuentes), Lewis MacAdams, Jr. (Robert Creeley), John R. Maier (John Gardner), Gerard Malanga (David Ignatow), Michael Manoll (Blaise Cendrars), Steven Marcus (Norman Mailer), Lucas Matthiessen (Irwin Shaw), Peter Matthiessen (William Styron), Sara Matthiessen (John Gardner), Larry McCaffery (Thomas McGuane), John McCall (Malcolm Cowley), J. D. McClatchy (John Hollander, James Merrill), Frank McConnell (John Gardner), Andrew McCord (Robert Fitzgerald), Pamela McCordick (Hortense Calisher), Jeanne McCulloch (Leon Edel), Molly McKaughan (J. P. Donleavy, John Hall Wheelock), David Michaelis (Kurt Vonnegut), Michael Millgate (Angus Wilson), Barbara Milton (Margaret Drabble), Julian Mitchell (Lawrence Durrell), Willie Morris (Irwin Shaw), Michael Newman (W. H. Auden), Elisabeth Niebuhr (Mary McCarthy), J. D. O'Hara (Donald Barthelme), John Phillips (Lillian Hellman), Robert Phillips (William Goyen, Philip Larkin, Joyce Carol Oates, Karl Shapiro), Darryl Pinckney (Elizabeth Hardwick), George Plimpton (John Barth, Malcolm Cowley, E. L. Doctorow, Joseph Heller, Ernest Hemingway, William Kennedy, Jerzy Kosinski, William Maxwell, Dorothy Parker, S. J. Perelman, William Styron, James Thurber, Kurt

NOTE

Vonnegut, E. B. White), Richard Poirier (Robert Frost), Dotson Rader (Tennessee Williams), Simon Raven (Graham Greene), Richard Rhodes (Kurt Vonnegut), Lloyd Richards (Athol Fugard), Charles Ruas (Carlos Fuentes), Christian Salmon (Milan Kundera), Charles Thomas Sammuels (John Updike), David Sanders (John Dos Passos), Karen Saum (May Sarton), W. I. Scobie (Christopher Isherwood), John Seabrook (William Maxwell), Frederick Seidel (Robert Lowell), James Sherwood, trans. (Louis-Ferdinand Cèline), Elisabeth Sifton (Robertson Davies), Robert B. Silvers (Françoise Sagan), Mona Simpson (Hortense Calisher, Philip Levine, Raymond Carver), Terry Southern (Nelson Algren, Henry Green), Elizabeth Spires (Elizabeth Bishop), Max Steele (James Thurber), Jean Stein (William Faulkner), John Steinbeck (from his letters), Daniel Stern (Bernard Malamud), Peter Stitt (John Ashbery, John Berryman, Stephen Spender, James Wright), Peter H. Stone (Gabriel García Márquez), Mira Stout (William Trevor), Rose Styron (Arthur Miller), Tom Teicholz (Cynthia Ozick), Barbara Thompson (Katherine Anne Porter, Peter Taylor), John Train (François Mauriac), Quentin Vest (Andrei Voznesensky), Elizabeth Vreeland (Jean Rhys), Linda Wagner (Robert Creeley), Eugene Walter (Isak Dinesen, Robert Penn Warren), Marina Warner (Rebecca West), Regina Weinreich (Francine du Plessix Gray), Jason Weiss (Julio Cortázar), Anthony Whittier (Frank O'Connor), George Wickes (Aldous Huxley, Henry Miller), Robert Hunter Wilbur (Conrad Aiken), A. Leslie Wilson (Heinrich Böll), William Crawford Woods (Robert Stone, Andrei Voznesensky), and Richard Ziegfield (James Laughlin).

CONTENTS

CONTENTS

INTRODUCTION

In 1953 *The Paris Review,* a fledgling literary quarterly, initiated a series of interviews with famous writers on their craft. For over thirty-five years it has continued to do so—with frequently a pair of interviews in each issue. Nearly two hundred novelists, poets, biographers, and essayists have talked about their work and how they go about it. Viking Penguin has collected many of these interviews in a series of volumes entitled *Writers at Work.*

The purpose of this present volume is to cull what the various authors have said about specific topics and present these under a series of headings—the focus on subject matter rather than author. Thus, if a reader is curious about the importance of "plot" to the novelist, under that heading in the *Chapbook* are to be found any number of comments and views on that particular subject. It saves browsing through all the issues of the *Review,* which in sum would stretch the length of a twenty-foot library shelf.

In a sense that is behind the choice of "Chapbook" for the book's title—that a volume is provided in which it is less time-consuming (and expensive) to find what one is looking for. There the comparison ends! The original chapbooks were sold in medieval times by a "chapman" (hence the common family name), an itinerant peddler who in the village square sold little rag-paper booklets about Tom Thumb, Reynard the Fox, and other such folk heroes.

A word about the arrangement of this book. It has been divided into four major sections. The first is a kind of general profile of the writer in which the major steps in a literary career are arranged chronologically—starting from earliest influences (childhood reading, early mentors) through the initial impulse for becoming a writer, then to the actual process of creation (the inspiration for a work, first drafts, work habits [the quintessential *Paris Review* question: Do you use a pen or a pencil?], and so forth) and finally on to publication and the effects of success or failure along with observations, quite pithy, on critics.

Next is a section in which the writers talk about the actual mechanics of writing: plot, characters, symbols, experimental work, writer's block, the use of artificial stimulants among them. Here we discover that when W. H. Auden took LSD experimentally, "nothing much happened, but I did get the distinct impression that some birds were trying to communicate with me."

In the third section the writers are concerned with different fields of writing—journalism, the theater, children's books, the short story, writing for the film, free-lancing. Of this last, John Cheever describes an assignment from the *Saturday Evening Post* to do an interview with Sophia Loren. He accepted the offer. "I got to kiss her. I've had other offers but nothing as good."

The final section focuses on the social life of the writer (writers' colonies, readings, teaching jobs, grants, and the like). In the interviews authors tended to talk most engagingly about their contemporaries; this section contains a number of these "portraits"—Malcolm Cowley on Ford Madox Ford, Aldous Huxley on James Joyce, Robert Frost on Ezra Pound, James Laughlin on Gertrude Stein, among them. The section concludes with some views on the future of the written word.

Since the various headings are fairly arbitrary and the authors' statements so often discursive, a cross-checking index has been provided so that under the heading "plot," for instance, the reader will find additional references in other parts of the book. The reader will also note that to provide even further insight into the various topics, each subject is prefaced by a collection of epigrams and quotations from authors as far back as John Heywood (1497?–1580).

A word about *The Paris Review*. The magazine, planned as a literary quarterly, was first published in the spring of 1953. Its policy from the start was to concentrate on publishing fiction and poetry rather than the critical essays which were the mainstay in almost all the literary magazines of the time. Its one concession to critical evaluation was that rather than getting a third party to provide an essay on a contemporary author, it would go to the authors themselves and, using the interview form, ask them firsthand about their work and their working methods. The first author *The Paris Review* went to see was E. M. Forster, then a senior fellow at King's College, Cambridge. He was an admirable choice. Perhaps the greatest living author at the time *(A Passage to India, Howard's End)*, in fact he had not published a novel since 1924. The interview, which was conducted by P. N. Furbank and F. J. H. Haskel, one scribbling down the answers while the other concentrated on the questions (tape recorders were still a few years away), was a feature in the first issue of the *Review* and raised an immediate stir. For in it Forster talked about the problems that made it so difficult for him to write fiction, namely what he called "fiction technicalities." The result furnished the best of patterns for the interviews that followed.

In the introduction to the first volume of *Writers at Work,* Malcolm Cowley suggested why such famous authors as Forster devoted so much of their time to a project from which they had very little to gain. "Some of them disliked the idea of being interviewed," he wrote, "but consented anyway, either out of friendship for someone on the *Review* or because they wanted to help a struggling magazine of the arts, perhaps in memory of their own early struggles to get published. . . . Authors are sometimes like tomcats: they distrust all the other toms, but they are kind to kittens."

Of particular importance to the series was that so many of the writers turned out to be absorbed by the writing process and glad to talk about it—almost as if they had never been asked, and perhaps thought it too self-indulgent to write about. In many cases they added additional material on their own; they were free to make what changes they wished since the intention of the editors was never to think of the interviews as inquisitions but rather as documentations of the authors-at-work.

The series gathered momentum. Because a number of distinguished writers agreed to be interviewed in its earliest numbers—E. M. Forster, François Mauriac, Graham Greene, Irwin Shaw, William Styron, Alberto Moravia, Joyce Cary, Ralph Ellison, Georges Simenon, James Thurber, Nelson Algren, William Faulkner were all in the first four years—the series began to assume the aura of a Pantheon. Writers were pleased to be asked to contribute. There were exceptions, of course—writers who made a point of their reclusivity: Samuel Beckett, J. D. Salinger, Alexander Solzhenitsyn, Thomas Pynchon—but many others agreed who rarely granted interviews: Faulkner, Hemingway, Henry Green. The length of the interviews increased. E. M. Forster's required only fourteen pages of the first issue. Many since have run to forty or fifty pages. The record is the interview of James Laughlin, the poet/publisher, whose reminiscences about his immersion in the literary world ran through two numbers of the magazine.

There is such diversity of opinion in the *Chapbook* that it may be hard to construct a composite writer out of the material at hand. The working habits are different: Hemingway rises at dawn to work; James Baldwin works late at night after the hour is quiet. Truman Capote, Paul Bowles, and Evelyn Waugh often work in bed. Robert Frost takes off a shoe and uses the sole for a desk. John Dos Passos rewrites a chapter seven or eight times. William Kennedy's rewrites of *Legs* stacked up to match the height of his six-year-old son. Yet Eudora Welty only corrects or changes an occasional word; to do more would make her feel that "someone would start looking over my shoulder." Writers have divergent views about the importance of plot. Norman Mailer doesn't work from plots. Neither does Elizabeth Hardwick. She says that if she wants a plot she'll watch the TV series *Dallas*. John Irving disagrees. So does Kurt Vonnegut, who doesn't believe a reader can be satisfied unless the rudiments of an old-fashioned plot are smuggled into the book someplace. Joseph Heller

INTRODUCTION

sees his novels in an astounding blast of insight provoked by a first line which evolves into a whole series of scenes, characters, resolutions. For a time James Merrill used a Ouija board for his creative impulses. E. M. Forster loses control of his characters. They wander away like disembodied puppets. John Cheever is contemptuous of this. So is Nabokov. He refers to his characters as galley slaves.

All this may be confusing to readers who hope to find direction for their own work in fiction or poetry. But then the vast complexity of material suggests that it is possible to come across ideas and comments with which associations can be made: "Ah, that seems to fit," and a key will be provided.

For the general reader, another matter. A reviewer once said of the *Writers at Work* series that a reader could dip into a volume and not reemerge for days. I have had very much that feeling compiling the material for the book. Reading through this series was a time of reacquaintance. The interview is obviously the most direct of relationships; the authors' voices are preeminent. One listens on a summer porch or in a library. It seemed almost an indignity to clip words out of their commentary. But the piles under various headings grew. Sometimes I even hoped the interview would be bland so that nothing had to be clipped. Never the case. The stacks increased. I tried grading the excerpts, thinking to cut down on them. A $-$, B $+$, A $-$, A, A, A $-$. A star class.

Interviews tend to be derided as a form. Too easy. Tape recorders do not necessarily catch true meanings. The interviewers set their machines down nervously on the coffee table. "Do you mind?" No matter. At the conclusion of his introduction to one of the *Writers at Work* volumes, Wilfrid Sheed wrote that he would trade half of *Childe Harold* for an interview with Lord Byron and all of *Adam Bede* for one with George Eliot. He said he was speaking for his "frivolous self," but I suspect he meant it. He would certainly have my support if he did.

—G. A. P.

The Writer: A Profile

ON READING

I never desire to converse with a man who has written more than
he has read.   —*Samuel Johnson*

Reading is to the mind what exercise is to the body.
                                                    —*Richard Steele*

Well, there's the early Joyce, P. G. Wodehouse, Evelyn Waugh,
Anthony Powell, Elizabeth Taylor and early Angus Wilson among
novelists. And poets . . . oh, Hardy I admire, but don't feel very warm
to—A. E. Housman, Philip Larkin, John Betjeman, the early R. S.
Thomas, parts of Robert Frost, parts of Robert Graves, some poems
by Yeats. It's not a complete list—in fact I was once worried by this,
that I couldn't name more than a dozen admired contemporaries. But
I mentioned it to Robert Graves, and he said, "Nonsense. You ought
to be concerned if you admire *more* than that number. It shows you
have no discrimination." Which is a good point!   —*Kingsley Amis*

The only poetry I had read, as a child, were certain books of sick
jokes—Belloc's *Cautionary Tales, Strubel Peter* by Hoffman, and Harry
Graham's *Ruthless Rhymes for Heartless Homes.* I had a favorite, which
went like this:

> *Into the drinking well*
> *The plumber built her*
> *Aunt Maria fell;*
> *We must buy a filter.*

3

Of course I read a good deal about geology and lead mining. Sopwith's *A Visit to Alston Moore* was one, *Underground Life* was another. I can't remember who wrote it. I read all the books of Beatrix Potter, and also Lewis Carroll. Andersen's *The Snow Queen* I loved, and also Haggard's *King Solomon's Mines*. And I got my start reading detective stories with Sherlock Holmes.　　　　　　　　　　　　　　　　—*W. H. Auden*

The great guides were the books I discovered in the Johns Hopkins Library, where my student job was to file books away. One was more or less encouraged to take a cart of books and go back into the stacks and not come out for seven or eight hours. So I read what I was filing. My great teachers (the best thing that can happen to a writer) were Scheherazade, Homer, Virgil, and Boccaccio; also the great Sanskrit taletellers. I was impressed forever with the width as well as the depth of literature—just what a kid from the sticks, from the swamp, in my case, needed.　　　　　　　　　　　　—*John Barth*

I remember a time when I used to come here [Borges's office in the Biblioteca Nacional] to read. I was a very young man, and I was far too timid to ask for a book. Then, I was rather, I won't say poor, but I wasn't too wealthy in those days—so I used to come every night here and pick out a volume of the *Encyclopaedia Britannica,* the old edition. The eleventh or twelfth because those editions are far above the new ones. They were meant to be *read.* Now they are merely reference books. While in the eleventh or twelfth edition of the *Encyclopaedia Britannica,* you had long articles by Macaulay, by Coleridge, De Quincey and so on. So that I used to take any volume from the shelves—there was no need to ask for them: they were reference books—and then I opened the book till I found an article that interested me, for example about the Mormons or about any particular writer. I sat down and read it because those articles were really monographs, really books or short books. The same goes for the German encyclopedias—Brockhaus or Meyers. When we got the new copy, I thought that was what they call the *Shorter Brockhaus,* but it wasn't. It was explained to me that because people live in small flats, there is no longer room for books in thirty volumes. Encyclopedias have suffered greatly; they have been packed in.

—*Jorge Luis Borges*

Oh, I used to read the Sears and Roebuck Catalogue, every year when it came out. But I learned early in life that you can be a reader or a writer. I decided to be a writer. —*Erskine Caldwell*

Anything, including labels and recipes and advertisements. I have a passion for newspapers . . . read all the New York dailies every day, and the Sunday editions of several foreign magazines too. The ones I don't buy I read standing at newsstands. I average about five books a week . . . the normal length novel takes me about two hours. I enjoy thrillers and would like someday to write one. Though I prefer first-rate fiction, for the last few years my reading seems to have been concentrated on letters and journals and biographies. It doesn't bother me to read while I am writing . . . I mean, I don't suddenly find another writer's style seeping out of my pen. Though once, during a lengthy spell of James, my own sentences *did* get awfully long.

—*Truman Capote*

Captain Lacroix . . . is an old sailor and his books are a feast. I've never had the luck to meet him. I looked for him in Nantes, at Saint-Nazaire. I was told that he is in his eighties and that he doesn't want to give up. When he was no longer able to navigate, he became a marine insurer, and it appears that he doesn't hesitate to put on a deep-sea diving rig in order to see for himself the state of his hulls. At his age, admirable. I imagine that the winter nights seemed long to him by the fireplace, when the wind from the sea poured down on his village of the Loire-Inférieure and blew around in his chimney, and I suppose it was to kill time that this man, who has knocked about on all the Seven Seas and aboard all sorts of ships possible and imaginable, began to write books. These are thick books, strongly built, full of solid documentation, sometimes a little too heavy but nearly always fresh, thus never tedious, all the less so in that the old seaman even searches out reproductions of illustrated post cards and photos of joyous ports of call of his youth, and he recounts things as they happened, his experience and all that he has learned and all that he has seen from Cape Horn to the China Sea, from Tasmania to Ushant, speaking of everything, of lighthouses, currents, wind, reefs, tempests, crews, traffic, shipwrecks, fish and birds, celestial phenomena and maritime catastrophes, history, customs, nations, people of the sea, relating thousands of anecdotes intimate or dramatic, all his life of an honest seaman carried along by the very movement of the sea and dominated by his exclusive love of ships. Ah, it is, certainly, not the work of a littérateur. His pen is a marlinspike, and each page brings you something, and there are ten big volumes! It's as moving as it can be and as simple as good morning. In a word, miraculous. One touches the globe with a finger. —*Blaise Cendrars*

The books that you really love give the sense, when you first open them, of having been there. It is a creation, almost like a chamber in the memory. Places that one has never been to, things that one has never seen or heard, but their fitness is so sound that you've been there somehow. —*John Cheever*

I read Edgar Allan Poe for the first time when I was only nine. I stole the book to read because my mother didn't want me to read it; she thought I was too young and she was right. The book scared me and I was ill for three months, because I believed in it . . . *dur comme fer* as the French say. For me, the fantastic was perfectly natural; I had no doubts at all. That's the way things were. When I gave those kinds of books to my friends, they'd say, "But no, we prefer to read cowboy stories." Cowboys were especially popular at the time. I didn't understand that. I preferred the world of the supernatural, of the fantastic. —*Julio Cortázar*

ON READING

I admire writers who are sometimes enviably self-indulgent, like Victor Hugo. Last summer, I was rereading *Les Misérables,* and really that book has sometimes as much as ninety pages about something which just happens to interest him, something political or religious or something of the sort. And you think, When is he ever going to get on with the story? But the story is so good that you put up with his digressions, and also he writes so fascinatingly about his odds and ends that you can't stop.

I'm very fond of Victor Hugo, and a book which I read when I was eleven years old which I've reread many times through my life and admired enormously is *Notre Dame de Paris.* I wish that people who see those many movies called *The Hunchback of Notre Dame* would read the novel. It's worth any of those movies twenty times over. A great nineteenth-century novelist like Balzac—infinitely enchanting. You cannot put him down. Even when he is telling you the details of rural newspaper publishing. Well, of course that is very interesting. It absolutely grips you. You cannot stop reading Balzac. You cannot stop reading any of the great Russians. The great English writers: Dickens more than Thackeray, but Thackeray is much finer than some people are prepared to admit. Trollope is endlessly gripping, though it's rather crunchy granola: you chomp your way resolutely through it, and it's worth it because the story is so good. It's the storytellers' quality that they have. Nabokov said that he thought that the most important element in a novelist's armory was what he called by a Russian word, *shamanstvo.* It means the enchanter-quality. The word *shamanen* is familiar to everyone. The enchanter-quality, the ability to keep people wanting more, it's not something which can be taught, and often it is associated with what critics call a "bad literary style," but it is irresistible. Dickens had it. Nobody praises Dickens's style, but who can resist his enchantment? Only professors, and only some of those.   —*Robertson Davies*

I always say Hemingway, because he taught me how sentences worked. When I was fifteen or sixteen I would type out his stories to learn how the sentences worked. I taught myself to type at the same time. A few years ago when I was teaching a course at Berkeley I reread *A Farewell to Arms* and fell right back into those sentences. I mean they're perfect sentences. Very direct sentences, smooth rivers, clear water over granite, no sinkholes.

Henry James wrote perfect sentences too, but very indirect, very complicated. Sentences *with* sinkholes. You could drown in them. I wouldn't dare to write one. I'm not even sure I'd dare to read James again. I loved those novels so much that I was paralyzed by them for a long time. All those possibilities. All that perfectly reconciled style. It made me afraid to put words down.   —*Joan Didion*

[Hemingway] and I used to read the Bible to each other. He began it. We read separate little scenes. From *Kings, Chronicles*. We didn't make anything out of it—the reading—but Ernest at that time talked a lot about style. He was crazy about Stephen Crane's *The Blue Hotel*. It affected him very much. I was very much taken with him. He took me around to Gertrude Stein's. I wasn't quite at home there. A Buddha sitting up there, surveying us. Ernest was much less noisy then than he was in later life. He felt such people were instructive.   —*John Dos Passos*

In 1926, I heard stories about Joyce's banned book *Ulysses* and what an oppressed author he was; nobody wanted to publish him. I sympathized; I explored. I finally got a smuggled copy. For a youth of eighteen the prose was dazzling. I thought of Joyce as a kind of Paganini of prose: a trickster who carried all English literature in his head. I was fascinated by the way Joyce tried to put the reader into the minds of his characters—that long soliloquy of Molly Bloom's, the way Joyce flitted from Bloom's thoughts into street smells and street incidents and then back into the stream of consciousness. Great stuff! Did I fall in love with Joyce? No, he wasn't lovable. But he was a great performer and youth likes performance. So I went to my favorite professor and announced I would write a dissertation on the "stream of consciousness" in Joyce. "Impossible," said the professor. Joyce was forty. His book wasn't available. There were only some poems, *Dubliners,* and *Portrait of the Artist as a Young Man.* And anyhow, he was alive; at that time you wrote dissertations only on the dead, whose work was complete and who could be fully appraised.

—*Leon Edel*

One night [at college] a friend lent me a book of short stories by Franz Kafka. I went back to the pension where I was staying and began to read *The Metamorphosis.* The first line almost knocked me off the bed, I was so surprised. The first line reads, "As Gregor Samsa awoke that morning from uneasy dreams, he found himself transformed in his bed into a gigantic insect. . . ." When I read the line I thought to myself that I didn't know anyone was allowed to write things like that. If I had known, I would have started writing a long time ago. So I immediately started writing short stories.

—*Gabriel García Márquez*

You know what made me want to become a journalist? Reading Evelyn Waugh's *Scoop* when I was about eleven. Enough to make anybody want to be a journalist!   —*Nadine Gordimer*

I still read, I still study, the *Cantos* of Pound. I found Pound in Texas when I was eighteen or nineteen through a young friend named William Hart. Hart was one of those prodigies, *enfants terribles,* that materialize in small towns, young men bearing a sense of art and poetry and life as naturally as others bore the instinct to compete and to copulate. He had a great deal to do with my early enlightenment and spiritual salvation in a lower middle class environment in an isolated (then) Texas town, where a boy's father considered him a sissy if he played the piano, as I've said, and questioned the sexual orientation of any youth who read poetry.

William Hart was a true pioneer; he brought me Pound, Eliot, and Auden. He was self-taught, finding things for himself out of hunger. He had a high-school education, barely, but afterwards he came and sat in my classes at Rice and listened. He knew more than the professors did sometimes—he really did . . . about Elizabethan drama, and medieval romances. He knew these things. He was a delicate boy, obviously, but not effete. He was French Cajun, from a poor family, and he was on the streets, and could have been in trouble a lot. But he ended up in the library. They felt they had a revolutionary in there. In the Houston Public Library at nineteen he would get up and speak about literature, and Archibald MacLeish, of all people. And oh, how this man Hart spoke. The whole library would turn and listen. He became that kind of town creature, one of those who go down in cities, unheralded . . . they go down into beds of ashes. Well, he brought me Pound.

Pound's *Cantos* hold for me madness and beauty, darkness and mystery, pain, heartbreak, nostalgia. Some of the most beautiful and most haunting were written as a prisoner. He made, above all, *songs,* and he told his stories lyrically, as I have felt driven to tell mine. By ordinary speech, ordinary people. I mean that it seems to me that Pound sometimes speaks from a sort of sub-tone in his poems like a con-man, a back-street hustler, using pieces of several languages, bits of myth, literary quotations and mixed dialects and plain beguiling nonsense. There is a stream, flowing and broken, of *voices* in Pound, echoes, town speech, songs, that deeply brought to me my own predicament, in the home of my parents and in the town where I lived. He helped show me a way to sing about it—it was, as most influences have been for me, as much a *tone,* a sound, a quality, as anything else.

The same for T. S. Eliot. He seemed then so much more American than Pound—but then Pound has the Chinese calligraphy and the heavy Greek and Latin. Eliot's wan songs broken suddenly by a crude word or a street phrase directly influenced me as a way to tell *The House of Breath;* and doom cut through by caprice shocked me and helped me survive in my own place until I could escape; showed me a way of managing the powerful life that I felt tearing through me, and trying to kill me. I saw a way: "Cry, what shall I cry?"—the dark Biblical overtone of the great poem; "the voice of one calling Stetson!" Oh, Eliot got hold of me at that early age and helped me speak for my own place.

The storytelling method of Eliot and Pound—darting, elliptical, circular, repetitive, lyric, self-revealing, simple speech within grand cadence and hyperbole, educated me and showed me a way to be taken out of my place, away from my obsessing relations: saved me from locality, from "regionalism." I knew then that it was "style" that would save me. I saw Pound as the most elegant of poets and the most elemental. Both. His madness partakes of both (elegance and elementalness) and is a quality of his poetry: "hast 'ou seen the rose in the steel dust / (or swansdown ever?) / so light is the urging, so ordered the dark / petals of iron / we who have passed over Lethe." That's Canto 74, from the *Pisan Cantos*.   —*William Goyen*

As far as I'm consciously aware, I forget everything I read at once, including my own stuff.   —*Henry Green*

As I have grown older I see myself as fortunate in many ways. It is fortunate to have had all my life this passion for studying and enjoying literature and for trying to add a bit to it as interestingly as I can. This passion has given me much joy, it has given me friends who care for the same things, it has given me employment, escape from boredom, everything. The greatest gift is the passion for reading. It is cheap, it consoles, it distracts, it excites, it gives you knowledge of the world and experience of a wide kind. It is a moral illumination.   —*Elizabeth Hardwick*

Mark Twain, Flaubert, Stendhal, Bach, Turgenev, Tolstoy, Dostoevsky, Chekhov, Andrew Marvell, John Donne, Maupassant, the good Kipling, Thoreau, Captain Marryat, Shakespeare, Mozart, Quevedo, Dante, Vergil, Tintoretto, Hieronymus Bosch, Brueghel, Patinir, Goya, Giotto, Cézanne, Van Gogh, Gauguin, San Juan de la Cruz,

Góngora—it would take a day to remember everyone. Then it would sound as though I were claiming an erudition I did not possess instead of trying to remember all the people who have been an influence on my life and work. This isn't an old dull question. It is a very good but a solemn question and requires an examination of conscience. I put in painters, or started to, because I learn as much from painters about how to write as from writers. You ask how this is done? It would take another day of explaining. I should think what one learns from composers and from the study of harmony and counterpoint would be obvious.   —*Ernest Hemingway*

I never got very much out of *Ulysses*. I think it's an extraordinary book, but so much of it consists of rather lengthy demonstrations of how a novel ought *not* to be written, doesn't it? He does show nearly every conceivable way it should not be written, and then goes on to show how it might be written.   —*Aldous Huxley*

The Amateur Gentleman and *The Broad Highway* were glorious works. So was *Captain Blood*. I think I read every one of Farnol's books and there must be twenty of them. And every one of Sabatini's.

Now I have no real idea of their merit. But I never enjoyed a novel more than *Captain Blood*. Nor a movie. Do you remember Errol Flynn as Captain Blood? Some years ago I was asked by a magazine what were the ten most important books in my development. The book I listed first was *Captain Blood*. Then came *Das Kapital*. Then *The Amateur Gentleman*.

I have learned a lot from E. M. Forster. You remember in *The Longest Journey* somewhere about the fourth chapter, you turn the page and read, "Gerald was killed that day. He was beaten to death in a football game."* It was quite extraordinary. Gerald had been very important through the beginning of the book. But now that he was suddenly and abruptly dead, everyone else's character began to

*Actually kicked in the head by a horse.—Ed.

shift. It taught me that personality was more fluid, more dramatic and startling, more inexact than I had thought. I was brought up on the idea that when you wrote a novel you tried to build a character who could be handled and walked around like a piece of sculpture. Suddenly character seemed related more closely to the paintings of the new realists. For instance I saw one recently which had a painted girl reclining on a painted bed, and there was a television set next to her in the canvas, a real one which you could turn on. Turning on the literal factual set changes the girl and the painting both. Well, Forster gives you something of that sensation in his novels.

—*Norman Mailer*

At eight or nine I was writing little stories in school and feeling the glow. To anyone of my friends who'd listen I'd recapitulate at tedious length the story of the last movie I'd seen. The movies tickled my imagination. As a writer I learned from Charlie Chaplin. Let's say the rhythm, the snap of comedy; the reserved comic presence—that beautiful distancing; the funny with sad; the surprise of surprise.

—*Bernard Malamud*

In Europe the *Paris Herald*—I get very American over there, and it's so concise. Here, I never learned how to read a newspaper. My first year away at school, I watched my classmates, some of them littler than I was, frowning over the war news or the financial page. They already knew how! I realized then and there I couldn't hope to catch up. I told this to Marianne Moore before introducing her at her Amherst reading in 1956. She looked rather taken aback, as I did myself, a half hour later, when in the middle of a poem she was reading—a poem I thought I knew—I heard my name. "Now Mr. Merrill," she was saying, "tells me he doesn't read a newspaper. That's hard for me to understand. The things one would miss! Why, only last week I read that our U.S. Customs Bureau was collecting all the egret and bird-of-paradise feathers we'd confiscated during the twenties and thirties—collecting them and sending them off to Nepal, where they're *needed*. . . ." And then she went right on with her poem.   —*James Merrill*

When I was about twelve, I think it was, my mother took me to a theater one afternoon. We lived in Harlem and in Harlem there were two or three theaters that ran all the time and many women would drop in for all or part of the afternoon performances. All I remember was that there were people in the hold of a ship, the stage was rocking—they actually rocked the stage—and some cannibal on the ship had a time bomb. And they were all looking for the cannibal: it was thrilling. The other one was a morality play about taking dope. Evidently there was much excitement in New York then about the Chinese and dope. The Chinese were kidnapping beautiful, blond, blue-eyed girls who, people thought, had lost their bearings morally; they were flappers who drank gin and ran around with boys. And they inevitably ended up in some basement in Chinatown where they were irretrievably lost by virtue of eating opium or smoking some pot. Those were the two masterpieces I had seen.   —*Arthur Miller*

That's hard to say, the writers I love are so diverse. They are the writers who are more than writers. They have this mysterious X quality which is metaphysical, occult, or whatnot—I don't know what term to use—this little extra something beyond the confines of literature. You see, people read to be amused, to pass the time, or to be instructed. Now I never read to pass the time, I never read to be instructed; I read to be taken out of myself, to become ecstatic. I'm always looking for the author who can lift me out of myself.
                                                                                                      —*Henry Miller*

I went to a convent in New York—The Blessed Sacrament. Convents do the same things progressive schools do, only they don't know it. They don't teach you how to read; you have to find out for yourself. At my convent we *did* have a textbook, one that devoted a page and a half to Adelaide Ann Proctor; but we couldn't read Dickens; he was vulgar, you know. But *I* read him and Thackeray, and I'm the one woman you'll ever know who's read every word of Charles Reade, the author of *The Cloister and the Hearth*. But as for helping me in the outside world, the convent taught me only that if you spit on a pencil eraser it will erase ink. And I remember the smell of oilcloth, the smell of nuns' garb. I was fired from there, finally, for a lot of things, among them my insistence that the Immaculate Conception was spontaneous combustion.

—*Dorothy Parker*

The greatness of a writer has nothing to do with subject matter itself, only with how much the subject matter touches the author. It is the density of style which counts. Through Hemingway's style you feel matter, iron, wood. I admire Hemingway but I prefer what I know of Faulkner. *Light in August* is a marvelous book. The character of the little pregnant woman is unforgettable. As she walks from Alabama to Tennessee something of the immensity of the South of the United States, of its essence, is captured for us who have never been there.

—*Boris Pasternak*

All the old houses that I knew when I was a child were full of books, bought generation after generation by members of the family. Everyone was literate as a matter of course. Nobody told you to read this or not to read that. It was there to read, and we read. I grew up in a sort of mélange. I was reading Shakespeare's sonnets when I was thirteen years old, and I'm perfectly certain that they made the most profound impression upon me of anything I ever read. For a time I knew the whole sequence by heart; now I can only remember two or three of them. That was the turning point of my life, when I read the Shakespeare sonnets, and then all at one blow, all of Dante—in that great big book illustrated by Gustave Doré. The plays I saw on the stage, but I don't remember reading them with any interest at all. Oh, and I read all kinds of poetry—Homer, Ronsard, all the old French poets in translation. We also had a very good library of—well, you might say secular philosophers. I was incredibly influenced by Montaigne when I was very young. And one day when I was about fourteen, my father led me up to a great big line of books and said, "Why don't you read this? It'll knock some of the nonsense out of you!" It happened to be the entire set of Voltaire's philosophical dictionary with notes by Smollett. And I plowed through it; it took me about five years.

And of course we read all the eighteenth-century novelists, though Jane Austen, like Turgenev, didn't really engage me until I was quite mature. I read them both when I was very young, but I was grown up before I really took them in. And I discovered for myself *Wuthering Heights;* I think I read that book every year of my life for fifteen years. I simply adored it. Henry James and Thomas Hardy were really my introduction to modern literature; Grandmother didn't much approve of it. She thought Dickens might do, but she was a little against Mr. Thackeray; she thought he was too trivial. So that was as far as I got into the modern world until I left home!   —*Katherine Anne Porter*

My education was as a chemist at Cornell and then an anthropologist at the University of Chicago. Christ—I was thirty-five before I went crazy about Blake, forty before I read *Madame Bovary,* forty-five before I'd even heard of Céline. Through dumb luck, I read *Look Homeward, Angel* exactly when I was supposed to—at the age of eighteen.

I grew up in a house crammed with books. But I never had to read a book for academic credit, never had to write a paper about it, never had to prove I'd understood it in a seminar. I am a hopelessly clumsy discusser of books. My experience is nil.   —*Kurt Vonnegut*

How They Brought the Good News from Aix to Ghent (at about age nine). I thought it was pretty nearly the height of human achievement. I didn't know whether I was impressed by riding a horse that fast or writing the poem. I couldn't distinguish between the two, but I knew there was something pretty fine going on. . . . Then *Lycidas.* . . .

By thirteen, something like that, I knew it wasn't what was happening in the poem that was important—it was the poem. I had crossed the line. —*Robert Penn Warren*

I enjoyed him [Ronald Firbank] very much when I was young. I can't read him now. I think there would be something wrong with an elderly man who could enjoy Firbank. —*Evelyn Waugh*

I was never a voracious reader and, in fact, have done little reading in my life. There are too many other things I would rather do than read. In my youth I read animal stories—William J. Long and Ernest Seton Thompson. I have read a great many books about small boat voyages—they fascinate me even though they usually have no merit. In the twenties, I read the newspaper columns: F.P.A., Christopher Morley, Don Marquis. I tried contributing and had a few things published. (As a child, I was a member of the St. Nicholas League and from that eminence was hurled into the literary life, wearing my silver badge and my gold badge.) My reading habits have not changed over the years, only my eyesight has changed. I don't like being indoors and get out every chance I get. In order to read, one must sit down, usually indoors. I am restless and would rather sail a boat than crack a book. I've never had a very lively literary curiosity, and it has sometimes seemed to me that I am not really a literary fellow at all. Except that I write for a living.

I admire anybody who has the guts to write anything at all. As for what comes out on paper, I'm not well equipped to speak about it. When I should be reading, I am almost always doing something else. It is a matter of some embarrassment to me that I have never read Joyce and a dozen other writers who have changed the face of literature. But there you are. I picked up *Ulysses* the other evening, when my eye lit on it, and gave it a go. I stayed with it only for about twenty minutes, then was off and away. It takes more than a genius to keep me reading a book. But when I latch onto a book like *They Live by the Wind,* by Wendell P. Bradley, I am glued tight to the chair. It is because Bradley wrote about something that has always fascinated (and uplifted) me—sailing. He wrote about it very well, too.

I was deeply impressed by Rachel Carson's *Silent Spring*. It may well be the book by which the human race will stand or fall.

—*E. B. White*

What writers influenced me as a young man? *Chekhov!*

As a dramatist? Chekhov! As a story writer? Chekhov! D. H. Lawrence, too, for his spirit, of course, for his understanding of sexuality, of life in general. —*Tennessee Williams*

ON FIRST EFFORTS

The first step is the hardest.
—*A comment made by Mme du Duffand, a celebrated 18th-century salon personage, on the legend of Saint Denis, who after his execution picked up his head and walked with it from Montmartre to the town which now bears his name a few miles north of Paris.*

Most of the basic material a writer works with is acquired before the age of fifteen.　　　　　　　　　　　　　—*Willa Cather*

When I was a child of about ten or eleven and lived near Mobile, I had to go into town on Saturdays to the dentist and I joined the Sunshine Club that was organized by the Mobile *Press Register*. There was a children's page with contests for writing and for coloring pictures and then every Saturday afternoon they had a party with free Nehi and Coca-Cola. The prize for the short story writing contest was either a pony or a dog, I've forgotten which, but I wanted it badly. I had been noticing the activities of some neighbors who were up to no good, so I wrote a kind of *roman à clef* called *Old Mr. Busybody* and entered it in the contest. The first installment appeared one Sunday, under my real name of Truman Streckfus Persons. Only somebody suddenly realized that I was serving up a local scandal as fiction, and the second installment never appeared. Naturally, I didn't win a thing.　　—*Truman Capote*

I painted a little in Africa, but every time I'd get to work someone would come and say an ox has died or something and I'd have to go out in the fields. I did write there to entertain myself and I told stories constantly to the natives, all kinds of nonsense: they loved it. I'd say, "Once there was a man who had an elephant with two heads," and right away the natives would say, "Oh? Yes, well, Mem-Sahib, how did he find it, and how did he manage to feed it," or whatever. They loved such invention. I delighted my people there by speaking in rime for them; they have no rime, you know, had never discovered it. I'd say things like "Wakamba na kula mamba"—"The such-and-such tribe eats snakes": which in prose would have infuriated them, but amused them mightily in rime. Afterwards they'd say, "Please, Mem-Sahib, talk like rain," so then I knew they liked it, for rain was very precious to us there. —*Isak Dinesen*

I never felt I wanted to be a writer . . . I didn't much like the literary world as I knew it. I studied architecture. I've always been a frustrated architect. But there are certain periods of life when you take in an awful lot of impressions. I kept a good diary—very usual sort of thing—and I was consistent about putting down my impressions. But I had no intention, really, of being a writer then. It may have been Barbusse that got me going. Or more likely something to keep the dry rot from settling in the brain. Robert Hillyer and I began what we called the Great Novel, or more simply the GN. Our schedule then at the front was twenty-four hours on, twenty hours off, and I remember we worked on the novel in a cement tank that protected us from the shelling. We wrote alternate chapters. I sent the manuscript up to the University of Virginia the other day. I didn't dare look at it. —*John Dos Passos*

One childhood episode stands out as particularly vivid, in Paris, in the 1930s. My father was an eccentric, extremely conservative Frenchman who deplored most aspects of the twentieth century, particularly the laxness of its education. And according to his wishes, I spent my first nine years confined to my room, tutored at home by a governess quite as tyrannical as my father. She was a rabid hypochondriac, convinced that the mere *sight* of another child might lead me to catch some deadly germ . . . I lived in extreme isolation. Once a week we commuted to a correspondence school where I'd receive the assignments for the following week—typically French, didactic, desiccating assignments, memorizing Latin verbs and the dates of battles won by Napoleon. But when I was eight years old an unprecedented event took place—a new teacher came in and gave us the following assignment: "Write a Story About Anything You Wish." I was filled with excitement and anguish by this novel freedom. I began as a severe minimalist. Here's the cautionary tale I wrote: "The little girl was forbidden by her parents to walk alone to the lake at the other end of the green lawn. But she wished to visit a green-eyed frog who could offer her the key to freedom. One day she disobeyed her parents and walked to the lake, and was immediately drowned. The End." The following day, during his daily visit to the study room my father perused the composition and raised a storm. "Pathetic dribble! You dare call that a story? What will become of you if you don't ever finish anything!" And he grabbed the paper from my little desk and tore it to shreds. It was a May evening in 1939, fourteen months before he died in the Resistance. My father had been the love of my life, and he'd warned me that I should never write again. I didn't attempt fiction again for over thirty years.

—*Francine du Plessix Gray*

I wanted to be a businessman and all sorts of other things; I wanted to prove to myself that I could do something else [than write]. The business career lasted for a fortnight. They were a firm, I remember, of tobacco merchants. I was to go up to Leeds to learn the business and then go abroad. I couldn't stand my companion. He was an insufferable bore. We would play double noughts and crosses and he always won. What finally got me was when he said: "We'll be able to play this on the way out, won't we?" I resigned immediately.

—*Graham Greene*

When I was nine, the teacher asked us to write a piece about our village *fête*. He read mine in class. I was encouraged and continued. I even wanted to write my memoirs at the age of ten. At twelve I wrote poetry, mostly about friendship—"Ode to Friendship." Then my class wanted to make a film and one little boy suggested that I write the script. It was a story about some children who invite some other children to a party, and they end up throwing all the furniture and the parents out of the window. Then I wrote a patriotic play, *Pro Patria*. You see how I went for the grand titles!

—*Eugène Ionesco*

I didn't have any other ambitions at all. Then I married Edmund Wilson, and after we'd been married about a week, he said, "I think you have a talent for writing fiction." And he put me in a little room. He didn't literally lock the door, but he said, "Stay in there!" And I did. I just sat down, and it just came. It was the first story I had ever written, really: the first story in *The Company She Keeps*. Robert Penn Warren published it in the *Southern Review*. And I found myself writing fiction to my great surprise.　　—*Mary McCarthy*

It was a science fiction novel about people on Earth taking a rocket ship to Mars. The hero had a name which sounded like Buck Rogers. His assistant was called Dr. Hoor. That's the way we used to pronounce whore in Brooklyn. He was patterned directly after Dr. Huer in Buck Rogers who was then appearing on radio. This novel filled two and a half paper notebooks. You know the type, about 7 × 10. They had soft shiny blue covers and they were, oh, only ten cents in those days, or a nickel. They ran to perhaps 100 pages each, and I used to write on both sides. My writing was remarkable for the way I hyphenated words. I loved hyphenating, so I would hyphenate "the" and make it th-e if it came at the end of the line. Or "they" would become the-y. Then I didn't write again for a long time. I didn't even try out for the high school literary magazine. I had friends who wrote short stories, and their short stories were far better than the ones I would write for assignments in high school English and I felt no desire to write. When I got to college I started again. The jump from Boys' High School in Brooklyn to Harvard came as a shock. I started reading some decent novels for the first time.

When I first began to write again at Harvard, I wasn't very good. I was doing short stories at the time. If there were fifty people in the class, let's say I was somewhere in the top ten. My teachers thought I was fair, but I don't believe they ever thought for a moment that I was really talented. Then in the middle of my sophomore year I started getting better. I got on the *Harvard Advocate,* and that gave me confidence, and about this time I did a couple of fairly good short stories for English A-1, one of which won *Story* magazine's college contest for that year. I must say that Robert Gorham Davis, who was my instructor then, picked the story to submit for the contest and was confident it would win.

And when I found out it had won—which was at the beginning of the summer after my sophomore year (1941)—well, that fortified me, and I sat down and wrote a novel. It was a very bad novel. I wrote it in two months. It was called *No Percentage.* It was just terrible. But I never questioned any longer whether I was *started* as a writer.   —*Norman Mailer*

The first play I wrote was in Michigan in 1935. It was written on a spring vacation in six days. I was so young that I dared do such things, begin it and finish it in a week. I'd seen about two plays in my life, so I didn't know how long an act was supposed to be, but across the hall there was a fellow who did the costumes for the University theater and he said, "Well, it's roughly forty minutes." I had written an enormous amount of material and I got an alarm clock. It was all a lark to me, and not to be taken too seriously . . . that's what I told myself. As it turned out, the acts were longer than that, but the sense of the timing was in me even from the beginning, and the play had a form right from the start.

Being a playwright was always the maximum idea. I'd always felt that the theater was the most exciting and the most demanding form one could try to master. When I began to write, one assumed inevitably that one was in the mainstream that began with Aeschylus, and went through about 2500 years of playwrighting. There are so few masterpieces in the theater, as opposed to the other arts, that one can pretty well encompass all of them by the age of nineteen.

—*Arthur Miller*

I had written something first about "the adder and the child with a bowl of porridge," and she [my mother] said, "Well, it won't do."

"All right," I said, "but I have to produce something." Cyril Connolly had asked me for something for *Horizon*. So I wrote "A Face." That is one of the few things I ever set down and it didn't give me any trouble. And she said, "I like it." I remember that.

Then, much before that, I wrote "The Buffalo." I thought it would probably outrage a number of persons because it had to me a kind of pleasing jerky progress. I thought, "Well, if it seems bad my brother will tell me, and if it has any point he'll detect it."

And he said, with a considerable gusto, "It takes my fancy." I was happy as could be.   —*Marianne Moore*

From the time I was nine or ten, it was a toss-up whether I was going to be a writer or a painter, and I discovered by the time I was sixteen or seventeen that paints cost too much money, so I became a writer because you could be a writer with a pencil and a penny notebook.   —*Frank O'Connor*

I started out with nothing in the world but a kind of passion, a driving desire. I don't know where it came from, and I do not know why—or why I have been so stubborn about it that nothing could deflect me. But this thing between me and my writing is the strongest bond I have ever had—stronger than any bond or any engagement with any human being or with any other work I've ever done.

—*Katherine Anne Porter*

One night I saw I. A. Richards on educational television reading a sonnet and explaining its form. I thought to myself, "I could do that, maybe; I could try." So I sat down and wrote a sonnet. The next day I wrote another one, and so forth. My doctor encouraged me to write more. "Don't kill yourself," he said. "Your poems might mean something to someone else someday." That gave me a feeling of purpose, a little cause, something to *do* with my life, no matter how rotten I was. —*Anne Sexton*

My early life was very strange. I was a solitary; radio fashioned my imagination. Radio narrative always has to embody a full account of both action and scene. I began to do that myself. When I was seven or eight, I'd walk through Central Park like Sam Spade, describing aloud what I was doing, becoming both the actor and the writer setting him into the scene. That was where I developed an inner ear. —*Robert Stone*

I remember a sentence I opened one story with, to show you how bad I was: "Monsieur Boule inserted a delicate dagger in Mademoiselle's left side and departed with a poised immediacy." I like to think I didn't take myself seriously then, but I did.

—*Eudora Welty*

When I was at Harvard in 1906, I was so influenced by Swinburne that I kept after my father, saying that I wanted to go over to England to see him. My father wasn't very well-off that year—it was a recession year—but he said, "Well, since you're so persistent you can go, but you'll have to go steerage; I can't afford to send you even cabin class." I said, "Well, that's fine with me," and I went over in the steerage and it wasn't bad at all. But I made the pilgrimage stupidly; I didn't get a letter of introduction. All I knew was that Swinburne was living with Theodore Watts-Dunton—a much lesser poet but quite well known as a critic—in "The Pines" in London, in a part of the city called Putney.

So I just went over and hung around "The Pines" for several days. I waited for I forget how many days, and then one August afternoon Swinburne appeared—this very short man wearing a turban—an odd idea, it was very hot—and I was disappointed because he was so short, almost giving the effect of being a dwarf—and he was talking to himself. At that time he must have been about seventy, and, of course, to me, as a youth, he seemed very old. As he came near me I thought I was going to faint, because my heart began palpitating so rapidly that I didn't know whether I'd be able to make it, I mean walk the rest of the distance without fainting. But I did, and as he passed me I touched his coat with my hand, and I hardly dared look at him. You must remember that I'd been reading Swinburne devoutly and knew many of his poems by heart. He had a very powerful influence on any poet, particularly a young poet, because he has such a marked style; I think after Pope probably the most marked style of any English poet. So, seeing the source of all this verbal magic and music, the poetry that so intoxicated me, was almost like, well, seeing God. I survived it, however, and passed him, and I went back to my room in a small, inexpensive hotel and lay down on the bed and just thought about it all the rest of the day. I went back for several days in the hope of seeing Swinburne again, thinking that I might even have the courage to say a word to him. I'd written him many letters, and also I'd written poems and an essay about him, which came out in *The Harvard Advocate,* and I had sent these to him. But, of course, I added in all my letters, "I would never forgive you if you answered this. Do not answer it, please." The *thought* of his being bothered to answer it—it was real hero-worship.   —*John Hall Wheelock*

I never knew for sure that I would follow a literary profession. I was twenty-seven or twenty-eight before anything happened that gave me any assurance that I could make a go of writing. I had *done* a great deal of writing, but I lacked confidence in my ability to put it to good use. I went abroad one summer and on my return to New York found an accumulation of mail at my apartment. I took the letters, unopened, and went to a Child's restaurant on 14th Street, where I ordered dinner and began opening my mail. From one envelope, two or three checks dropped out, from *The New Yorker*. I suppose they totaled a little under a hundred dollars, but it looked like a fortune to me. I can still remember the feeling that "this was it"—I was a pro at last. It was a good feeling and I enjoyed the meal.

—*E. B. White*

ON MOTIVATION:
WHY I WRITE

I was too slow a mover. It was much easier to be a poet.

—*T. S. Eliot*
on giving up boxing in college

I don't want to be a doctor, and live by men's diseases; nor a minister to live by their sins; nor a lawyer to live by their quarrels. So I don't see there's anything left for me but to be an author.

—*Nathaniel Hawthorne*

Sir, no man but a blockhead ever wrote except for money.

—*Samuel Johnson*

The role of the writer is not to say what we can all say, but what we are unable to say.   —*Anaïs Nin*

My main reason for adopting literature as a profession was that, as the author is never seen by his clients, he need not dress respectably.   —*George Bernard Shaw*

When starting to think about any novel, part of the motive is: I'm going to show them, this time. Without that, a lot of what passes under the name of creative energy would be lost. It's an egotistical self-assertion, if you like—the mere act of writing a book is that.

• • •

There's always vanity. You remember that Orwell said, when he was answering his own question, why I write, that his leading motive was the desire to be thought clever, to be talked about by people he had never met. I don't think he was being arrogant, I think he was being very honest.   —*Kingsley Amis*

ON MOTIVATION

Something that irritates you and won't let you go. That's the anguish of it. Do this book, or die. You have to go through that. Talent is insignificant. I know a lot of talented ruins. Beyond talent lie all the usual words: discipline, love, luck, but, most of all, endurance.

. . .

When you're writing, you're trying to find out something which you don't know. The whole language of writing for me is finding out what you don't want to know, what you don't want to find out. But something forces you to anyway.   —*James Baldwin*

It's a combination of an almost obscene self-confidence and an on-going terror. You remember the old story of how Hemingway would always record the number of words he wrote each day. When I learned that detail about Hemingway I understood why the poor chap went bonkers and did himself in at the end. The average professional, whether he's good or mediocre, learns enough confidence in himself so that he no longer fears the blank page. About my own fiction: my friend John Hawkes once said of it that it seems spun out against nothingness, simply so that there should not be silence. I understand that. It's Scheherazade's terror: the terror that comes from the literal or metaphorical equating of telling stories with living, with life itself. I understand that metaphor to the marrow of my bones. For me there is always a sense that when this story ends maybe the whole world will end; I wonder whether the world's really there when I'm not narrating it. Well, at this stage of my life I have enough confidence in myself to know that the page will fill up. Indeed, because I'm not a very consistent fiction writer (my books don't resemble one another very much), I have an ongoing curiosity about what will happen next. Stendhal said that once when he wanted to commit suicide, he couldn't abide to do it because he wanted to find out what would happen next in French politics. I have a similar curiosity . . . when this long project is over, what will fill the page next? I've never been able to think that far ahead; I can't do it until the project in hand is out of the shop and going through the publisher's presses. Then I begin to

think about what will be next. I'm just as curious as the next chap.
Maybe more so.   —*John Barth*

Emotion. Savy, the biologist, said something appropriate: In the
beginning there was emotion, and the verb wasn't there at all. When
you tickle an amoeba she withdraws, she has emotion, she doesn't
speak but she does have emotion. A baby cries, a horse gallops. Only
us, they've given us the verb. That gives you the politician, the writer,
the prophet. The verb's horrible. You can't smell it. But to get to
the point where you can translate this emotion, that's a difficulty no
one imagines. . . . It's ugly. . . . It's superhuman. . . . It's a trick that'll
kill a guy.   —*Louis-Ferdinand Céline*

One time, again some years ago, Franz Kline was being questioned—
not with hostility but with intensity, by another friend—and finally
he said, "Well, look, if I paint what *you* know, then that will simply
bore you, the repetition from me to you. If I paint what *I* know, it
will be boring to myself. Therefore I paint what I don't know." Well,
I believe that. I write what I don't know. Communication is a word
one would have to spend much time defining. For example, can you
make a blind man see? That has always been a question in my own
mind. And if it is true that you cannot tell someone something he
has no experience of, then the act of reading is that one is reading
with someone. I feel when people read my poems most sympathetically,
they are reading *with* me. So communication is mutual feeling with
someone, not a didactic process of information.   —*Robert Creeley*

I wrote stories from the time I was a little girl, but I didn't want to
be a writer. I wanted to be an actress. I didn't realize then that it's
the same impulse. It's make-believe. It's performance. The only difference being that a writer can do it all alone. I was struck a few
years ago when a friend of ours—an actress—was having dinner
here with us and a couple of other writers. It suddenly occurred to
me that she was the only person in the room who couldn't plan what

she was going to do. She had to wait for someone to ask her, which is a strange way to live.   —*Joan Didion*

I subscribe to what Henry James tries to indicate when he gives that wonderful example of a young woman who has led a sheltered life walking along beside an army barracks and hearing a snatch of soldier's conversation coming through the window. On the basis of that, said James, if she's a novelist she's capable of going home and writing a perfectly accurate novel about army life. I've always subscribed to that idea. We're supposed to be able to get into other skins. We're supposed to be able to render experiences not our own and warrant times and places we haven't seen. That's one justification for art, isn't it—to distribute the suffering? Writing teachers invariably tell students, Write about what you know. That's, of course, what you have to do, but on the other hand, how do you know what you know until you've written it? Writing is knowing. What did Kafka know? The insurance business? So that kind of advice is foolish, because it presumes that you have to go out to a war to be able to do war. Well, some do and some don't. I've had very little experience in my life. In fact, I try to avoid experience if I can. Most experience is bad.   —*E. L. Doctorow*

It doesn't really matter whether you're first rate, second rate, or third rate, but it's of vital importance that the water finds its own level and that you do the very best you can with the powers that are given you. It's idle to strive for things out of your reach, just as it's utterly immoral to be slothful about the qualities you have. You see, I'm not fundamentally interested in the artist. I use him to try to become a happy man, which is a good deal harder for me. I find art easy. I find life difficult.   —*Lawrence Durrell*

He must never be satisfied with what he does. It never is as good as it can be done. Always dream and shoot higher than you know you can do. Don't bother just to be better than your contemporaries or predecessors. Try to be better than yourself. An artist is a creature driven by demons. He doesn't know why they choose him and he's usually too busy to wonder why. He is completely amoral in that he will rob, borrow, beg, or steal from anybody and everybody to get the work done.

The writer's only responsibility is to his art. He will be completely ruthless if he is a good one. He has a dream. It anguishes him so much he must get rid of it. He has no peace until then. Everything goes by the board: honor, pride, decency, security, happiness, all, to get the book written. If a writer has to rob his mother, he will not hesitate; the "Ode on a Grecian Urn" is worth any number of old ladies.   —*William Faulkner*

If the work weren't difficult I'd die of boredom. After *The Recognitions,* where there is a great deal of authorial intrusion and little essays along the way, on alchemy or what have you, I found it was too easy and I didn't want to do it again. I wanted to write something different. I wanted to do something which was challenging, to create other problems, to force this discipline on myself.   —*William Gaddis*

As I tried to make plain in *On Moral Fiction,* I think that the difference right now between good art and bad art is that the good artists are the people who are, in one way or another, creating, out of deep and honest concern, a vision of life-in-the-twentieth-century that is worth pursuing. And the bad artists, of whom there are many, are whining or moaning or staring, because it's fashionable, into the dark abyss. If you believe that life is fundamentally a volcano full of baby skulls, you've got two main choices as an artist: you can either stare into the volcano and count the skulls for the thousandth time and tell everybody, "There are the skulls; that's your baby, Mrs. Miller." Or you can try to build walls so that fewer baby skulls go in. It seems to me that the artist ought to hunt for positive ways of surviving, of living. You shouldn't lie. If there aren't any, so far as you can see, you should say so, like the *Merdistes.* But I don't think the *Merdistes*

ON MOTIVATION

are right—except for Céline himself, by accident, because Céline (as character, not as author) is comic; a villain so outrageous—miserable, and inept—that we laugh at him and at all he so earnestly stands for. I think the world is not all merde. I think it's possible to make walls around at least some of the smoking holes.

• • •

The ones that last are the ones that are true. You look at Faulkner and John O'Hara. John O'Hara outsold Faulkner, he circled Faulkner at the time they were writing. Ten years after his death, O'Hara's books are out of print. We all read Faulkner, nobody reads O'Hara. Dreiser in some ways, some of the time, is one of the worst writers who ever lived. *An American Tragedy,* for instance, is an endless book with terrible sentences like "He found her extremely intellectually interesting." But by the time you finish the book, you've sopped your vest. He's a great writer, though he wrote badly. But what he does morally, that is to say what he does in terms of analysis of character and honest statement about the way the world is, is very good. Of course, some writers last a long time because of their brilliance, their style; Fitzgerald is a good example—a fine stylist. But he never quite got to the heart of things. *That's* what should concern the critics. If a critic is concerned with only how well the sentences go, or how neat the symbolic structure is, or how new the devices are, he's going to exaggerate the importance of mediocre books. Samuel Beckett— surely one of the great writers of our time despite my objections— is loved by critics, but except for John Fowles, I hear no one pointing out that the tendency of all he says is wrong. He says it powerfully, with comi-tragic brilliance, and he believes it, but what he says is not quite sound. Every night Samuel Beckett goes home to his wife, whom he's lived with all these years; he lies down in bed with her, puts his arms around her, and says, "No meaning again today . . ." Critics can say, and do say, well, it doesn't matter what he says, it's how well he says it. But I think in the long run Beckett is in for it. Because great writers tell the truth exactly—and get it right.

—*John Gardner*

I can't imagine *not* writing. Writing simply is a way of life for me. The older I get, the more a way of life it is. At the beginning, it was totally a way of life excluding everything else. Now it's gathered to it marriage and children and other responsibilities. But still, it is simply a way of life before all other ways, a way to observe the world and to move through life, among human beings, and to record it all above all and to shape it, to give it sense, and to express something of myself in it. Writing is something I cannot imagine living without, nor scarcely would want to. Not to live daily as a writing person is inconceivable to me. —*William Goyen*

Over the years I've come to realize that my greatest fear in life is a dread of a certain kind of solitude, of abandonment. And I've come to know that by writing I'm creating a presence which fills that solitude, which takes the place of some ideal Other. Mind you, I'm not afraid of any *chosen* solitude—I'm fiercely independent, I love traveling alone, going to restaurants and theater alone—I'm only terrified of abandonment. This is rooted certainly in the evenings of my childhood. Night was a very threatening time. I don't remember having one single dinner with my parents during all of my childhood in Paris. They were each off in a different direction every night, and there I was in the dark apartment alone with this terrifying predatory governess who I felt was always ready to ravage, destroy me. So the act of writing—I'm dealing with the most primitive, elemental fears here—the act of writing, this creation of a *controllable* presence, seems to be a mature way of exorcising the fear of abandonment, the dread of annihilation which filled my early years. The text in progress is like a fire in the room, an animal, it speaks, hollers, barks, growls back at me, like a magical dog guarding my body from evils, guarding me against the threat of void, of extinction.

. . .

Rousseau made the point that writing becomes necessary when speech fails to protect our identity. The written word may be a weak second best to lived experience, but it's still pretty powerful—our only path to meaning and inner order. I keep being haunted by this phrase of Valéry's: "I thought to erect a minor monument of language on the menacing shore of the ocean of gibberish."

—*Francine du Plessix Gray*

The purpose of art is to produce something alive, in my case, in print, but with a separate, and of course one hopes, with an everlasting life of its own. The miracle is that it should live in the person who reads it. And if it is real and true it does, for five hundred years, for generation after generation. It's like having a baby, but in print. If it's really good, you can't stop its living. Indeed once the thing is printed, you simply cannot strangle it, as you could a child, by putting your hands around its little wet neck.   —*Henry Green*

Talent, even of a very high order, cannot sustain an achievement, whereas a ruling passion gives to a shelf of novels the unity of a system.   —*Graham Greene*

A writer without a sense of justice and of injustice would be better off editing the Year Book of a school for exceptional children than writing novels. Another generalization. You see; they are not so difficult when they are sufficiently obvious. The most essential gift for a good writer is a built-in, shock-proof shit detector. This is the writer's radar and all great writers have had it.

—*Ernest Hemingway*

There are lots of excellent story-tellers who are simply story-tellers, and I think it's a wonderful gift, after all. I suppose the extreme example is Dumas: that extraordinary old gentleman, who sat down and thought nothing of writing six volumes of *The Count of Monte Cristo* in a few months. And my God, *Monte Cristo* is damned good! But it isn't the last word. When you can find story-telling which carries at the same time a kind of parable-like meaning (such as you get, say, in Dostoevsky or in the best of Tolstoy), this is something extraordinary, I feel. I'm always flabbergasted when I re-read some of the short things of Tolstoy, like *The Death of Ivan Ilych*. What an astounding work that is! Or some of the short things of Dostoevsky, like *Notes from Underground*.

• • •

Fiction, history, and biography are *immensely* important, not only for their own sake, because they provide a picture of life now and of life in the past, but also as vehicles for the expression of general philosophic ideas, religious ideas, social ideas. My goodness, Dostoevsky is six times as profound as Kierkegaard, because he writes *fiction*. In Kierkegaard you have this Abstract Man going on and on—like Coleridge—why, it's *nothing* compared with the really profound Fictional Man, who has always to keep these tremendous ideas *alive* in a concrete form. In fiction you have the reconciliation of the absolute and the relative, so to speak, the expression of the general in the particular. And this, it seems to me, is the exciting thing—both in life and in art.

—*Aldous Huxley*

Any literary work that aspires to the condition of art must forget politics, religion, and, ultimately, morals. Otherwise it will be a pamphlet, a sermon, or a morality play. Even the greatest moralist of our century, Joseph Conrad, was first and foremost an entertainer. Solzhenitsyn is a failed artist but a very successful moralist. His novels are pretentious junk, but his political writing, *The Gulag Archipelago* books, for example, are precious masterpieces of indictment. George Orwell is a failure as an artist, but a superb pamphleteer. His political essays, together with Camus's, are the best written in Europe since World War II. These men are heroes because they fight swords with words—but that doesn't make them artists.

—*Guillermo Cabrera Infante*

I can't do anything else. I have always regretted having gotten involved with literature up to my neck. I would have preferred to have been a monk; but, as I said, I was torn between wanting fame and wishing to renounce the world. The basic problem is that if God exists, what is the point of literature? And if He *doesn't* exist, what is the point of literature? Either way, my writing, the only thing I have ever succeeded in doing, is invalidated.   —*Eugène Ionesco*

I'm old-fashioned. I believe in plot, of all things; in narrative, all the time; in storytelling; in character. Very traditional forms interest me. This nonsense about the novel being about "the word" . . . what can that mean? Are we novelists going to become like so many modern poets, writing only for and to each other, not comprehensible to anyone who isn't another writer? I have only a prep school education in the poems of John Milton. Yet I can read Milton; I really understand him. All that time has passed, and yet he's still clear. But when I read the poems of someone my own age and can't understand a single thing, is that supposed to be a failure of my education, or of the poetry?

                                    •   •   •

A writer is a vehicle. I feel the story I am writing existed before I existed; I'm just the slob who finds it, and rather clumsily tries to do it, and the characters, justice. I think of writing fiction as doing justice to the people in the story, and doing justice to *their* story— it's not *my* story. It's entirely ghostly work; I'm just the medium. As a writer, I do more listening than talking. W. H. Auden called the first act of writing "noticing." He meant the vision—not so much what we make up but what we *witness*. Oh, sure: writers "make up" the language, the voice, the transitions, all the clunking bridges that span the story's parts—that stuff, it's true, is invented. I am still old-fashioned enough to maintain that what *happens* in a novel is what distinguishes it, and what happens is what we *see*. In that sense, we're all just reporters. Didn't Faulkner say something like it was necessary only to write about "the human heart in conflict with itself" in order to write well? Well, I think that's all we do: we find more than we create, we simply see and expose more than we fabulate and invent. At least I do. Of course, it's necessary to make the atmosphere of a novel more real than real, as we say. Whatever its *place* is, it's got to feel, concretely, like a place with richer detail than any place we can actually remember. I think what a reader likes best is memories, the more vivid the better. That's the role of atmosphere in fiction: it provides details that feel as good, or as terrifying, as memories. Vienna, in my books, is more Vienna than Vienna; St. Cloud's is more Maine than Maine.   —*John Irving*

I think I'm a very unobservant person, one who goes straight to concepts about people and ignores evidence to the contrary and the bric-a-brac surrounding that person. Stephen Spender said an amusing thing about Yeats—that he went for days on end without noticing anything, but then, about once a month, he would look out of a window and suddenly be aware of a swan or something, and it gave him such a stunning shock that he'd write a marvelous poem about it. That's more the kind of way I operate: suddenly something pierces the reverie and self-absorption that fill my days, and I see with a tremendous flash the extraordinariness of that person or object or situation.   —*Christopher Isherwood*

I used to say on Thursday afternoons when I was on my day off from the Albany *Times Union* and I was waiting for the muse to descend and I discovered that it was the muse's day off too, you have to beat the bastards. I didn't even know who the bastards were, but you have to beat somebody. You have to beat your own problematic imagination, to discover what it is you're saying and how to say it and move forward into the unknown. I always knew that (a) I wanted to be a writer and (b) if you persist in doing something, sooner or later you will achieve it. It's just a matter of persistence—and a certain amount of talent. You can't do anything without talent, but you can't do anything without persistence, either. Bellow and I once talked about that. We were talking just in general about writing and publishing and so on, and he said there's a certain amount of talent that's necessary. After that, it's character. I said, "What do you mean by character?" He smiled at me and never said anything. So I was left to define what he meant that night. What I concluded was that character is equivalent to persistence. That you just refuse to give up. Then, the game's not over. You know, I had an enormous success in everything I'd done in life . . . up until the time I decided to be a writer. I was a good student; I was a good soldier; I was good at this and that. I got a hole-in-one one day on the golf course. I bowled 299, just like Billy Phelan. I was a very good newspaperman. I became a managing editor. Anything I wanted to do in journalism, it seemed to work; it just fell into place. So I didn't understand why I was so successful as a journalist and yet zilch as a novelist and a short-story writer. It was just that time was working against me. You just have to learn. It's such a complicated craft . . . such a complicated thing to understand what you're trying to bring out of your own imagination, your own life.   —*William Kennedy*

The great European novel started out as entertainment, and every true novelist is nostalgic for it. In fact, the themes of those great entertainments are terribly serious—think of Cervantes! In *The Farewell Party*, the question is, does man deserve to live on this earth? Shouldn't one "free the planet from man's clutches"? My lifetime ambition has been to unite the utmost seriousness of question with the utmost lightness of form. Nor is this purely an artistic ambition. The combination of a frivolous form and a serious subject immediately unmasks the truth about our dramas (those that occur in our beds as well as those that we play out on the great stage of History) and their awful insignificance. We experience the unbearable lightness of being.

Every one of my novels could be entitled *The Unbearable Lightness of Being* or *The Joke* or *Laughable Loves*; the titles are interchangeable, they reflect the small number of themes that obsess me, define me, and, unfortunately, restrict me. Beyond these themes, I have nothing else to say or to write.   —*Milan Kundera*

You've been reading Auden: "To ask the hard question is simple." The short answer is that you write because you have to. If you rationalize it, it seems as if you've seen this sight, felt this feeling, had this vision, and have got to find a combination of words that will preserve it by setting it off in other people. The duty is to the original experience. It doesn't feel like self-expression, though it may look like it. As for *whom* you write, well, you write for everybody. Or anybody who will listen.

• • •

I think a young poet, or an old poet, for that matter, should try to produce something that pleases himself personally, not only when he's written it but a couple of weeks later. Then he should see if it pleases anyone else, by sending it to the kind of magazine he likes reading. But if it doesn't, he shouldn't be discouraged. I mean, in the seventeenth century every educated man could turn a verse and play the lute. Supposing no one played tennis because they wouldn't make Wimbledon? First and foremost, writing poems should be pleasure. So should reading them, by God.

• • •

You must realize I've never had "ideas" about poetry. To me it's always been a personal, almost physical release or solution to a complex pressure of needs—wanting to create, to justify, to praise, to explain, to externalize, depending on the circumstances. And I've never been much interested in other people's poetry—one reason for writing, of course, is that no one's written what you want to read.

Probably my notion of poetry is very simple. Some time ago I agreed to help judge a poetry competition—you know, the kind where they get about 35,000 entries, and you look at the best few thousand. After a bit I said, Where are all the love poems? And nature poems? And they said, Oh, we threw all those away. I expect they were the ones I should have liked.

• • •

ON MOTIVATION

I think a poet should be judged by what he does with his subjects, not by what his subjects are. Otherwise you're getting near the totalitarian attitude of wanting poems about steel production figures rather than *"Mais où sont les neiges d'antan?"* Poetry isn't a kind of paint-spray you use to cover selected objects with. A good poem about failure is a success.

—*Philip Larkin*

I have never begun a novel without hoping that it would be the one that would make it unnecessary for me to write another. I have had to start again from scratch with each one. What had gone before didn't count. . . . I was not adding to a fresco. Like a man who has decided to start his life over again, I have told myself that I had so far accomplished nothing: for I have always believed that my *chef d'oeuvre* would be the novel I was working on at the time.

—*François Mauriac*

It's the nature of the work that a poem is getting at something mysterious, which no amount of staring at straight-on has ever solved, something like death or love or treachery or beauty. And we keep doing this corner-of-the-eye thing. I remember when we were in training to be night fliers in the Navy, I learned, very strangely, that the rods of the eye perceive things at night in the corner of the eye that we can't see straight ahead. That's not a bad metaphor for the vision of art. You don't stare at the mystery, but you *can* see things out of the corner of your eye that you weren't supposed to see.

—*William Meredith*

I knew early on that I was going to be a writer. I think it's something rather like a curse that you're born with. I knew I wanted to be a writer and my father was far too intelligent to tell me not to be one. Instead of that, he said, "Of course you'll be a writer. Of course you'll be a very successful writer but just till you make a fortune by writing, just divorce a few people. You know, just a few. There's nothing in it." He thought that writers' wives led such terrible lives because the writer was always at home brewing tea and stumped for words. And he said, "Your marriage will be much happier if you go down to Temple tube station and go to the law courts and divorce people." And he told me there was really nothing to being a lawyer except a certain amount of common sense, and relatively clean fingernails. You see, I was practically born into the divorce courts. My father was the *doyen* of the divorce barristers. He was an extremely erudite and very famous divorce barrister. So that when I was a little boy in the nursery, instead of a story like "Snow White and the Seven Dwarfs," I used to get "The Duchess and the Seven Co-Respondents." My father used to return to me glowing with his triumphs in the divorce courts and give me wonderful lines which I was afterwards able to use in a play I wrote about him. He did really come home to me one night in the nursery and say, "I had a wonderful day in court, John. Terrific trial," he said. "Managed to prove adultery by evidence of inclination and opportunity," he said. "The only piece of evidence we had was a pair of footprints upside down on the dashboard of an Austin 711 parked in a Hampstead garden suburb."

—*John Mortimer*

I really got into this row, big, at the novel conference at Harvard when I had a couple of people talking about the various types of novel—and analyzing them, and then we had a novelist get up and speak about the responsibilities of the novelist. I was with Anthony West on the stage and I was gradually getting into hysterics. It's never happened to me before in public; I was giggling, I couldn't stop myself. And, "all right," I said at the end of it, "if there are any of my students here I'd like them to remember that writing is fun." That's the reason you do it, because you enjoy it, and you read it because you enjoy it. You don't read it because of the serious moral responsibility to read, and you don't write it because it's a serious moral responsibility. You do it for exactly the same reason that you paint pictures or play with the kids. It's a creative activity.

—*Frank O'Connor*

It seems as if I was fated to write . . . Which is horrible. But I can only do one thing. I'm rather useless, but perhaps not as useless as everyone thinks. I tried to be an actress—a chorus girl—and the whole thing ended when I was handed a line to say: "Oh Lottie, don't be epigrammatic." But, when the cue came, the words just disappeared. That was that. I was interested in beauty—cosmetics— but when I tried to make a face cream, it blew up.   —*Jean Rhys*

Writing novels is not the road to power. I don't believe that, in my society, novels effect serious changes in anyone other than the handful of people who are writers, whose own novels are of course seriously affected by other novelist's novels. I can't see anything like that happening to the ordinary reader, nor would I expect it to. Novels provide readers with something to read. At their best writers change the *way* readers read. That seems to me the only realistic expectation. It also seems to me quite enough. Reading novels is a deep and singular pleasure, a gripping and mysterious human activity that does not require any more moral or political justification than sex.

• • •

A writer needs his poisons. The antidote to his poisons is often a book.   —*Philip Roth*

Writing is like a contact sport, like football. Why do kids play football? They can get hurt on any play, can't they? Yet they can't wait until Saturday comes around so they can play on the high-school team, or the college team, and get smashed around. Writing is like that. You can get hurt, but you enjoy it.   —*Irwin Shaw*

In the later years before I began to publish, my brother gave me a number of rules about writing which seem to me sacred. Not that these rules cannot be broken once in a while, but it's good to remember them. One of his rules was that while facts never become obsolete or stale, commentaries *always* do. When a writer tries to explain too much, to psychologize, he's already out of time when he begins. Imagine Homer explaining the deeds of his heroes according to the old Greek philosophy, or the psychology of his time. Why, nobody would read Homer! Fortunately, Homer just gave us the images and the facts, and because of this the *Illiad* and the *Odyssey* are fresh in our time. And I think this is true about all writing. Once a writer tries to explain what the hero's motives are from a psychological point of view, he has already lost. This doesn't mean that I am against the psychological novel. There are some masters who have done it well. But I don't think it is a good thing for a writer, especially a young writer, to imitate them.　　　　—*Isaac Bashevis Singer*

"Fiction must justify itself in every line." Yes. I'm beginning to frame one—and along rather Conradian lines. Prose fiction must first of all perform the traditional functions of storytelling. We *need* stories. We can't identify ourselves without them. We're always telling ourselves stories about who we are: that's what history is, what the idea of a nation or an individual is. The purpose of fiction is to help us answer the question we must constantly be asking ourselves: who do we think we are and what do we think we're doing?

　　　　—*Robert Stone*

I think of my books not as sermons or directives in a war of ideas but as objects, with different shapes and textures and the mysteriousness of anything that exists. My first thought about art, as a child, was that the artist brings something into the world that didn't exist before, and that he does it without destroying something else. A kind of refutation of the conservation of matter. That still seems to me its central magic, its core of joy.　　　　—*John Updike*

ON MOTIVATION

Once you start illustrating virtue as such you had better stop writing fiction. Do something else, like Y-work. Or join a committee. Your business as a writer is not to illustrate virtue but to show how a fellow may move toward it—or away from it.

—*Robert Penn Warren*

An artist must be a reactionary. He has to stand out against the tenor of the age and not go flopping along; he must offer some little opposition. Even the great Victorian artists were all anti-Victorian, despite the pressures to conform.

—*Evelyn Waugh*

A writer should concern himself with whatever absorbs his fancy, stirs his heart, and unlimbers his typewriter. I feel no obligation to deal with politics. I do feel a responsibility to society because of going into print: a writer has the duty to be good, not lousy; true, not false; lively, not dull; accurate, not full of error. He should tend to lift people up, not lower them down. Writers do not merely reflect and interpret life, they inform and shape life.

• • •

The writer's role is what it has always been: he is a custodian, a secretary. Science and technology have perhaps deepened his responsibility but not changed it. In "The Ring of Time," I wrote: "As a writing man, or secretary, I have always felt charged with the safekeeping of all unexpected items of worldly or unworldly enchantment, as though I might be held personally responsible if even a small one were to be lost. But it is not easy to communicate anything of this nature."

A writer must reflect and interpret his society, his world; he must also provide inspiration and guidance and challenge. Much writing today strikes me as deprecating, destructive, and angry. There are good reasons for anger, and I have nothing against anger. But I think some writers have lost their sense of proportion, their sense of humor, and their sense of appreciation. I am often mad, but I would hate to be nothing but mad: and I think I would lose what little value I may have as a writer if I were to refuse, as a matter of principle, to accept the warming rays of the sun, and to report them, whenever, and if ever, they happen to strike me. One role of the writer today is to sound the alarm. The environment is disintegrating, the hour is late, and not much is being done. Instead of carting rocks from the moon, we should be carting the feces out of Lake Erie.   —*E. B. White*

It seems to me that there has to be a sudden, confident sense that there is an exploitable and interesting relationship between something perceived out there and something in the way of incipient meaning within you. And what you see out there has to be seen freshly, or the process is not going to be provoked. Noting a likeness or resemblance between two things in nature can provide this freshness, but I think there must be more. For example, to perceive that the behavior of certain tree leaves is like the behavior of birds' wings is not, so far as I am concerned, enough to justify the sharpening of the pencil. There has to be a feeling that some kind of idea is implicit within that resemblance. It is strange how confident one can be about this. I always detest it when artists and writers marvel at their own creativity, but I think this is a very strange thing which most practiced artists would have in common, the certainty which accompanies these intitial, provocative impressions. I am almost always right in feeling that there is a poem in something if it hits me hard enough. You can spoil your material, of course, but that doesn't mean the original feeling was false.   —*Richard Wilbur*

I suspect that all writers have some didactic intention. That starts the motor. Or let us say: many of the things we eat are cooked over a gas stove, but there is no taste of gas in the food.

. . .

I think I write in order to discover on my shelf a new book which I would enjoy reading, or to see a new play that would engross me.

ON MOTIVATION

That is why the first months of work on a new project are so delightful:
you see the book already bound, or the play already produced, and
you have the illusion that you will read or see it as though it were
a work by another that will give you pleasure.

—*Thornton Wilder*

ON WORK HABITS

I like writing with a Peacock's Quill; because its Feathers are all
Eyes.   —*Thomas Fuller,* Gnomologia

I put a piece of paper under my pillow, and when I could not
sleep I wrote in the dark.   —*Henry David Thoreau*

I never travel without my diary. One should always have something
sensational to read in the train.   —*Oscar Wilde*

I compelled myself all through to write an exercise in verse, in a
different form, every day of the year. I turned out my page every
day, of some sort—I mean I didn't give a damn about the meaning,
I just wanted to master the form—all the way from free verse, Walt
Whitman, to the most elaborate of villanelles and ballad forms. Very
good training. I've always told everybody who has ever come to me
that I thought that was the first thing to do. And to study all the
vowel effects and all the consonant effects and the variation in vowel
sounds. For example, I gave Malcolm Lowry an exercise to do at
Cuernavaca, of writing ten lines of blank verse with the caesura
changing one step in each line. Going forward, you see, and then
reversing on itself. I still have a group of them sent to me at his
rented house in Cuernavaca, sent to me by hand from the bar with
a request for money, and in the form of a letter—and unfortunately
not used in his collected letters; very fine, and very funny. As an
example of his attention to vowel sounds, one line still haunts me,
"Airplane or aeroplane, or just plain plane." Couldn't be better.
                                              —*Conrad Aiken*

There's a time to go to the typewriter. It's like a dog—the way a dog before it craps wanders around in circles—a piece of earth, an area of grass, circles it for a long time before it squats. It's like that—figuratively circling the typewriter getting ready to write, and then finally one sits down. I think I sit down to the typewriter when it's time to sit down to the typewriter. That isn't to suggest that when I do finally sit down at the typewriter, and write out my plays with a speed that seems to horrify all my detractors and half of my well-wishers, that there's no work involved. It *is* hard work, and one *is* doing all the work oneself. Still, I know playwrights who like to kid themselves into saying that their characters are so well formed that *they* just take over. *They* determine the structure of the play. By which is meant, I suspect, only that the unconscious mind has done its work so thoroughly that the play just has to be filtered through the conscious mind. But there's work to be done—and discovery to be made. Which is part of the pleasure of it. It's a form of pregnancy I suppose, and to carry that idea further, there are very few people who are pregnant who can recall specifically the moment of conception of the child—but they discover that they are pregnant, and it's rather that way with discovering that one is thinking about a play.

—*Edward Albee*

I don't like the phone very much, and never stay on long if I can help it. You get some people who simply will not get off the line! I remember the story of the man who answered the phone and was kept prisoner for what seemed an age. The lady talked and talked. Finally, in desperation, he told her, "Really, I must go. I hear the phone ringing!"

—*W. H. Auden*

I start working when everyone has gone to bed. I've had to do that ever since I was young—I had to wait until the kids were asleep. And then I was working at various jobs during the day. I've always had to write at night. But now that I'm established I do it because I'm alone at night.

—*James Baldwin*

I write in longhand. My Baltimore neighbor Anne Tyler and I are maybe the only two writers left who actually write with a fountain pen. She made the remark that there's something about the muscular movement of putting down script on the paper that gets her imagination back in the track where it was. I feel that too, very much so. My sentences in print, as in conversation, tend to go on a while before they stop: I trace that to the cursiveness of the pen. The idea of typing out first drafts, where each letter is physically separated by a little space from the next letter, I find a paralyzing notion. Good old script, which connects this letter to that, and this line to that— well, that's how good plots work, right? When this loops around and connects to that . . .   —*John Barth*

I don't use a typewriter. It's too heavy, too much trouble. I use a notebook, and I write in bed. Ninety-five percent of everything I've written has been done in bed.   —*Paul Bowles*

My eight-year-old son said the other day: "Dad, why don't you write for *fun*?" Even he divined that the process as I practice it is prone to irritability and despair. I suppose, apart from my marriage, I was happiest when I was doing a teaching job and had nothing much to think about in the vacations. The anxiety involved is intolerable. And—I differ here from Simenon—the financial rewards just don't make up for the expenditure of energy, the damage to health caused by stimulants and narcotics, the fear that one's work isn't good enough. I think if I had enough money, I'd give up writing tomorrow.   —*Anthony Burgess*

I have a red rug in my room. Wherever I've lived in life, I've carried my red rug with me. I keep it in excellent shape. I have it vacuumed; I have it dry-cleaned. We are sitting on it now, in fact. Why is it here? We have a very good carpet underneath. But I've got a reason for wanting it here. It's part of my life. Back in the early days I had to live on cold and splintery floors. There was a hardwood floor in Maine that was especially cold because the room I worked in was unheated. Now, an unheated room in a New England winter is sort of a difficult dungeon. Then, in South Carolina, I was confined to write for a while in a rented room with a linoleum floor. The linoleum was cracked and it bristled with splinters. Anytime I didn't have my shoes on, I'd get a splinter in my foot. Well, as soon as I could afford to get a good rug, I bought my red one. And I decided then that I'd carry my red rug with me wherever I went.

•   •   •

I used to have all kinds of schedules. Years ago, in the state of Maine, I chose to write my book on even days and work outside on odd days. When winter came, I shoveled snow and slept a little during the day, then stayed up all night to write. Another early method I used was to take a trip to write a short story. I'd ride a bus, from Boston to Cleveland maybe, and get off at night once in a while to write. I'd do a story that way in about a week's time. Then, for a while, I took the night boats between Boston and New York. The Fall River Line, the New Bedford Line, the Cape Cod Line, all going to New York at night. The rhythm of the water might have helped my sentence structure a little; at least I thought it did.

—*Erskine Caldwell*

I suppose my superstitiousness could be termed a quirk. I have to add up all numbers: there are some people I never telephone because their number adds up to an unlucky figure. Or I won't accept a hotel room for the same reason. I will not tolerate the presence of yellow roses . . . which is sad because they're my favorite flower. I can't allow three cigarette butts in the same ashtray. Won't travel on a plane with two nuns. Won't begin or end anything on a Friday. It's endless, the things I can't and won't. But I derive some curious comfort from obeying these primitive concepts.

•   •   •

I am a completely horizontal author . . . I can't think unless I'm lying down, either in bed or stretched on a couch and with a cigarette and coffee handy. I've got to be puffing and sipping. As the afternoon wears on, I shift from coffee to mint tea to sherry to martinis. I write my first version in long-hand (pencil). Then I do a complete revision, also long-hand. Essentially I think of myself as a stylist and stylists can become notoriously obsessed with the placing of a comma, the weight of a semi-colon. Obsessions of this sort, and the time I take over them, irritate me beyond endurance.

Then I type a third draft on yellow paper, a very special certain kind of yellow paper. I don't get out of bed to do this . . . I balance the machine on my knees. I can manage a hundred words a minute. Well, when the yellow draft is finished, I put the manuscript away for a while, a week, a month, sometimes longer. When I take it out again, I read it as coldly as possible, then read it aloud to a friend or two, and decide what changes I want to make and whether or not I want to publish it. I've thrown away rather a few short stories, an entire novel, and half of another. But if all goes well, I type the final version on white paper and that's that.   —*Truman Capote*

A writer should never install himself before a panorama, however grandiose it may be. . . . Like Saint Jerome, a writer should work in his cell. Turn the back. Writing is a view of the spirit. . . . "The world is my representation." Humanity lives in its fiction. This is why a conqueror always wants to transform the face of the world into his image. Today, I even veil the mirrors.

The workroom of Rémy de Gourmont was on a court, 71 rue des Saints-Pères, in Paris. At 202 Boulevard Saint-Germain, Guillaume Apollinaire, who had a vast apartment with large rooms and with a belvedere and terrace on the roof, wrote by preference in his kitchen, at a little card table where he was very uncomfortable, having had to shrink this little table even smaller in order to succeed in sliding it under a bull's-eye window in the mansard, which was also on a court. Edouard Peisson, who has a nice little house in the hills near Aix-en-Provence, does not work in one of the front rooms where he could enjoy a beautiful view of the valley and the play of light in the distance, but has had a little library corner constructed in back, the window of which gives on an embankment bordered with lilacs. And myself, in the country, in my house at Tremblay-sur-Mauldre, I've never worked on the upper floor, which looks out on the orchards, but in the lower room, which looks in one direction on an impasse behind a stable and in another on a wall which encloses my garden.

Among the very few writers I've had occasion to see much of, only one man of letters, celebrated for his frenetic cult of Napoleon, installed himself before a panorama to work—a historical one—the window of his study had a full view of the Arc de Triomphe. But this window was most often closed because the living spectacle of the glory of his great man, far from inspiring him, clipped his wings. He could be heard through the door coming and going in his study, beating his sides, roaring his phrases, trying out phrases and cadences, groaning, weeping, laboring himself sick like Flaubert in his "*gueuloir.*" His wife then said to the servants, "Pay no attention. It is Monsieur castigating his style."

. . .

I like long sea voyages, and the unique life at sea, too much to ever dream of working. It's the apotheosis of idleness; a triumph—to do nothing while the deck rocks, the boat moves, the engines knock, the ocean rolls, the wind blows, the earth revolves with the heavens and the stars, and the entire universe rushes to open for you to pass. I'm never in a hurry to arrive, and I've tried dozens of times to seduce the captain into taking his boat elsewhere than the designated port. "There's no way, alas!" an old Dutchman told me. "For thirty years I've been making the trip between Rotterdam and Buenos Aires, as if I was the engineer of a train. Impossible to change anything, the route is set in advance, the timetable fixed, I must get there on such a day at such a time, it's outlined in advance by the company, who are masters after God. But the most annoying thing is that it's always the same people who get on, always the same heads I'm obliged to have at my table—the same chargés d'affaires, the same diplomats, the same nabobs, the same big bankers. After thirty years, I know them too well! If only I had the courage to follow your infernal ideas, swing the helm and point elsewhere, to the east or the west, no matter . . . pass the Cape, dive into the southern seas."

All that to tell you that on board, I don't write.

—*Blaise Cendrars*

Almost all of them are certainly procrastinators, but a few people really like to write. Kay Boyle used to say that she loved the smell of paper. Anthony Trollope trained himself to turn out forty-nine pages of manuscript a week, seven pages a day, and he was so rigorous about keeping to that exact number of pages that if he finished a novel halfway through the last day, he'd write the title of a new book and "Chapter One" on the next page and go right on until he'd done his proper quota of seven pages. —*Malcolm Cowley*

Allen Ginsberg, for example, can write poems anywhere—trains, planes, in any public place. He isn't the least self-conscious. In fact, he seems to be stimulated by people around him. For myself, I need a very kind of secure quiet. I usually have some music playing, just because it gives me something, a kind of drone that I like, as relaxation. I remember reading that Hart Crane wrote at times to the sound of records because he liked the stimulus and this pushed him to a kind of openness that he could use. In any case, the necessary environment is that which secures the artist in the way that lets him be *in* the world in a most fruitful manner. —*Robert Creeley*

Another thing I need to do, when I'm near the end of the book, is sleep in the same room with it. That's one reason I go home to Sacramento to finish things. Somehow the book doesn't leave you when you're asleep right next to it. In Sacramento nobody cares if I appear or not. I can just get up and start typing.

—*Joan Didion*

During the German occupation of Denmark I thought I should go mad with boredom and dullness. I wanted so to be amused, to amuse myself, and besides I was short of money, so I went to my publisher in Copenhagen and said, look here, will you give me an advance on a novel, and send me a stenographer to dictate it to? They said they would, and she appeared and I started dictating. I had no idea at all of what the story would be about when I began. I added a little every day, improvising. It was very confusing to the poor stenographer.

I'd start one day by saying, "Then Mr. So-and-So entered the room," and the stenographer would cry out, "Oh dear, but he can't. He died yesterday in Chapter Seventeen."   —*Isak Dinesen*

The best job that was ever offered to me was to become a landlord in a brothel. In my opinion it's the perfect milieu for an artist to work in. It gives him perfect economic freedom; he's free of fear and hunger; he has a roof over his head and nothing whatever to do except keep a few simple accounts and to go once every month and pay off the local police. The place is quiet during the morning hours, which is the best time of the day to work. There's enough social life in the evening, if he wishes to participate, to keep him from being bored; it gives him a certain standing in his society; he has nothing to do because the madam keeps the books; all the inmates of the house are females and would defer to him and call him "sir." All the bootleggers in the neighborhood would call him "sir." And he could call the police by their first names.

So the only environment the artist needs is whatever peace, whatever solitude, and whatever pleasure he can get at not too high a cost. All the wrong environment will do is run his blood pressure up; he will spend more time being frustrated or outraged. My own experience has been that the tools I need for my trade are paper, tobacco, food, and a little whiskey.   —*William Faulkner*

I am a great believer in diaries, if only in the sense that bar exercises are good for ballet dancers: it's often through personal diaries (however embarassing they are to read now) that the novelist discovers his true bent—that he can narrate real events and distort them to please himself, describe character, observe other beings, hypothesize, invent, all the rest. I think that is how I became a novelist, eventually.   —*John Fowles*

I never write except with a writing board. I've never had a table in my life. And I use all sorts of things. Write on the sole of my shoe.   —*Robert Frost*

When I was working for *El Espectador* in Bogotá, I used to do at least three stories a week, two or three editorial notes every day, and I did movie reviews. Then at night, after everyone had gone home, I would stay behind writing my novels. I liked the noise of the Linotype machines, which sounded like rain. If they stopped, and I was left in silence, I wouldn't be able to work. Now, the output is comparatively small. On a good working day, working from nine o'clock in the morning to two or three in the afternoon, the most I can write is a short paragraph of four or five lines, which I usually tear up the next day.   —*Gabriel García Márquez*

I get very tense working, so I often have to get up and wander around the house. It is very bad on my stomach. I have to be mad to be working well anyway, and then I am mad about the way things are going on the page in addition. My ulcer flourishes and I have to chew lots of pills. When my work is going well, I am usually sort of sick.   —*William Gass*

I can't understand writers who feel they shouldn't have to do any of the ordinary things of life, because I think that this is necessary;

one has got to keep in touch with that. The solitude of writing is also quite frightening. It's quite close sometimes to madness, one just disappears for a day and loses touch. The ordinary action of taking a dress down to the dry cleaner's or spraying some plants infected with greenfly is a very sane and good thing to do. It brings one back, so to speak. It also brings the world back. I have formed the habit, over the last two books I've written, of spending half an hour or so reading over what I'd written during the day just before I go to bed at night. Then, of course, you get tempted to fix it up, fuss with it, at night. But I find that's good. But if I've been with friends or gone out somewhere, then I won't do that. The fact is that I lead a rather solitary life when I'm writing.

—*Nadine Gordimer*

Everything is made by hand—with one exception: this nasty plastic triple file which was given me as a present. I've put it here out of politeness for two or three weeks, then it will disappear. Almost everything else is made by hand. Oh yes, the books have been printed, but many have been printed by hand—in fact some I printed myself. Apart from the electric light fixtures, everything else is handmade; nowadays very few people live in houses where anything at all is made by hand. One secret of being able to think is to have as little as possible around you that is not made by hand.

—*Robert Graves*

I keep a small sheath of 3 × 5 cards in my billfold. If I think of a good sentence, I'll write it down. It won't be an idea ("have him visit a brothel in New Orleans"). What I put down is an actual line of intended text ("In the brothel in New Orleans was like the time in San Francisco"). Of course, when I come back to it, the line may change considerably. Occasionally, there's one that sings so perfectly the first time that it stays, like "My boy has stopped speaking to me and I don't think I can bear it." I wrote that down on a 3 × 5 card, perhaps on a bus, or after walking the dog. I store them in filing cabinets. The file on *Something Happened* is about four inches deep, the one on *Catch-22* about the length of a shoe-box.

• • •

I have to be alone. A bus is good. Or walking the dog. Brushing my teeth is marvelous—it was especially so for *Catch-22*. Often when I am very tired, just before going to bed, while washing my face and brushing my teeth, my mind gets very clear . . . and produces a line for the next day's work, or some idea way ahead. I don't get my best ideas while actually writing . . . which is the agony of putting down what I think are good ideas and finding the words for them and the paragraph forms for them . . . a laborious process. I don't think of myself as a naturally gifted writer when it comes to using language. I distrust myself. Consequently I try every which way with a sentence, then a paragraph, and finally a page, choosing words, selecting pace (I'm obsessed with that, even the pace of a sentence). I say to myself what I hope to put down on paper, but I hope not aloud. I think sometimes I move my lips, not only when I'm writing, but when I'm thinking of what I'm going to be having for dinner.

—*Joseph Heller*

When I am working on a book or a story I write every morning as soon after first light as possible. There is no one to disturb you and it is cool or cold and you come to your work and warm as you write. You read what you have written and, as you always stop when you know what is going to happen next, you go on from there. You write until you come to a place where you still have your juice and know what will happen next and you stop and try to live through until the next day when you hit it again. You have started at six in the morning, say, and may go on until noon or be through before that. When you stop you are as empty, and at the same time never empty but filling, as when you have made love to some-one you love. Nothing can hurt you, nothing can happen, nothing means anything until the next day when you do it again. It is the wait until the next day that is hard to get through.

—*Ernest Hemingway*

I work in the morning. I sit comfortably in an armchair, opposite my secretary. Luckily, although she's intelligent, she knows nothing about literature and can't judge whether what I write is good or worthless. I speak slowly, as I'm talking to you, and she takes it down. I let characters and symbols emerge from me, as if I were dreaming. I always use what remains of my dreams of the night before. Dreams are reality at its most profound, and what you invent is truth because invention, by its nature, can't be a lie. Writers who try to prove something are unattractive to me, because there is nothing to prove and everything to imagine. So I let words and images emerge from within. If you do that, you might prove something in the process. As for dictating the text to my secretary, for twenty-five years I wrote by hand. But now it is impossible for me; my hands shake and I am too nervous. Indeed, I am so nervous that I kill my characters immediately. By dictating, I give them the chance to live and grow.

—*Eugène Ionesco*

I am compulsive about writing, I need to do it the way I need sleep and exercise and food and sex; I can go without it for a while, but then I need it. A novel is such a long involvement; when I'm beginning a book, I can't work more than two or three hours a day. I don't know more than two or three hours a day about a new novel. Then there's the middle of a book. I can work eight, nine, twelve hours then, seven days a week—if my children let me; they usually don't. One luxury of making enough money to support myself as a writer is that I can afford to have those eight-, nine-, and twelve-hour days. I resented having to teach and coach, not because I disliked teaching or coaching or wrestling but because I had no time to write. Ask a doctor to be a doctor two hours a day. An eight-hour day at the typewriter is easy; and two hours of reading over material in the evening, too. That's routine. Then when the time to finish the book comes, it's back to those two and three hour days. Finishing, like beginning, is more careful work. I write very quickly; I rewrite very slowly. It takes me nearly as long to rewrite a book as it does to get the first draft. I can write more quickly than I can read.

—*John Irving*

I get up earlier than most guys—between seven and eight—but only because I like to go out in the afternoons while there's still sun. After I get up it takes me an hour and a half of fiddling around before I can get up the courage and nerve to go to work. I smoke half a pack of cigarettes, drink six or seven cups of coffee, read over what I wrote the day before. Finally there's no further excuse. I go to the typewriter. Four to six hours of it. Then I quit and we go out. Or stay home and read.

—*James Jones*

I had a ritual once of lighting a candle and writing by its light and blowing it out when I was done for the night . . . also kneeling and praying before starting (I got that from a French movie about George Frederick Handel) . . . but now I simply hate to write. My superstition? I'm beginning to suspect that full moon. Also I'm hung up on the number 9 though I'm told a Piscean like myself should stick to number 7; but I try to do 9 touchdowns a day, that is, I stand on my head in the bathroom, on a slipper, and touch the floor 9 times with my toe tips, while balanced. This is incidentally more than Yoga, it's an athletic feat, I mean imagine calling me "unbalanced" after that. Frankly I do feel that my mind is going. So another "ritual," as you call it, is to pray to Jesus to preserve my sanity and my energy so I can help my family: that being my paralyzed mother, and my wife, and the ever-present kitties. Okay?

—*Jack Kerouac*

ON WORK HABITS

My life is as simple as I can make it. Work all day, cook, eat, wash up, telephone, hack writing, drink, television in the evenings. I almost never go out. I suppose everyone tries to ignore the passing of time: some people by doing a lot, being in California one year and Japan the next; or there's my way—making every day and every year exactly the same. Probably neither works.   —*Philip Larkin*

There was a period when Delmore Schwartz wrote a sonnet every day. He didn't really like sonnets, but he wrote them for discipline. It certainly helped him. If you look at his best short poems, they're not sonnets, but they're very well structured. So too with Pound. There was a time early on when Ezra used to chant his lines to a metronome, though he gave it up after a while—another way to learn verbal discipline and control.   —*James Laughlin*

I like a room with a view, preferably a long view. I dislike looking out on gardens. I prefer looking at the sea, or ships, or anything which has a vista to it. Oddly enough, I've never worked in the mountains.   —*Norman Mailer*

I prefer small messy rooms that don't look out on anything interesting. I wrote the last two sections of *They Came Like Swallows* beside a window looking out on a tin roof. It was perfect. The roof was so boring it instantly drove me back to my typewriter.
              —*William Maxwell*

I generally go to work right after breakfast. I sit right down to the machine. If I find I'm not able to write, I quit.   —*Henry Miller*

I tried to keep one [a notebook] but I never could remember where I put the damn thing. I always say I'm going to keep one tomorrow.   —*Dorothy Parker*

I don't ask writers about their work habits. I really don't care. Joyce Carol Oates says somewhere that when writers ask each other what time they start working and when they finish and how much time they take for lunch, they're actually trying to find out "Is he as crazy as I am?" I don't need that question answered.   —*Philip Roth*

I sometimes start the day with the letters. Just to get the oil into the machine.

Music. I play records, mostly eighteenth-century music. I find that the Romantics—Beethoven—don't work for me. I love them to listen to, but not to work with, alongside of, whereas Mozart, Bach, Albinoni . . . Haydn, I love. I feel the tremendous masculine joy of Haydn. That gets me going.   —*May Sarton*

I might, if I felt the poem come on, put on a certain record, sometimes the "Bachianas Brasileiras" by Villa-Lobos. I wrote to that for about three or four years. It's my magic tune.   —*Anne Sexton*

The beginning will be always the same; it is almost a geometrical question: I have such a man, such a woman, in such surroundings. What can happen to them to oblige them to go to their limit? That's the question. It will be sometimes a very simple incident, anything which will change their lives. Then I write my novel chapter by chapter. When I am doing a novel now I don't see anybody, I don't speak to anybody, I don't take a phone call—I live just like a monk. All the day I am one of my characters. I feel like him. And it's almost unbearable after five or six days. That is one of the reasons my novels are so short; after eleven days I can't— It's impossible. I have to— It's physical. I am too tired. And it's awful. That is why, before I start a novel—this may sound foolish here, but it is the truth— generally a few days before the start of a novel I look to see that I don't have any appointments for eleven days. Then, I call the doctor. He takes my blood pressure, he checks everything. And he says, "Okay." Because I have to be sure that I am good for the eleven days. He thinks it is all right but unhealthy to do it too often. Sometimes he will say, "Look, after this novel take two months off."

For example, yesterday he said, "Okay, but how many novels do you want to do before you go away for the summer?" I said, "Two." "Okay," he said.   —*Georges Simenon*

The poet Walter de la Mare said that if there is a leak of attention when you are trying to concentrate, the leak can be stifled by smoking a cigarette, or in Schiller's case, by inhaling the rotten apples which he kept in a drawer.   —*Stephen Spender*

On the third finger of my right hand I have a great callus just from using a pencil for so many hours every day. It has become a big lump by now and it doesn't ever go away. Sometimes it is very rough and other times, as today, it is as shiny as glass. It is peculiar how touchy one can become about little things. Pencils must be round. A hexagonal pencil cuts my fingers after a long day. You see I hold a pencil for about six hours every day. This may seem strange but it is true. I am really a conditioned animal with a conditioned hand.

—*John Steinbeck*

I don't have to do the sort of thing Fitzgerald did with *The Last Tycoon*—the voluminous, the tiny and meticulous notes, the long descriptions of character. I can keep all these things in my mind. I wouldn't have to write down "three roses in a vase," or something, or a man's middle name. Henry James dictated notes just the way that I write. His note-writing was part of the creative act, which is why his prefaces are so good. He dictated notes to see what it is that they might come to.   —*James Thurber*

I often read for an hour or two. Clearing the mind. I'm always reluctant to start work, and reluctant to stop. The most interesting thing about writing is the way that it obliterates time. Three hours seem like three minutes. Then there is the business of surprise. I never know what is coming next. The phrase that sounds in the head changes when it appears on the page. Then I start probing it with a pen, finding new meanings. Sometimes I burst out laughing at what is happening as I twist and turn sentences. Strange business, all in all. One never gets to the end of it. That's why I go on, I suppose. To see what the next sentences I write will be.　　—*Gore Vidal*

I don't schedule. Nobody does. In Russia, everything is improvisation. Nobody can tell where he'll be on Friday night. Let me give you an example. When I came to America, I wanted very much to visit my dear friend Robert Lowell's grave. We drove out from Boston in the late afternoon—a dinner had been arranged for that evening. It was dark by the time we found the grave in the forest. I was with a young poet from Boston, and I said to him, "Please, I'm sorry, excuse me, it is impolite, but leave me alone, go to your car, I want half-an-hour alone." Then I began to write poetry. Later I asked him to find a phone and call the people and tell them we wouldn't come to dinner. They were all friends of Lowell's and they were very upset with me. But how could I have gone to a dinner party and broken the mood of that encounter?　　—*Andrei Voznesensky*

My memory is certainly in my hands. I can remember things only if I have a pencil and I can write with it and I can play with it. I think your hand concentrates for you. I don't know why it should be so.　　—*Rebecca West*

Delay is natural to a writer. He is like a surfer—he bides his time, waits for the perfect wave on which to ride in. Delay is instinctive with him. He waits for the surge (of emotion? of strength? of courage?) that will carry him along. I have no warm-up exercises, other than to take an occasional drink. I am apt to let something simmer for a while in my mind before trying to put it into words. I walk around, straightening pictures on the wall, rugs on the floor—as though not until everything in the world was lined up and perfectly true could anybody reasonably expect me to set a word down on paper.

• • •

ON WORK HABITS

There are two faces to discipline. If a man (who writes) feels like going to a zoo, he should by all means go to a zoo. He might even be lucky, as I once was when I paid a call at the Bronx Zoo and found myself attending the birth of twin fawns. It was a fine sight, and I lost no time writing a piece about it. The other face of discipline is that, zoo or no zoo, diversion or no diversion, in the end a man must sit down and get the words on paper, and against great odds. This takes stamina and resolution. Having got them on paper, he must still have the discipline to discard them if they fail to measure up; he must view them with a jaundiced eye and do the whole thing over as many times as is necessary to achieve excellence, or as close to excellence as he can get.   —*E. B. White*

Writers say two things that strike me as nonsense. One is that you must follow an absolute schedule every day. If you're not writing well, why continue it? I just don't think this grinding away is useful. The other thing they say: I write because I must. Well, I have never felt that, and I doubt most of them do either. I think they are mouthing a cliché. I don't think most people write because they must; perhaps economically they must, but spiritually? I wonder. I think many writers would be perfectly happy to lay down their pens and never write again if they could maintain their prestige, professorship and PEN membership.   —*Edmund White*

I proceed as Dylan Thomas once told me he proceeded—it is a matter of going to one's study, or to the chair in the sun, and starting a new sheet of paper. On it you put what you've already got of a poem you are trying to write. Then you sit and stare at it, hoping that the impetus of writing out the lines that you already have will get you a few lines farther before the day is done. I often don't write more than a couple of lines in a day of, let's say, six hours of staring at the sheet of paper. Composition for me is, externally at least, scarcely distinguishable from catatonia.

• • •

There are some circumstances under which it is easier to translate than to try to go ahead with a poem of your own. I think that in order to work on your own poem you need to baby yourself sort of totally, not to have the telephone ring, not otherwise to be vulnerable. I somehow can't work on poetry, which is the most important thing in my life, until I've taken care of all the unimportant things: written that silly letter, marked the class papers, *mowed the lawn!* At any rate, I've gotten into that fussy frame of mind now, whereas I can translate Molière riding on a plane, sitting in a motel. I have with me on this trip a translation of *The Learned Ladies,* which has almost reached the end of the second act, and in a frustrating recent day full of flights, limousines, and buses I got four lines done to my satisfaction. And that's a fair average even if one were sitting in a living room. Some days you get sixteen lines done, some days none.

—*Richard Wilbur*

Many writers have told me that they have built up mnemonic devices to start them off on each day's writing task. Hemingway once told me he sharpened twenty pencils; Willa Cather that she read a passage from the Bible (not from piety, she was quick to add, but to get in touch with fine prose; she also regretted that she had formed this habit, for the prose rhythms of 1611 were not those she was in search of). My springboard has always been long walks. I drink a great deal, but I do not associate it with writing.   —*Thornton Wilder*

In Key West I get up just before daybreak, as a rule. I like being completely alone in the house in the kitchen when I have my coffee and ruminate on what I'm going to work on. I usually have two or three pieces of work going at the same time, and then I decide which to work on that day.

I go to my studio. I usually have some wine there. And then I carefully go over what I wrote the day before. You see, baby, after a glass or two of wine I'm inclined to extravagance. I'm inclined to excesses because I drink while I'm writing, so I'll blue pencil a lot the next day. Then I sit down, and I begin to write.

My work is *emotionally* autobiographical. It has no relationship to the actual events of my life, but it reflects the emotional currents of my life. I try to work every day because you have no refuge but writing. When you're going through a period of unhappiness, a broken love affair, the death of someone you love, or some other disorder in your life, then you have no refuge but writing.

—*Tennessee Williams*

ON INSPIRATION:
THE STARTING POINT

It is not *in*spiration; it is expiration. [the gaunt, fine hands on the thorax; evacuation of the chest; a great breathing out from himself]
—*Jean Cocteau*

A poem is never a put-up job so to speak. It begins as a lump in the throat, a sense of wrong, a homesickness, a love sickness. It is never a thought to begin with.
—*Robert Frost*

Listening to the rhythm of his water drinking [her dog, Basset's] made me recognize the difference between sentences and paragraphs, that paragraphs are emotional and sentences are not.
—*Gertrude Stein*

We are stricken by memory sometimes, and old affections rush back on us as vivid as in the time when they were our daily talk.
—*William Makepeace Thackeray*

I remember when I was in Okinawa and the war was over and we went out to one of the invasion beaches near Buckner Bay, me and my co-flyers, and we went swimming and there was an old amtrack there in ten feet of water that the Japanese had stove in—big holes in the sides of it—and I swam down and sat in the driver's seat. That image stayed with me and years later, twenty or twenty-five years later, I wrote "The Driver."
—*James Dickey*

What's so hard about that first sentence is that you're stuck with it. Everything else is going to flow out of that sentence. And by the time you've laid down the first *two* sentences, your options are all gone.

Yes, and the last sentence in a piece is another adventure. It should open the piece up. It should make you go back and start reading from page one. That's how it *should* be, but it doesn't always work. I think of writing anything at all as a kind of highwire act. The minute you start putting words on paper you're eliminating possibilities. Unless you're Henry James.

I suppose that's part of the dynamic. I start a book and I want to make it perfect, want it to turn every color, want it to *be the world*. Ten pages in, I've already blown it, limited it, made it less, marred it. That's very discouraging. I hate the book at that point. After a while I arrive at an accommodation: well, it's not the ideal, it's not the perfect object I wanted to make, but maybe—if I go ahead and finish it anyway—I can get it right next time. Maybe I can have another chance.   —*Joan Didion*

Well, it can be anything. It can be a voice, an image; it can be a deep moment of personal desperation. For instance, with *Ragtime* I was so desperate to write something, I was facing the wall of my study in my house in New Rochelle and so I started to write about the wall. That's the kind of day we sometimes have, as writers. Then I wrote about the house that was attached to the wall. It was built in 1906, you see, so I thought about the era and what Broadview Avenue looked like then: trolley cars ran along the avenue down at the bottom of the hill; people wore white clothes in the summer to stay cool. Teddy Roosevelt was President. One thing led to another and that's the way that book began, through desperation to those few images. With *Loon Lake,* in contrast, it was just a very strong sense of place, a heightened emotion when I found myself in the Adirondacks after many, many years of being away . . . and all this came to a point when I saw a sign, a road sign: Loon Lake. So it can be anything. . . . I liked the sound of the two words together—loon lake. I had these opening images of a private railroad train on a single track at night going up through the Adirondacks with a bunch of gangsters on board, and a beautiful girl standing, naked, holding a white dress up in front of a mirror to see if she should put it on. I didn't know where these gangsters came from. I knew where they were going—to this rich man's camp. Many years ago the very wealthy discovered the wilderness in the American eastern mountains. They built these extraordinary camps—C. W. Post, Harriman, Morgan— they made the wilderness their personal luxury. So I imagined a camp like this, with these gangsters, these lowdown people going up there on a private railroad train. That's what got me started. I published this material in the *Kenyon Review*, but I wasn't through. I kept thinking about the images and wondering where they'd come from. The time was in the 1930s, really the last era a man would have had his own railroad car, as some people today have their own jetliners. There was a depression then, so the person to see this amazing train was obviously a hobo, a tramp. So then I had my character, Joe, out there in this chill, this darkness, seeing the headlamp of the engine coming around the bend and blinding him, and then as the train goes by seeing these people at green baize tables being served drinks and this girl standing in a bedroom compartment holding the dress. And at dawn he follows the track in the direction the train has gone. And he's off and running, and so am I.   —*E. L. Doctorow*

I remember the day when I started *A Singular Man.* I was sitting in the sunroom of a house out in the west of Ireland, near Clifden in County Galway, and out my window I could see the Atlantic. I was in the middle of my litigations with the Olympia Press over *The Ginger Man* then and I could see the mailman on his bicycle on the winding mountain road coming to me four hours before he arrived, and I'd sit and wonder what bad news he had for me.

I think it must have been the glamour of America, the glamour of New York, as opposed to the isolation and poverty of Ireland that started me on the book. There was a cemetery just over a couple of fields where there were no gravestones. When anyone was buried they'd just pile some boulders on the grave. There were no markings, nothing. One was so isolated out there that I remember that day when the local farmer came rushing across the lawn, pointing up to the sky, and yelling, "There's a dog up there." My two children, Philip and Karen, were playing in front of the house. I remember warning my wife that the children should be pulled inside because there was a maniac wandering around. I was struck with terror. I had no contact with the outside world and no way of knowing that the Russians had sent a dog up in a spaceship. In Ireland when you buy a newspaper, as often as not they put a recent cover on it, but inside will be an old, old newspaper. They think news is news and vintage news is better than anything. Indeed, in Ireland, to read a local paper that's 50 years old is not much different than reading today's. In that kind of isolation *A Singular Man* came into being. —*J. P. Donleavy*

It's simply a sort of premonitory sense that one day one was going to put one's whole shoulder behind a particular punch. But one had to be patient and wait and let it [*The Quartets*] form up, and not catch it in the early jelly stage before it had set properly, and ruin it by a premature thing. That explains why I have hung around in the Foreign Service for so long—keeping the machine running by writing other sorts of things, but waiting patiently, and now I suddenly felt this was it, and this was the moment, and bang—at least I hope, bang. —*Lawrence Durrell*

You begin, I suppose, the way all storytellers begin. Remember, a biography is a narrative, and the biographer has a story to tell. Inside the mind there is the classical beginning: "Once upon a time..." In my Thoreau, I found my first sentence an expression of my thematic sense of Thoreau's narcissism. I began something like this: "Of the creative spirits that flourished in Concord, Massachusetts, it might be said that Hawthorne loved men but felt estranged from them,

Emerson loved ideas even more than men, and Thoreau loved himself."
A cruel beginning, but I think the reader wants to go right on.
—*Leon Edel*

[*The Sound and the Fury*] began with a mental picture. I didn't realize at the time it was symbolical. The picture was of the muddy seat of a little girl's drawers in a pear tree, where she could see through a window where her grandmother's funeral was taking place and report what was happening to her brothers on the ground below. By the time I explained who they were and what they were doing and how her pants got muddy, I realized it would be impossible to get all of it into a short story and that it would have to be a book. And then I realized the symbolism of the soiled pants, and that image was replaced by the one of the fatherless and motherless girl climbing down the rainpipe to escape from the only home she had, where she had never been offered love or affection or understanding.

I had already begun to tell the story through the eyes of the idiot child, since I felt that it would be more effective as told by someone capable only of knowing what happened, but not why. I saw that I had not told the story that time. I tried to tell it again, the same story through the eyes of another brother. That was still not it. I told it for the third time through the eyes of the third brother. That was still not it. I tried to gather the pieces together and fill in the gaps by making myself the spokesman. It was still not complete, not until fifteen years after the book was published, when I wrote as an appendix to another book the final effort to get the story told and off my mind, so that I myself could have some peace from it. It's the book I feel tenderest towards. I couldn't leave it alone, and I never could tell it right, though I tried hard and would like to try again, though I'd probably fail again.

• • •

I don't know anything about inspiration, because I don't know what inspiration is—I've heard about it, but I never saw it.
—*William Faulkner*

ON INSPIRATION

I think first it was that towering kind of confidence of being quite young, that one can do anything—"All's brave that youth mounts and folly guides," as we're told in *As You Like It*. *The Recognitions* started as a short piece of work, quite undirected, but based on the Faust story. Then as I got into the idea of forgery, the entire concept of forgery became—I wouldn't say an obsession—but a central part of everything I thought and saw; so the book expanded from simply the central character of the forger to the forgery, falsification, and cheapening of values and what have you, everywhere. Looking at it now with its various faults, I suppose excess would be the main charge. I remember Clive Bell looking back on his small fine book, *Art,* thirty-five years after it was published in 1913, and listing *its* faults, finding it too confident and aggressive, even too optimistic—I was never accused of that!—but still feeling, as he said, "a little envious of the adventurous young man who wrote it."　　　—*William Gaddis*

One of the most difficult things is the first paragraph. I have spent many months on a first paragraph and once I get it, the rest just comes out very easily. In the first paragraph you solve most of the problems with your book. The theme is defined, the style, the tone. At least in my case, the first paragraph is a kind of sample of what the rest of the book is going to be. That's why writing a book of short stories is much more difficult than writing a novel. Every time you write a short story, you have to begin all over again.

　　　—*Gabriel García Márquez*

I thought I was going to die in the war. I was on a terrible ship. It was the *Casablanca*, the first baby flattop. There were always holes in it, and people dying and it was just the worst place for me to be. I really was desperate. I just wanted to jump off. I thought I was going to die anyway, be killed, and I wanted to die because I couldn't endure what looked like an endless way of life with which I had nothing to do—the war, the ship, and the water . . . I have been terrified of water all my life. I would have fits when I got close to it.

Suddenly—it was out on a deck in the cold—I saw the breath that came from me. And I thought that the simplest thing that I know is what I belong to and where I came from and I just called out to my family as I stood there that night, and it just . . . I saw this breath come from me and I thought—in that breath, in that call is *their* existence, is their reality . . . and I must shape that and I must write about them—*The House of Breath.*

I saw this whole thing. I saw what was going to be four or five years' work. Isn't that amazing? But I knew it was there. Many of my stories happen that way. It's dangerous to tell my students this because then these young people say, "Gee, all I've got to do, if I really want to write, is wait around for some ship in the cold night, and I'll blow out my breath, and I've got my thing."

—*William Goyen*

Some people have gifts, like a friend of mine who can balance a glass on his finger and make it turn round by just looking at it. I have the gift of being occasionally able to put myself back in the past and see what's happening. That's how historical novels should be written. I also have a very good memory for anything I want to remember, and none at all for what I don't want to remember. *Wife to Mr. Milton*— my best novel—started when my wife and I were making a bed in 1943 and I suddenly said: "You know, Milton must have been a trichomaniac"—meaning a hair-fetishist. The remark suddenly sprang out of my mouth. I realized how often his imagery had been tricho- manic. So I read all I could find about him, and went into the history of his marriages. I'd always hated Milton, from earliest childhood; and I wanted to find out the reason. I found it. His jealousy. It's present in all his poems . . . Marie Powell had long hair with which he could not compete.

—*Robert Graves*

I got the idea of *Loving* from a manservant in the Fire Service during the war. He was serving with me in the ranks, and he told me he had once asked the elderly butler who was over him what the old boy most liked in the world. The reply was: "Lying in bed on a summer morning, with the window open, listening to the church bells, eating buttered toast with cunty fingers." I saw the book in a flash.

—*Henry Green*

I was lying in bed in my four-room apartment on the West Side when suddenly this line [the first line of *Catch-22*] came to me: "It was love at first sight. The first time he saw the chaplain, Someone fell madly in love with him." I didn't have the name Yossarian. The chaplain wasn't necessarily an army chaplain—he could have been a *prison* chaplain. But as soon as the opening sentence was available, the book began to evolve clearly in my mind—even most of the particulars . . . the tone, the form, many of the characters, including some I eventually couldn't use. All of this took place within an hour and a half. It got me so excited that I did what the cliché says you're supposed to do: I jumped out of bed and paced the floor. That morning I went to my job at the advertising agency and wrote out the first chapter in long hand. Before the end of the week I had typed it out and sent it to Candida Donadio, my agent. One year later, after much planning, I began chapter two. I don't understand the process of imagination—though I know that I am very much at its mercy. I feel that these ideas are floating around in the air and they pick me to settle upon. The ideas come to me; I don't produce them at will. They come to me in the course of a sort of controlled daydream, a directed reverie. It may have something to do with the disciplines of writing advertising copy (which I did for a number of years) where the limitations involved provide a considerable spur to the imagination. There's an essay of T. S. Eliot's in which he praises the disciplines of writing, claiming that if one is forced to write within a certain framework the imagination is taxed to its utmost and will produce its richest ideas. Given total freedom however, the chances are good that the work will sprawl.

. . .

As for *Something Happened*, in 1962 I was sitting on the deck of a house on Fire Island. I was frightened. I was worried because I had lost interest in my job then—which was writing advertising and promotion copy. *Catch-22* was not making much money. It was selling steadily (eight hundred to two thousand copies a week)—mostly by word-of-mouth—but it had never come close to the *The New York Times* best-seller list. I had a wife and two children. I had no idea for another book. I was waiting for something to happen(!), wishing I had a book to start. My novels begin in a strange way. I don't begin with a theme, or even a character. I begin with a first sentence that is independent of any conscious preparation. Most often nothing comes out of it: a sentence will come to mind that doesn't lead to a second sentence. Sometimes it will lead to thirty sentences which then come to a dead end. I was alone on the deck. As I sat there worrying and wondering what to do, one of those first lines suddenly came to mind: "In the office in which I work, there are four people of whom I am afraid. Each of these four people is afraid of five people." Immediately, the lines presented a whole explosion of possibilities and choices—characters (working in a corporation), a tone, a mood of anxiety or insecurity. In that first hour (before someone came along and asked me to go to the beach) I knew the beginning, the ending, most of the middle, the whole scene of that particular "something" that was going to happen; I knew about the brain-damaged child, and especially, of course, about Bob Slocum, my protagonist, and what frightened him, that he wanted to be liked, that his immediate hope was to be allowed to make a three-minute speech at the company convention. Many of the actual lines through-out the book came to me—the entire "something happened" scene with those solar plexus lines (beginning with the doctor's statement and ending with "Don't tell my wife" and the rest of them) all coming to me in that first hour on that Fire Island deck. Eventually I found a different opening chapter with a different first line ("I get the willies when I see closed doors") but I kept the original, which had spurred everything, to start off the second section. —*Joseph Heller*

I think the first impulse comes from some deep emotion. It may be anger, it may be some sort of excitement. I recognize in the real world around me something that triggers such an emotion, and then the emotion seems to cast up pictures in my mind that lead me towards a story. To give you an example, the impulse to write *The Wall* came from seeing some camps in Eastern Europe when I was working as a correspondent in Moscow for *Time*. We were taken first to Estonia, and there we saw a camp where the Germans had had orders to kill everybody before they left; they had done it in a crude and awful way, making the prisoners build their own pyres before shooting them. We went later to Poland, and though the Warsaw ghetto itself was completely razed, we saw a couple of camps where the same thing had happened, the Germans had been ordered to kill everybody. In each case, there had been a few survivors to talk to. This came at a time when the West had not yet known very much about the Holocaust; there had been some vague rumors of the camps, but we had no real pictures of them. To see these bodies, to hear from the people who survived, created a sense of horror and anger in me that made me want to write. I thought at first to write about one of the camps like Auschwitz, and I did a lot of research on that; then it appeared to me, later on, that the life in the ghettos was at least something like real life for a long time, and so would, I thought, lend itself better to a novel. But it was the sense of distress, fear, anger that I felt seeing those camps that got me launched on that work. —*John Hersey*

I don't believe for a moment that creativity is a neurotic symptom. On the contrary, the neurotic who succeeds as an artist has had to overcome a tremendous handicap. He creates in spite of his neurosis, not because of it. —*Aldous Huxley*

I begin by telling the truth, by remembering real people, relatives and friends. The landscape detail is pretty good, but the people aren't quite interesting enough—they don't have quite enough to do with one another; of course, what unsettles me and bores me is the absence of plot. . . . And so I find a little something that I exaggerate, a little; gradually, I have an autobiography on its way to becoming a lie. The lie, of course, is more interesting. I become much more interested in the part of the story I'm making up, in the "relative" I never had. And then I begin to think of a novel; that's the end of the diary. I promise I'll start another one as soon as I finish the novel. Then the same thing happens; the lies become much more interesting—always.

• • •

Henry Robbins, my late editor at E. P. Dutton, called this my enema theory: keep from writing the book as long as you can, make yourself *not begin,* store it up. This is an advantage in historical novels. *Setting Free the Bears* and *The Cider House Rules,* for example. I had to learn so much before I could begin those books; I had to gather so much information, take so many notes, see, witness, observe, study—whatever—that when I finally was able to begin writing, I knew everything that was going to happen, in advance. That never hurts. I want to know how a book feels after the main events are over. The authority of the storyteller's voice—of mine, anyway—comes from knowing how it all comes out before you begin. It's very plodding work, really.
                                                               —*John Irving*

Burroughs and I were sitting in a bar one night and we heard a newscaster saying . . . "and so the Egyptians attacked blah blah . . . and meanwhile there was a great fire in the zoo in London and the fire raced across the fields and the hippos were boiled in their tanks! Goodnight everyone!" That's Bill, he noticed that. Because he notices them kind of things.
                                                               —*Jack Kerouac*

What triggered "King of the River," I recall, was a brief report in *Time* of some new research on the aging process of the Pacific salmon.

ON INSPIRATION

I wrote the poem in Provincetown one fall—my favorite writing season. The very first lines came to me with their conditional syntax and suspended clauses, a winding and falling movement. The rest seemed to flow, maybe because I'm never very far from the creature world. Some of my deepest feelings have to do with plants and animals. In my bad times they've sustained me. It may be pertinent that I experienced a curious elation while confronting the unpleasant reality of being mortal, the inexorable process of my own decay. Perhaps I had managed to "distance" my fate—the salmon was doing my dying for me.

A poem has secrets that the poet knows nothing of. It takes on a life and a will of its own. It might have proceeded differently—towards catastrophe, resignation, terror, despair—and I still would have no claim to it. Valéry said that poetry is a language within a language. It is also a language beyond language, a meta-medium—that is, metabolic, metaphoric, metamorphic. A poet's collected work is his book of changes. The great meditations on death have a curious exaltation. I suppose it comes from the realization, even on the threshold, that one isn't done with one's changes.

· · ·

The poem in the head is always perfect. Resistance starts when you try to convert it into language. Language itself is a kind of resistance to the pure flow of self. The solution is to become one's language. You cannot write a poem until you hit upon its rhythm. That rhythm not only belongs to the subject matter, it belongs to your interior world, and the moment they hook up there's a quantum leap of energy. You can ride on that rhythm, it will carry you somewhere strange. The next morning you look at the page and wonder how it all happened. You have to triumph over all your diurnal glibness and cheapness and defensiveness. —*Stanley Kunitz*

I remember what "On the Edge" came out of very clearly . . . a lecture on Edgar Allan Poe, delivered in French, a language I don't understand. I sat right in the front; I didn't know it was going to be in French. The speaker was a very nice young man, an Argentine I'd met; there was almost no one there—maybe ten people—so once he began in French I couldn't leave, it would have been too rude; so I sat through fifty minutes, an academic hour. I focused on small things, like the delightful way he said Poe's name in this French way, ED-ga-PO . . . so much more delicious than Edgar Allan Poe in a heavy Midwestern voice, the way my high school lit teacher had said it. So musical, ED-ga-PO. The French take Poe much more seriously than we do. I've always thought of Poe as the last poet in the world I would want to be, so I just imagined myself as Poe. The poem also came out of not writing. I was going through one of my extensive three month dry spells or maybe I was simply dissatisfied with what I was writing. So I became Poe. The poem is really, I guess, about not writing, about the power one gains by not committing oneself; one becomes almost God-like. That was the vision of the poem, for God won't commit himself. We don't see Him, we have these rumors of His existence, hints of his immense power, we're told of his enormous concern for us, and we don't see it. So I said, Well, maybe I'll be God-like, I will remain silent, I will give away nothing. I'm sure the idea came from my encounters with certain people who never seem to commit themselves and gain a temporary power, especially over a loudmouth like me.   —*Philip Levine*

Some bit of scenery or something you've felt. Almost the whole problem of writing poetry is to bring it back to what you really feel, and that takes an awful lot of maneuvering. You may feel the doorknob more strongly than some big personal event, and the doorknob will open into something that you can use as your own. A lot of poetry seems to me very good in the tradition but just doesn't move me very much because it doesn't have personal vibrance to it. I probably exaggerate the value of it, but it's precious to me. Some little image, some detail you've noticed—you're writing about a little country shop, just describing it, and your poem ends up with an existentialist account of your experience. But it's the shop that started it off. You didn't know why it meant a lot to you. Often images and often the sense of the beginning and end of a poem are all you have—some journey to be gone through between those things: you know that, but you don't know the details. And that's marvelous; then you feel the poem will come out. It's a terrible· struggle, because what you really feel hasn't got the form, it's not what you can put down in a poem. And the poem you're equipped to write concerns nothing that you care very much about or have much to say on. Then the great moment comes when there's enough resolution of your technical equipment, your way of constructing things, and what you can make a poem out of, to hit something you really want to say. You may not know you have it to say.

—*Robert Lowell*

When I start something it's like being a bird dog getting a smell; it's a matter of running it down in prose and then trying to figure out what the thing is that's out there. Sometimes it might be a picture. This morning when I was writing I was chasing down one of those images. It was just a minute thing that happened to me while I was recently down in Alabama. We had rented a little cottage on the edge of Mobile Bay and at one point there was stormy weather out on the bay; I wandered out to see what kind of weather it was and the door blew closed and locked me out of the cottage. I thought about getting back inside and I sat down and there was one of those semi-tropical warm summer rains starting to come down like buck-shot. Somehow the image of stepping outside to see what's going on and having the wind blow the door shut has stuck in my head. I don't know what that image *is* exactly, or what it means, but I know that ever since I came home I've been trying to pursue that image in language, find out what it is. That image begins to ionize the prose and narrative particles around it so that words are drawn in, people and language begin to appear. That's when things are going well. When that's happening, any reader will recognize that flame-edge of discovery, that excitement of proceeding on the page that is shared between the reader, the writer, and the page.   —*Thomas McGuane*

An appropriate image for me might be that I start with the idea of constructing a treehouse and end with a skyscraper made of wood. With *The Naked and the Dead*, I wanted to write a short novel about a long patrol. All during the war I kept thinking about this patrol. I even had the idea before I went overseas. Probably it was stimulated by a few war books I had read: John Hersey's *Into the Valley*, Harry Brown's *A Walk in the Sun*, and a couple of others I no longer remember. Out of these books came the idea to do a novel about a long patrol. And I began to create my characters. All the while I was overseas a part of me was working on this long patrol. I even ended up in a reconnaissance outfit which I had asked to get into. A reconnaissance outfit, after all, tends to take long patrols. Art kept traducing life. At any rate, when I started writing *The Naked and the Dead* I thought it might be a good idea to have a preliminary chapter or two in which to give the reader a chance to meet my characters before they went on patrol. But the next six months and the first five hundred pages went into that, and I remember in the early days I was annoyed at how long it was taking me to get to the patrol.   —*Norman Mailer*

When I start I have a pretty well-developed idea what the book is about and how it ought to go, because generally I've been thinking about it and making notes for months if not years. Generally I have the ending in mind, usually the last paragraph almost verbatim. I begin at the beginning and stay close to the track, if it is a track and not a whalepath. If it turns out I'm in the open sea, my compass is my narrative instinct, with assistance from that astrolabe, theme. The destination, wherever it is, is, as I said, already defined. If I go astray it's not a long excursus, good for getting to know the ocean if not the world. The original idea, altered but recognizable, on the whole remains.   —*Bernard Malamud*

When I was at Harvard I got to know Robert Fitzgerald, and I used to show my poems to him. In spite of the fact that I was older than he was—I was a graduate student and he was a sophomore—

I had enormous respect for him. He was better educated than I was, and intransigent, and he despised anything that wasn't first rate. One day he looked at my poem and then he looked at me, rather in the way you look at children who present a problem, and he said, "Why don't you write prose?" I was so happy that he thought I could write *anything* that I just turned to and wrote prose—as if he'd given me permission to try. The prose took the form of fiction because I do like stories and don't have a very firm grasp on ideas.

—*William Maxwell*

Whether you're at your desk or not when a poem's under way, isn't there that constant eddy in your mind? If it's strong enough all sorts of random flotsam gets drawn into it, how selectively it's hopeless to decide at the time. I try to break off, get away from the page, into the kitchen for a spell of mixing and marinating which gives the words a chance to sort themselves out behind my back. But there's really no escape, except perhaps the third drink. On "ordinary" days, days when you've nothing on the burner, it might be safe to say that you're not a poet at all: more like a doctor at a dinner party, just another guest until his hostess slumps to the floor or his little beeper goes off. Most of those signals are false alarms—only they're not. Language *is* your medium. You can be talking or writing a letter, and out comes an observation, a "sentence-sound" you rather like. It needn't be your own. And it's not going to make a poem, or even fit into one. But the *twinge* it gives you—and it's this, I daresay, that distinguishes you from the "citizen"—reminds you you've got to be careful, that you've a condition that needs watching.

—*James Merrill*

Each man has his own way. After all, most writing is done away from the typewriter, away from the desk. I'd say it occurs in the quiet, silent moments, while you're walking or shaving or playing a game or whatever, or even talking to someone you're not vitally interested in. You're working, your mind is working, on this problem in the back of your head. So, when you get to the machine it's a mere matter of transfer.

What is an artist? He's a man who has antennae, who knows how to hook up to the currents which are in the atmosphere, in the cosmos; he merely has the facility for hooking on, as it were. Who is original? Everything that we are doing, everything that we think, exists already, and we are only intermediaries, that's all, who make use of what is in the air. Why do ideas, why do great scientific discoveries often occur in different parts of the world at the same time? The same is true of the elements that go to make up a poem or a great novel or any work of art. They are already in the air, they have not been given voice, that's all. They need *the* man, *the* interpreter, to bring them forth.   —*Henry Miller*

"Get black on white," used to be Maupassant's advice—that's what I always do. I don't give a hoot what the writing's like; I write any sort of rubbish which will cover the main outlines of the story, then I can begin to see it. When I write, when I draft a story, I never think of writing nice sentences about, "It was a nice August evening when Elizabeth Jane Moriarty was coming down the road." I just write roughly what happened, and then I'm able to see what the construction looks like. It's the design of the story which to me is most important, the thing that tells you there's a bad gap in the narrative here and you really ought to fill that up in some way or another. I'm always looking at the design of a story, not the treatment. Yesterday I was finishing off a piece about my friend A. E. Coppard, the greatest of all the English storytellers, who died about a fortnight ago. I was describing the way Coppard must have written these stories, going around with a notebook, recording what the lighting looked like, what that house looked like, and all the time using metaphor to suggest it to himself: "The road looked like a mad serpent going up the hill," or something of the kind, and, "she said so-and-so, and the man in the pub said something else." After he had written them all out, he must have got the outline of his story and he'd start working in all the details. Now, I could never do that at all. I've got to see what these people did, first of all, and then I start thinking of whether it was a nice August evening or a spring evening. I have to wait for the theme before I can do anything. —*Frank O'Connor*

I can't remember exactly how a given play developed in my mind. I think what happens is that I write in a very high state of excitement and frustration. I follow what I see on the paper in front of me— one sentence after another. That doesn't mean I don't have a dim, possible overall idea—the image that starts off doesn't just engender what happens immediately, it engenders the possibility of an overall happening, which carries me through. I've got an idea of what *might* happen—sometimes I'm absolutely right, but on many occasions I've been proved wrong by what does actually happen. Sometimes I'm going along and I find myself writing "C. comes in" when I didn't know that he was going to come in; he *had* to come in at that point, that's all. —*Harold Pinter*

The truth is, I have never written a story in my life that didn't have a very firm foundation in actual human experience—somebody else's experience quite often, but an experience that became my own by hearing the story, by witnessing the thing, by hearing just a word perhaps. It doesn't matter, it just takes a little—a tiny seed. Then it takes root, and it grows. It's an organic thing. That story ["Flowering Judas"] had been on my mind for years, growing out of this one little thing that happened in Mexico. It was forming and forming in my mind, until one night I was quite desperate—people are always so sociable, and I'm sociable too, and if I live around friends . . . Well, they were insisting that I come and play bridge. But I was very firm, because I knew the time had come to write that story, and I had to write it.

Something I saw as I passed a window one evening. A girl I knew had asked me to come and sit with her, because a man was coming to see her, and she was a little afraid of him. And as I went through the courtyard, past the flowering judas tree, I glanced in the window and there she was sitting with an open book on her lap, and there was this great big fat man sitting beside her. Now Mary and I were friends, both American girls living in this revolutionary situation. She was teaching at an Indian school, and I was teaching dancing at a girls' technical school in Mexico City. And we were having a very strange time of it. I was more skeptical, and so I had already begun to look with a skeptical eye on a great many of the revolutionary leaders—oh, the idea was all right, but a lot of men were misapplying it.

And when I looked through that window that evening, I saw something in Mary's face, something in her pose, something in the whole situation, that set up a commotion in my mind. Because until that moment I hadn't really understood that she was not able to take care of herself, because she was not able to face her own nature and was afraid of everything.

I don't know why I saw it. I don't believe in intuition. When you get sudden flashes of perception, it is just the brain working faster than usual. But you've been getting ready to know it for a long time, and when it comes, you feel you've know it always.

—*Katherine Anne Porter*

It is hard to describe. I have an idea of the beginning. I write the first line and continue to the last. I correct a great deal, work hard and write several drafts, but I never question the finished work. So I start with the first words which will be the first words of the book, but I never know how it will develop or end. The first idea is vague, but I know that it is the generating force—later everything can change. I can well imagine Proust writing: "For a long time I used to go to bed early. . ." and not knowing what story he was going to tell.

—*Alain Robbe-Grillet*

Many of my poems are love poems. I'm only able to write poetry, for the most part, when I have a Muse, a woman who focuses the world for me. She may be a lover, may not. In one case it was a person I saw only once, at lunch in a room with a lot of other people, and I wrote a whole book of poems. Many of these poems have not been published. But this is the mystery. Something happens which touches the source of poetry and ignites it. Sometimes it is the result of a long love affair, as with "The Divorce of Lovers" poems, the sonnet sequence. But not always. So who is the audience for my poetry? The audience is the loved one for me. But usually "the loved one" isn't really interested in the poems. —*May Sarton*

Watching, listening, remembering. A lot of them from my friends or people I meet. Sometimes from a general feeling or belief which is strong enough to make me invent characters and situations to state it. For example, my story *The Eighty-Yard Run,* which was about an ex-football player, a minor hero, who turns into a complete failure by the age of thirty-five, came as a result of my seeing around me so many men, all of whose best moments had come in their youth. I wanted to express that and show the subtle disappointments and inadequacies which bring so many promising young men to failure so early. Americans are at their best in their youth, and for me, at least, nothing is more characteristic of that best side and best moment of Americans than the race down the football field under a kickoff, in which are mingled gaiety, grace, recklessness, good-humored ferocity, skill at high speed, all taking place in a particular atmosphere of health and holiday that is duplicated nowhere else in the world. It was a productive symbol both for me and for the reader, and I built my story around the feelings of past joy and present regret that remembering it gave me. —*Irwin Shaw*

There are two theories of inspiration. One idea is that poetry can actually be dictated to you, like it was to William Blake. You are in a hallucinated state, and you hear a voice or you are in communication with something outside, like James Merrill's new poem, which he says is dictated through the Ouija board by Auden and other people.

The other idea is Paul Valéry's, what he calls *une ligne donnée*, that you are given one line and you try to follow up this clue, pulling the whole poem out of it. My own experience is that a rhythm or something comes into my head which I feel I must do, I must write it, create it.

For example, I recall looking out of a railway window and seeing an industrial landscape, factories, slag heaps, and the line coming into my head: "A language of flesh and roses." The thought at the back of this was that the industrial landscape was a language, what people have made out of nature, the contrast of nature and the industrial, "A language of flesh and roses." The problem of the poem was to work this connection out, trying to go back to remember what you really thought at that instant, and trying to re-create it. If I think of a poem, I may spend six months writing, but what I am really trying to do is remember what I thought of at that instant.

— *Stephen Spender*

Something I read or see stays in my head for five or six years. I always remember the date, the place, the room, the road, when I first was struck. For instance, *World Enough and Time*. Katherine Anne Porter and I were both at the Library of Congress as Fellows. We were in the same pew, had offices next to each other. She came in one day with an old pamphlet, the trial of Beauchamp for killing Colonel Sharp. She said, "Well, Red, you better read this." There it was. I read it in five minutes. But I was six years making the book. Any book I write starts with a flash but takes a long time to shape up. All of your first versions are in your head so by the time you sit down to write you have some line developed in your head.

— *Robert Penn Warren*

The process by which the idea for a play comes to me has always been something I really couldn't pinpoint. A play just seems to materialize, like an apparition it gets clearer and clearer and clearer. It's very vague at first, as in the case of *Streetcar*, which came after

Menagerie. I simply had the vision of a woman in her late youth. She was sitting in a chair all alone by a window with the moonlight streaming in on her desolate face, and she'd been stood up by the man she planned to marry.

I believe I was thinking of my sister because she was madly in love with some young man at the International Shoe Company who paid her court. He was extremely handsome, and she was profoundly in love with him. Whenever the phone would ring, she'd nearly faint. She'd think it was he calling for a date, you know? They saw each other every other night, and then one time he just didn't call anymore. That was when Rose first began to go into a mental decline. From that vision *Streetcar* evolved. I called it, at the time, *Blanche's Chair in the Moon,* which is a very bad title. But it was from that image, you know, of a woman sitting by a window that *Streetcar* came to me.

—*Tennessee Williams*

ON THE AUDIENCE

I've written some poetry I don't understand myself.

—*Carl Sandburg*

To have great poets, there must be great audiences, too.

—*Walt Whitman*

I just try to put the thing out and hope somebody will read it. Someone says: "Whom do you write for?" I reply: "Do you read me?" If they say "Yes," I say, "Do you like it?" If they say "No," then I say, "I don't write for you." —*W. H. Auden*

In bed last night I was reading a collection of articles by Stendhal. One of them amused me very much, touched me. Stendhal was saying how lucky writers were in the age of Louis XIV not to have anyone take them very seriously. Their obscurity was very valuable. Corneille had been dead for several days before anyone at court considered the fact important enough to mention. In the 19th century, says Stendhal, there would have been several public orations, Corneille's funeral covered by all the papers. There are great advantages in not being taken *too* seriously. Some writers are excessively serious about themselves. They accept the ideas of the "cultivated public." There is such a thing as overcapitalizing the A in Artist. Certain writers and musicians understand this. Stravinsky says the composer should practice his trade exactly as a shoemaker does. Mozart and Haydn accepted commissions—wrote to order. In the 19th century, the artist loftily waited for Inspiration. Once you elevate yourself to the rank of a cultural institution, you're in for a lot of trouble.

ON THE AUDIENCE

• • •

I have in mind another human being who will understand me. I count on this. Not on perfect understanding, which is Cartesian, but on approximate understanding, which is Jewish. And on a meeting of sympathies, which is human. But I have no ideal reader in my head, no. Let me say just this, too. I seem to have the blind self-acceptance of the eccentric who can't conceive that his eccentricities are not clearly understood.   —Saul Bellow

My "imaginary reader" can be "uneducated," but with a vacillating optimism that sometimes approaches pessimism. I still consider language to be a means of communication with this reader. Even complicated events—which form topics in essays or reviews—are communicable to the "uneducated" reader. [The most difficult aspect of writing], considering my "imaginary reader," is being able to be understood without having to compromise by making something easy that isn't easy, or by making something unnecessarily difficult when it is easy in the first place.   —Heinrich Böll

Perhaps a few personal friends of mine. Not myself because I never reread what I've written. I'm far too afraid to feel ashamed of what I've done.   —Jorge Luis Borges

As I write I think about Auden, what he would say—would he find it rubbish, or kind of entertaining? Auden and Orwell.
                                    —Joseph Brodsky

The ideal reader of my novels is a lapsed Catholic and failed musician, short-sighted, color-blind, auditorially biased, who has read the books that I have read. He should also be about my age.
                                    —Anthony Burgess

All sorts of pleasant and intelligent people read the books and write thoughtful letters about them. I don't know who they are, but they are marvelous and seem to live quite independently of the prejudices of advertising, journalism, and the cranky academic world. Think of the books that have enjoyed independent lives. *Let Us Now Praise Famous Men. Under the Volcano. Henderson the Rain King.* A splendid book like *Humboldt's Gift* was received with confusion and dismay, but hundreds of thousands of people went out and bought hardcover copies. The room where I work has a window looking into a wood, and I like to think that these earnest, lovable, and mysterious readers are in there.   —*John Cheever*

You are always concentrated on the inner thing. The moment one becomes aware of the crowd—performs for the crowd—it is spectacle. It is *fichu.*   —*Jean Cocteau*

I suppose very isolated, lonely folk. I remember one letter from a girl in a midwestern town who read one of my books and thought she had discovered it—that no one had ever read it or knew about it. Then one day in her local library she found cards for one or two of my other books. They were full of names—the books were borrowed all the time. She resented this a bit and then walked around the town looking in everybody's face and wondering if they were the ones who were reading my books. That is someone I write for.

—*J. P. Donleavy*

What really annoys me are the ones who write to say, I am doing your book for my final examinations and could you please tell me what the meaning of it is. I find it just so staggering—that you're supposed to explain the meaning of your book to some total stranger! If I knew what the meanings of my books were, I wouldn't have bothered to write them.   —*Margaret Drabble*

I myself am too busy to care about the public. I have no time to wonder who is reading me. I don't care about John Doe's opinion on my or anyone else's work. Mine is the standard which has to be met, which is when the work makes me feel the way I do when I read *La Tentation de Saint-Antoine,* or the Old Testament. They make me feel good. So does watching a bird make me feel good. You know that if I were reincarnated, I'd want to come back a buzzard. Nothing hates him or envies him or wants him or needs him. He is never bothered or in danger, and he can eat anything.

—*William Faulkner*

When I write I *don't* think of the audience. After the fact I think, "Well there. I hope they like it." —*William Gaddis*

In general I think you usually do write for someone. When I'm writing I'm always aware that this friend is going to like this, or that another friend is going to like that paragraph or chapter, always thinking of specific people. In the end all books are written for your friends. The problem after writing *One Hundred Years of Solitude* was that now I no longer know whom of the millions of readers I am writing for; this upsets and inhibits me. It's like a million eyes are looking at you and you don't really know what they think.

—*Gabriel García Márquez*

I don't think much about the reader. Ways of reading are adversaries—those theoretical ways. As far as writing something is concerned, the reader really doesn't exist. The writer's business is somehow to create in the work something which will stand on its own and make its own demands; and if the writer is good, he discovers what those demands are, and he meets them, and creates this thing which readers can then do what they like with. Gertrude Stein said, "I write for myself and strangers," and then eventually she said that she wrote only for herself. I think she should have taken one further step. You don't write *for* anybody. People who send you bills do that. People who want to sell you things so they can send you bills do that. People who want to tell you things so they can sell you things so they can send you bills do that. You are advancing an art—the art. That is what you are trying to do.   —*William Gass*

I suppose it's that audience which has no tradition by which to measure their experience but the intensity and clarity of their inner lives. That's the audience I'd like to be good enough to write for.
          —*Norman Mailer*

There are some biological laws in the theater which can't be violated. It should not be made into an activated chess game. You can't have a theater based upon anything other than a mass audience if it's going to succeed. The larger the better. It's the law of the theater. In the Greek audience fourteen thousand people sat down at the same time, to see a play. Fourteen thousand people! And nobody can tell me that those people were all readers of *The New York Review of Books*! Even Shakespeare was smashed around in his time by university people. I think for much the same reasons—because he was reaching for those parts of man's makeup which respond to melodrama, broad comedy, violence, dirty words, and blood. Plenty of blood, murder, and not very well motivated at that.

· · ·

People are pretty primitive—they really want the thing to turn out all right. After all, for a century and half *King Lear* was played in England with a happy ending. I wrote a radio play about the boy who wrote that version—William Ireland—who forged Shakespeare's plays, and edited *King Lear* so that it conformed to a middleclass view of life. They thought, including all but Malone, who was the first good critic, that this was the real Shakespeare. He was an expert forger. He fixed up several of the other plays, but this one he really rewrote. He was seventeen years old. And they produced it—it was a big success—and Boswell thought it was the greatest thing he'd ever seen, and so did all the others. They only one was Malone, who on the basis of textual impossibilities—aside from the fact that he sensed it was a bowdlerization—proved that it couldn't have been Shakespeare. It's what I was talking about before: the litmus paper of the playwright: you see Ireland sensed quite correctly what those people really wanted from *King Lear*, and he gave it to them. He sentimentalized it; took out any noxious references. It ended with a kind of happy family reunion . . . like a Jewish melodrama. A family play.

. . .

There's a wonderful naivete that the Parisian theater public has; they're not bored to death. They're not coming in out of the rain, so to speak, with nothing better to do. When they go to the theater, it has great weight with them. They come to see something that'll change their lives. Ninety percent of the time, of course, there's nothing there, but they're open to a grand experience. This is not the way we go to the theater.   —*Arthur Miller*

I found writing novels rather a lonely business. You very rarely actually catch anyone reading them. I've heard of a novelist who got onto the tube at Piccadilly Circus for the purpose of getting out at Green Park, a distance of one stop. And as he got onto the tube he found himself sitting next to a girl who was in fact reading one of his novels. And he knew that two hundred pages further on there was a joke. So he sat on till Cockfosters, the end of the line, in the faint hope of hearing a laugh which never came.   —*John Mortimer*

When you are writing you are not conscious of the reader, so that you don't feel embarrassed. I'm sure Joyce had a most heady and wonderful time writing the last fifty pages of *Ulysses*—glorious Molly Bloom. He must have written it in one bout, thinking: I'll show the women of the world that I am omniscient!   —*Edna O'Brien*

I hold out for some sort of contractual relationship between novelist and reader, however flawed, misapprehended or fragmentary. Perhaps the contract is ultimately narratological, perhaps not. But something keeps—or fails to keep—the reader reading the next sentence. Even

the "antinovel" presupposes some sort of contractual venture at the very moment the "antinovelist" is attacking narrativity. Such a venture implies that the writer is up to something, going abroad like Don Quixote—if only to attack windmills—and that the reader is with him. Otherwise why would the latter bother? The antinovelist is like a Protestant. His protests might be valid, but where would he be without the Catholic Church? I have no objection to "antistory" novels. What I object to is any excursion by the author which violates the novelistic contract between writer and reader which I take to be an intersubjective transaction entailing the transmission of a set of symbols, a text. The writer violates the contract when he trashes the reader by pornography or scatological political assaults, e.g., depicting President Nixon in a novel buggering Ethel Rosenberg in Times Square, or LBJ plotting the assassination of JFK. Take pornography, a difficult, slippery case. It is not necessary to get into a discussion of First Amendment rights—for all I know it has them. And for all I know, pornography has its uses. All I suggest is that pornography and literature stimulate different organs. If we can agree that a literary text is a set of signals transmitted from sender to receiver in a certain code, pornography is a different set of signals and a different code.
—*Walker Percy*

I don't know if that grocer on my shoulder digs all the references, but other than him, I write pretty much for myself. If, at the close of business each evening, I myself can understand what I've written, I feel the day hasn't been totally wasted.   —*S. J. Perelman*

I occasionally have an anti-Roth reader in mind. I think, "How he is going to hate this!" That can be just the encouragement I need.
—*Philip Roth*

This situation of not having a very large audience has something good in it too. I mean that it educates you in a certain way: not to consider that great audiences are the most important reward on this earth. I consider that even if I have three people who read me, I mean really read me, it is enough. That reminds me of a conversation I had once upon a time during the only glimpse I ever had of Henri Michaux. It was when he had a stop-over in Athens, coming from Egypt, I think. He came ashore while his ship was in Piraeus just in order to have a look at the Acropolis. And he told me on that occasion: "You know, my dear, a man who has only one reader is not a writer. A man who has two readers is not a writer either. But a man who has *three* readers (and he pronounced "three readers" as though they were three million), that man is *really* a writer."

• • •

I'm sorry to say that I never felt I was the spokesman for anything or anybody. There are no credentials which appoint anybody to be a spokesman for something. Now others consider that a sort of function which must be performed; but I think that is, after all, why I have written so little. I've never felt the obligation; I have to consider only that I am not dried up as a poet and to write. I mean that has been my feeling from the very beginning. I remember when I published my first book, there were lots of people who said: "Mr. Seferis, you must now try to show us that you can do more." I answered them: "Gentlemen, you must consider that every poem published by me is the last one. I never have any feeling about its continuation." My last poem. And if I write another one, it's a great blessing.

—*George Seferis*

I wrote "The Girls in Their Summer Dresses" one morning while my wife Marian was lying in bed and reading. And I knew I had something good there, but I didn't want her to read it, knowing that the reaction would be violent, to say the least, because it's about a man who tells his wife that he's going to be unfaithful to her. So I turned it facedown, and I said, "Don't read this yet. It's not ready." It was the only copy I had. Then I went out and took a walk, had a drink, and came back. She was raging around the room. She said, "It's a lucky thing you came back just now, because I was going to open the window and throw it out." Since then she's become reconciled to it, and I think she reads it with pleasure, too.

• • •

I have a fine play in mind I'll write for them [theater audiences] someday. The curtain slides up on a stage bare except for a machine gun facing the audience. Then after a pause in which the audience is given time to rustle their paper bags and their programs, wheeze and cough and settle in their seats, the actor enters. He's a tall man dressed in evening clothes. He comes downstage to the footlights and after a little bow smiles charmingly at the audience, giving them more time to mumble and rustle and cough and whisper and settle in their seats. Then he walks upstage, adjusts the machine gun, and blasts them.   —*Irwin Shaw*

I've always tried out my material on my dogs first. You know, with Angel, he sits there and listens and I get the feeling he understands everything. But with Charley, I always felt he was just waiting to get a word in edgewise. Years ago, when my red setter chewed up the manuscript of *Of Mice and Men,* I said at the time that the dog must have been an excellent literary critic.   —*John Steinbeck*

Faulkner doesn't give enough help to the reader. I'm all for the complexity of Faulkner, but not for the confusion. That goes for Joyce, too. All that fabulously beautiful poetry in the last part of *Finnegans Wake* is pretty much lost to the world simply because not many people are ever going to put up with the chaos that precedes it. As for *The Sound and the Fury,* I think it succeeds in spite of itself. Faulkner often simply stays too damn intense for too long a time. It ends up being great stuff, somehow, though, and the marvel is how it could be so wonderful being pitched for so long in that one high, prolonged, delirious key.

—*William Styron*

Someone once wrote a definition of the difference between English and American humor. I wish I could remember his name. I thought his definition very good. He said that the English treat the commonplace as if it were remarkable and the Americans treat the remarkable as if it were commonplace. I believe that's true of humorous writing. Years ago we did a parody of *Punch* in which Benchley did a short piece depicting a wife bursting into a room and shouting "The primroses are in bloom"—treating the commonplace as remarkable, you see. In *The Secret Life of Walter Mitty* I tried to treat the remarkable as commonplace. —*James Thurber*

When I write, I aim in my mind not toward New York but toward a vague spot a little to the east of Kansas. I think of the books on library shelves, without their jackets, years old, and a countryish teen-aged boy finding them, and having them speak to him. The reviews, the stacks in Brentano's, are just hurdles to get over, to place the books on that shelf. —*John Updike*

At the time of writing, I don't write for my friends or myself, either; I write for *it*, for the pleasure of *it*. I believe if I stopped to wonder what So-and-so would think, or what I'd feel like if this were read by a stranger, I would be paralyzed. I care what my friends think, very deeply—and it's only after they've read the finished thing that I really can rest, deep down. But in the writing, I have to just keep going straight through with only the *thing* in mind and what it dictates.

It's so much an inward thing that reading the proofs later can be a real shock. When I received them for my first book—no, I guess it was for *Delta Wedding*—I thought, *I* didn't write this. It was a page of dialogue—I might as well have never seen it before. I wrote to my editor, John Woodburn, and told him something had happened to that page in the typesetting. He was kind, not even surprised—maybe this happens to all writers. He called me up and read me from the manuscript—word for word what the proofs said. Proofs don't shock me any longer, yet there's still a strange moment with every book when I move from the position of writer to the position of reader, and I suddenly see my words with the eyes of the cold public. It gives me a terrible sense of exposure, as if I'd gotten sunburned.

—*Eudora Welty*

I think it was a Spanish poet—it may have been Calderón—who said that all his life he had been like a swimmer who could only use one arm, because with the other arm he had to hold his poems up over the waters. The things that he really cared about. It's strange, but we live in a world which is even more alienated from poetry than it used to be; most people don't care or know anything about poetry. Most civilized, cultivated people know something about painting, they go to galleries; they know something about music, they go to concerts; but no one cares or knows anything about poetry except the poets themselves. Since the poets don't expect anyone else to read them, many of them have devised a way of communicating with one another through their poems, and readers often find such poetry difficult. Prose is, of course, easier. —*John Hall Wheelock*

ON PERFORMANCE

When my horse is running good, I don't stop to give him sugar.
　　　　　　　　　　　　　　　　　　　　—*William Faulkner*

When I described how Emma Bovary poisoned herself, I had such
a strong taste of arsenic in my mouth, I was so poisoned myself,
that I had two attacks of indigestion, one after the other, very real
attacks, for I vomited my entire dinner.　　　—*Gustave Flaubert*

How do I know what I think until I see what I say?
　　　　　　　　　　　　　　　　　　　　　—*E. M. Forster*

We are all apprentices in a craft where no one ever becomes a
master.　　　　　　　　　　　　　　　　　—*Ernest Hemingway*

Who casts a living line, must sweat.　　　　　　—*Ben Jonson*

The idea is to get the pencil moving quickly.　—*Bernard Malamud*

There is no need for the writer to eat a whole sheep to be able to
tell what mutton tastes like. It is enough if he eats a cutlet.
　　　　　　　　　　　　　　　　　　　　—*Somerset Maugham*

Nothing, unless it is difficult, is worth while.　　　　—*Ovid*

Naturally, no writer who's any good at all would sit down and put
a sheet of paper in a typewriter and start typing a play unless he
knew what he was writing about. But at the same time, writing has
got to be an act of discovery. Finding out things about what one is
writing about. To a certain extent I imagine a play is completely
finished in my mind—in my case at any rate—without my knowing
it, before I sit down to write. So in that sense, I suppose, writing a

play is *finding out* what the play is. I always find that the better answer
to give. It's a question I despise, and it always seems to me better
to slough off the answer to a question which I consider to be a terrible
invasion of privacy—the kind of privacy that a writer must keep for
himself. If you intellectualize and examine the creative process too
carefully, it can evaporate and vanish. It's not only terribly difficult
to talk about, it's also dangerous. You know the old story about the—
I think it's one of Aesop's Fables, or perhaps not, or a Chinese story—
about the very clever animal that saw a centipede that he didn't like.
He said, "My God, it's amazing and marvelous how you walk with
all those hundreds and hundreds of legs. How do you do it? How do
you get them all moving that way?" The centipede stopped and
thought and said, "Well, I take the left front leg and then I—" and
he thought about it for a while, and he couldn't walk.

—*Edward Albee*

It is simply this: a writer has to take all the risks of putting down
what he sees. No one can tell him about that. No one can control
that reality. It reminds me of something Pablo Picasso was supposed
to have said to Gertrude Stein while he was painting her portrait.
Gertrude said, "I don't look like that." And Picasso replied, "You
will." And he was right.

•   •   •

I have a pretty good sense of where the book is going to go. By
temperament I am an incorrigible formalist, not inclined to embark
on a project without knowing where I'm going. It takes me about
four years to write a novel. To embark on such a project without
some idea of what the landfall and the estimated time of arrival were
would be rather alarming. But I have learned from experience that
there are certain barriers that you cannot cross until you get to them;
in a thing as long and complicated as a novel you may not even know
the real shape of the obstacle until you heave in sight of it, much
less how you're going to get around it. I can see in my plans that
there will be this enormous pothole to cross somewhere around the

third chapter from the end; I'll get out my little pocket calculator and estimate that the pothole will be reached about the second of July, 1986, let's say, and then just trust to God and the muses that by the time I get there I'll know how to get around it.

—*John Barth*

Work is the only device I know of. Writing has laws of perspective, of light and shade, just as painting does, or music. If you are born knowing them, fine. If not, learn them. Then rearrange the rules to suit yourself. Even Joyce, our most extreme disregarder, was a superb craftsman; he could write *Ulysses because* he could write *Dubliners.* Too many writers seem to consider the writing of short stories as a kind of finger exercise. Well, in such cases, it is certainly only their fingers they are exercising.

. . .

Since each story presents its own technical problems, obviously one can't generalize about them on a 2 × 2 = 4 basis. Finding the right form for your story is simply to realize the most *natural* way of telling the story. The test of whether or not a writer has divined the natural shape of his story is just this: after reading it, can you imagine it differently, or does it silence your imagination and seem to you absolute and final? As an orange is final. As an orange is something nature has made just right.

—*Truman Capote*

I feel myself inhabited by a force or being—very little known to me. *It gives* the orders; I follow. The conception of my novel *Les Enfants Terribles* came to me from a friend, from what he told me of a circle: a family closed from societal life. I commenced to write: exactly seventeen pages per day. It went well. I was pleased with it. Very. There was in the original life story some connection with America, and I had something I wanted to say about America. Poof! The being in me did not want to write that! Dead halt. A month of stupid staring at paper unable to say anything. One day it commenced again in its own way.

. . .

When it goes well—the euphoria of such moments has been much the most intense and joyous of my life experience.   —*Jean Cocteau*

It's like improvising in jazz. You don't ask a jazz musician, "But what are you going to play?" He'll laugh at you. He has a theme, a series of chords he has to respect, and then he takes up his trumpet or his saxophone and he begins. It's not a question of *idea*. He performs through a series of different internal pulsations. Sometimes it comes out well, sometimes it doesn't. It's the same with me. I'm a bit embarrassed to sign my stories sometimes. The novels, no, because the novels I work on a lot; there's a whole architecture. But my stories, it's as if they were dictated to me by something that is in me, but it's not me who's responsible. Well, since it does appear they are mine even so, I guess I should accept them!   —*Julio Cortázar*

I do know the story when I begin, but I don't know how it's going to end. I know about two-thirds of it, and then the end emerges as I go on. I shrink from saying this, but I've agreed to come here and talk about it, and it's true: I hear the story, I am told the story, I record the story. I don't pretend that some remarkable person some- where else is whispering in my ear, or that a beautiful lady in a diaphanous garment is telling me what I should write. It is just part of my own creative process which I am not immediately in touch with and certainly not in full control of. And so the story emerges. There can be no two ways about how it's going to end. It just ends the way it's going to end. I don't think that that is very mysterious, for if the story is any good, it must have an inevitability, although some critics dispute that. They say they're full of coincidence and this, that or the other; but the fact is that my life seems to be much fuller of coincidence and curious happenings than the lives of critics. What I mean is, the kind of mind which makes a critic is an analytical, cool, infinitely, unenviably, cautious mind. A recent professorial crit- icism of *What's Bred in the Bone* was very severe with me for my attraction to arcane lore and weird belief—no use explaining that to me the arcane lore isn't arcane at all, and makes wonderful sense, and that almost all belief is strange, if you catch it with the light falling on it in a certain way. I wish professorial critics, who often write so dully, would give me the credit for a minimum of wits, and stop elevating themselves as the standard by which all belief and understanding should be measured! What sort of books would Balzac and Dickens have written if they had listened to such stuff?

• • •

My family background was Welsh, and the Welsh are very, very fond of storytelling and tend to be rather good at it. They're also fond of children, but they are not in the modern way infinitely tolerant of children. They think children need to be *taught* and they *teach* them. They teach them very often through stories. I feel that this quality of storytelling is basic to the novelist's art. Sometimes I am asked to talk to groups of students about writing, and the poor souls are filled to the brim with all the complex business about theories and types of narrative and this, that and the other. What I say to them is, "If you're a writer, a real writer, you're a descendant of those medieval storytellers who used to go into the square of a town and spread a little mat on the ground and sit on it and beat on a bowl and say, 'If you give a copper coin I will tell you a golden tale.' If the storyteller had what it took, he collected a little group and told them a golden tale until it got to the most exciting point and then he passed the bowl again. That was the way he made his living, and if he failed to hold his audience, he was through and had to take up some other line of work. Now this is what a writer must do." I get so sick of writers who make tedious demands on their readers and expect them to bear with them through infinitely refined analyses of meaning and this, that and the other. You really must have a story and you must tell it, or people will just put the book down and they will find it to be one of those books (unlike the ones you sometimes read about in book reviews) that once put down is impossible to take up again.
                                                              —*Robertson Davies*

One of the difficulties in writing poetry is to maintain your sense of excitement and discovery about what you write. American literature is full of people who started off excited about poetry and their own contribution to it and their own relationship to poetry and have had, say, a modicum of success and have just gone on writing poetry as a kind of tic, a sort of reflex, when they've lost all their original excitement and enthusiasm for what they do. They do it because they have learned to do it, and that's what they *do*. You have to find private stratagems to keep up your original enthusiasm, no matter what it takes. As you get older, that's tougher and tougher to do. You want to try to avoid, if you possibly can, the feeling of doing it simply because you *can* do it.   —James Dickey

As the book goes on it becomes inevitable. Your choices narrow, the thing picks up speed. And there's the exhilaration of a free ride— like a downhill ski run. You know before you get there what the last scene is. Sometimes what the last line is. But even if none of that happens, even if you find yourself at the end before you expected to, a kind of joy breaks over you, spills out of your eyes. And you realize you've finished. And then you want to be sure, you see. You need confirmation. You ask somebody you love to read it and see if it works. I remember when I finished *The Book of Daniel*. We were living in a house on the beach in Southern California. One of those houses with sliding glass doors for windows. I asked my wife if she would read the manuscript. She said she would be pleased to. And I left her sitting and reading with the sun coming through those big windows, and I went for a walk on the beach. It was a Sunday and the beach was crowded; they really use their beaches in California, every inch of them. Back toward the road were the volleyball players and the kite flyers. Boys throwing footballs or Frisbees. Then the sunbathers, the children with their sandpails, the families. Then the runners splashing along at the edge of the surf. Or the people looking for little shells in the tide pools in the rocks. Then the swimmers. Beyond them the surfers in their wet suits waiting on their boards.

ON PERFORMANCE

Further out snorkelers' flags bobbing in the water. Out past the buoys the water skiers tearing along. Or rising into the air in their parachutes. And beyond that sailboats, flotillas of them, to the horizon. And all in this light. It was like a Brueghel, a Southern Californian Brueghel. I walked for several hours and thought about my book, and worried in my mind, in that California light worrying about this dark book, very much a New York City book. Was it done? Was it any good? And I came back to the house in the late afternoon, the house in shadows now, and there was Helen sitting in the same chair and the manuscript was all piled upside down on the table and she couldn't speak; she was crying, there were these enormous tears running down her cheeks, and it was the most incredible moment—never before had I known such happiness   —*E. L. Doctorow*

You get a great deal off your chest—emotions, impressions, opinions. Curiosity urges you on—the driving force. What is collected must be got rid of. That's one thing to be said about writing. There is a great sense of relief in a fat volume.   —*John Dos Passos*

I've often worried about this—if one got really very happy in life, one might not want to write at all. I think grief is creative. And, in some awful way, boredom is creative. When I'm really deeply bored (inevitably I'm rather miserable at the same time) I find this a creative phase because one's got to get something. One's got to rise out of it in some way. And the way that I'm most familiar with is by writing.   —*Margaret Drabble*

Poetry is form, and the wooing and seduction of form is the whole game. You can have all the apparatus in the world, but what you finally need is something like a—I don't know what—a lasso . . . a very delicate thing, for catching wild deer. Oh, no, I'll give you an analogy for it. To write a poem is like trying to catch a lizard without its tail falling off. In India when I was a boy they had great big green lizards there, and if you shouted or shot them their tails would fall off. There was only one boy in the school who could catch lizards intact. No one knew quite how he did it. He had a special soft way of going up to them, and he'd bring them back with their tails on. That strikes me as the best analogy I can give you. To try and catch your poem without its tail falling off.　　　—*Lawrence Durrell*

It's a little like falling in love; at any rate that's the way it usually begins. You never know how long the affair or the infatuation will last. Of course, it's a one-sided love affair since the love object is dead or, if alive, relatively unwooable. Most biographies are begun out of enchantment or affection; you read a poem and want to find the poet, you hear a statesman and are filled with admiration, or you are stirred by the triumphs of a general or an admiral. In the writing of the life changes occur, discoveries are made. Realities emerge. The love affair, however exhilarating, has to be terminated if a useful biography is to emerge. Sometimes there is disenchantment and even hate; the biographer feels deceived. Isn't that the way all love affairs run—from dream and cloud-journey to earth-firmness?

—*Leon Edel*

People will not realize how little conscious one is of these things; how one flounders about. They want us to be so much better informed than we are. If critics could only have a course on writers' *not* thinking things out—a course of lectures.　　　—*E. M. Forster*

Very first one I wrote I was walking home from school and I began to make it—a March day—and I was making it all afternoon and making it so I was late at my grandmother's for dinner. I finished it, but it burned right up, just burned right up, you know. And what started that? what burned it? So many talk, I wonder how falsely, about what it costs them, what agony it is to write. I've often been quoted: "No tears in the writer, no tears in the reader. No surprise for the writer, no surprise for the reader." But another distinction I made is: however sad, no grievance, grief without grievance. How could I, how could anyone have a good time with what cost me too much agony, how could they? What do I want to communicate but what a *hell* of a good time I had writing it? The whole thing is performance and prowess and feats of association. Why don't critics talk about those things?—what a feat it was to turn that that way, and what a feat it was to remember that, to be reminded of that by this? Why don't they talk about that?

Scoring. You've got to *score*. They say not, but you've got to score—in all the realms—theology, politics, astronomy, history, and the country life around you.

• • •

I look at a poem as a performance. I look on the poet as a man of prowess, just like an athlete. He's a performer. And the things you can do in a poem are very various. You speak of figures, tones of voice varying all the time. I'm always interested, you know, when I have three or four stanzas, in the way I *lay* the sentences in them. I'd hate to have the sentences all lie the same in the stanzas. Every poem is like that: some sort of achievement in performance. Somebody has said that poetry among other things is the marrow of wit. That's probably way back somewhere—marrow of wit. There's got to be wit. And that's very, very much left out of a lot of this labored stuff. It doesn't sparkle at all. Another thing to say is that every thought, poetical or otherwise, every thought is a feat of association. They tell of old Gibbon—as he was dying he was the same Gibbon at his historical parallels. All thought is a feat of association: having what's in front of you bring up something in your mind that you almost didn't know you knew. Putting this and that together. That click.

—*Robert Frost*

Bernard Malamud and I had a conversation one time in which he said that he doesn't know how he does those magnificent things he sometimes does. He just keeps writing until it comes out right. If that's the way a writer works, then that's the way he has to work and that's fine. But I like to be in control as much of the time as possible. One of the first things you have to understand when you are writing fiction—or teaching writing—is that there are different ways of doing things, and each one has a slightly different effect. A misunderstanding of this leads you to the Bill Gass position: that fiction can't tell the truth, because every way you say the thing changes it. I don't think that's to the point. I think that what fiction does is sneak up on the truth by telling it six different ways and finally releasing it. That's what Dante said, that you can't really get at the poetic, inexpressible truths, that the way things are leaps up like steam between them. So you have to determine very accurately the potential of a particular writer's style and help that potential develop at the same time, ignoring what you think of his moral stands.

· · · ·

I get great pleasure out of stealing other people's writings. Actually, I do that at least partly because of a peculiar and unfortunate quality of my mind: I remember things. Word for word. I'm not always aware of it. Once in college, I wrote a paragraph of a novel which was word for word out of Joyce's "The Dead," and I wasn't aware of it at all. I absolutely wasn't. My teacher at the time said why did you do this? He wasn't accusing me of plagiarism, he was just saying it was a very odd thing to do. I realized then that I had a problem. Of course, it was a big help when I was a teacher, because I could quote long passages of Beowulf and things like that. Once I realized that I also accidentally quote, that I'm constantly alluding to things I'm not consciously aware of, I began to develop this allusive technique—at least when it's fiction—so that nobody could accuse me of plagiarism since it's so obvious that I'm alluding. In fact, sometimes I have great fun with it. Particularly in *Jason and Medeia,* where I took long sections of writing by Bill Gass, whom I'm enormously fond of, and with whom I completely disagree on almost everything unimportant, and altered a few words to mess up his arguments. And in *The Wreck of Agathon* I took long sections out of Jean-Paul Sartre, changed all the images, but kept the rest directly translated. So I use everything.

—*John Gardner*

ON PERFORMANCE

The leading atomic scientist in Australia agreed with me the other day that time does not really exist. The finished poem is present before it is written and one corrects it. It is the final poem that dictates what is right, what is wrong.   —*Robert Graves*

I'm not sure I understand the process of writing. There is, I'm sure, something strange about imaginative concentration. The brain slowly begins to function in a different way, to make mysterious connections. Say, it is Monday, and you write a very bad draft, but if you keep on trying, on Friday, words, phrases, appear almost unexpectedly. I don't know why you can't do it on Monday, or why I can't. I'm the same person, no smarter, I have nothing more at hand. I think it's true of a lot of writers. It's one of the things writing students don't understand. They write a first draft and are quite disappointed, or often *should* be disappointed. They don't understand that they have merely begun, and that they may be merely beginning even in the second or third draft.   —*Elizabeth Hardwick*

If a writer stops observing he is finished. But he does not have to observe consciously nor think how it will be useful. Perhaps that would be true at the beginning. But later everything he sees goes into the great reserve of things he knows or has seen. If it is any use to know it, I always try to write on the principle of the iceberg. There is seven-eighths of it underwater for every part that shows. Anything you know you can eliminate and it only strengthens your iceberg. It is the part that doesn't show. If a writer omits something because he does not know it then there is a hole in the story.

The Old Man and the Sea could have been over a thousand pages long and had every character in the village in it and all the processes of how they made their living, were born, educated, bore children, etc. That is done excellently and well by other writers. In writing you are limited by what has already been done satisfactorily. So I have tried to learn to do something else. First I have tried to eliminate everything unnecessary to conveying experience to the reader so that after he or she has read something it will become a part of his or her experience and seem actually to have happened. This is very hard to do and I've worked at it very hard.

. . .

The stories you mention I wrote in one day in Madrid on May sixteenth when it snowed out the San Isidro bullfights. First I wrote "The Killers," which I'd tried to write before and failed. Then after lunch I got in bed to keep warm and wrote "Today Is Friday." I had so much juice I thought maybe I was going crazy and I had about six other stories to write. So I got dressed and walked to Fornos, the old bullfighters' café, and drank coffee and then came back and wrote "Ten Indians." This made me very sad and I drank some brandy and went to sleep. I'd forgotten to eat and one of the waiters brought me up some *bacalao* and a small steak and fried potatoes and a bottle of Valdepeñas.

The woman who ran the Pension was always worried that I did not eat enough and she had sent the waiter. I remember sitting up in bed and eating, drinking the Valdepeñas. The waiter said he would bring up another bottle. He said the Señora wanted to know if I was going to write all night. I said no, I thought I would lay off for a while. Why don't you try to write just one more, the waiter asked. I'm only supposed to write one, I said. Nonsense, he said. You could write six. I'll try tomorrow, I said. Try it tonight, he said. What do you think the old woman sent the food up for?

I'm tired, I told him. Nonsense, he said (the word was not nonsense). You tired after three miserable little stories. Translate me one.

Leave me alone, I said. How am I going to write it if you don't leave me alone? So I sat up in bed and drank the Valdepeñas and thought what a hell of a writer I was if the first story was as good as I'd hoped.   —*Ernest Hemingway*

When the writing is really working, I think there is something like dreaming going on. I don't know how to draw the line between the conscious management of what you're doing and this state. It usually takes place in the earlier stages, in the drafting process. I would say that it's related to day-dreaming. When I feel really engaged with a passage, I become so lost in it that I'm unaware of my real surroundings, totally involved in the pictures and sounds that that passage evokes. So I think it's a kind of dream state of some sort, though it has baffled most people who've tried to analyze just what takes place in the creative process. Even Freud, who gave up on almost nothing, seemed to have given up on that. It remains mysterious; and it's probably a good thing that it does. It may be that the mystery is among the things that attract those of us who write.

—John Hersey

If I stop working and just try to enjoy myself, I get very neurotic and guilt-ridden. Orwell was the same. Like the man who, if he stops running, becomes afraid. Or the shark which must move to breathe. But I love playing games like Scrabble. That's not wasting time because it's an effort. Like climbing mountains, which I used to do too. Everything which is an effort is virtuous, is work, and is worth doing. *—Arthur Koestler*

I think the longest uninterrupted stretch I ever had was twenty-seven hours. I wrote nineteen pages of *The Painted Bird* which in the drafts that followed shrank to one page. On an average I probably "produce" about a page, maybe a page and a half, in a sitting. I write very much the way some of my poet friends do. I select from the novel's master plan, from its topography, a fragment of a scene I find most inspiring at the given time, and then write it moving either "above it" or "below it." Since I start with an image, let's say, of a man being driven in his car through the West Virginia countryside— I might first write about the rain, or his car, or what he felt at the end of the drive, and only then confront the scene's dramatic center. I usually start a novel by writing its opening and its end, which seem to survive relatively unchanged through all the following drafts and galley-proof changes. *—Jerzy Kosinski*

Over the course of my writing life the process has changed. When I was a kid speaking poetry I never wrote it down; those poems began with a phrase and then I would try to employ the vocabulary and the structure of the phrase to create a fabric of repetitions. When I started writing poetry at eighteen the poems seemed to spring outward from a visual image; it was that precise visual image I was out to capture; that's what excited me; the poem became the means for pushing forward the images I wanted the reader to devour. Then Yeats set me on fire. I mean the language is exalted, yet it sounds like somebody talking and singing at the same time. I thought, *this is it*. And I still kind of feel *this is it*. This is the perfection of form. It's got speech, song, it's high rhetoric and yet it doesn't sound remote or false. A poem like "Easter, 1916." I said, Jesus Christ, this is so much what I want. It doesn't matter about his stupid attitudes. He wrote one poem about his daughter, such a sexist poem. But it's so beautifully done. I remember telling a woman friend of mine, isn't this an incredible poem? and she got very angry with me; she said it's so sexist, look at this! I said, sure, it's like Eliot's anti-Semitic stuff, "the Jew squats on the windowsill," fuck you Eliot, but the poem is exquisite.

Then somewhere in my forties I hit a kind of phase of automatic writing. I would really be taken, sort of seized, and just write the stuff! It would just come pouring out, hundreds of lines. Then the process of making a poem became quite different: it became seeing what was inside this great blast of language and imagery, and finding the core.   —*Philip Levine*

You delight me by saying some of my poems sound as though they had come in a rush, but none of them have with the exception of "You, Andrew Marvell," which was there at the end of a morning and finished by night. I am sure—I mean I am not sure at all but I believe—the master poets must come at their poems as a hawk on a pigeon in one dive. I can't. I chip away like a stonemason who has got it into his head that there is a pigeon in that block of marble.

ON PERFORMANCE

But there's a delight in the chipping. At least there's a delight in it when your hunch that the pigeon in there is stronger than you are carries you along. There is no straining then nor *are* you strained—all assurance and confidence. Oh, you can be fooled, of course—there may be nothing there but a stone. But until you are...

· · ·

The first discipline is the realization that there *is* a discipline—that all art begins and ends with discipline, that any art is first and foremost a craft. We have gone far enough on the road to self-indulgence now to know that. The man who announces to the world that he is going to "do his thing" is like the amateur on the high-diving platform who flings himself into the void shouting at the judges that he is going to do whatever comes naturally. He will land on his ass. Naturally. You'd think, to listen to the loudspeakers which surround us, that no man had ever tried to "do his thing" before. Every poet worth reading has, but those really worth reading have understood that to do your thing you have to learn first what your thing is and second how to go about doing it. The first is learned by the difficult labor of living, the second by the endless discipline of writing and rewriting and rewriting. There are no shortcuts. Young writers a while back, misreading Bill Williams, decided to ignore the fact that poems are made of words as sounds as well as of words as signs—decided not to learn the art of words as sounds, not to be bothered with it. They were not interested in poems. They were interested in doing their thing. They did—and that was that.

· · ·

A book takes on its own life in the writing. It has its laws, it becomes a creature to you after a while. One feels a bit like a master who's got a fine animal. Very often I'll feel a certain shame for what I've done with a novel. I won't say it's the novel that's bad; I'll say it's I who was bad. Almost as if the novel did not really belong to me, as if it was something raised by me like a child. I know what's potentially beautiful in my novel, you see. Very often after I've done the novel I realize that that beauty which I recognize in it is not going to be recognized by the reader. I didn't succeed in bringing it out. It's very odd—it's as though I had let the novel down, owed it a duty which I didn't fulfill.   —Archibald MacLeish

Occasionally I have to look something up. But I'm always unhappy about that and mistrust the writing which comes out of it. I feel in a way that one's ignorance is part of one's creation, too. I don't know quite how to put it, but for instance if I, as a Jew, am writing about other Jews, and if my knowledge of Jewish culture is exceptionally spotty, as indeed it is, I am not so sure that that isn't an advantage in creating a modern American Jew. Because *his* knowledge of Jewish culture is also extremely spotty, and the way in which his personality is composed may be more in accordance with my ignorance than with a cultivated Jew's immersion in the culture. So in certain limited ways one's ignorance can help to buttress the validity of a novel.
                                                                —Norman Mailer

Frederick Buechner gave me a Ouija board as a birthday present in 1953. As I recall, we sat down then and there to try it, and got a touching little story from a fairly simple soul—that engineer "dead of cholera in Cairo," who'd met Goethe. I used it in the first thing I ever wrote about the Ouija board (a poem called "Voices from the Other World"), although by that time the *experiences* behind this poem were mine and David's. We started in the summer of 1955. But the spirit *we* contacted—Ephraim—was anything but simple. So much so that for a long time I felt that the material he dictated really couldn't be used—then or perhaps ever. I felt it would be like cheating, or plagiarizing from some unidentifiable source. Oh, I put a few snippets of it into *The Seraglio,* but that was just a novel, and didn't count. Twenty years later, though, I was yet again trying to tell the whole story as fiction, through a set of characters bearing little resemblance to David or me. I'd got about fifty pages done, hating every bit of it. I'm not a novelist, and never was. No accident, then, that I simply "forgot" the manuscript in a taxi in Atlanta, and never recovered it—well, all that's described in "The Book of Ephraim." But I went on, I didn't take the hint. I put together all the drafts and notes for those lost pages, and proceeded to forget *these* in a hotel room in Frankfurt! By now I was down to just two pages of an opening draft. As I sat glaring at them, the prose began to dissolve into verse. I marked the line-breaks with a pencil, fiddled a bit, typed it up, and showed the two versions to a friend who said quite firmly: "You must never write prose again." At that point "The Book of Ephraim" crystallized, and got written without any particular trouble.

Most of the time, we never knew what to expect. Last summer, for instance, we were about to sit down at the board—no, I was already in my chair—when David called from the kitchen. He can never keep abreast of the rising postal rates, and wanted to know which stamp to put on his letter. I called back, "Put on an Edna St. Vincent Millay"—I'd bought a sheet of her commemoratives just that week. And when we started at the board, there she was. Very embarrassing on both sides, as it dawned on the poor creature that we hadn't meant to talk to *her* at all.

An overturned teacup is our pointer. The commercial boards come with a funny see-through planchette on legs. I find them too cramped. Besides, it's so easy to make your own—just write out the alphabet, and the numbers, and your YES and NO (punctuation marks too, if you're going all out) on a big sheet of cardboard. Or use brown paper—it travels better. On our Grand Tour, whenever we felt lonely in the hotel room, David and I could just unfold our instant company. He puts his right hand lightly on the cup, I put my left, leaving the right free to transcribe, and away we go. We get, oh, 500 to 600 words an hour. Better than gasoline.   —*James Merrill*

Dostoevsky was always in a miserable state, but you can't say he deliberately chose psychological discomforts. No, I doubt that strongly. I don't think anyone chooses these things, unless unconsciously. I do think many writers have what you might call a demonic nature. They are always in trouble, you know, and not only while they're writing or because they're writing, but in every aspect of their lives, with marriage, love, business, money, everything. It's all tied together, all part and parcel of the same thing. It's an aspect of the creative personality. —*Henry Miller*

Oh, I never knew anyone who had a passion for words who had as much difficulty in saying things as I do. I very seldom say them in a manner I like. If I do it's because I don't know I'm trying.

. . .

I do enjoy writing, yes. A great deal. And I feel somewhat at a loss, aimless and foolishly sentimental, and disconnected, when I've finished one work and haven't yet become absorbed in another. All of us who write work out of a conviction that we are participating in some sort of communal activity. Whether my role is writing, or reading and responding, might not be very important. I take seriously Flaubert's statement that we must love one another in our art as the mystics love one another in God. By honoring one another's creation we honor something that deeply connects us all, and goes beyond us.

Of course writing is only one activity out of a vast number of activities that constitute our lives. It seems to be the one that some of us have concentrated on, as if we were fated for it. Since I have a great deal of faith in the processes and the wisdom of the unconscious, and have learned from experience to take lightly the judgments of the ego, and its inevitable doubts, I never find myself constrained to answer such questions. Life is energy, and energy is creativity. And even when we as individuals pass on, the energy is retained in the work of art, locked in it and awaiting release if only someone will take the time and the care to unlock it. —*Marianne Moore*

One must be pitiless about this matter of "mood." In a sense the writing will *create* the mood. If art is, as I believe it to be, a genuinely transcendental function—a means by which we rise out of limited, parochial states of mind—then it should not matter very much what states of mind or emotion we are in. Generally, I've found this to be true: I have forced myself to begin writing when I've been utterly exhausted, when I've felt my soul as thin as a playing-card, when nothing has seemed worth enduring for another five minutes . . . and somehow the activity of writing changes everything. Or appears to do so. Joyce said of the underlying structure of *Ulysses*—the Odyssean parallel and parody—that he really didn't care whether it was plausible, so long as it served as a bridge to get his "soldiers" across. Once they were across, what does it matter if the bridge collapses? One might say the same thing about the use of one's self as a means for the writing to get written. Once the soldiers are across the stream . . .   —*Joyce Carol Oates*

The old apothegm that easy writing makes hard reading is as succinct as ever. I used to know several eminent writers who were given to boasting of the speed with which they created. It's not a lovable attribute, to put it mildly, and I'm afraid our acquaintanceship has languished.   —*S. J. Perelman*

Beginning a book is unpleasant. I'm entirely uncertain about the character and the predicament, and a character in his predicament is what I have to begin with. Worse than not knowing your subject is not knowing how to treat it, because that's finally everything. I type out beginnings and they're awful, more of an unconscious parody of my previous book than the breakaway from it that I want. I need something driving down the center of a book, a magnet to draw everything to it—that's what I look for during the first months of writing something new. I often have to write a hundred pages or more before there's a paragraph that's alive. Okay, I say to myself, that's your beginning, start there; that's the first paragraph of the book. I'll go over the first six months of work and underline in red a paragraph, a sentence, sometimes no more than a phrase, that has some life in it, and then I'll type all these out on one page. Usually it doesn't come to more than one page, but if I'm lucky, that's the start of page one. I look for the liveliness to set the tone. After the awful beginning come the months of freewheeling play, and after the play come the crises, turning against your material and hating the book.   —*Philip Roth*

It's a little mad, but I believe I am many people. When I am writing a poem, I feel I am the person who should have written it. Many times I assume these guises; I attack it the way a novelist might. Sometimes I become someone else and when I do, I believe, even in moments when I'm not writing the poem, that I am that person. When I wrote about the farmer's wife, I lived in my mind in Illinois; when I had the illegitimate child, I nursed it—in my mind—and gave it back and traded life. When I gave my lover back to his wife, in my mind, I grieved and saw how ethereal and unnecessary I had been. When I was Christ, I felt like Christ. My arms hurt, I desperately wanted to pull them in off the Cross. When I was taken down off the Cross, and buried alive, I sought solutions; I hoped they were Christian solutions.   —*Anne Sexton*

Now let me give you the benefit of my experience in facing 400 pages of blank stock—the appalling stuff that must be filled. The following are some of the things I have had to do to keep from going nuts.

1. Abandon the idea that you are ever going to finish. Lose track of the 400 pages and write just one page for each day; it helps. Then when it gets finished, you are always surprised.

2. Write freely and as rapidly as possible and throw the whole thing on paper. Never correct or rewrite until the whole thing is down. Rewrite in process is usually found to be an excuse for not going on. It also interferes with flow and rhythm which can only come from a kind of unconscious association with the material.

3. Forget your generalized audience. In the first place, the nameless, faceless audience will scare you to death and in the second place,

ON PERFORMANCE

unlike the theater, it doesn't exist. In writing, your audience is one single reader. I have found that sometimes it helps to pick out one person—a real person you know, or an imagined person and write to that one.

4. If a scene or a section gets the better of you and you still think you want it—bypass it and go on. When you have finished the whole you can come back to it and then you may find that the reason it gave trouble is because it didn't belong there.

5. Beware of a scene that becomes too dear to you, dearer than the rest. It will usually be found that it is out of drawing.

6. If you are using dialogue—say it aloud as you write it. Only then will it have the sound of speech.   —*John Steinbeck*

I guess like everybody I'm emotionally fouled up most of the time, but I find I do better when I'm relatively placid. It's hard to say, though. If writers had to wait until their precious psyches were completely serene there wouldn't be much writing done. Actually—though I don't take advantage of the fact as much as I should—I find that I'm simply the happiest, the placidest, *when* I'm writing, and so I suppose that that, for me, is the final answer. When I'm writing I find it's the only time that I feel completely self-possessed, even when the writing itself is not going too well. It's fine therapy for people who are perpetually scared of nameless threats as I am most of the time—for jittery people. Besides, I've discovered that when I'm not writing I'm prone to developing certain nervous tics, and hypochondria. Writing alleviates those quite a bit. I think I resist change more than most people. I dislike traveling, like to stay settled. When I first came to Paris all I could think about was going home, home to the old James River. One of these days I expect to inherit a peanut farm. Go back home and farm them old peanuts and be real old Southern whiskey gentry.   —*William Styron*

I never quite know when I'm not writing. Sometimes my wife comes up to me at a party and says, "Dammit, Thurber, stop writing." She usually catches me in the middle of a paragraph. Or my daughter will look up from the dinner table and ask, "Is he sick?" "No," my wife says. "He's writing something." I have to do it that way on account of my eyes. I still write occasionally—in the proper sense of the word—using black crayon on yellow paper and getting perhaps twenty words to the page. My usual method, though, is to spend the mornings turning over the text in my mind. Then in the afternoon, between 2 and 5, I call in a secretary and dictate to her. I can do about 2,000 words. It took me about 10 years to learn.

. . .

Hervey Allen, you know, the author of the big best-seller *Anthony Adverse,* seriously told a friend of mine who was working on a biographical piece on Allen that he could close his eyes, lie down on a bed and hear the voices of his ancestors. Furthermore there was some sort of angel-like creature that danced along his pen while he was writing. He wasn't balmy by any means. He just felt he was in communication with some sort of metaphysical recorder. So you see the novelists have all the luck. I never knew a humorist who got any help from his ancestors. Still, the act of writing is either something the writer dreads or actually likes, and I actually like it. Even re-writing's fun. You're getting somewhere, whether it seems to move or not. I remember Elliot Paul and I used to argue about re-writing back in 1925 when we both worked for the *Chicago Tribune* in Paris. It was his conviction you should leave the story as it came out of the typewriter, no changes. Naturally, he worked fast. Three novels he could turn out, each written in three weeks' time. I remember once he came to the office and said that a 60,000 word manuscript had been stolen. No carbons existed, no notes. We were all horrified. But it didn't bother him at all. He'd just get back to the typewriter and bat away again.   —*James Thurber*

I don't find it easy. You see there are always words going round in my head; some people think in pictures, some in ideas. I think entirely in words. By the time I come to stick my pen in my ink pot these words have reached a stage of order which is fairly presentable.

—*Evelyn Waugh*

Some things I let alone from first to last—the kernel of the story. You know enough not to touch something if it's right. The hardest thing for me is getting people in and out of rooms—the mechanics of a story. A simple act of putting on clothes is almost impossible for me to describe without many false starts. You have to be quick and specific in conveying that sort of action or fact, and also as neat and quiet about it as possible so that it doesn't obtrude. And I find that very challenging, especially to describe an action that I don't do very well myself, like sewing. I made Aunt Lexie in *Losing Battles* a poor sewer so that I wouldn't have to describe it too well. The easiest things to write about are emotions. For a writer those things are what you start with. You wouldn't have started a story without that awareness—that's what made you begin. That's what makes a character, projects the plot. Because you write from the inside. You can't start with how people look and speak and behave and come to know how they feel. You must know exactly what's in their hearts and minds before they ever set visible foot on the stage. You must know all, then not tell it all, or not tell too much at once; simply the right thing at the right moment. And the same character would be written about entirely differently in a novel as opposed to a short story. In a story you don't go into a character in order to develop him. He was born full grown, and he's present there to perform his part in the story. He's subservient to his function, and he doesn't exist outside it. But in a novel, he may. So you may have to allow for his growth and maybe hold him down and not tell everything you know, or else let him have his full sway—make room for a hero, even, in more spacious premises.

—*Eudora Welty*

I wish I were more at home with writing. I can go a year or two or three without picking up my pen and I'm perfectly content. The minute I have to write I become neurotic and grouchy and ill; I become like a little wet, drenched bird, and I put a blanket over my shoulders and I try to write and I hate myself and I hate what I'm writing. Writing depends upon a fairly quiet life, whereas I am a sociable person. I think every writer goes back and forth on this question; it's a constant struggle to find the right balance between solitude and society and I don't think anyone ever does. I find it reassuring to read the complaints of Chekhov: "My country house is full of people, they never leave me alone; if only they would go away I could be a good writer." He's writing this close to the end of his life.   —*Edmund White*

When I write, everything is visual, as brilliantly as if it were on a lit stage. And I talk out the lines as I write.

When I was in Rome, my landlady thought I was demented. She told Frank (Merlo), "Oh, Mr. Williams has lost his mind! He stalks about the room talking out loud!"

Frank said, "Oh, he's just writing." She didn't understand *that*.

—*Tennessee Williams*

I love writing. I never feel really comfortable unless I am either actually writing or have a story going. I could not stop writing.

—*P. G. Wodehouse*

ON REVISING:
SELF-EVALUATION

Let your literary compositions be kept from the public eye for nine years at least. —*Horace*

Read over your compositions and, when you meet a passage which you think is particularly fine, strike it out. —*Samuel Johnson*

The players often mention it as an honor to Shakespeare that in his writing, whatsoever he penned, he never blotted out a line. My answer hath been, "Would he had blotted a thousand." —*Ben Jonson*

The wastepaper basket is the writer's best friend. —*Isaac Bashevis Singer*

Fall seven times, stand up eight. —*Japanese proverb*

Occasionally I've discarded and then resurrected. I would find a crumpled yellow ball of paper in the wastebasket, in the morning, and open it to see what the hell I'd been up to; and occasionally it was something that needed only a very slight change to be brought off, which I'd missed the day before. —*Conrad Aiken*

I used to labor over what's done a great deal, but because of my strong desire to avoid all unnecessary work, I have somehow trained myself not to write something that I will either have to discard or be forced to work a great deal over. I like the idea of being as close to the original thought or voice as possible and not to falsify it by editing. Here is something I just read by Max Jacob, quoted by André Salmon in the notes to Jacob's book *La Défense de Tartuffe*. He talks about composing novels or stories in a notebook while taking long walks through Paris. I'll translate: "The ideas I found in this way seemed sacred to me and I didn't change a comma. I believe that prose which comes directly from meditation is a prose which has the form of the brain and which it is forbidden to touch."

—*John Ashbery*

I do a lot of rewriting. It's very painful. You know it's finished when you can't do anything more to it, though it's never exactly the way you want it. . . . Most of the rewrite is cleaning. Don't describe it, show it. That's what I try to teach all young writers—take it out! Don't describe a purple sunset, make me see that it is purple. The hardest thing in the world is simplicity. And the most fearful thing, too. You have to strip yourself of all your disguises, some of which you didn't know you had. You want to write a sentence as clean as a bone. That is the goal. —*James Baldwin*

At first I did [revisions]. Then I found out that when a man reaches a certain age he has found his real tone. Nowadays, I try to go over what I've written after a fortnight or so and of course there are many slips and repetitions to be avoided, certain favorite tricks that should not be overworked. But I think that what I write nowadays is always on a certain level and that I can't better it very much nor can I spoil it very much either. Consequently I let it go, forget all about it, and think about what I'm doing at the time.

• • •

We know that [Kafka] was very dissatisfied with his own work. Of course, when he told his friend, Max Brod, that he wanted his manuscripts to be burned, as Vergil did, I suppose he knew that his friend wouldn't do that. If a man wants to destroy his own work, he throws it into a fire, and there it goes. When he tells a close friend of his: "I want all the manuscripts to be destroyed," he knows that the friend will never do that, and the friend knows that he knows

and that he knows that the other knows that he knows and so on
and so forth.　　　　　　　　　　　　　　　　—*Jorge Luis Borges*

There's not much that I like better than to take a story that I've
had around the house for a while and work it over again. It's the
same with the poems I write. I'm in no hurry to send something off
just after I write it, and I sometimes keep it around the house for
months doing this or that to it, taking this out and putting that in.
It doesn't take that long to do the first draft of the story, that usually
happens in one sitting, but it does take a while to do the various
versions of the story. I've done as many as twenty or thirty drafts of
a story. Never less than ten or twelve drafts. It's instructive, and
heartening both, to look at the early drafts of great writers. I'm
thinking of the photographs of galleys belonging to Tolstoy, to name
one writer who loved to revise. I mean, I don't know if he loved it
or not, but he did a great deal of it. He was always revising, right
down to the time of page proofs. He went through and rewrote *War
and Peace* eight times and was still making corrections in the galleys.
Things like this should hearten every writer whose first drafts are
dreadful, like mine are.　　　　　　　　　—*Raymond Carver*

I do a lot of revising. Certain chapters six or seven times. Occasionally
you can hit it right the first time. More often, you don't. George
Moore rewrote entire novels. In my own case I usually write to a
point where the work is getting worse rather than better. That's the
point to stop and the time to publish.　　　　—*John Dos Passos*

I suffer from terrible nausea about my own work, purely physical
nausea. It sounds stupid, but the fact is I write at a terrific speed,
and . . . you cross inner resistances like you cross a shoal of trans-
mitters when you are fiddling with the dial on a radio. By the time
the thing is in typescript, it is really with physical nausea that I regard
it. When the proofs come back I have to take an aspirin before I can
bring myself really to read it through. Occasionally when I'm asked

to correct or edit a version, I always ask someone to do it for me. I don't know why. I just have a nausea about it. Perhaps when one day I get something I really do like, I won't have to take aspirin.

—*Lawrence Durrell*

My editor at Random House used to tell me, "Stanley, less is more." I had to fight him tooth and nail in the better restaurants to maintain excess because I don't believe that less is more. I believe that *more* is more. I believe that less is less, fat fat, thin thin and enough is enough. There's a famous exchange between Fitzgerald and Thomas Wolfe in which Fitzgerald criticizes Wolfe for one of his novels. Fitzgerald tells him that Flaubert believed in the *mot précis* and that there are two kinds of writers—the putter-inners and the taker-outers. Wolfe, who probably was not as good a writer as Fitzgerald but evidently wrote a better letter, said, "Flaubert me no Flauberts. Shakespeare was a putter-inner, Melville was a putter-inner." I can't remember who else was a putter-inner, but I'd rather be a putter-inner than a taker-outer.

—*Stanley Elkin*

All of us failed to match our dream of perfection. So I rate us on the basis of our splendid failure to do the impossible. In my opinion, if I could write all my work again, I am convinced that I would do it better, which is the healthiest condition for an artist. That's why he keeps on working, trying again; he believes each time that this time he will do it, bring it off. Of course he won't, which is why this condition is healthy. Once he did it, once he matched the work to the image, the dream, nothing would remain but to cut his throat, jump off the other side of that pinnacle of perfection into suicide.

—*William Faulkner*

I am more interested in achievement than in advance on it and decline from it. And I am more interested in works than in authors. The paternal wish of critics to show how a writer dropped off or picked up as he went along seems to me misplaced. I am only

interested in myself as a producer. What was it Mahler said?—
"anyone will sufficiently understand me who will trace my development through my nine symphonies." This seems odd to me; I
couldn't imagine myself making such a remark; it seems too uncasual.
Other authors find themselves much more an object of study. I am
conceited, but not interested is myself in this particular way. Of
course I like reading my own work, and often do it. I go gently over
the bits I think are bad.   —*E. M. Forster*

What I tend to do is not so much pick at a thing but sit down and
rewrite it completely. Both for *A Single Man* and *A Meeting by the River*
I wrote three entire drafts. After making notes on one draft I'd sit
down and rewrite it again from the beginning. I've found that's much
better than patching and amputating things. One has to rethink the
thing completely. They say D. H. Lawrence used to write second
drafts and never look at the first.   —*Christopher Isherwood*

I presented my editor with *Legs,* which was then about one hundred
pages. He bought it. Then it took me six years to finish it. I wrote
it eight times and seven times it was no good. Six times it was
especially no good. The seventh time out it was pretty good, though
it was way too long. My son was six years old and so was my novel
and they were both the same height. I was wounded many times in
the writing of that novel.   —*William Kennedy*

I keep depressing my text, deescalating the language. I count words
the way Western Union does; often, I'm afraid my prose tends to
resemble a night letter. Every word is there for a reason, and if not,
I cross it out. I do rewrite—often entirely—my galley pages, even
page proofs. The publishers complain, but I argue that every new
draft keeps improving my own as well as their book. Still, I am never
certain whether my English prose is sufficiently clear. Also, I rarely

allow myself to use English in an unchecked, spontaneous way. I always have a sense of trembling—but so does a compass, after all.

—*Jerzy Kosinski*

I formed the habit long ago of putting new poems into a desk drawer and letting them lie there to ripen (or the opposite) like apples. I suppose everyone else does the same thing. I learned early and by sad experience never to publish a green poem. Who in hell wrote *that*? Instead, I pull them out after a few weeks or months and say, "Well . . . possibly . . ." and start all over. Or consign the whole thing to the wood fire and hope the seed, whatever it was, will sow itself again. I doubt if it does. It's sick of me by that time. —*Archibald MacLeish*

First drafts are for learning what your novel or story is about. Revision is working with that knowledge to enlarge and enhance an idea, to re-form it. D. H. Lawrence, for instance, did seven or eight drafts of *The Rainbow*. The first draft of a book is the most uncertain— where you need guts, the ability to accept the imperfect until it is better. Revision is one of the true pleasures of writing. "The men and things of today are wont to lie fairer and truer in tomorrow's memory," Thoreau said. —*Bernard Malamud*

When I'm revising, I use a pen and ink to make changes, cross out, insert. The manuscript looks wonderful afterwards, like a Balzac. Then I retype, and in the process of retyping I make more changes. I prefer to retype everything myself, because even when I think I've made all the changes I want, the mere mechanical business of touching the keys sharpens my thoughts, and I find myself revising while doing the finished thing. In a way the machine acts as a stimulus; it's a cooperative thing. —*Henry Miller*

I don't approve of my "enigmas," or as somebody said, "the not ungreen grass."

I said to my mother one time, "How did you ever permit me to let this be printed?"

And she said, "You didn't ask my advice." —*Marianne Moore*

I cut adjectives, adverbs, and every word which is there just to make an effect. Every sentence which is there just for the sentence. You know, you have a beautiful sentence—cut it. Every time I find such a thing in one of my novels it is to be cut. Sometimes I've changed the names while writing: a woman will be Helen in the first chapter and Charlotte in the second, you know; so in revising I straighten this out. And then, cut, cut, cut. —*Georges Simenon*

Occasionally, I can write a poem straight off. Usually I revise a great deal—a hundred or more rewritings. One good remark Virginia Woolf makes somewhere in her journals is that too much rewriting is symptomatic of a failure of imagination. *Mea culpa.* But if you put a poem aside, when you look at it again it tends to rewrite itself, because your remembered intention criticizes the failures of expression. —*Stephen Spender*

My wife took a look at the first version of something I was doing not long ago and said: "Goddam it, Thurber, that's high-school stuff." I have to tell her to wait until the seventh draft, it'll work out all right. I don't know why that should be so, that the first or second draft of everything I write reads as if it was turned out by a char-woman. I wrote a thing called *File and Forget* in one afternoon. But only because it was a series of letters just as one would ordinarily dictate. And I'd have to admit that the last letter of the series, after doing all the others that one afternoon, took me a week. It was the end of the piece and I had to fuss over it.

Brevity in any case—whether the work is supposed to be humorous or not—would seem to me to be desirable. Most of the books I like are short books: *The Red Badge of Courage, Turn of the Screw,* Conrad's short stories, *A Lost Lady,* Joseph Hergesheimer's *Wild Oranges,* Victoria

Lincoln's *February Hill, The Great Gatsby*. . . . You know, Fitzgerald once wrote Thomas Wolfe: "You're a putter-inner and I'm a taker-outer." I stick with Fitzgerald. I don't believe, as Wolfe did, that you have to turn out a massive work before being judged a writer. Wolfe once told me at a cocktail party I didn't know what it was to be a writer. My wife, standing next to me, complained about that. "But my husband *is* a writer," she said. Wolfe was genuinely surprised. "He is?" he asked. "Why all I ever see is that stuff of his in *The New Yorker*." In other words he felt that prose under 5,000 words was certainly not the work of a writer . . . it was some kind of doodling in words. If you said you were a writer, he wanted to know where the books were, the great big long books. He was really genuine about that.   —*James Thurber*

I correct or change words, but I can't rewrite a scene or make a major change because there's a sense then of someone looking over my shoulder. It's necessary, anyway, to trust that moment when you were sure at last you had done all you could, done your best for that time. When it's finally in print, you're delivered—you don't ever have to look at it again. It's too late to worry about its failings. I'll have to apply any lessons this book has taught me toward writing the next one.   —*Eudora Welty*

I revise a great deal. I know when something is right because bells begin ringing and lights flash. I'm not at all sure what the "necessary equipment" is for a writer—it seems to vary greatly with the individual. Some writers are equipped with extra-sensory perception. Some have a good ear, like O'Hara. Some are equipped with humor—although not nearly as many as think they are. Some are equipped with a massive intellect, like [Edmund] Wilson. Some are prodigious. I do think the ability to evaluate one's own stuff with reasonable accuracy is a helpful piece of equipment. I've known good writers who've had it, and I've known writers who were utterly convinced that anything at all, if it came from their pen, was the work of genius and as close to being right as anything can be.   —*E. B. White*

It is a struggle when I have to cut. I reduce nine hundred pages to one hundred sixty pages. I also enjoy cutting. I do it with a masochistic pleasure although even when you cut, you don't. Writing is not like painting, where you add. It is not what you put on the canvas that the reader sees. Writing is more like a sculpture where you remove, you eliminate in order to make the work visible. Even those pages you remove somehow remain. There is a difference between a book of two hundred pages from the very beginning, and a book of two hundred pages which is the result of an original eight hundred pages. The six hundred pages are there. Only you don't see them.

—*Elie Wiesel*

I forget which of the great sonneteers said: "One line in the fourteen comes from the ceiling; the others have to be adjusted around it." Well, likewise there are passages in every novel whose first writing is pretty much the last. But it's the joint and cement, between those spontaneous passages, that take a great deal of rewriting.

—*Thornton Wilder*

ON EDITORS

An editor should tell the author his writing is better than it is. Not
a lot better, a little better.   —*T. S. Eliot*

No passion in the world is equal to the passion to alter someone
else's draft.   —*H. G. Wells*

Ah! don't say you agree with me. When people agree with me I
always feel that I must be wrong.   —*Oscar Wilde*

Dear Herr Doctor:
   You are already 10 months behind with the manuscript of *Das
Kapital,* which you have agreed to write for us. If we do not receive the manuscript within 6 months, we shall be obliged to commission another to do this work.
                —*Letter to Karl Marx from his Leipzig publisher*

We have read your manuscript with boundless delight. If we were
to publish your paper, it would be impossible for us to publish any
work of lower standard. And as it is unthinkable that in the next
thousand years we shall see its equal, we are, to our regret, etc.
                —*Rejection slip from a Chinese economics journal,
                quoted in the* Financial Times

I remember standing on a street corner with the black painter Beau-
ford Delaney down in the Village waiting for the light to change, and
he pointed down and said, "Look." I looked and all I saw was water.
And he said, "Look again," which I did, and I saw oil on the water
and the city reflected in the puddle. It was a great revelation to me.
I can't explain it. He taught me how to see, and how to trust what

I saw. Painters have often taught writers how to see. And once you've had that experience, you see differently. —*James Baldwin*

What gave me the courage to forget about poetry was a chap by the name of Louis Untermeyer. I had such admiration for him that I sent him some of my poems. He wrote to me and said that every young man is entitled to write poetry, but the sooner he gives it up, the better he's going to be as a man. So I took his advice. —*Erskine Caldwell*

He [Harold Ross of *The New Yorker*] asked preposterous queries on a manuscript—everyone's written about that—something like thirty-six queries on a story. The author always thought it outrageous, a violation of taste, but Ross really didn't care. He liked to show his hand, to shake the writer up. Occasionally he was brilliant. In "The Enormous Radio" he made two changes. A diamond is found on the bathroom floor after a party. The man says, "Sell it, we can use a few dollars." Ross had changed "dollars" to "bucks," which was absolutely perfect. Brilliant. Then I had "the radio came softly" and Ross penciled in another "softly." "The radio came softly, softly." He was absolutely right. But then there were twenty-nine other suggestions like, "This story has gone on for twenty-four hours and no one has eaten anything. There's no mention of a meal." A typical example of this sort of thing was Shirley Jackson's "The Lottery," about the stoning ritual. He hated the story; he started turning vicious. He said there was no town in Vermont where there were rocks of that sort. He nagged and nagged and nagged. It was not surprising. Ross used to scare the hell out of me. I would go in for lunch. I never knew Ross was coming, until he'd bring in an egg cup. I'd sit with my back pressed against my chair. I was really afraid. He was a scratcher and a nose picker, and the sort of man who could get his underwear up so there was a strip of it showing between his trousers and his shirt. He used to hop at me, sort of jump about in his chair. It was a creative, destructive relationship from which I learned a great deal, and I miss him.

• • •

Everyone keeps saying about my stories, "Oh, they're so sad." My agent, Candida Donadio, called me about a new story and said, "Oh, what a beautiful story, it's so sad." I said, "All right, so I'm a sad man." The sad thing about "The Brigadier and the Golf Widow" is the woman standing looking at the bomb shelter in the end of the story and then being sent away by a maid. Did you know that *The New Yorker* tried to take that out? They thought the story was much more effective without my ending. When I went in to look at page proofs, I thought there was a page missing. I asked where the end of the story was. Some girl said, "Mr. Shawn thinks it's better this way." I went into a very deep slow burn, took the train home, drank a lot of gin, and got one of the editors on the telephone. I was by then loud, abusive, and obscene. He was entertaining Elizabeth Bowen and Eudora Welty. He kept asking if he couldn't take this call in another place. Anyhow, I returned to New York in the morning. They had reset the whole magazine—poems, newsbreaks, cartoons—and replaced the scene.

• • •

My definition of a good editor is a man I think charming, who sends me large checks, praises my work, my physical beauty, and my sexual prowess, and who has a stranglehold on the publisher and the bank.
—*John Cheever*

These days there's a good deal more directed writing in which bright young publishers or editors dream up an idea for a book and then think of somebody to write it. Part of the creative process, at least in nonfiction, has moved over from the writer to the editor . . . If an editor begins to let the concept of catering to the public weigh on him he becomes, to me, a bad editor. An editor should have an idea of what meets his own taste; that should provide the criterion. The whole notion of divining the public taste has been one of the deadliest ideas of publishing. When *True Confessions* was at the height of its success, a new fiction editor was picked every month. She would be one of the typists in the office, preferably the youngest, because it was felt that if she followed her own honest feeling about what was good, that was what the public wanted. After a month or so, she would become too sophisticated and then they would fire her as the fiction editor and take on another typist. That was cynicism carried to the extreme, but it may well have produced better results than an editor guessing at what the public might like.   —*Malcolm Cowley*

He [Ezra Pound] would send books at times which would be useful. *The History of Money* by Alexander Del Mar, which I read, and thought about. He was very helpful. It was very flattering to be taken at all seriously by him. [William Carlos] Williams was always much more specific. At times he would do things which would . . . not *dismay* me —but my own ego would be set back. I remember one time I wrote him a very stern letter—some description about something I was going to do, or *this* was the way things were, *blah blah*. And he returned me the sheets of the letter and he had marked on the margin of particular sections, "Fine. Your style is tightening."   —*Robert Creeley*

He [Ezra Pound] was a marvelous critic because he didn't try to turn you into an imitation of himself. He tried to see what you were trying to do.   —*T. S. Eliot*

There was, of course, Ezra Pound and his fondness for the *Odyssey*. He had helped W. H. D. Rouse. Rouse was trying to do a prose version and there was a correspondence between them. I always felt that Pound was really dissatisfied and disappointed in the end with what Rouse did. Before I went to Europe, I went to see Pound at St. Elizabeths. I wanted to tell him what I was going to try to do. I told him what I felt at the time—which was that there was no point in trying to do every line. I would do what I could. I'd hit the high spots. He said, "Oh no, don't do that. Let him say everything he wanted to say." So I had to rethink it and eventually I did let Homer say everything he wanted to say. I sent Pound the first draft of the first book when I got that done in Italy that fall. I got a post card back, a wonderful post card, saying, "Too much iambic will kill any subject matter." After that, I was very careful about getting singsong again. Keep the verse alive, that was the main thing.   —*Robert Fitzgerald*

Miss Stein wrote at some length and with considerable inaccuracy about her influence on my work. It was necessary for her to do this after she had learned to write dialogue from a book called *The Sun Also Rises*. I was very fond of her and thought it was splendid she had learned to write conversation. It was no new thing to me to learn from everyone I could, living or dead, and I had no idea it would affect Gertrude so violently. She already wrote very well in other ways. Ezra was extremely intelligent on the subjects he really knew. Doesn't this sort of talk bore you? This backyard literary gossip while washing out the dirty clothes of thirty-five years ago is disgusting to me. It would be different if one had tried to tell the whole truth. That would have some value. Here it is simpler and better to thank Gertrude for everything I learned from her about the abstract relationship of words, say how fond I was of her, reaffirm my loyalty to Ezra as a great poet and a loyal friend, and say that I cared so much for Max Perkins that I have never been able to accept that he is dead. He never asked me to change anything I wrote except to remove certain words which were not then publishable. Blanks were left, and anyone who knew the words would know what they were. For me he was not an editor. He was a wise friend and a wonderful companion. I liked the way he wore his hat and the strange way his lips moved.   —*Ernest Hemingway*

One of the things that has been bad for American publishing was the invention of the person called a copy-editor, an expert who knows grammar and can spot inconsistencies: a technician of text. Many copy-editors are very good at what they do, but the creation of that function has taken away from the principal editor a basic interest in the text. Most editors, with some notable exceptions, have become packagers now, rather than close editors. And I think that publishers are more interested in acquisitions from their editors than they are in developing to the fullest extent the craft of each writer they deal with. Publishing has changed in my years. I've worked since the era of Alfred Knopf Sr., who had as contemporaries people like Alfred Harcourt, Horace Liveright, Charles Scribner Sr., all essentially book men. In the case of Knopf, he was dazzled by authorhood; he cared more about his relationship with authors than he did about his relationship with books. His concern was the full career of the writer. He lost many authors, he was crusty, many writers moved on to other firms. But Knopf's concern was always for the growth of the person as a craftsman. Now—again with some worthy exceptions—the heads of firms are more apt to be businessmen. That's been a loss, I think.   —*John Hersey*

I shouldn't normally show what I'd written to anyone: what would be the point? You remember Tennyson reading an unpublished poem to Jowett; when he had finished, Jowett said, "I shouldn't publish that if I were you, Tennyson." Tennyson replied, "If it comes to that, Master, the sherry you gave us at lunch was downright filthy." That's about all that can happen.   —*Philip Larkin*

I'd gone to call on Frost with a huge epic on the First Crusade, all written out in clumsy longhand on lined paper. He read a page of that and said, "You have no compression." Then he read me a very short poem of Collins, "How Sleep the Brave," and said, "That's not a great poem, but it's not too long." He was very kindly about it. You know his point about the voice coming into poetry: he took a very unusual example of that, the opening of *Hyperion;* the line about the Naiad, something about her pressing a cold finger to her cold lips, which wouldn't seem like a voice passage at all. And he said, "Now Keats comes alive here." That was a revelation to me; what had impressed me was the big Miltonic imitation in *Hyperion.* I don't know what I did with that, but I recoiled and realized that I was diffuse and monotonous. —*Robert Lowell*

By "editor" I suppose you mean proofreader. Among these I have known limpid creatures of limitless tact and tenderness who would discuss with me a semi-colon as if it were a point of honor—which, indeed, a point of art often is. But I have also come across a few pompous avuncular brutes who would attempt to "make suggestions" which I countered with a thunderous "stet!" —*Vladimir Nabokov*

He [Harold Ross of *The New Yorker*] was a professional lunatic, but I don't know if he was a great man. He had a profound ignorance. On one of Mr. Benchley's manuscripts he wrote in the margin opposite "Andromache," "Who he?" Mr. Benchley wrote back, "You keep out of this." —*Dorothy Parker*

Apart from Fordie [Ford Madox Ford] rolling on the floor undecorously and holding his head in his hands, and groaning on one occasion, I don't think anybody helped me through my manuscripts. Ford's stuff appeared too loose then, but he led the fight against tertiary archaisms.

· · ·

Once out at Rapallo I tried for God's sake to prevent him [W. B. Yeats] from printing a thing. I told him it was rubbish. All he did was print it with a preface saying that I *said* it was rubbish. —*Ezra Pound*

The editors I had at *The New Yorker* quietly helped me in peculiar, small ways. One thing they taught me was the value of cutting out the last paragraph of stories, something I pass down as a tip to all writers. The last paragraph in which you tell what the story is about is almost always best left out. —*Irwin Shaw*

He [Harold Ross of *The New Yorker*] wasn't the man to develop a writer. He was an unread man. Well, he'd read Mark Twain's *Life on the Mississippi* and several other books he told me about—medical books—and he took the Encyclopaedia Britannica to the bathroom with him. I think he was about up to H when he died. But still his effect on writers was considerable. When you first met him you couldn't believe he was the editor of *The New Yorker* and afterwards you couldn't believe that anyone else could have been. The main thing he was interested in was clarity. Someone once said of *The New Yorker* that it never contained a sentence that would puzzle an intelligent 14-year-old or in any way affect her morals badly. Ross didn't like that, but nevertheless he was a purist and perfectionist and it had a tremendous effect on all of us: it kept us from being sloppy. When I first met him he asked me if I knew English. I thought he meant French or a foreign language. But he repeated, "Do you know English?" As Andy White mentioned in his obituary, Ross approached the English sentence as though it was an enemy, something that was going to throw him. He used to fuss for an hour over a comma. He'd call me in for lengthy discussions about the Thurber colon. And as for poetic license, he'd say, "Damn any license to get things wrong." In fact, Ross read so carefully that often he didn't get the sense of your story. I once said: "I wish you'd read my stories for pleasure, Ross." He replied he hadn't time for that.   —*James Thurber*

I never met anybody with whom I could have discussed books before or after. One doesn't have people on one's wavelength as completely as that. I very rarely found *The New Yorker* editors any good.

—*Rebecca West*

Once or twice books were turned down by Mr. Scribner because he was jealous of keeping his imprint free from anything that seemed unworthy or tasteless. He was a man of great courage; he would take chances, but there were some things that he was adamant about. When Scott Fitzgerald's first book, *This Side of Paradise,* came in, Mr. Scribner, after reading it, simply did not want his imprint on it. Only our great determination—and that of some of the other editors—

that the book should be published made Mr. Scribner change his mind, and only on the condition that Fitzgerald cut and rewrite the book in certain sections. Even then, Mr. Scribner was not quite sure.

The story of *The Sun Also Rises* is more striking. At a meeting in his office, Mr. Scribner said that he did not care to have his imprint on the book. There was a long silence. Max Perkins could be very silent and not feel that he had to talk, not even to relieve embarrassment. Max was standing. Mr. Scribner, who was seated at his desk, looked up at him and said: "Max, you haven't said anything. I'm turning the book down. Haven't you got something you'd like to say?" Max finally said, "Yes, I'd like to say this: That if we are going to turn down such a talent we might as well go out of the publishing business. We cannot go on publishing Richard Harding Davis, Thomas Nelson Page, George Cable, Henry Van Dyke, and other worthies. If we're going to be publishers, we have to move along with the talents of the time, even though they may offend . . . well, even though they might offend our kind of taste." Finally Mr. Scribner asked Max: "Will Hemingway change some of the four-letter words? Take them out?" Max said, "Yes, he will take some of them out, I'm quite sure." "Which words will he take out?" said Mr. Scribner. Whereupon Max hastened to his office, got a piece of paper, came back and wrote down the words. Mr. Scribner looked at him (he had a very mischievous sense of humor) and he said: "Max—if Ernest knew that you couldn't say those words, that you had to write them down, he'd disown you!"

•   •   •

Max, of course, saw more of Thomas Wolfe than I did. In fact, Wolfe absorbed so much of Max's time, and indeed of the time of everyone connected with the editorial department, that Mr. Scribner felt he'd have to let him go because other authors resented the excess attention Thomas Wolfe was getting. He slept in the office; he lived there, he was a tremendous talker; he would go from one office to another with this endless flow of language. He was an impetuous, impulsive man who in his normal state of mind, which was most of

the time, could be very charming. But when he had a drink or two (and he was rather inclined to drink more as he tired from his tremendous labors), he could be really paranoiac, and almost manic. But the feeling that Max Perkins had for Wolfe as a writer was extraordinary . . . I always felt there was more to the relationship: Max had no son; and he had a strange attitude about women which is hard to reconcile with his courtesy and his affection for his wife, but the fact was he regarded women as inferior, he seemed in some ways to resent them. He could be very severe with his wife. They had five daughters, so he sat down to breakfast with six women. He really longed for a son and he made Tom his son. As you know, Tom in the end betrayed him. Well, "betrayal" perhaps is the wrong word. But in his paranoiac state of mind, he conceived the idea that Max had ruined his books by playing so large a part in editing them and helping him. Max had objected to certain points-of-view in *Look Homeward, Angel* which reflected Tom's interest in communism . . . involving Eugene, the hero of the book, in communist and liberal movements at a time when according to the background framework of the novel, no such things were going on. Because of this Tom got the idea that Max was an old Tory and was taming his book and had ruined it. He wrote letters to Max that were really dreadful. They were not found until after Max's death because Max was so ashamed of them he had hidden them in his desk. But, as you know, on his deathbed, Tom wrote that famous letter to Max which made all the difference. He admitted that Max was the one who had made his work possible, and he asked forgiveness and said: "Let's think of the day we walked over Brooklyn Bridge together, and the book had been published, and the first reviews were coming in, and the world with all its glory and beauty lay before us, and we were happy. That's the way I think of you now. I've met the dark man, and I don't think I was too afraid of him. But I know I have to go and I wanted you to get this before that happened."
—*John Hall Wheelock*

ON PUBLICATION:
SUCCESS, FAILURE, ETC.

Posterity—what you write for after being turned down by
publishers.   —*George Ade*

For several days after my first book was published I carried it
about in my pocket, and took surreptitious peeps at it to make
sure the ink had not faded.   —*Sir James M. Barrie*

There is a great discovery still to be made in Literature, that of
paying literary men by the quantity they do not write.
                                               —*Thomas Carlyle*

While we are asleep, we are all equal.   —*Miguel de Cervantes*

If you aspire to the highest place it is no disgrace to stop at the
second, or even the third.   —*Cicero*

Success is a rare paint; hides all the ugliness.   —*Sir John Suckling*

A friend of mine, Dorothy Day, had been put in the women's prison
at 6th Avenue and 8th Street, for her part in a protest. Well, once
a week at this place, on a Saturday, the girls were marched down
for a shower. A group were being ushered in when one, a whore,
loudly proclaimed:

> *Hundreds have lived without love,*
> *But none without water*

A line from a poem of mine which had just appeared in *The New Yorker*. When I heard this I knew I hadn't written in vain!

—*W. H. Auden*

In my time it was unusual to be published when you were very young. Of course, there were one or two examples, such as Radiguet, who was a prodigy. Sartre himself wasn't published until he was about thirty-five, when *Nausea* and *The Wall* were brought out. When my first more or less publishable book was rejected, I was a bit discouraged. And when the first version of *She Came to Stay* was rejected, it was very unpleasant. Then I thought that I ought to take my time. I knew many examples of writers who were slow in getting started. And people always spoke of the case of Stendhal, who didn't begin to write until he was forty. —*Simone de Beauvoir*

I don't like to agree with the going view that if you write a bestseller it's because you betrayed an important principle or sold your soul. I know that sophisticated opinion believes this. And although I don't take much stock in sophisticated opinion, I have examined my conscience. I've tried to find out whether I had unwittingly done wrong. But I haven't yet discovered the sin. I do think that a book like *Herzog*, which ought to have been an obscure book with a total sale of 8000, has such a reception because it appeals to the unconscious sympathies of many people. I know from the mail I've received that the book described a common predicament. *Herzog* appealed to Jewish readers, to those who have been divorced, to those who talk to themselves, to college graduates, readers of paperbacks, autodidactics, to those who yet hope to live a while, etc. —*Saul Bellow*

You have to believe in your stuff—every day has to be the new day on which the new poem may be *it*. Well, fame supports that feeling. It gives self-confidence, it gives a sense of an actual, contemporary audience, and so on. On the other hand, unless it is sustained, it can cause trouble—and it is very seldom sustained. If your first book is a smash, your second book gets kicked in the face, and your third book, and lots of people, like Delmore [Schwartz], can't survive that disappointment. From that point of view, early fame is very dangerous indeed, and my situation, which was so painful to me for many years, was really in a way beneficial.

I overestimated myself, as it turned out, and felt bitter, bitterly neglected; but I had certain admirers, certain high judges on my side from the beginning, so that I had a certain amount of support. Moreover, I had a kind of indifference on my side—much as Joseph Conrad did. A reporter asked him once about reviews, and he said, "I don't read my reviews. I measure them." Now, until I was about thirty-five years old, I not only didn't read my reviews, I didn't measure them, I never even looked at them. That is so peculiar that close friends of mine wouldn't believe me when I told them. I thought that was indifference, but now I'm convinced that it was just that I had no skin on—you know, I was afraid of being killed by some remark. Oversensitivity. But there was an *element* of indifference in it, and so the public indifference to my work was countered with a certain amount of genuine indifference on my part, which has been very helpful since I became a celebrity. Auden once said that the best situation for a poet is to be taken up early and held for a considerable time and then dropped after he has reached the level of indifference.

Something else is in my head; a remark of Father Hopkins to Bridges. Two completely unknown poets in their thirties—fully mature—Hopkins, one of the great poets of the century, and Bridges, awfully good. Hopkins with no audience and Bridges with thirty readers. He says, "Fame in itself is nothing. The only thing that matters is virtue. Jesus Christ is the only true literary critic. But," he said, "from any lesser level or standard than that, we must recognize that fame is the true and appointed setting of men of genius." That seems to me appropriate. This business about geniuses in neglected garrets is for the birds. The idea that a man is somehow no good just because he becomes very popular, like Frost, is nonsense, also.

There are exceptions, Chatterton, Hopkins, of course, Rimbaud, you can think of various cases, but on the whole, men of genius were judged by their contemporaries very much as posterity judges them. So if I were talking to a young writer, I would recommend the cultivation of extreme indifference to both praise and blame because praise will lead you to vanity, and blame will lead you to self-pity, and both are bad for writers.   —*John Berryman*

A_h, listen, I'll say something I shouldn't say because no one will believe it, but success isn't a pleasure for me. I'm glad to be able to live from what I write, so I have to put up with the popular and critical side of success. But I was happier as a man when I was unknown. Much happier. Now I can't go to Latin America or to Spain without being recognized every ten yards, and the autographs, the embraces. . . . It's very moving, because they're readers who are frequently quite young. I'm happy that they like what I do, but it's terribly distressing for me on the level of privacy. I can't go to a beach in Europe; in five minutes there's a photographer. I have a physical appearance that I can't disguise; if I were small I could shave and put on sunglasses, but with my height, my long arms and all that, they discover me from afar. On the other hand, there are very beautiful things: I was in Barcelona a month ago, walking around the gothic quarter one evening, and there was an American girl, very pretty, playing the guitar very well and singing. She was seated on the ground singing to earn her living. She sang a bit like Joan Baez, a very pure, clear voice. There was a group of young people from Barcelona listening. I stopped to listen to her, but I stayed in the shadows. At one point, one of these young men who was about twenty, very young, very handsome, approached me. He had a cake in his hand. He said, "Julio, take a piece." So I took a piece and I ate it, and I told him, "Thanks a lot for coming up and giving that to me." He said to me, "But, listen, I give you so little next to what you've given me." I said, "Don't say that, don't say that," and we embraced and he went away. Well, things like that, that's the best recompense for my work as a writer. That a boy or a girl comes up to speak to you and to offer you a piece of cake, it's wonderful. It's worth the trouble of having written.   —*Julio Cortázar*

I keep hoping I'll be compensated in some way. Once I wrote a piece that tried to sum up the joys and vexations of being eighty, but I left out one of the worst vexations—which is to become a national scholarly resource. I never expected to become a national scholarly resource—but you can't escape the destiny of your dotage. Simply by having outlived your great contemporaries, you find that you have a field all to yourself; or if you don't have a field, at least you have a stable in one corner of the field. Hundreds of scholars then come into the field who are writing dissertations, monographs, biographies—all sorts of things—and for each one they want to have a little reinforcement, a little supplement; they want to have a word straight from the horse's mouth. So they come to me and say, "Well, you are the horse—won't you please share your memories? Won't you please answer this little questionnaire of five single-spaced typed pages?" or, "Won't you let us put your memories on tape?" There is no enrichment from this sort of thing. Not one of them thinks of filling the horse's feed-box with oats or of putting a little hay in the manger. They assume, I guess, that a horse can just forage for himself—if he has time; certainly nobody gives him an offer to earn an easy living by putting himself out to stud.

                    —*Malcolm Cowley*

Luck plays an enormous part in it. It's not like business, though luck has a very strong place in business too. You can write one good poem by luck or hazard that's going to make people want your work. Whether or not you can produce anything good later on is not the important thing. It's that you struck it right then. It's the same with a novel—I wrote *Deliverance*. The movies bought it; it was serialized, written into a dozen languages; it's the best novel I can write, but there's also an enormous element of luck in it. I wrote the right book at the right time. People were caught up in a savage fable of decent men fighting for their lives and killing and getting away with it. My next novel could be a failure.

—*James Dickey*

Fame invades your private life. It takes away from the time that you spend with friends, and the time that you can work. It tends to isolate you from the real world. A famous writer who wants to continue writing has to be constantly defending himself against fame. I don't really like to say this because it never sounds sincere, but I would really have liked for my books to have been published after my death, so I wouldn't have to go through all this business of fame and being a great writer. In my case, the only advantage in fame is that I have been able to give it a political use. Otherwise, it is quite uncomfortable. The problem is that you're famous for twenty-four hours a day and you can't say, "Okay, I won't be famous until tomorrow" or press a button and say, "I won't be famous here or now."

I was asked the other day if I would be interested in the Nobel Prize, but I think that for me it would be an absolute catastrophe. I would certainly be interested in deserving it, but to receive it would be terrible. It would just complicate even more the problems of fame. The only thing I really regret in life is not having a daughter.

—*Gabriel García Márquez*

It [*The Days to Come*] was an absolute horror of a failure. I mean the curtain wasn't up ten minutes and catastrophe set in. It was just an awful failure. Mr. William Randolph Hearst caused a little excitement by getting up in the middle of the first act and leaving with his party of ten. I vomited in the back aisle. I did. I had to go home and change my clothes. I was drunk.

—*Lillian Hellman*

I detest and despise success, yet I cannot do without it. I am like a drug addict—if nobody talks about me for a couple of months I have withdrawal symptoms. It is stupid to be hooked on fame, because it is like being hooked on corpses. After all, the people who come to see my plays, who create my fame, are going to die.   —*Eugène Ionesco*

You get to the point where you realize that personal fame is not at all what you're concerned with really—that old Robert [Frost] was right when he said he hoped to leave half a dozen poems which would be hard to get rid of. Wonderful way of saying it. You begin to see that what is really going to happen is not that half a dozen but two, three, four poems, or maybe lines of poems, or fragments— some things may get shelved, shored up, or left behind. But left behind not alone but in a conjunction. So that you begin to think of yourself in terms of the others who were with you in this place— your contemporaries. "Oh living men, Remember me, Receive me among you." And you realize that's how you are really going to end up. You're going to be part of that, of them. And finally you begin to think, that's the way it ought to be. You ought to make the world fruitful that way. Rot! Leaving those fragments—those few poems that will be hard to get rid of.

· · ·

I don't know if there is anything I can say about it, but by God something ought to be said. Let me begin with two people whom I knew, one very well and one quite well: Ernest Hemingway and Scott Fitzgerald. The tragedy—and it is a tragedy—of Hemingway's fame is that his life and his dramatization of himself have been built up, not by him, or let me say, not altogether by him, to such a point that the myth of the man is more important than the achievement— the work. And the same thing is true of Scott, Scott having done less about dramatizing himself, but having had more done for him. In each case the *Literary Figure*—capital "L," capital "F"—has been so blown up, so exaggerated, that the work has been diminished. You would know better than I how permanently, but in any case damage has been done. And the same thing is true of Robert Frost. Robert was himself the villain there, because, as anybody who knew him knows, he worked very hard at his own reputation even when he had no need to—when his greatness was acknowledged. This was damaging only to him. But the real question is what you do about this sort of thing. I don't know that pontificating about it does any good. My own conviction is that the literary person as such just doesn't count—doesn't matter. Some are interesting and some are dull. The only thing that matters is the work. And the amplification of the amplifying device, which is the man himself, is not good for the art of writing, is not good for the writer, is not good. Ernest used to love to come up and go to the nightclubs in New York. Why? To be recognized? But, for God's sake, he had been recognized in better ways before. I am not throwing off on Ernest. He is still the great prose stylist of the century. But if ever there was a cult of personality . . . ! Well, the one thing a young writer ought to swear to on his sword never to do is never to dramatize himself, whatever he may want to do about his work. —*Archibald MacLeish*

Booze, pot, too much sex, too much failure in one's private life, too much attrition, too much recognition, too little recognition, frustration. Nearly everything in the scheme of things works to dull a first-rate talent. But the worst probably is cowardice—as one gets older, one becomes aware of one's cowardice, the desire to be bold which once was a joy gets heavy with caution and duty. And finally there's apathy. About the time it doesn't seem too important anymore to be a great writer, you know you've slipped far enough to be doing your work now on the comeback trail. —*Norman Mailer*

Almost all the works die while the men remain. We seldom read any more of Rousseau than his *Confessions,* or of Chateaubriand than his *Mémoires d'outre-tombe.* They alone interest us. I have always been and still remain a great admirer of Gide. It already appears, however, that only his journal and *Si le grain ne muert,* the story of his childhood, have any chance of lasting. The rarest thing in literature, and the only success, is when the author disappears and his work remains. We don't know who Shakespeare was, or Homer. People have worn themselves out writing about the life of Racine without being able to establish anything. He is lost in the radiance of his creation. That is quite rare.   —*François Mauriac*

The first notice I got—and I don't like notices; they make me very frightened—was by a man called Daniel George who wrote in *The Daily Express,* "Not for fifteen years have I found so certain a touch." Now if I got that nowadays I would be absolutely delighted. But when I got that when I was twenty-three I was absolutely furious. I thought, "Who is this swine whom he read fifteen years ago who had such wonderful writing?"   —*John Mortimer*

It is only by the grace of God, and perhaps willpower, that one comes through each time. Many wonderful writers write one or two books and then kill themselves. Sylvia Plath for instance. She was much younger than Virginia Woolf when she committed suicide, but if she had survived that terrible crisis, I feel she would have written better books. I have this theory that Woolf feared that the flame of her talent was extinguished or dwindling because her last book, *Between the Acts,* lacked the soaring genius of the others. When a writer, or an artist, has the feeling that he can't do it anymore, he descends into hell. So you must keep in mind that although it may stop, it can come back. When I was a child in Ireland, a spring would suddenly appear and yield forth buckets of beautiful clear water, then just as suddenly it would dry up. The water-diviners would come with their rods and sometimes another spring would be found. One has to be one's own water-diviner. It is hard, especially as writers are always anxious, always on the run—from the telephone, from people, from responsibilities, from the distractions of this world. The other thing that can destroy talent is too much grief. Yeats said, "Too much sorrow can make a stone of the heart." I often wonder, if Emily Brontë had lived to be fifty, what kind of books would she have written? Her life was so penalizing—and Charlotte's too—utterly without sex. Emily was thirty when she wrote *Wuthering Heights.* I think the grinding suffering might have killed her talent later. It is not that you have to be happy—that would be asking too much—but if it gets too painful that sense of wonderment, or joy, dies, and with it the generosity so necessary to create. —*Edna O'Brien*

Don't take rejection slips too seriously. I don't think they ought to send them out at all. I think a very amusing anthology might be gotten up of rejection letters alone. It's largely a question of remembering, when you send something out, that So-and-so is on the other end of this one, and he has certain interests. To give an example of what I mean on this rejection business, I had a story accepted by a magazine. So I wrote it over again as I always do, and sent it back. Well, someone else got it and I got this very nice letter saying that they couldn't use it, but that they'd be very interested in seeing anything else I wrote in the future. —*Frank O'Connor*

One *must* avoid ambition *in order to* write. Otherwise something else is the goal: some kind of power beyond the power of language. And the power of language, it seems to me, is the only kind of power a writer is entitled to. —*Cynthia Ozick*

Failure is inevitable for the writer. Any writer. I don't care who he is, or how great he is, or what he's written. Sooner or later he's going to flop and everybody who admired him will try to write him off as a bum. He can't help it. He's bound to write something bad. Shakespeare wrote a few bad plays. Tolstoy was turning out some pretty dreadful stuff at the end of his life. Name me one great writer who hasn't had some failure. . . . Everybody forgets that a writer who has had success, even one who's made a lot of money on one book, may have waited fifteen years for that one book, and before he can produce another one, it may be another fifteen years, if ever. And I'm not only talking about commercial or critical failure. There's the kind of running failure that dogs a writer all his life—ideas that only get half-written, false beginnings, first drafts that suddenly go dead and have to be thrown away, even crucial paragraphs that stiffen under your hand and refuse to be revived. And then, whole books, even if they've been well-received, that nag you long after they've been published, because you see where you could have done something better with them. And then, American writers, more than any others, are haunted by the fear of failure, because it's such a common pattern in America. The ghost of Fitzgerald, dying in Hollywood, with his comeback book unfinished, and his best book, *Tender Is the Night,* scorned—his ghost hangs over every American typewriter. An absolutely necessary part of a writer's equipment, almost as necessary as talent, is the ability to stand up under punishment, both the punishment the world hands out and the punishment he inflicts upon himself. If he doesn't have the faith in himself, the energy, the ambition, to shake it off or absorb it and plow ahead, he'll wind up a one-book man or a two-book man, and hitting the bottle instead of the typewriter. Failure is more consistent—for everybody—than success. It's like living in a rainy belt—there are some sunny days, but most of the time it's wet outside and you'd better carry your umbrella. Anyway, failure is apt to produce self-pity and it's been my experience that self-pity can be very productive. —*Irwin Shaw*

One bulls-eye and you're rich and famous. The rich get more famous and the famous get richer. You're the talk of the town. The taxi drivers have read about you and they remember you for a fortnight. You get to be photographed for *Vogue* with new clothes and Vuitton luggage, if that's your bag. If it's a new play, everyone owes the writer, they celebrate him—the theater owners, the producers, the actors. Even the stage doorman is somehow touched by the wand. The sense of so much depending on success is very hard to ignore, perhaps impossible. It leads to disproportionate anxiety and disproportionate relief or disappointment. The British are more phlegmatic about these things. You know about British phlegm. —*Tom Stoppard*

ON PUBLICATION

The other day two little boys accosted me in the street and said to me, "You are the lady who wrote *Mary Poppins,* aren't you?" And I admitted it, and said, "How do you know?" And they said, "Because we sing in the choir, and the vicar told us." So, clearly, they had thrown off their surplices and rushed after me to catch me. So I said, "Well, do you like her?" And they both nodded vigorously. I then said, "What is it you like about her?" And one of them said, "Well, she's so *ordinary* and then . . ." and having said "and then" he looked around for the proper word, and couldn't find it. And I said, "You don't have to say any more. That 'and then' says everything." And the other little boy said, "Yes, and I'm going to marry her when I grow up." And I saw the first one clench his fists and look very belligerent. I felt there might be trouble and so I said, "Well, we'll just have to see what *she* thinks about it, won't we? And in the meantime, my house is just there—come in and have a lemonade." So they did.
—*P. L. Travers*

I'm interviewed too much. I fight them off, but even one is too many. In any interview, you do say more or less than you mean. You leave the proper ground of your strength and become one more gassy monologist. Unlike Mailer and Bellow, I don't have much itch to pronounce on great matters, to reform the country, to get elected Mayor of New York, or minister to the world with laughter like the hero of "The Last Analysis." My life is, in a sense, trash, my life is only that of which the residue is my writing.
—*John Updike*

A cousin of mine wrote to my professor of English at Whittier College and to my poor mother (who had been so proud that her daughter had a book published) to say, first of all, no Milhous had ever said "ain't." Second, it was degrading to the Quaker faith to have Jess pray louder than was necessary. Actually, he was not really shouting to God, you know, he was trying to make himself heard above the organ. Third, I often used dirty words. I said that a duck (and it was a Quaker duck too) deposited duck dung on the steps, and that Jess didn't like ducks for that reason. My cousin felt I could have found some other way to say it, in spite of the alliteration.

—*Jessamyn West*

ON CRITICS

You know who critics are—the men who have failed in literature
and art.   —*Benjamin Disraeli*

Monsieur Flaubert is not a writer.   —*Le Figaro,* on *Madame Bovary*

Some reviews give pain. That is regrettable, but no author has the
right to whine. He was not obliged to be an author. He invited
publicity, and he must take the publicity that comes along.
                                            —*E. M. Forster*

It is advantageous to an author that his book should be attacked as
well as praised. Fame is a shuttlecock. If it be struck at only one
end of the room, it will soon fall to the ground. To keep it up, it
must be struck at both ends.   —*Samuel Johnson*

You do not publish your own verses, Laelius; you criticise mine.
Pray cease to criticise mine, or else publish your own.   —*Martial*

It's a short walk from the hallelujah to the hoot.
                                            —*Vladimir Nabokov*

I love every bone in their heads.   —*Eugene O'Neill*

A drama critic is a man who leaves no turn unstoned.
                                            —*George Bernard Shaw*

Indeed it is true that a number of the movie critics of *Who's Afraid
of Virginia Woolf?* have repeated the speculation that the play was
written about four homosexuals disguised as heterosexual men and
women. This comment first appeared around the time the play was
produced. I was fascinated by it. I suppose what disturbed me about

157

it was twofold: first, nobody has ever bothered to ask *me* whether it was true; second, the critics and columnists made no attempt to document the assertion from the text of the play. The facts are simple: *Who's Afraid of Virginia Woolf?* was written about two heterosexual couples. If I had wanted to write a play about four homosexuals, I would have done so. Parenthetically, it is interesting that when the film critic of *Newsweek* stated that he understood the play to have been written about four homosexuals, I had a letter written to him suggesting he check his information before printing such speculations. He replied, saying, in effect, two things: first, that we all know that a critic is a far better judge of an author's intention than the author; second, that seeing the play as being about four homosexuals was the only way that he could live with the play, meaning that he could not accept it as a valid examination of heterosexual life. Well, I'm sure that all the actresses from Uta Hagen to Elizabeth Taylor who've played the role of Martha would be absolutely astonished to learn they've been playing men.   —*Edward Albee*

Before publication, and if provided by persons whose judgment you trust, yes, of course criticism helps. But after something is published all I want to read or hear is praise. Anything less is a bore, and I'll give you fifty dollars if you produce a writer who can honestly say he was ever helped by the prissy carpings and condescensions of reviewers. I don't mean to say that none of the professional critics are worth paying attention to . . . but few of the good ones review on a regular basis. Most of all, I believe in hardening yourself against opinion. I've had, and continue to receive, my full share of abuse, some of it extremely personal, but it doesn't faze me anymore . . . I can read the most outrageous libel about myself and never skip a pulsebeat. And in this connection there is one piece of advice I strongly urge: never demean yourself by talking back to a critic, never. Write those letters to the editor in your head, but don't put them on paper.   —*Truman Capote*

ON CRITICS

I don't really read very many reviews of anything I write. If somebody comes up to me and says, "Jim, there's a fabulous review in the *Atlantic* and you must read it; he's crazy about the book," then I'll read it. If the guy says it's a horrible review and that I'm the anti-Christ himself, then I don't read it, because I don't want to go around filled with resentment against some stranger. That bleeds off your energies; you take them out in useless hatred. I need the energy for other things. I've known writers who are absolutely destroyed by adverse opinion, and I think this is a lot of shit. You shouldn't allow that to happen to yourself, and if you do, then it's *your* fault. My course is set; I know what I'm going to do. As Stephen Dedalus says, in *A Portrait of the Artist as a Young Man,* "I'm ready to make a lifelong mistake." I believe in making a lifelong mistake, but I don't believe in being guided by people who write about me. Why, there's not anything that could ever be said about a person either good or bad that hasn't been said about me. But it doesn't matter. I'm going to write my way, and if that doesn't agree with people's sensibilities or even their digestions, it doesn't make any difference to me. If it's a lifelong mistake, it won't be the first one that's been made.

—*James Dickey*

Donoghue was someone who used to come into my rooms at Trinity and see something in the typewriter and glance at it. I'd ask him, "What do you think of that, Donoghue?" and he'd say, "It stinks!" This went on for days and days every time he'd come in trying to get food from me. And then—he was a classicist—one night I typed out some Plato and left it in my typewriter, and I had it ready for him as he popped in. And I said, "Okay, Donoghue, there is the typewriter. Now let's have your opinion on that." "That stinks too." "Look, Donoghue, I've tried awfully hard with this." He'd say, "Doesn't matter. You're never going to make it." I made him give it a second reading, but he said it still stunk. Then I revealed to him it was Plato. And that stopped him staring at my typewriter.

He finally conceded, "What the hell, you work hard, maybe you'll make it."
—*J. P. Donleavy*

People sometimes send me articles about myself, and I bundle them off after a while to the University of Virginia for the professors to mull over. Occasionally I look at things, but I've generally managed to avoid stuff written about my work because there just isn't time to fuss with it. I don't think I've lost very much sleep by what you would call the critical reception of my work. I've been very fortunate in a way. If a thing is knocked in one place, somebody else may like it somewhere else. *The Great Days* was very much ignored in this country, but it went quite well in England and in Germany. I wouldn't have been able to make a living without the international market.
—*John Dos Passos*

I find what they call "constructive" criticism helpful. Occasionally you come across somebody who says, "Why didn't she do so and so?" And you think, "God, why didn't I?" And he says, "Why doesn't she do so and so next time?" And you think, "Yes, why don't I?"
—*Margaret Drabble*

[If I pay any attention to critics], I get blocks. I have discovered quite recently that the characteristic Freudian resistances to confessions of any sort, which are very well represented in all the writing blocks one goes through—the dizzy fits, the nauseas, and so on and so forth, which almost every writer has recorded—are a standard pattern for all kinds of creative things. They are simply forms of egotism. And egotism can be inflamed very easily by a good review, or a bad review for that matter, and you can get a nice tidy block which will cost you two days of work. And when you've got to get the money for the work, you can't afford it. So I don't read reviews unless they're sent to me. Usually they go to my agent because they help sell foreign rights. And it sounds very pompous, but really I think they have a bad influence on one, and even the good ones make you a bit ashamed. In fact I think the best regimen is to get up early, insult yourself a bit in the shaving-mirror, and then pretend you're cutting wood, which is really just about all the hell you are doing— if you see what I mean. But all the Jungian guilt about the importance of one's message, and all that sort of thing—well, you get a nice corpulent ego standing in the way there, telling you that you're so damn clever that you're almost afraid to write it down, it's so wonderful. And the minute you get that, where are your checks going to come from for next month's gas, light, and heat? You can't afford it. *—Lawrence Durrell*

They've never had any effect on me, for the simple reason that I've never read them. I've never made a point of writing for any particular person or audience; I've simply tried to do the best job I could and let it go at that. The critics don't interest me because they're concerned with what's past and done, while I'm concerned with what comes next. I've never reread my early novels, for example. Perhaps I should read them one of these days. *—Aldous Huxley*

I have a friend who says that reviewers are the tickbirds of the literary rhinoceros—but he is being kind. Tickbirds perform a valuable service to the rhino and the rhino hardly notices the birds. Reviewers perform no service to the writer and are noticed too much. I like what Cocteau said about them. "Listen very carefully to the first criticism of your work. Note just what it is about your work that the reviewers don't like; it may be the only thing in your work that is original and worthwhile." *—John Irving*

I was thirty-seven years old. I had the baby and the galleys together, and I sat at my desk—the same desk I use now, the same desk I inherited from my brother when I was eight years old—correcting the galleys with my right hand, and rocking the baby carriage with my left. I felt stung when the review in *Time,* which had a big feature on first novels that season, got my age wrong and added a year. I hated being so old; beginning when I thought I'd be so far along. I've had age-sorrow all my life. —*Cynthia Ozick*

When the articles were agreeable I read them through. I never learned anything at all from them but I was astonished by their imagination and fecundity. They saw intentions I never had.

—*Françoise Sagan*

Auden himself had total self-confidence, of course. He just thought that he was cleverer than anyone else, but without arrogance really, just out of his own judgment, which may or may not have been right, but which nevertheless was never arrogant. He knew exactly what he was doing, and he was totally indifferent to what anyone said about it. And then being a "psychoanalyst" helped him a great deal. For instance, when he was so attacked by Randall Jarrell in 1947 or so, he said, "He must be in love with me; I can't think of any other explanation." Well, that isn't what one usually thinks about being attacked in print. He was genuinely puzzled. He didn't think it was a damaging attack in any way. —*Stephen Spender*

From the writer's point of view, critics should be ignored, although it's hard not to do what they suggest. I think it's unfortunate to have critics for friends. Suppose you write something that stinks, what are they going to say in a review? Say it stinks? So if they're honest they do, and if you were friends you're still friends, but the knowledge of your lousy writing and their articulate admission of it will be always something between the two of you, like the knowledge between a man and his wife of some shady adultery. I know very few critics, but I usually read their reviews. Bad notices always give me a sense of humility, or perhaps humiliation, even when there's a tone of envy or sour grapes or even ignorance in them, but they don't help me much. When *Lie Down in Darkness* came out, my home-town paper scraped up the local literary figure to review the book, a guy who'd written something on hydraulics, I think, and he came to the conclusion that I was a decadent writer. Styron is a decadent writer, he said, because he writes a line like "the sea sucking at the shore," when for that depraved bit he should have substituted "the waves lapping at the shore." Probably his hydraulic background. No, I'm afraid I don't think much of critics for the most part, although I have to admit that some of them have so far treated me quite kindly. Look, there's only one person a writer should listen to, pay any attention to. It's not any damn critic. It's the reader. And that doesn't mean any compromise or sell-out. The writer must criticize his own work as a reader. Every day I pick up the story or whatever it is I've been working on and read it through. If I enjoy it as a reader then I know I'm getting along all right. —*William Styron*

Slapstick may be a very bad book. I am perfectly willing to believe that. Everybody else writes lousy books, so why shouldn't I? What was unusual about the reviews was that they wanted people to admit now that I had never been any good. The reviewer for the Sunday *Times* actually asked critics who had praised me in the past to now admit in public how wrong they'd been. All of a sudden, critics wanted me squashed like a bug. And it wasn't just that I had money all of a sudden, either. The hidden complaint was that I was barbarous, that I wrote without having made a systematic study of great literature, that I was no gentleman, since I had done hack writing so cheerfully for vulgar magazines—that I had not paid my academic dues. It was dishonorable enough that I perverted art for money. I then topped that felony by becoming, as I say, fabulously well-to-do. Well, that's just too damn bad for me and for everybody. I'm completely in print, so we're all stuck with me and stuck with my books.

—*Kurt Vonnegut*

The important thing is that you make sure that neither the favorable nor the unfavorable critics move into your head and take part in the composition of your next work. —*Thornton Wilder*

I always read them really carefully. You do get tips from them. Now that last Jeeves book of mine, *Jeeves and the Tie That Binds,* I forget which critic it was, but he said that the book was dangerously near to self-parody. I know what he meant. I had exaggerated Jeeves and Bertie. Jeeves always reciting some poetry or something. I'll correct that in the next one. I do think one can learn from criticism. In fact, I'm a pretty good critic of my own work. I know when it isn't as good as it ought to be. —*P. G. Wodehouse*

Technical Matters

ON BEGINNINGS
AND ENDINGS

A bad beginning makes a bad ending.   *—Euripides,* Aeolus

My way is to begin with the beginning.   *—Lord Byron,* Don Juan

I always wanted to write a book that ended with the word
mayonnaise.   *—Richard Brautigan*

My greatest trouble is getting the curtain up and down.
                                        —T. S. Eliot

Great is the art of beginning, but greater the art is of ending.
                           —Thomas Fuller, Gnomologia

The last thing one knows when writing a book is what to put first.
                                     —Blaise Pascal

As for curtain lines, well, I suppose there are playwrights who do
build toward curtain lines. I don't think I do that. In a sense, it's the
same choice that has to be made when you wonder when to start a
play. And when to end it. The characters' lives have gone on before
the moment you chose to have the action of the play begin. And
their lives are going to go on after you have lowered the final curtain
on the play, unless you've killed them off. A play is a parenthesis
which contains all the material you think has to be contained for the
action of the play. Where do you end that? Where the characters
seem to come to a pause . . . where they seem to want to stop—
rather like, I would think, the construction of a piece of music.
                                       —Edward Albee

A gag that's probably gone unnoticed turns up in the last sentence of the novel I wrote with James Schuyler. Actually it's my sentence. It reads: "So it was that the cliff dwellers, after bidding their cousins good night, moved off towards the parking area, while the latter bent their steps toward the partially rebuilt shopping plaza in the teeth of the freshening foehn." *Foehn* is a kind of warm wind that blows in Bavaria that produces a fog. I would doubt that many people know that. I liked the idea that people, if they bothered to, would have to open the dictionary to find out what the last word in the novel meant. They'd be closing one book and opening another.

—*John Ashbery*

When you've finished a novel it means, "The train stops here, you have to get off here." You never get the book you wanted, you settle for the book you get. I've always felt that when a book ended there was something I didn't see, and usually when I remark the discovery it's too late to do anything about it.   —*James Baldwin*

Ends always give me trouble. Characters run away with you, and so won't fit on to what is coming.   —*E. M. Forster*

I always start a novel by writing its first page and its last page, which seem to survive almost intact through all the following drafts and changes.   —*Jerzy Kosinski*

Offhand I think of "None of them knew the color of the sky," which is *The Open Boat,* and "All the sisters lay dreaming of horses," which is *National Velvet.* And the wonderful first line of *Pride and Prejudice.* "It is a truth universally acknowledged, that a single man in possession of a good fortune must be in want of a wife."

—*William Maxwell*

It's pure instinct. The curtain comes down when the rhythm seems right—when the action calls for a finish. I'm very fond of curtain lines, of doing them properly.   —*Harold Pinter*

ON BEGINNINGS AND ENDINGS

If I didn't know the ending of a story, I wouldn't begin. I always write my last lines, my last paragraph, my last page first, and then I go back and work towards it. I know where I'm going. I know what my goal is. And how I get there is God's grace.

. . .

Any true work of art has got to give you the feeling of reconciliation—what the Greeks would call catharsis, the purification of your mind and imagination—through an ending that is endurable because it is right and true. Oh, not in any pawky individual idea of morality or some parochial idea of right and wrong. Sometimes the end is very tragic, because it needs to be. One of the most perfect and marvelous endings in literature—it raises my hair now—is the little boy at the end of *Wuthering Heights,* crying that he's afraid to go across the moor because there's a man and woman walking there.

—*Katherine Anne Porter*

I truly do not care about a book once it is finished. Any money or fame that results has no connection in my feeling with the book. The book dies a real death for me when I write the last word. I have a little sorrow and then go on to a new book which is alive. The rows of my books on the shelf are to me like very well embalmed corpses. They are neither alive nor mine. I have no sorrow for them because I have forgotten them, forgotten in its truest sense.

—*John Steinbeck*

Curtain lines tend to be produced under the pressure of the preceding two or three acts, and usually they seem so dead right, to me anyway, that it really is as if they were in the DNA, unique and inevitable. Some of my favorite curtain lines are "The son of a bitch stole my watch" [from *The Front Page*]—I quote from memory—and "You that way; we this way" [from *Love's Labour's Lost*].

—*Tom Stoppard*

ON NAMES
AND TITLES

The Ancient Mariner would not have taken so well if it had been called *The Old Sailor*.   —*Samuel Butler*

There are little local and private jokes. Indeed, I did name the two lead characters of *Virginia Woolf* George and Martha because there is contained in the play—not its most important point, but certainly contained within the play—an attempt to examine the success or failure of American revolutionary principles. Some people who are historically and politically and sociologically inclined find them. Now in one play—*Virginia Woolf* again—I named a very old Western Union man "Little Billy"—"Crazy Billy" rather. And I did that because as *you* might recall, Mr. Flanagan,* you used to deliver telegrams for Western Union, and you are very old and your name is Billy. Things like that—lots of them going on in the plays. In *Zoo Story,* I named two characters Peter and Jerry. I know two people named Peter and Jerry. But then the learned papers started coming in, and of course Jerry is supposed to be Jesus . . . which is much more interesting, I suppose, to the public than the truth.   —*Edward Albee*

I don't consider that very important. I chose the name Xavière in *She Came to Stay* because I had met only one person who had that name. When I look for names, I use the telephone directory or try to remember the names of former pupils.   —*Simone de Beauvoir*

*William Flanagan, Albee's interviewer.

ON NAMES AND TITLES

I can't begin if I don't know the name. That's my problem at the moment. I have a plan in mind, something, a novel. I should have five or six names already that I don't have yet. Certainly I can help myself out—and that's not bad either—just by calling them all Schmitz, just to get going. But I can't think about names too much. It's an awkward mistake to try to make a name significant or characteristic of the person in question. The name of a person is really sacrosanct to me. A lot of things are ruined because I can't find a name. Sometimes I improvise on the typewriter, just as one improvises on the piano. I think, well, it starts with a D, then I put down an E, and then an N and so forth. So then he's named Denger or some such name.

· · ·

The title comes afterwards, usually with considerable difficulty. I remember that *The Train Was on Time* had a totally different working title; it was called *Between Lemberg and Czernowitz*. The publisher said, "My God, two place names." I was persuaded to change it, but not against my will; I agreed to it then. A working title often changes.

—*Heinrich Böll*

I have two methods: one of them is to work in the names of my grandfathers, great-grandfathers, and so on. To give them a kind of, well, I won't say immortality, but that's one of the methods. The other is to use names that somehow strike me. For example, in a story of mine, one of the characters who comes and goes is called Yarmolinsky because the name struck me—it's a strange word, no? Then another character is called Red Scharlach because Scharlach means *scarlet* in German and he was a murderer; he was doubly red, no? Red Scharlach: Red Scarlet.　　　　—*Jorge Luis Borges*

The name of the Angel Heurtebise, in the book of poems *L'Ange Heurtebise*, which was written in an unbroken automatism from start to finish, was taken from the name of an elevator stop where I happened to pause once. And I have named characters after desig-

nations on those great old-fashioned glass jars in a pharmacy in
Normandy.   —*Jean Cocteau*

Sometimes I use characters from real life, and sometimes I use their
real names—when I do, it's always in celebration of people that I
like. Once or twice, as in *October Light,* I've borrowed other people's
fictional characters. Naming is only a problem, of course, when you
make the character up. It seems to me that every character—every
person—is an embodiment of a very complicated, philosophical way
of looking at the world, whether conscious or not. Names can be
strong clues to the character's system. Names are magic. If you name
a kid John, he'll grow up a different kid than if you named him
Rudolph. I've used real characters in every single novel, except in
Grendel, where it's impossible—they didn't have our kinds of names
in those days—but even in *Grendel* I used jokes and puns that give
you clues to who I'm talking about. For instance there's a guy named
Red Horse, which is really a sorrel, which is really George Sorel.
                                                 —*John Gardner*

I make a list of titles *after* I've finished the story or the book—
sometimes as many as a hundred. Then I start eliminating them,
sometimes all of them.   —*Ernest Hemingway*

Yes, names are very important, aren't they? And the most unlikely
names keep turning up in real life, so one must be careful. I can
explain some of the names in *After Many a Summer.* Take Virginia
Maunciple. That name was suggested to me by Chaucer's manciple—
what is a manciple, anyhow? a kind of steward—it's the sort of a
name that a movie starlet would choose, in the hope of being unique,
custom-made. She's called Virginia because she appears so virginal to
Jeremy, and so obviously isn't, in fact; also because of her devotion
to the Madonna. Dr. Sigmund Obispo: here the first name obviously

refers to Freud, and Obispo I took from San Luis Obispo for local color and because it has a comical sound. And Jeremy Pordage. There's a story connected with that name. When I was an undergraduate at Oxford, Professor Walter Raleigh (who was a marvelous teacher) had me do a piece of research on the literature connected with the Popish Plot. One of the authors mentioned by Dryden under the name of "lame Mephibosheth" was called Pordage. His poetry, when I read it at the Bodleian, turned out to be unbelievably bad. But the name was a treasure. As for Jeremy, that was chosen for the sound: combined with Pordage it has a rather spinsterish ring. Propter came from the Latin for "on account of"—because, as a wise man, he is concerned with ultimate causes. Another reason why I chose the name was its occurrence in a poem of Edward Lear, "Incidents in the Life of My Uncle Arly." Let's see, how does it go now?

> Like the ancient Medes and Persians,
> Always by his own exertions
>   He subsisted on those hills;
> Whiles, by teaching children spelling,
> Or at times by merely yelling,
> Or at intervals by selling
>   "Propter's Nicodemus Pills."

Pete Boone doesn't mean anything in particular. It's just a straightforward American name that suits the character. Jo Stoyte, too—the name simply means what it sounds like.   —*Aldous Huxley*

The title always comes first, to me and to the reader. I've written many stories and articles just by doggedly following the title. Sometimes I use a working title, sometimes I find a title suitable for a given subject. Take my most recent novel, *La habana para un infante difunto* (1979). It had a different title when I began: *Las confesiones de agosto*, a clever allusion to confession and to Saint Augustine's *Confessions*. I had begun writing the book in August, so that was included as well. Then one day I heard a title, *La habana para un infante difunto*, just like that, the same way Saint Augustine heard the voice in the garden. With the new title in mind, I rewrote the whole book.

—*Guillermo Cabrera Infante*

I have been unwise enough to use names that are very well known in my part of the country, around Bordeaux. So far, I have been able to avoid the great embarrassments that this system could have caused me.   —*François Mauriac*

As I was writing the poem "Eighteen Days Without You"—the last poem in *Love Poems*—my husband said to me, "I can't stand it any longer, you haven't been with me for days." That poem originally was 'Twenty-one Days Without You" and it became "Eighteen Days" because he had cut into the inspiration; he demanded my presence back again, into his life, and I couldn't take that much from him.

—*Anne Sexton*

Sometimes I'll come up with a title that doesn't sound good in itself, but it's the only title that really fits the meaning of the play. Like *A House Not Meant to Stand* isn't a beautiful title. But the house it refers to in the play is in a terrible state of disrepair, virtually leaking rain water everywhere. That house, and therefore the title, is a metaphor for society in our times. And, of course, the critics don't like that sort of thing, nor do they dare to openly approve it. They know who butters their bread.

Some titles come from dialogue as I write a play, or from the setting itself. Some come from poetry I've read. When I need a title I'll usually reread the poetry of Hart Crane. I take a copy of Crane's work with me when I travel. A phrase will catch my eye and seem right for what I'm writing. But there's no system to it. Sometimes a line from the play will serve as its title. I often change titles a number of times until I find one that seems right.

There is a Catholic church in Key West named "Mary, Star of the Sea." That would make a lovely title for a play.

—*Tennessee Williams*

ON STYLE

The greatest masterpiece in literature is only a dictionary out of order.   *—Jean Cocteau*

A work that aspires, however humbly, to the condition of art should carry its justification in every line.
      —Joseph Conrad,
         The Nigger and the Narcissus, *Preface*

All the fun's in how you say a thing.   *—Robert Frost*

This is what I'd like to put in my letter: "Beautiful Marquise, your beautiful eyes make me die of love," but I'd like to put it in an elegant way, I want it prettily tuned.   *—Molière*

When we come across a natural style, we are surprised and delighted; for we expected an author, and we find a man.
      —Blaise Pascal

Proper words in proper places make the true definition of a style.
      —Jonathan Swift

The difference between the right word and the nearly right word is the same as that between lightning and the lightning bug.
      —Mark Twain

I never used a carbon because that made me self-conscious. I can remember discussing the effect of the typewriter on our work with Tom Eliot because he was moving to the typewriter about the same time I was. And I remember our agreeing that it made for a slight change of style in the prose—that you tended to use more periodic sentences, a little shorter, and a rather choppier style—and that one must be careful about that. Because, you see, you couldn't look ahead quite far enough, for you were always thinking about putting your fingers on the bloody keys. But that was a passing phase only. We both soon discovered that we were just as free to let the style throw itself into the air as we had been writing manually. —*Conrad Aiken*

W‌ell, I haven't consciously tried to develop it. The only thing I've consciously tried to do was put myself in a position to hear the people I wanted to hear talk talk. I used the police line-up for I don't know how many years . . . they finally stopped me . . . the card got ragged as hell, pasted here and there, you couldn't read it . . . the detective who sat at the door stopped me and said, "What happened, you mean you're still looking for the guy?" This was like seven years later, and I said, "Hell yes, I lost fourteen dollars," so he let me go ahead. —*Nelson Algren*

W‌hen I began writing, I thought that everything should be defined by the writer. For example to say "the moon" was strictly forbidden; that one had to find an adjective, an epithet for the moon. (Of course, I'm simplifying things. I know it, because many times I have written "la luna," but this is a kind of symbol of what I was doing.) Well, I thought everything had to be defined and that no common terms of phrase should be used. I would never have said "So-and-so came in and sat down," because that was far too simple and far too easy. I thought I had to find out some fancy way of saying it. Now I find out that those things are generally annoyances to the reader. But I think the whole root of the matter lies in the fact that when a writer is young he feels somehow that what he is going to say is rather silly or obvious or commonplace, and then he tries to hide it under baroque ornament, under words taken from the seventeenth-century writers; or, if not, and he sets out to be modern, then he does the contrary: he's inventing words all the time, or alluding to airplanes, railway trains, or the telegraph and telephone because he's doing his best to be modern. Then as time goes on, one feels that one's ideas, good or bad, should be plainly expressed, because if you have an idea you must try to get that idea or that feeling or that mood into the mind of the reader. If, at the same time, you are trying to be, let's say, Sir Thomas Browne or Ezra Pound, then it can't be done. So that I think a writer always begins by being too complicated: he's playing at several games at the same time. He wants to convey a peculiar mood; at the same time he must be a contemporary and if not a contemporary, then he's a reactionary and a classic. As to the vocabulary, the first thing a young writer, at least in this country, sets out to do is to show his readers that he possesses a dictionary, that he knows all the synonyms; so we get, for example, in one line, *red,* then we get *scarlet,* then we get other different words, more or less, for the same color: *purple.*

Whenever I find an out-of-the-way word, that is to say, a word that may be used by the Spanish classics or a word used in the slums of Buenos Aires, I mean a word that is different from the others, then I strike it out and I use a common word. I remember that Stevenson wrote that in a well-written page all the words should look the same way. If you write an uncouth word or an astonishing or an archaic word, then the rule is broken; and what is far more important, the attention of the reader is distracted by the word. One should be able to read smoothly in it, even if you're writing metaphysics or philosophy or whatever.

● ● ●

I think that Mark Twain was one of the really great writers but I think he was rather unaware of the fact. But perhaps in order to write a really great book, you *must* be rather unaware of the fact. You can slave away at it and change every adjective to some other adjective, but perhaps you can write better if you leave the mistakes. I remember what Bernard Shaw said, that as to style, a writer has as much style as his conviction will give him and not more. Shaw thought that the idea of a game of style was quite nonsensical, quite meaningless. He thought of Bunyan, for example, as a great writer because he was convinced of what he was saying. If a writer disbelieves what he is writing, then he can hardly expect his readers to believe it. In this country [Argentina], though, there is a tendency to regard any kind of writing—especially the writing of poetry—as a game of style. I have known many poets here who have written well—very fine stuff—with delicate moods and so on—but if you talk with them, the only thing they tell you is smutty stories or speak of politics in the way that everybody does, so that really their writing turns out to be a kind of sideshow. They had learned writing in the way that a man might learn to play chess or to play bridge. They were not really poets or writers at all. It was a trick they had learned and they had learned it thoroughly. They had the whole thing at their finger ends. But most of them—except four or five I should say—seemed to think of life as having nothing poetic or mysterious about it. They take things for granted. They know that when they have to write, then, well, they have to suddenly become rather sad or ironic.

—*Jorge Luis Borges*

To write in the first person seems the easiest. As all young journal-writers assume. Actually it may be hardest—there are so many hazards. Garrulity. Lack of shape, or proportion. Or even of judgment. On the other hand, when you're really riding that horse well, it can feel as if you're on Bucephalus. And you really feel the wind on you.   —*Hortense Calisher*

I mean [by control] maintaining a stylistic and emotional upper hand over your material. Call it precious and go to hell, but I believe a story can be wrecked by a faulty rhythm in a sentence (especially if it occurs toward the end) or a mistake in paragraphing, even punctuation. Henry James is the maestro of the semi-colon. Hemingway is a first-rate paragrapher. From the point of view of ear, Virginia Woolf never wrote a bad sentence. I don't mean to imply that I successfully practice what I preach . . . I try, that's all.

•   •   •

What is style? And "what" as the Zen Koan asks, "is the sound of one hand clapping?" No one really *knows;* yet either you *know* or you don't. For myself, if you will excuse a rather cheap little image, I suppose style is the mirror of an artist's sensibility . . . more so than the *content* of his work. To some degree all writers have style. . . . Ronald Firbank, bless his heart, had little else, and thank God he realized it. But the possession of style, *a* style, is often a hindrance, a negative force, not as it should be, and as it is . . . with, say E. M. Forster and Colette and Flaubert and Mark Twain and Hemingway and Isak Dinesen, a reinforcement. Dreiser, for instance, has *a* style—but oh, Dio Buono! And Eugene O'Neill. And Faulkner, brilliant as he is. They all seem to me triumphs over strong but negative styles . . . styles that do not really add to the communication between writer and reader. Then there is the styleless stylist . . . which is very difficult, very admirable, and *always* very popular: Graham Greene, Maugham, Thornton Wilder, John Hersey, Willa Cather, Thurber, Sartre (remember, we're *not* discussing content), J. P. Marquand and so on. But yes, there *is* such an animal as a nonstylist. Only they're not writers. They're typists. Sweaty typists blacking up pounds of Bond with formless, eyeless, earless messages. Well, who are some of the younger writers who seem to know that style exists? P. H. Newby, Françoise Sagan, somewhat. Bill Styron. Flannery O'Connor . . . she has some fine moments, that girl. James Merrill. William Goyen . . . if he'd stop being hysterical. J. D. Salinger . . . especially in the colloquial tradition. Colin Wilson? Another typist.

No, I don't think that style is consciously arrived at. Any more than one arrives at the color of one's eyes. After all, your style *is* you. At the end the personality of a writer has so much to do with the work. The personality has to be humanly there. Personality is a debased word, I know, but it's what I mean. The writer's individual humanity, his word or gesture toward the world, has to appear almost like a character that makes contact with the reader. If the personality is vague or confused or merely literary, *ça ne va pas.* Faulkner, McCullers— they project their personality at once.   —*Truman Capote*

I don't think anyone can, you know, develop a style consciously. I read with amazement, for example, of old Maugham solemnly writing out a page of Swift every day when he was trying to learn the job, in order to give himself a stylistic purchase as it were. It struck me as something I could never do. No. When you say "consciously," I mean it's like "Do you consciously dream?" One doesn't know very much about these processes at all. I think the writing itself grows you up, and you grow the writing up, and finally you get an amalgam of everything you have pinched with a new kind of personality which is your own, and then you are able to pay back these socking debts with a tiny bit of interest—which is the only honorable thing for a writer to do—at least a writer who is a thief like me.

—*Lawrence Durrell*

He [Henry James] began dictating directly to the typewriter. It's a case of the medium being the message and with dictation he ran into longer sentences, and parenthetical remarks, and when he revised what he had dictated he tended to add further flourishes. In the old days when he wrote in longhand he was much briefer and crisper, but now he luxuriated in fine phrases and he was exquisitely baroque. It's a grand style but not to everyone's taste.   —*Leon Edel*

The notion that a perfect form, like a sort of god, hovers over all of us, which we either cling or pay lip service to, I dislike intensely. I think whatever form is chosen by each writer is "perfect" for him or her, however imperfect it may seem to those under the delusion of some general "perfect form" and its attainability. That sort of myth of a perfect form, applicable to all, seems to me one of those things modern art has sunk beyond resurrection. I certainly try to make the form I put things in suit their matter, but I agree totally with E. M. Forster that forcing matter into some supposed general idea of the form best suited to it is wrong. Novels in a sense are like new scientific theories. Of course there are ways in which they have to pay homage to the past, to high past standards; but they also have to disobey and question them, to break new ground. Nothing in their cultural pasts could have allowed for a predicted, say, *Tristram Shandy* or *Ulysses*.   —*John Fowles*

After *The Evil Hour* I did not write anything for five years. I had an idea of what I always wanted to do, but there was something missing and I was not sure what it was until one day I discovered the right tone—the tone that I eventually used in *One Hundred Years of Solitude*. It was based on the way my grandmother used to tell her stories. She told things that sounded supernatural and fantastic, but she told them with complete naturalness. When I finally discovered the tone I had to use, I sat down for eighteen months and worked every day. What was most important was the expression she had on her face. She did not change her expression at all when telling her stories and everyone was surprised. In previous attempts to write *One Hundred Years of Solitude,* I tried to tell the story without believing in it. I discovered that what I had to do was believe in them myself and write them with the same expression with which my grandmother told them: with a brick face.   —*Gabriel García Márquez*

Whoever thinks about the English language and tries to discover its principles, and also pulls a whole lot of writers to pieces to show how badly they write, can't afford to write badly himself. In 1959, I entirely rewrote *Goodbye to All That*—every single sentence—but no one noticed. Some said: "What a good book that is, after all. How well it's lasted." It hasn't lasted at all. It's an entirely new product. One of those computer analyses of style couldn't possibly decide that my historical novels were all written by the same hand. They're completely different in vocabulary, syntax and language-level.   —*Robert Graves*

We must all struggle against all that is curious, already-seen, fatigued, shopworn. I battle against what my admirable colleague William Gass calls "pissless prose," prose that lacks the muscle, the physicality, the gait of a good horse, for pissless prose is bodiless and has no soul. Of course this holds equally true for fiction as for essays, reporting, a letter to a friend, a book review, a decent contribution to art criticism—in sum I search for language in which faith intertwines with desire, faith that we can recapture, with erotic accuracy, that treasured memory or vision which is the object of our desire. I'm keen on the word "voluptuous," a word too seldom heard in this society founded on puritanical principles. I think back to a phrase of Julia Kristeva's, the most interesting feminist thinker of our time, who speaks of "the voluptuousness of family life." I would apply the same phrase to the prose I most admire, prose I can caress and nurture and linger on, diction which is nourished by the deep intimacy of familiar detail, and yet is constantly renewed by the force of the writer's love and fidelity to language.   —*Francine du Plessix Gray*

His [the writer's] style is himself, and we are all of us changing every day—developing, we hope! We leave our marks behind us like a snail.   —*Henry Green*

The prose written by poets is one of my passions. I like the offhand flashes, the absence of the lumber in the usual prose . . . the quickness, the deftness, confidence, and even the relief from spelling everything out, plank by plank. Here is a beautiful sentence, just right, inspired, a bit of prose I've memorized. It is by Pasternak. It goes: "The beginning of April surprised Moscow in the white stupor of returning winter. On the seventh, it began to thaw for the second time, and on the fourteenth when Mayakovsky shot himself, not everyone had yet become accustomed to the novelty of spring." I love the rhythm of "the beginning of April . . . on the seventh . . . on the fourteenth" and the way the subject, Mayakovsky's suicide, is honored by the beauty of this introduction to the account. It's in *Safe Conduct,* Pasternak's autobiographical writing.   —*Elizabeth Hardwick*

That is a long-term tiring question and if you spent a couple of days answering it you would be so self-conscious that you could not write. I might say that what amateurs call a style is usually only the unavoidable awkwardness in first trying to make something that has not heretofore been made. Almost no new classics resemble other previous classics. At first people can see only the awkwardness. Then they are not so perceptible. When they show so very awkwardly people think these awkwardnesses are the style and many copy them. This is regrettable.   —*Ernest Hemingway*

My style flows from the fingers. The eye and ear approve or amend.   —*Bernard Malamud*

I have very seldom asked myself about the technique I was using. When I begin to write I don't stop and wonder if I am interfering too directly in the story, or if I know too much about my characters, or whether or not I ought to judge them. I write with complete naïveté, spontaneously. I've never had any preconceived notion of what I could or could not do. . . . I believe that my younger fellow novelists are greatly preoccupied with technique. They seem to think a good novel ought to follow certain rules imposed from outside. In fact, however, this preoccupation hampers them and embarrasses them in their creation. The great novelist doesn't depend on anyone but himself. Proust resembled none of his predecessors and he did not have, he could not have, any successors. The great novelist breaks his mold; he alone can use it. Balzac created the "Balzacian" novel; its style was suitable only for Balzac.

There is a close tie between a novelist's originality in general and the personal quality of his style. A borrowed style is a bad style. American novelists from Faulkner to Hemingway invented a style to express what they wanted to say—and it is a style that can't be passed on to their followers.   —*François Mauriac*

ON STYLE

I've been called a stylist until I really could tear my hair out. And I simply don't believe in style. The style is you. Oh, you can cultivate a style, I suppose, if you like. But I should say it remains a cultivated style. It remains artificial and imposed, and I don't think it deceives anyone. A cultivated style would be like a mask. Everybody knows it's a mask, and sooner or later you must show yourself—or at least, you show yourself as someone who could not afford to show himself, and so created something to hide behind. Style is the man. Aristotle said it first, as far as I know, and everybody has said it since, because it is one of those unarguable truths. You do not create a style. You work, and develop yourself; your style is an emanation from your own being. —*Katherine Anne Porter*

I don't know about method. The *what* is so much more important than how. —*Ezra Pound*

I used to spend a lot of time worrying over word order, trying to create beautiful passages. I still believe in the value of a handsome style. I appreciate the sensibility which can produce a nice turn of phrase, like Scott Fitzgerald. But I'm not interested anymore in turning out something shimmering and impressionistic—Southern, if you will—full of word-pictures, damn Dixie baby-talk, and that sort of thing. I guess I just get more and more interested in people. And story. —*William Styron*

It comes down to what is language? Up to now, until this age of mass literacy, language has been something spoken. In utterance there's a minimum of slowness. In trying to treat words as chisel strokes you run the risk of losing the quality of utterance, the rhythm of utterance, the happiness. A phrase out of Mark Twain—he describes a raft hitting a bridge and says that it "went all to smash and scatteration like a box of matches struck by lightning." The beauty of "scatteration" could only have occurred to a talkative man, a man who had been brought up among people who were talking and who loved to talk himself. I'm aware myself of a certain dryness of this reservoir, this backlog of spoken talk. A Rumanian once said to me that Americans are always telling stories. I'm not sure this is as true as it once was. Where we once used to spin yarns, now we sit in front of the T.V. and receive pictures. I'm not sure the younger generation even knows how to gossip. But, as for a writer, if he has something to tell, he should perhaps type it almost as fast as he could talk it. We must look to the organic world, not the inorganic world, for metaphors; and just as the organic world has periods of repose and periods of great speed and exercise, so I think the writer's process should be organically varied. But there's a kind of tautness that you should feel within yourself no matter how slow or fast you're spinning out the reel.   —*John Updike*

I'm not familiar with books on style. My role in the revival of Strunk's book was a fluke—just something I took on because I was not doing anything else at the time. It cost me a year out of my life, so little did I know about grammar. I don't think [style] can be taught. Style results more from what a person is than from what he knows. But there are a few hints that can be thrown out to advantage. They would be the twenty-one hints I threw out in Chapter V of *The Elements of Style*. There was nothing new or original about them, but there they are, for all to read.*   —*E. B. White*

*These are (1) Place yourself in the background; (2) Write in a way that comes naturally; (3) Work from a suitable design; (4) Write with nouns and verbs; (5) Revise and rewrite; (6) Do not overwrite; (7) Do not overstate; (8) Avoid the use of qualifiers; (9) Do not affect a breezy manner; (10) Use orthodox spelling; (11) Do not explain too much; (12) Do not construct awkward adverbs; (13) Make sure the reader knows who is speaking; (14) Avoid fancy words; (15) Do not use dialect unless your ear is good; (16) Be clear; (17) Do not inject opinion; (18) Use figures of speech sparingly; (19) Do not take shortcuts at the cost of clarity; (20) Avoid foreign languages; (21) Prefer the standard to the offbeat.

These are headings in Chapter V of *The Elements of Style* and are followed by explanatory texts.—Ed.

ON PLOT

What I am trying to achieve is a voice sitting by a fireplace telling you a story on a winter's evening. —*Truman Capote*

The French writers do not burden themselves too much with plot, which has been reproached to them as a fault. —*John Dryden*

With me, it's story, story, story. —*Bernard Malamud*

I've always figured the only way I could finish a book and get a plot was just to keep making it longer and longer until something happens . . . you know, until it finds its own plot . . . because you can't outline and then fit the thing into it. I suppose it's a slow way of working. —*Nelson Algren*

In my case, the work changes constantly, since I seldom have a firm plot or any idea at all about the ending. But there is a clear, almost mathematically conceptual idea that determines length—the length or brevity of a literary work being comparable to the size of the frame needed by a picture. —*Heinrich Böll*

I don't work with plots. I work with intuition, apprehension, dreams, concepts. Characters and events come simultaneously to me. Plot implies narrative and a lot of crap. It is a calculated attempt to hold the reader's interest at the sacrifice of moral conviction. Of course, one doesn't want to be boring . . . one needs an element of suspense. But a good narrative is a rudimentary structure, rather like a kidney. —*John Cheever*

Yes, it is. I start with a tingle, a kind of feeling of the story I will write. Then come the characters, and they take over, they make the story. But all this ends by being a plot. For other writers, that seems an unnatural thing. But a proper tale has a shape and an outline. In a painting the frame is important. Where does the picture end? What details should one include? Or omit! Where does the line go that cuts off the picture? People always ask me, they say, "In 'The Deluge at Norderney,' were those characters drowned or saved at the end?" (You remember they are trapped in a loft during a flood and spend the night recounting their stories while awaiting rescue.) Well, what can I reply? How can I tell them? That's outside the story. I really don't know! —*Isak Dinesen*

It's like driving a few stakes in the ground; you haven't got to that point in the construction yet, so you run ahead fifty yards, and you plant a stake in to show roughly the direction your road is going, which helps to give you your orientation. But they are very far from planned in the exact sense. —*Lawrence Durrell*

The novelist should, I think, always settle when he starts what is going to happen, what his major event is to be. He may alter this event as he approaches it, indeed he probably will, indeed he probably had better, or the novel becomes tied up and tight. But the sense of a solid mass ahead, a mountain round or over or through which the story must somehow go, is most valuable and, for the novels I've tried to write, essential. There must be something, some major object towards which one is to approach. When I began *A Passage to India* I knew that something important happened in the Malabar Caves, and that it would have a central place in the novel—but I didn't know what it would be. The Malabar Caves represented an area in which concentration can take place. A cavity. Something to focus everything up: to engender an event like an egg. —*E. M. Forster*

ON PLOT

When you teach creative writing, you teach people, among other things, how to plot. You explain the principles, how it is that fiction *thinks*. And to give the kids a sense of how a plot works, you just spin out plot after plot. In an hour session, you may spin out forty possible plots, one adhering to the real laws of energeia, each one a balance of the particular and general—and not one of them a story that you'd really want to write. Then one time, you hit one that catches you for some reason—you hit on the story that expresses your unrest. When I was teaching creative writing at Chico State, for instance, one of many plots I spun out was *The Resurrection*.

One plot will just sort of rise above all the others for reasons that you don't fully understand. All of them are interesting, all of them have interesting characters, all of them talk about things that you could talk about; but one of them catches you like a nightmare. Then you have no choice but to write it; you can't forget it. It's a weird thing. If it's the kind of plot you really don't want to do because it involves your mother too closely, or whatever, you can try to do something else. But the typewriter keeps hissing at you and shooting sparks, and the paper keeps wrinkling and the lamp goes off and nothing else works, so finally you do the one that God said you've got to do. And once you do it, you're grounded.

—*John Gardner*

As to plotting or thinking ahead, I don't in a novel. I let it come page by page, one a day, and carry it in my head. When I say carry I mean the proportions—that is, the length. This is the exhaustion of creating. Towards the end of the book your head is literally bursting. But try and write out a scheme or plan and you will only depart from it. My way you have a chance to set something living.

—*Henry Green*

I don't have many plots and perhaps as a justification I sometimes think: if I want a plot I'll watch "Dallas." I think it's mood. No, I mean tone. Tone arrived at by language. I can't write a story or an essay until I can, by revision after revision, get the opening tone right. Sometimes it seems to take forever, but when I have it I can usually go on. It's a matter of the voice, how you are going to approach the task at hand. It's all language and rhythm and the establishment of the relation to the material, of who's speaking, not speaking as a person exactly, but as a mind, a sensibility.   —*Elizabeth Hardwick*

I have great difficulty in inventing plots. Some people are born with an amazing gift for storytelling; it's a gift which I've never had at all. One reads, for example, Stevenson's accounts of how all the plots for his stories were provided in dreams by his subconscious mind (what he calls the "Brownies" working for him), and that all he had to do was to work up the material they had provided. I've never had any Brownies. The great difficulty for me has always been creating situations.

• • •

I work away a chapter at a time, finding my way as I go. I know very dimly when I start what's going to happen. I just have a very general idea, and then the thing develops as I write. Sometimes— it's happened to me more than once—I will write a great deal, then find it just doesn't work, and have to throw the whole thing away. I like to have a chapter finished before I begin on the next one. But I'm never entirely certain what's going to happen in the next chapter until I've worked it out. Things come to me in driblets, and when the driblets come I have to work hard to make them into something coherent.   —*Aldous Huxley*

I have last chapters in my mind before I see first chapters, too. I usually begin with endings, with a sense of aftermath, of dust settling, of epilogue. I love plot, and how can you plot a novel if you don't know the ending first? How do you know how to introduce a character if you don't know how he *ends up*? You might say I back into a novel. All the important discoveries—at the end of a book—those are the things I have to know before I know where to begin. I knew that

Garp's mother would be killed by a stupid man who blindly hates women; I knew Garp would be killed by a stupid woman who blindly hates men. I didn't even know which of them would be killed first; I had to wait to see which of them was the main character. At first I thought Jenny was the main character; but she was too much of a saint for a main character—in the way that Wilbur Larch is too much of a saint to be the main character of *The Cider House Rules*. Garp and Homer Wells are flawed; by comparison to Jenny and Dr. Larch, they're weak. They're main characters. Actors know how they end up—I mean how their *characters* end up—before they speak the opening lines. Shouldn't writers know at least as much about their characters as actors know? I think so.   —*John Irving*

My plots are always rudimentary. Whatever I've accomplished certainly does not depend on my virtuosity with plot. Generally I don't even have a plot. What happens is that my characters engage in an action, and out of that action little bits of plot sometimes adhere to the narrative.   —*Norman Mailer*

I've always enjoyed crime fiction. I think that much of the best writing being done today is in crime novels. The plot and discipline essential to a crime novel save it from the terrible traps of being sensitive and stream-of-consciousness and all of that stuff. You do need that discipline, I think, and plot! Life happens in plots all the time; life is absolutely composed of plots!   —*John Mortimer*

I don't bother with charts and so forth. Elliot Nugent, on the other hand, was a careful constructor. When we were working on *The Male Animal* together, he was constantly concerned with plotting the play. He could plot the thing from back to front—what was going to happen here, what sort of a situation would end the first act curtain, and so forth. I can't work that way. Nugent would say: "Well, Thurber, we've got our problem, we've got all these people in the living room. Now what are we going to do with them?" I'd say that

I didn't know and couldn't tell him until I'd sat down at the typewriter and found out. I don't believe the writer should know too much where he's going. If he does, he runs into old man blueprint . . . old man propaganda.

—*James Thurber*

I guarantee you that no modern story scheme, even plotlessness, will give a reader genuine satisfaction, unless one of those old-fashioned plots is smuggled in somewhere. I don't praise plots as accurate representations of life, but as ways to keep readers reading. When I used to teach creative writing, I would tell the students to make their characters want something right away—even if it's only a glass of water. Characters paralyzed by the meaninglessness of modern life still have to drink water from time to time. One of my students wrote a story about a nun who got a piece of dental floss stuck between her lower left molars, and who couldn't get it out all day long. I thought that was wonderful. The story dealt with issues a lot more important than dental floss, but what kept readers going was anxiety about when the dental floss would finally be removed. Nobody could read that story without fishing around in his mouth with a finger.

—*Kurt Vonnegut*

I'll tell you what I think my greatest weakness is. I don't think I'm a very good plotter: I mean, of the mechanics of the story. I was in Hollywood for nine months during the making of *The Friendly Persuasion*. I remember Mr. William Wyler, who directed it, saying to me, "Jessamyn (actually, I think he said 'Miss West'), we've got to get one more 'will he? won't he?' into this." I tend not to do enough of that and I think this is what a reader wants. —*Jessamyn West*

I do think modern novels are boring on the whole. Somebody told me I ought to read a wonderful thing about how a family of children buried Mum in a cellar under concrete and she began to smell. But that's the sole point of the story. Mum just smells. That's all that happens. It is not enough. —*Rebecca West*

ON PLOT

What shouldn't you do if you're a young playwright? *Don't bore the audience!* I mean, even if you have to resort to totally arbitrary killing on stage, or pointless gunfire, at least it'll catch their attention and keep them awake. Just keep the thing going any way you can.

—*Tennessee Williams*

ON CHARACTER

A good novel tells us the truth about its hero; but a bad novel tells us the truth about its author.　　　　—G. K. Chesterton

A novelist is a person who lives in other people's skins.
　　　　　　　　　　　　　　　　—E. L. Doctorow

Human beings have their great chance in the novel.
　　　　　　　　　　　　　　　　—E. M. Forster

You can never know enough about your characters.
　　　　　　　　　　　　　　—Somerset Maugham

Graham Greene said he would find an episode or a character turning up after the first ten thousand words which he had no idea how to use. But then thirty thousand words later it would come up. And experience had taught him never to destroy what he had written, because it would always be fitted into the design later.

　　　　　　　　　　　　　　　　—Kingsley Amis

I have no influence over them. I'm only an observer, recording. The story is always being told by the characters themselves. In fact, I'm often critical, or maybe ashamed, of what some of them say and do— their profanity or their immorality. But I have no control over it.

　　　　　　　　　　　　　　　　—Erskine Caldwell

The legend that characters run away from their authors—taking up drugs, having sex operations, and becoming president—implies that the writer is a fool with no knowledge or mastery of his craft. This is absurd. Of course, any estimable exercise of the imagination draws upon such a complex richness of memory that it truly enjoys the expansiveness—the surprising turns, the response to light and darkness—of any living thing. But the idea of authors running around helplessly behind their cretinous inventions is contemptible.

—*John Cheever*

It's the characters who direct me. That is, I see a character, he's there, and I recognize someone I knew, or occasionally two who are a bit mixed together, but then that stops. Afterwards, the character acts on his own account. He says things . . . I never know *what* any of them are going to say when I'm writing dialogue. Really, it's up to them. Me, I'm just typing out what they're saying. Sometimes I burst out laughing, or I throw out a page and say, "There, there you've said silly things. Out!" And I put in another page and start over again with their dialogue.   —*Julio Cortázar*

I find it difficult to write about very stupid people. I'm aware that my characters tend to be not only intelligent, but intelligent about themselves. One of the things that I really admire is the ability to write with dignity and understanding about people who are not aware of themselves. I think most people are more intelligent than they are given credit for, but that they don't express themselves in a way people find accessible. I look at some people and I don't know what their minds contain. And that I find a problem.

And men. Writing about men. I used to find it difficult because I didn't trust myself to know what they were like. I still feel uneasy when I describe men's clothes and their offices. I have to do research, find out what they really look like, how they talk, and what kind of work pattern they have.   —*Margaret Drabble*

We all like to pretend we don't use real people, but one does actually. I used some of my family. Miss Bartlett was my Aunt Emily— they all read the book but they none of them saw it. Uncle Willie turned into Mrs. Failing. He was a bluff and simple character [*correcting himself*]—bluff without being simple. Miss Lavish was actually a Miss Spender. Mrs. Honeychurch was my grandmother. The three Miss Dickinsons condensed into two Miss Schlegels. Philip Herriton I modeled on Professor Dent. He knew this, and took an interest in his own progress. I have used several tourists.

In no book have I got down more than the people I like, the person I think I am, and the people who irritate me. This puts me among the large body of authors who are not really novelists, and have to get on as best they can with these three categories. We have not the power of observing the variety of life and describing it dispassionately. There are a few who have done this. Tolstoy was one, wasn't he?

A useful trick is to look back upon such a person with half-closed eyes, fully describing certain characteristics. I am left with about two-thirds of a human being and can get to work. A likeness isn't aimed at and couldn't be obtained, because a man's only himself amidst the particular circumstances of his life and not amid other circumstances. So that to refer back to Dent when Philip was in difficulties with Gino, or to ask one and one-half Miss Dickinsons how Helen should comport herseslf with an illegitimate baby would have ruined the atmosphere and the book. When all goes well, the original material soon disappears, and a character who belongs to the book and nowhere else emerges.
—*E. M. Forster*

In every novel, the character is a collage: a collage of different characters that you've known, or heard about or read about. I read everything that I could find about Latin American dictators of the last century, and the beginning of this one. I also talked to a lot of people who had lived under dictatorships. I did that for at least ten years. And when I had a clear idea of what the character was going to be like, I made an effort to forget everything I had read and heard, so that I could invent, without using any situation that had occurred in real life. I realized at one point that I myself had not lived for any period of time under a dictatorship, so I thought if I wrote the book in Spain, I could see what the atmosphere was like living in an established dictatorship. But I found that the atmosphere was very different in Spain under Franco from that of a Caribbean dictatorship. So the book was kind of blocked for about a year. There was something missing and I wasn't sure what it was. Then overnight, I decided that the best thing was that we come back to the Caribbean. So we all moved back to Barranquilla in Colombia. I made a statement to the journalists which they thought was a joke. I said that I was coming back because I had forgotten what a guava smelled like. In truth, it was what I really needed to finish my book. I took a trip through the Caribbean. As I went from island to island, I found the elements which were the ones that had been lacking from my novel.   —*Gabriel García Márquez*

The first thing that makes a reader read a book is the characters. Say you're standing in a train station, or an airport, and you're leafing through books; what you're hoping for is a book where you'll like the characters, where the characters are interesting. To establish powerful characters, a writer needs a landscape to help define them; so setting becomes important. Setting is also a powerful vehicle of thematic concerns; in fact, it's one of the most powerful. If you're going to talk about the decline of Western civilization or at least the possibility of that decline, you take an old place that's sort of worn out and run-down. For instance, Batavia, New York, where the Holland Land Office was . . . the beginning of a civilization . . . selling the land in this country. It was, in the beginning, a wonderful, beautiful place with the smartest Indians in America around. Now it's this old, run-down town which has been urban-renewalized just about out of existence. The factories have stopped and the people are poor and sometimes crabby; the elm trees are all dead, and so are the oaks and maples. So it's a good symbol. You choose the setting that suits and illuminates your material.   —*John Gardner*

Henry James could have been a woman. E. M. Forster could have been. George Eliot could have been a man. I used to be too insistent on this point that there's no sex in the brain; I'm less insistent now—perhaps I'm being influenced by the changing attitude of women toward themselves in general? I don't think there's anything that women writers don't know. But it may be that there are certain aspects of life that they can deal with a shade better, just as I wonder whether any woman writer, however great, could have written the marvelous war scenes in *War and Peace*. By and large, I don't think it matters a damn what sex a writer is, so long as the work is that of a real *writer*. I think there *is* such a thing as "ladies' writing," for instance, feminine writing; there are "authoresses" and "poetesses." And there are men, like Hemingway, whose excessive "manliness" is a concomitant part of their writing. But with so many of the male writers whom I admire, it doesn't matter too much. There doesn't seem to be anything *they* don't know, either. After all, look at Molly Bloom's soliloquy. To me, that's the ultimate proof of the ability of either sex to understand and convey the inner workings of the other. No woman was ever "written" better by a woman writer. How did Joyce know? God knows how and it doesn't matter.

—*Nadine Gordimer*

One never knows enough about characters in real life to put them into novels. One gets started and then, suddenly, one can not remember what toothpaste they use; what are their views on interior decoration, and one is stuck utterly. No, major characters emerge: minor ones may be photographed. —*Graham Greene*

I don't think characters turn out the way you think they are going to turn out. They don't always go your way. At least they don't go my way. If I wanted to start writing about you, by page ten I probably wouldn't be. I don't think you start with a person. I think you start with the parts of many people. Drama has to do with conflict in people, with denials. —*Lillian Hellman*

ON CHARACTER

If I explained how that [the process of turning a real-life character into a fictional one] is sometimes done, it would be a handbook for libel lawyers.

—*Ernest Hemingway*

I try to imagine how certain people I know would behave in certain circumstances. Of course I base my characters partly on the people I know—one can't escape it—but fictional characters are oversimplified; they're much less complex than the people one knows.

—*Aldous Huxley*

By the time I'm done with them, they're not like anybody else but themselves. It would be better to say I use them as springboards. It's funny; I've been accused by various reviewers or critical writers of portraying myself—autobiographically—in nearly all of my characters. It's been said that I was Prewitt; it's been said that I was Warden; it's been said that I was Dave Hirsh. I couldn't be them all. I've actually had people, who of course romanticized Prewitt as a hero, flatly refuse to believe I didn't draw Prewitt from myself, even when I told them I hadn't. I guess it's true that when I was younger and more romantic, I would have liked to have been Prewitt, and Warden too for that matter. On the other hand, I certainly wouldn't want to be Dave Hirsh. But by and large I guess I take my characters from people I've known at one time or another. Sometimes, though, it's simply an event which strikes me and then I try to imagine a character who would fit into that event. For instance, the man who was killed by Fatso Judson in the Stockade, Blues Berry; I never knew him at all.

—*James Jones*

When you begin to dwell on why he or she acted in this particular way—that is what moves you forward to the next page. That's the way it happens with me, because what's most interesting is not the plot. Who cares about the plot? Who? Forster in *The Art of the Novel* dismissed it as a faintly contemptible thing you have to have, somehow, but that's really not where the story exists. The character does something which is new, and then, the story begins to percolate. If I knew at the beginning how the book was going to end, I would probably never finish. I knew that Legs Diamond was going to die at the end of the book, so I killed him on page one.   —*William Kennedy*

I try to put the model in situations which have very little to do with his real situations in life. Very quickly the model disappears. His private reality can't hold up. For instance, I might take somebody who is a professional football player, a man let's say whom I know slightly, and make him a movie star. In a transposition of this sort, everything which relates particularly to the professional football player quickly disappears, and what is left, curiously, is what is *exportable* in his character. But this process while interesting in the early stages is not as exciting as the more creative act of allowing your characters to grow once they're separated from the model. It's when they become almost as complex as one's own personality that the fine excitement begins. Because then they are not really characters any longer— they're beings, which is a distinction I like to make. A character is someone you can grasp as a whole, you can have a clear idea of him, but a being is someone whose nature keeps shifting. Like a character of Forster's. In *The Deer Park* Lulu Myers is a being rather than a character. If you study her closely you will see that she is a different person in every scene. Just a little different. I don't know whether initially I did this by accident or purposefully, but at a certain point I made the conscious decision *not* to try to straighten her out, she seemed right in her change-ableness.   —*Norman Mailer*

My characters run away but not far. Their guise is surprises.
    —*Bernard Malamud*

There is almost always a real person in the beginning, but then he changes so that sometimes he no longer bears the slightest resemblance to the original. In general, it is only the secondary characters who are taken directly from life.   —*François Mauriac*

ON CHARACTER

I was reading E. M. Forster who was writing about plot, and he said the awful thing is you create these wonderful characters and then they won't do anything; they won't be bothered to get involved in a plot! —*John Mortimer*

It was not he [E. M. Forster] who fathered that trite little whimsy about characters getting out of hand; it is as old as the quills, although of course one sympathizes with *his* people if they try to wriggle out of that trip to India or wherever he takes them. My characters are galley slaves. —*Vladimir Nabokov*

Women are better at emotions and the havoc those emotions wreak. But it must be said that Anna Karenina is the most believable heroine. The last scene where she goes to the station and looks down at the rails and thinks of Vronski's rejection is terrible in its depiction of despair. Women, on the whole, are better at plumbing the depths. A woman artist can produce a perfect gem, as opposed to a huge piece of rock carving a man might produce. It is not a limitation of talent or intelligence, it is just a different way of looking at the world. —*Edna O'Brien*

I've tried very hard and I've never found any resemblance between the people I know and the people in my novels. I don't search for exactitude in portraying people. I try to give to imaginary people a kind of veracity. It would bore me to death to put into my novels the people I know. It seems to me that there are two kinds of trickery: the "fronts" people assume before one another's eyes and the "front" a writer puts on the face of reality. —*Françoise Sagan*

It is very natural. You construct characters and set them going in their own interior landscape, and what they find to talk about and what confronts them are, of course, things that concern you most. —*Robert Stone*

E. M. Forster refers to "flat" and "round" characters. I try to make all of mine round. It takes an extrovert like Dickens to make flat characters come alive. But story as such has been neglected by today's introverted writers. Story and character should grow together; I think I'm lucky so far in that in practically everything I've tried to write these two elements have grown together. They must, to give an impression of life being lived, just because each man's life is a story, if you'll pardon the cliché. —William Styron

Well, I think it does seem to me that the only way you can create a character is through observation. I don't think there is any other route. And what you observe is not quite like just meeting someone on a train, having a conversation and then going away. I mean, really, a kind of adding up of people you notice. I think there's something *in* writers of fiction that makes them notice things and store them away all the time. Writers of fiction are collectors of useless information. They are the opposite of good, solid, wise citizens who collect good information and put it to good use. Fiction writers remember tiny little details, some of them almost malicious, but very telling. It's a way of endlessly remembering. A face comes back after years and years and years, as though you've taken a photograph. It's as though you have, for the moment, thought: "I know that person very well." You could argue that you have some extraordinary insight, but actually it's just a very hard-working imagination. It's almost like a stress in you that goes on, nibbling and nibbling, gnawing away at you, in a *very* inquisitive way, wanting to know. And of course while all that's happening you're stroking in the colors, putting a line here and a line there, creating something which moves further and further away from the original. The truth emerges, the person who is created is a different person altogether—a person in their own right.
—*William Trevor*

Every character is a mixture of people you've known. Characters come to me—and I think this is behind the Madeleine business in

Proust—when people are talking to me. I feel I have heard this, this tone of voice, in other circumstances. And, at the risk of seeming rude, I have to hold on to this and chase it back until it clicks with someone I've met before. The second secretary at the embassy in Bangkok may remind me of the chemistry assistant at Oxford. And I ask myself, what have they in common? Out of such mixtures I can create characters.   —*Angus Wilson*

I only intended to use him [Jeeves] once. His first entrance was: "Mrs. Gregson to see you, Sir," in a story called *Extricating Young Gussie*. He only had one other line, "Very good, Sir. Which suit will you wear?" But then I was writing a story, *The Artistic Career of Corky*, about two young men, Bertie Wooster and his friend Corky, getting into a lot of trouble, and neither of them had brains enough to get out of the trouble. I thought: Well, how can I get them out? And I thought: "Suppose one of them had an omniscient valet?" I wrote a short story about him, then another short story, then several more short stories and novels. That's how a character grows. I think I've written nine Jeeves novels now and about thirty short stories.

—*P. G. Wodehouse*

ON SYMBOLS

INTERVIEWER: What is the symbolic significance of the birds in so many of your sex scenes—the white bird that flies out of the gondola...?

HEMINGWAY (shouting): You think you can do any better??

It's nearly always unintentional. I look back at it and think, "Oh, that relates to that." When you're writing in a certain vein, everything grows out of the same source. Occasionally it's more deliberate. I was very much aware when I got to the end of *The Ice Age* that it would be nice to have another bird. I had put a bird on the first page; it seemed obvious to put a bird on the last. And there were a lot of dead dogs in that book, but then there were just a lot of dead dogs around that year. It's a natural associative process, really. It's not exactly symbolism, it's just how life is. You notice one thing and then you notice the same thing again tomorrow.

—*Margaret Drabble*

When I was about a hundred pages into *Boswell,* I suddenly discovered that I had Boswell in a lot of elevators, and because I had been trained in the New Criticism I decided, hey, this is pretty neat! Elevators. Makes a nice pattern. And so I was conscious of the elevator motif and kept moving him in and out of elevators. In a way it works because a great deal of novelistic fiction is about ascent. Since Boswell was a guy on the make and had this sort of excelsior personality, it was quite fitting for him to be in elevators, on up escalators, and to climb stairs. There's one scene in *Boswell* where he's in a Jewish

204

community in Brooklyn, as I recall, to meet a miracle rabbi, and he can't get past the front door. He is not permitted to climb those stairs and is stalled. Sure, I'm conscious of symbols and patterns in my work. But this is something I've sometimes come on to only after the fact and then made the most of. —*Stanley Elkin*

There are certain themes, symbols, and images which are based on folk material. For example, there is the old saying among Negroes: If you're black, stay back; if you're brown, stick around; if you're white, you're right. And there is the joke Negroes tell on themselves about their being so black they can't be seen in the dark. In my book this sort of thing was merged with the meanings which blackness and light have long had in Western mythology: evil and goodness, ignorance and knowledge, and so on. In my novel the narrator's development is one through blackness to light; that is, from ignorance to enlightenment: invisibility to visibility. He leaves the South and goes North; this, as you will notice in reading Negro folk tales, is always the road to freedom—the movement upward. You have the same thing again when he leaves his underground cave for the open.

It took me a long time to learn how to adapt such examples of myth into my work—also ritual. The use of ritual is equally a vital part of the creative process. I learned a few things from Eliot, Joyce and Hemingway, but not how to adapt them. When I started writing, I knew that in both *The Waste Land* and *Ulysses* ancient myth and ritual were used to give form and significance to the material; but it took me a few years to realize that the myths and rites which we find functioning in our everyday lives could be used in the same way. In my first attempt at a novel—which I was unable to complete—I began by trying to manipulate the simple structural unities of *beginning, middle,* and *end,* but when I attempted to deal with the psychological strata—the images, symbols, and emotional configurations—of the experience at hand, I discovered that the unities were simply cool points of stability on which one could suspend the narrative line— but beneath the surface of apparently rational human relationships there seethed a chaos before which I was helpless. People rationalize what they shun or are incapable of dealing with; these superstitions and their rationalizations become ritual as they govern behavior. The rituals become social forms, and it is one of the functions of the artist to recognize them and raise them to the level of art.

I don't know whether I'm getting this over or not. Let's put it this way: Take the "Battle Royal" passage in my novel, where the boys are blindfolded and forced to fight each other for the amusement of the white observers. This is a vital part of behavior pattern in the South, which both Negroes and whites thoughtlessly accept. It is a ritual in preservation of caste lines, a keeping of taboo to appease the gods and ward off bad luck. It is also the initiation ritual to which all greenhorns are subjected. This passage states what Negroes will see I did not have to invent; the patterns were already there in society so that all I had to do was present them in a broader context of meaning. In any society there are many rituals of situation which, for the most part, go unquestioned. They can be simple or elaborate, but they are the connective tissue between the work of art and the audience.   —*Ralph Ellison*

I suppose there are symbols since critics keep finding them. If you do not mind I dislike talking about them and being questioned about them. It is hard enough to write books and stories without being asked to explain them as well. Also it deprives the explainers of work. If five or six or more good explainers can keep going why should I interfere with them? Read anything I write for the pleasure of reading it. Whatever else you find will be the measure of what you brought to the reading.   —*Ernest Hemingway*

The dove signifies the dove and the guitar signifies a musical instrument called the guitar.   —*Pablo Neruda*

I never consciously took or adopted a symbol in my life. I certainly did not say, "This blooming tree upon which Judas is supposed to have hanged himself is going to be the center of my story." I named "Flowering Judas" after it was written, because when reading back over it I suddenly saw the whole symbolic plan and pattern of which I was totally unconscious while I was writing. There's a pox of symbolist theory going the rounds these days in American colleges in the writing courses. Miss Mary McCarthy, who is one of the wittiest and most acute and in some ways the worst-tempered woman in American letters, tells about a little girl who came to her with a story. Now Miss McCarthy is an extremely good critic, and she found this to be a good story, and she told the girl that it was—that she considered it a finished work, and that she could with a clear conscience go on to something else. And the little girl said, "But Miss McCarthy, my writing teacher said, 'Yes, it's a good piece of work, but now we must go back and put in the symbols!' " I think that's an amusing story, and it makes my blood run cold.

—*Katherine Anne Porter*

ON DIALOGUE

Discourse, the sweeter banquet of the mind.   —*Alexander Pope*

Dialogue's a very powerful weapon, isn't it? Again, traditionally the novelist has to characterize people quite quickly by the way they talk: their various idioms, whether they talk plainly or in a flowery style. But I do find dialogue quicker to write than narrative—narrative I always find rather painful. Dialogue is more fun . . . but I always try over the phrases, fooling the reader into believing that this is how people actually talk. In fact, inevitably, it's far more coherent than any actual talk. I don't say I succeed all that often, but when in doubt I will repeat a phrase to myself seven or eight times, trying to put myself in the place of an actor speaking the part. And all these "I mean's" and "sort of's" and "you know's" are important because there are characters who find it difficult to lay their tongues on what they mean the first time, and I think this should be indicated.

—*Kingsley Amis*

Dialogue is almost too easy. For me. So much so that it makes me suspicious of it, so I have to be careful with it. I *could* find myself evading problems of true expression because dialogue's so easy for me to do. There are many important issues and points of sublety about people, about human behavior, that I want to make in writing, and it's easy to evade these—or do them superficially, do them halfway—by simply writing good dialogue. And it becomes increasingly easy as I get to know the people better. But good dialogue just isn't enough to explain the subtler ramifications of the characters and

208

incidents which I'm trying to work out now. Not *realistic* dialogue, anyway. Perhaps if you used some kind of surrealistic dialogue, but then it would read like a dream episode. It wouldn't be real talk. For instance, it's obvious enough that in almost any conversation things are happening to the people in the conversation which they do not and cannot express. In a play it is possible for a good actor to imply that he is thinking something other than what he is saying. But it's pretty slipshod and half-assed, because he cannot convey what he's thinking *explicitly*. In prose, and especially in the novel form, this can be done. If the man is using a subterfuge, it can be explained explicitly, and why. Actually, in life, conversation is more often likely to be an attempt at deliberate evasion, deliberate confusion, rather than communication. We're all cheats and liars, really. And the novelist can show just how and why we are.   —*James Jones*

Dialogue is very important to me because I've always loved it in novels. Lots of people read novels racing from dialogue to dialogue. In fact, I would like to really compress the prose in a novel, without getting too arch about it. Some people, like Manuel Puig, have written novels almost entirely in dialogue, but it gets to be a little too much sometimes since readers need to know where they are a bit. At any rate, writing dialogue is probably the best thing I do, and I'm always trying to work up an aesthetic for my fiction that will acknowledge that fact. Of course, Hemingway was really a great dialogue writer, it's one of the reasons we read him. Dialogue is a very useful tool to reveal things about people, and novels are about people and about what they do to each other. That's what novels are for. They're not pure text for deconstructionists. One day, that will be clear again.
                                —*Thomas McGuane*

If you're the sort of person that meets a girl in the street and instantly notices the color of her eyes and of her hair and the sort of dress she's wearing, then you're not in the least like me. I just notice a feeling from people. I notice particularly the cadence of their voices, the sort of phrases they'll use, and that's what I'm all the time trying to hear in my head, how people word things—because everybody speaks an entirely different language, that's really what it amounts to. I have terribly sensitive hearing and I'm terribly aware of voices. If I remember somebody, for instance, that I was very fond of, I don't remember what he or she looked like, but I can absolutely take off the voice. I'm a good mimic; I've a bit of the actor in me, I suppose, that's really what it amounts to. I cannot pass a story as finished unless I connect it myself, unless I know how everybody in it spoke, which, as I say, can go quite well with the fact that I couldn't tell you in the least what they looked like. If I use the right phrase and the reader hears the phrase in his head, he sees the individual.

—*Frank O'Connor*

In its beginning, dialogue's the easiest thing in the world to write when you have a good ear, which I think I have. But as it goes on, it's the most difficult, because it has so many ways to function. Sometimes I needed to make a speech do three or four or five things at once—reveal what the character said but also what he thought he said, what he hid, what others were going to think he meant, and what they misunderstood, and so forth—all in his single speech. And the speech would have to keep the essence of this one character, his whole particular outlook in concentrated form. This isn't to say I succeeded. But I guess it explains why dialogue gives me my greatest pleasure in writing. I used to laugh out loud sometimes when I wrote it—the way P. G. Wodehouse is said to do. I'd think of some things my characters would say, and even if I couldn't use it, I would write the scene out just to let them loose on something—my private show.

. . .

Familiarity. Memory of the way things get said. Once you have heard certain expressions, sentences, you almost never forget them. It's like sending a bucket down the well and it always comes up full. You don't know you've remembered, but you have. And you listen for the right word, in the present, and you hear it. Once you're into a story everything seems to apply—what you overhear on a city bus is exactly what your character would say on the page you're writing. Wherever you go, you meet part of your story. I guess you're tuned in for it, and the right things are sort of magnetized—if you can think of your ears as magnets. I could hear someone saying—and I had to cut this out—"What, you never ate goat?" And someone answering, "Goat! Please don't say you serve *goat* at this reunion. I wasn't told it was *goat* I was served. I thought—" and so on, and then the recipe, and then it ended up with—I can't remember exactly now—it ended with, "You can do a whole lot of things with vinegar." Well, all these things I would just laugh about and think about for so long and put them in. And then I'd think, that's just plain indulgence. Take it out! And I'd take it out.　　　　*—Eudora Welty*

Always get to the dialogue as soon as possible. I always feel the thing to go for is speed. Nothing puts the reader off more than a great slab of prose at the start. I think the success of every novel— if it's a novel of action—depends on the high spots. The thing to do is to say to yourself, "Which are my big scenes?" and then get every drop of juice out of them. The principle I always go on in writing a novel is to think of the characters in terms of actors in a play. I say to myself, if a big name were playing this part, and if he found that after a strong first act he had practically nothing to do in the second act, he would walk out. Now, then, can I twist the story so as to give him plenty to do all the way through? I believe the only way a writer can keep himself up to the mark is by examining each story quite coldly before he starts writing it and asking himself if it is all right *as a story*. I mean, once you go saying to yourself, "This is a pretty weak plot as it stands, but I'm such a hell of a writer that my magic touch will make it OK," you're sunk. If they aren't in interesting situations, characters can't be major characters, not even if you have the rest of the troop talk their heads off about them.

—P. G. Wodehouse

ON SEX

To enlarge or illustrate this power of effect of love is to set a candle in the sun.   —*Robert Burton*

Sex annihilates identity, and the space given to sex in contemporary novels is an avowal of the absence of character.
                                                        —*Mary McCarthy*

Cover that breast, it offends my eye.   —*Molière*

Sex as an institution, sex as a general notion, sex as a problem, sex as a platitude—all this is something I find too tedius for words. Let's skip sex.   —*Vladimir Nabokov*

I shy away from explicit sex mainly because it's socially embarrassing. The comparison I usually draw is with being told these things by an acquaintance—and after all, the novelist is only an acquaintance, isn't he, as far as the reader's concerned?—and to be told in detail what he's been up to for over half an hour—the equivalent of a chapter, say—would be embarrassing, wouldn't it? *I* would find it embarrassing.   —*Kingsley Amis*

My aversion to describing amorous details in my work is probably that I treasure physical love so highly I don't want to let strangers in on it. For, after all, when we describe copulation we're describing our own experiences. I like privacy. I think that other writers should do what they can do, and if they can spend—as one of my American girl students did—ten pages on the act of fellatio without embarrassing themselves, very good luck to them. But I think there's more artistic pleasure to be gained from the ingenious circumvention of a taboo than from what is called total permissiveness. When I wrote my first Enderby novel, I had to make my hero say "For cough," since "Fuck off" was not then acceptable. With the second book the climate had changed, and Enderby was at liberty to say "Fuck off." I wasn't happy. It was too easy. He still said "For cough," while others responded with "Fuck off." A compromise. Literature, however, thrives on taboos, just as all art thrives on technical difficulties.

—*Anthony Burgess*

He [Hemingway] was *always* concerned with four-letter words. It never bothered me particularly. Sex can be indicated with asterisks. I've always felt that was as good a way as any.   —*John Dos Passos*

I certainly think the erotic was very important for Hardy. The avoiding any direct contact with it (or expression of it), the slipping round it, plays an enormous part in his novels. He was obviously a shy and repressed man. He liked the tryst, that first secret meeting or instinctual attraction between lovers, so much more than the fully physical side, what we should call the sex. I suppose I am the same, that is, haunted, both ravished and tormented, by the erotic; yet happiest when it is left three quarters hidden, in secret. I spent a year of my life once writing an erotic novel, in common terms a pornographic one. One day, when it was virtually complete, I took it and all its drafts into the garden and burnt the lot. It would no doubt have made me a great deal of money, and I was rather proud of it, for what it was. It was not prudishness that made me burn; but much more a feeling of blasphemy, an error of bad taste. It broke that secret, bared the hidden part. That is why I dislike what I see as the unnecessary sexual explicitness in so much American fiction; it becomes infantile, destructive of the truly erotic, in the end.

Mantissa was meant to make fun of that, in part; and also of the poor novelists, like Hardy, Fournier, D. H. Lawrence, Henry Miller, and countless others, laboring under this monstrous erotic succubus (the idiot's illusion: "I must be a great writer because I make a lot of money") are the two main danger points for the male writer.

—*John Fowles*

I think writers should research sex in the same way they research historical characters. It's not difficult to write about. What is difficult to write about is the actual pornographic element of sex. That ceases to be interesting. What you need to do is find the surrounding elements. Yet another struggle of the genitals is hardly worth writing about. It's done on every streetcorner, fifty-five times a magazine. So that's not the point. On the contrary, it's when you discover a character like Kiki Roberts who is Legs Diamond's girlfriend and you look at her and discover this incredible beauty, obviously a great sex object for Diamond, who endangered his life many times for her. And she, reciprocating, constantly. She was a fugitive from justice with him. When you look at that woman, you can begin to imagine what it was about her that led him to behave that way. That was quite a pleasant thing for me—to reimagine Kiki Roberts.

—*William Kennedy*

I've led a good rich sexual life, and I don't see why it should be left out.

—*Henry Miller*

His [Harold Ross's of *The New Yorker*] idea was that sex is an incident. "If you can prove it," I said, "we can get it in a box on the front page of *The New York Times*." Now I don't want to say that in private life Ross was a prude. But as regards the theater or the printed page he certainly was. For example, he once sent an office memorandum to us in a sealed envelope. It was an order: "When you send me a memorandum with four-letter words in it, *seal it*. There are women in this office." I said, "Yah, Ross, and they know a lot more of these words than you do." When women were around he was very conscious

ON SEX

of them. Once my wife and I were in his office and Ross was discussing a man and woman he knew much better than we did. Ross told us: "I have every reason to believe that they're s-l-e-e-p-i-n-g together." My wife replied: "Why, Harold Ross, what words you do spell out." But honest to goodness that was genuine. Women are either good or bad, he once told me, and the good ones must not hear these things. —*James Thurber*

A great friend of mine at the beginning of our friendship (he was himself a poet) said to me very defiantly, "I have to tell you that I *loathe* children's books." And I said to him, "Well, won't you just read this just for my sake?" And he said grumpily, "Oh, very well, send it to me." I did, and I got a letter back saying: "Why didn't you *tell* me? Mary Poppins with her cool green core of sex has me enthralled forever." —*P. L. Travers*

I would have thought that [the awkwardness in writing about sex] was completely true of Kafka who couldn't write about sex or value its place in life. I think there's an awful lot of nonsense in Lawrence when he writes about Mexican sacrifices and sexual violence. Their only relevance was to the Mexicans' lack of protein, as in the South Sea Islands. Funny, that's a wonderful thing. I don't know why more people don't write about it: how the whole of life must have been different when four-footed animals came in. They had just a few deer before, but not enough to go round, and so they prevented the deer from becoming extinct by making them sacred to the kings. It's much more interesting to write about that than about sex, which most of your audience knows about. —*Rebecca West*

ON EXPERIMENTAL
WRITING

It's not wise to violate the rules until you know how to observe
them.   —*T. S. Eliot*

I'd just as soon play tennis with the net down.   —*Robert Frost*

Here lies that peerless paper peer Lord Peter,
Who broke the laws of God and man and metre.
         —*Sir Walter Scott*

Zounds! I was never so bethumped with words!
        —*William Shakespeare*

Fiction *is* experimentation; when it ceases to be that, it ceases to be
fiction. One never puts down a sentence without the feeling that it
has never been put down before in such a way, and that perhaps
even the substance of the sentence has never been felt. Every sentence
is an innovation.   —*John Cheever*

I don't think that [Gertrude Stein] moved on from her remarkable
early work. She got deeper and deeper into automatic writing, which
she was beginning at the time I worked for her. Automatic writing
is a dead end. You go on writing "automatically" and what do you
write? If you look at those later books that Yale published for her
after she gave them her papers, they're pretty boring.

I used to watch Gertrude at it. That last summer I spent in Savoie
writing those press releases for *Lectures in America,* I'd watch her sitting
in a bath chair on her terrace with a big notebook, writing just as

fast as she could, the pen flying, no pauses whatsoever. No rewriting. And then Alice B. Toklas, sweet person—well, not all that sweet, *sort* of sweet—would be given these notebooks to type out. Her best work came early: *Three Lives, The Blood on the Dining-Room Floor,* parts of *The Making of Americans, Portrait of Mabel Dodge. Four Saints in Three Acts* was beautiful, and some of the other plays, the opera plays. She really needed someone like Virgil Thomson, whom she respected, to sit on her a bit and make her devise some plot. In the automatic writing pieces there's no plot movement; they just roll on and become tedious.

—*James Laughlin*

No, I think all writing is experimental. The very obvious sort of experimental writing is not really more experimental than that of a conventional writer like myself. I experiment all the time but the experiments are hidden. Rather like abstract art: you look at an abstract picture, and then you look at a close-up of a Renaissance painting and find the same abstractions.

—*William Trevor*

What is "experimental writing"? James Joyce didn't do "experimental writing"—he wrote *Ulysses.* Eliot didn't do "experimental writing"—he wrote *The Waste Land.* When you fail at something you call it an "experiment," an elite word for flop. Just because lines are uneven or capitals missing doesn't mean experiment. Literary magazines devoted to experimental writing are usually filled with works by middle-aged or old people. Or young fogeys. In one way, of course, all writing that is any good *is* experimental; that is, it's a way of seeing what is possible—what poem, what novel is possible. Experiment—they define it as putting a question to nature, and that is true of writing undertaken with seriousness. You put the question to human nature—and especially your own nature—and see what comes out. It is unpredictable. If it is predictable—not experimental in that sense—then it will be worthless.

—*Robert Penn Warren*

Experiment? God forbid! Look at the results of experiment in the case of a writer like Joyce. He started off writing very well, then you can watch him going mad with vanity. He ends up a lunatic.

—*Evelyn Waugh*

ON HUMOR

Among all kinds of writing, there is none in which authors are more apt to miscarry than in works of humour, as there is none in which they are more ambitious to excel.　　—*Joseph Addison*

Master, shall I begin with the usual jokes
That the audience always laugh at?　　—*Aristophanes*

Aristotle said melancholy men of all others are most witty.
　　—*Robert Burton*

'Tis a strange undertaking, to make the gentry laugh.　　—*Molière*

Humor is emotional chaos remembered in tranquility.
　　—*James Thurber*

There are several kinds of stories, but only one difficult kind—the humorous.　　—*Mark Twain*

The best way to cheer yourself up is to try to cheer somebody else up.　　—*Mark Twain*

There's one obvious one [pitfall]: you must never make one character laugh at what another says or does. Dornford Yates's "Berry" novels, which are quite good fun in a sedate sort of way, are ruined by everybody collapsing with merriment whenever Berry shows up. The other pitfall is: you must never offer the reader anything simply *as* funny and nothing more. Make it acceptable as information, comment, narrative, et cetera, so that if the joke flops the reader has still got *something*. Wodehouse understood this perfectly, even better than Shakespeare did.　　—*Kingsley Amis*

Humor is really one of the hardest things to define, very hard. And it's very ambiguous. You have it or you don't. You can't attain it. There are terrible forms of professional humor, the humorists' humor. That can be awful. It depresses me because it is artificial. You can't always be humorous, but a professional humorist must. That is a sad phenomenon.   —*Heinrich Böll*

My pull is toward comedy. And I have a very high opinion of comedy: comedy is fully as revealing in its probing of human problems as is tragedy. The thing about comedy which I greatly value is that it is infinitely harder to fake than tragedy. It is extremely easy to be gloomy and to say, This is a terrible situation and everybody has got to be serious about it, and because I'm being serious about it, I am a writer of consequence. True, I have not often pulled out the *vox humana* and the *voix céleste* stops, but I know I have made quite a few people laugh a lot, and that is not the easiest thing to do. To see that life is funny and not to mock or jeer at somebody's predicament, cruelly and without understanding, simply because some aspects of it are funny—that takes a bit of doing. I saw an instance today on Fifth Avenue, a situation that was either comic or tragic depending on how you want to take it. This girl was sitting there in the rain begging, and she had a big sign which said what her trouble was. It was a quite ordinary tale of betrayal and misery and this, that and the other—if it was true, and I don't know if it was true. But the person sitting in the rain looking wretched, even if she was not an honest beggar, was tragic. That someone of her age should be sitting on the sidewalk begging may mean not that she can't do something else, but that she has chosen to do that. It's tragic. You have to balance these two things against one another. Life is, as you said, a very rum thing.   —*Robertson Davies*

Inconsequential is the operative word there. Consequence to me is when the bone doesn't heal, when the germ does not do what the penicillin wants it to. Consequence is pain. There can be no consequences in comedy. Tom and Jerry chase each other; Tom falls off the Empire State Building and shatters like a dish. In the next loop he has reconstituted himself. Now, I don't laugh at Tom and Jerry, but in a simplistic way, that's the model for all comedy. Nothing bad may happen. There is safety in comedy. —*Stanley Elkin*

If you can make the reader laugh he is apt to get careless and go on reading. So you as the writer get a chance to get something on him. —*Henry Green*

Georges Duhamel used to say that "Humor is the courtesy of despair." Humor is therefore very important. At the same time, I can understand people who can't laugh anymore. How can you, with the carnage that is going on in the world—in the Middle East, in Africa, in South America, everywhere? There is awfully little that is conducive to mirth. —*Eugène Ionesco*

One uses humor to make people laugh. In my case, I don't know whether they in fact do. The trouble is, it makes them think you aren't being serious. That's the risk you take. —*Philip Larkin*

The funny bone is universal. I doubt humorists think of individual taste when they're enticing the laugh. With me humor comes unexpectedly, usually in defense of a character, sometimes because I need cheering up. When something starts funny I can feel my imagination eating and running. I love the distancing—the guise of invention—that humor gives fiction. Comedy, I imagine, is harder to do consistently than tragedy, but I like it spiced in the wine of sadness. —*Bernard Malamud*

I don't want to be classed as a humorist. It makes me feel guilty. I've never read a good tough quotable female humorist, and I never was one myself. I couldn't do it. A "smartcracker" they called me, and that makes me sick and unhappy. There's a hell of a distance between wisecracking and wit. Wit has truth in it; wisecracking is simply calisthenics with words. I didn't mind so much when they were good, but for a long time anything that was called a crack was attributed to me—and then they got the shaggy dogs.

—*Dorothy Parker*

Well, it must be thoroughly apparent how many more people wrote humor for the printed page in the twenties. The form seems to be passing, and there aren't many practitioners left. The only magazine nowadays that carries any humor worthy of the name, in my estimation, is *The New Yorker*. Thirty years ago, on the other hand, there were *Judge, Life, Vanity Fair, College Humor,* and one or two others. I think the explanation for the paucity of written humor is simply that very few fledgling writers deign to bother with it. If someone has a flair for comedy, he usually goes into television or what remains of motion pictures. There's far more loot in those fields, and while it's ignominious to be an anonymous gagman, perhaps, eleven hundred dollars a week can be very emollient to the ego. The life of the freelance writer of humor is highly speculative and not to be recommended as a vocation. In the technical sense, the comic writer is a cat on a hot tin roof. His invitation to perform is liable to wear out at any moment; he must quickly and constantly amuse in a short span, and the first smothered yawn is a signal to get lost. The fiction writer, in contrast, has much more latitude. He's allowed to sideslip into exposition, to wander off into interminable byways and browse around endlessly in his characters' heads. The development of a comic idea has to be swift and economical; consequently, the pieces are shorter than conventional fiction and fetch a much smaller stipend.

. . .

It may surprise you to hear me say—and I'll thank you not to confuse me with masters of the paradox like Oscar Wilde and G. K. Chesterton—that I regard my comic writing as serious. For the past thirty-four years, I have been approached almost hourly by damp people with foreheads like Rocky Ford melons who urge me to knock off my frivolous career and get started on that novel I'm burning to write. I have no earthly intention of doing any such thing. I don't believe in the importance of scale; to me the muralist is no more valid than the miniature painter. In this very large country, where size is all and where Thomas Wolfe outranks Robert Benchley, I am content to stitch away at my embroidery hoop. I think the form I work can have its own distinction, and I would like to surpass what I have done in it.   —S. J. Perelman

With humor you have to look out for traps. You're likely to be very gleeful with what you've first put down, and you think it's fine, very funny. One reason you go over and over it is to make the piece sound less as if you were having a lot of fun with it yourself. You try to play it down. In fact, if there's such a thing as a *New Yorker* style, that would be it—playing it down.   —James Thurber

I find difficulty with the word "humor" and with the word "humorist" to peg a writer. I was taken aback, the other day, when I looked in *Who's Who* to discover Frank Sullivan's birthday and found him described as "humorist." It seemed a wholly inadequate summary of the man. Writing funny pieces is a legitimate form of activity, but the durable humor in literature, I suspect, is not the contrived humor of a funnyman commenting on the news but the sly and almost imperceptible ingredient that sometimes gets into writing. I think of Jane Austen, a deeply humorous woman. I think of Thoreau, a man of some humor along with his bile.   —E. B. White

I think character [makes a story funny] mostly. You know instinctively what's funny and what isn't if you're a humorous writer. I don't think a man can deliberately sit down to write a funny story unless he has got a sort of slant on life that leads to funny stories. If you take life fairly easily, then you take a humorous view of things. It's probably because you were born that way. Lord Emsworth and his pig—I *know* they're funny.   —P. G. Wodehouse

ON WRITER'S
BLOCK

If you are in difficulties with a book, try the element of surprise: attack it at an hour when it isn't expecting it.   —*H. G. Wells*

Facing it—always facing it—that's the way to get through it! Face it!   —*Joseph Conrad*

Tom Birch is as brisk as a bee in conversation, but no sooner does he take a pen in his hand, than it becomes a torpedo to him, and benumbs all faculties.   —*Samuel Johnson*

If there is no wind, row.   —*Latin proverb*

Inhibitions or blocks have recently become second nature with me. It has to do with the situation on earth. I live in a country which has the greatest concentration of atomic weapons on earth—and now more masses of new atomic weapons are to be added. That can take away your breath, and your enjoyment of life, and give you pause about whether writing makes any sense. For a time music, classical music, helped me to overcome a block—Beethoven's *breath,* for example, in which I sense something very West European and Rhine-like. The persistent problem with my writing is that I never know how something is going to come out; even when I write a short review, I always have to start all over. I have no mastery. But it's actually beneficial—it prevents things from becoming routine.

—*Heinrich Böll*

You can always write something. You write limericks. You write a love letter. You do something to get you in the habit of writing again, to bring back the desire.   —*Erskine Caldwell*

ON WRITER'S BLOCK

They tell me that success is a terrible test of people. Thank God I've never had to undergo it. But nationwide success with money pouring in will kill lots of writers. Ross Lockridge, who wrote *Raintree County*, and Thomas Heggen, the author of that novel about a ship, *Mister Roberts*, both committed suicide. It was always said that Gilbert Seldes's review of *The Great Gatsby*, which was ecstatic, probably damaged Scott Fitzgerald. The trouble is that after something like that, every work has to count . . . every word has to live up to this marvelous praise. The poor author gets stage fright.

—*Malcolm Cowley*

Then, of course, she [Carson McCullers] was terribly affected by not being able to write. It was a murderous thing, a death blow, that block. She said she just didn't have anything to write. And really, it was as though she had never written. This happens to writers when there are dead spells. We die sometimes. And it's as though we're in a tomb; it's a death. That's what we all fear, and that's why so many of us become alcoholics or suicides or insane—or just no-good philanderers. It's amazing that we survive, though I think survival in some cases is kind of misgiven and it's a bore. It was written recently about Saul Bellow that one of the best things about him is that he survived, he didn't become an alcoholic, he didn't go mad and so forth. And that the true heroism of him lies simply in his endurance. That's the way we look at artists in America.

—*William Goyen*

I wonder, when a writer's blocked and doesn't have any resources to pull himself out of it, why doesn't he jump in his car and drive around the U.S.A.? I went last winter for 7000 miles and it was lovely. Inexpensive too. A lot of places—even good motels—are only twenty-five dollars in the winter, and food isn't much because there aren't any good restaurants. You pack along a bunch of stomach remedies and a bottle of whiskey.

—*Jim Harrison*

I've come close. There was a period after I left *The New Yorker* for the first time, when I thought I knew enough about writing stories to be able to make a living by it, but it turned out that every idea I had for a story was in some way too close to home. The stories I did write weren't bought. I began to feel that my hands were tied. I guess, though, I have always believed that if the material interested me enough to want to write about it, then it was all right; it wouldn't go away and so I should just keep working on it. Updike said once, riding in a taxi—he was talking about the reviewers, who had been scolding him for not writing what they thought he ought to be writing—"All I have to go on," he said, "is something I caught a glimpse of out of the corner of my eye." That seemed a very nice way of describing the way material comes to you. That glimpse, it's all you have. I don't think a writer's block is anything more than a loss of confidence. It certainly isn't a loss of talent.

—*William Maxwell*

Okay, I am stuck. The question is, am I dead, as Messrs. A.B.C. might wish? In case I conk out, this is provisionally what I have to do: I must clarify obscurities; I must make clearer definite ideas or dissociations. I must find a verbal formula to combat the rise of brutality—the principle of order versus the split atom. There was a man in the bughouse, by the way, who insisted that the atom had never been split.

An epic is a poem containing history. The modern mind contains heteroclite elements. The past epos has succeeded when all or a great many of the answers were assumed, at least between author and audience, or a great mass of audience. The attempt in an experimental age is therefore rash. Do you know the story: "What are you drawing, Johnny?"

"God!"

"But nobody knows what He looks like."

"They will when I get through!"
That confidence is no longer obtainable. *—Ezra Pound*

It is usual that the moment you write for publication—I mean one of course—one stiffens in exactly the same way one does when one is being photographed. The simplest way to overcome this is to write it *to* someone, like me. Write it as a letter aimed at one person. This removes the vague terror of addressing the large and faceless audience and it also, you will find, will give a sense of freedom and a lack of self-consciousness. *—John Steinbeck*

Well, the characteristic fear of the American writer is not so much that as it is the process of aging. The writer looks in the mirror and examines his hair and teeth to see if they're still with him. "Oh my God," he says, "I wonder how my writing is. I bet I can't write today." The only time I met Faulkner he told me he wanted to live long enough to do three more novels. He was 53 then, and I think he *has* done them. Then Hemingway says, you know, that he doesn't expect to be alive after sixty. But he doesn't look forward *not* to being. When I met Hemingway with John O'Hara in Costello's Bar 5 or 6 years ago we sat around and talked about how *old* we were getting. You see it's constantly on the minds of American writers. I've never known a woman who could weep about her age the way the men I know can.

Coupled with this fear of aging is the curious idea that the writer's inventiveness and ability will end in his fifties. And of course it often does. Carl Van Vechten stopped writing. The prolific Joseph Hergesheimer suddenly couldn't write anymore. Over in Europe that's never been the case.—Hardy, for instance, who started late and kept going. Of course Keats had good reason to write, *When I have fears that I may cease to be Before my pen has glean'd my teeming brain.* That's the great classic statement. But in America the writer is more likely to fear that his brain may cease to glean. I once did a drawing of a man at his typewriter, you see, and all this crumpled paper is on the floor, and he's staring down in discouragement. "What's the matter," his wife is saying. "Has your pen gleaned your teeming brain?"

—*James Thurber*

ON ARTIFICIAL
STIMULANTS

I pray thee let me and my fellow have
A hair of the dog that bit me last night.   —*John Heywood*

One of the disadvantages of wine is that it makes a man mistake
words for thoughts.   —*Samuel Johnson*

Some American writers who have known each other for years have
never met in the daytime or when both were sober.

—*James Thurber*

I've tried it long ago, with hashish and peyote. Fascinating, yes, but
no good, no. This, as we find in alcohol, is an *escape* from awareness,
a cheat, a momentary substitution, and in the end a destruction of
it. With luck, someone might have a fragmentary Kubla Khan vision.
But with no meaning. And with the steady destruction of the observing
and remembering mind.   —*Conrad Aiken*

I find writing very nervous work. I'm always in a dither when starting
a novel—that's the worst time. It's like going to the dentist, because
you do make a kind of appointment with yourself. And this is one
of the things I've learnt to recognize more and more with experience:
that you realize it's got to be . . . next week. Not today—but if you
don't sit down by the end of next week, it'll go off the boil slightly.
Well, it can't be next Wednesday, because somebody from *The Paris
Review* is coming to interview you, so it had better be Thursday. And
then, quaking, you sit down at the typewriter. And that's when a
glass of Scotch can be very useful as a sort of artistic ice-

breaker . . . artificial infusion of a little bit of confidence which is necessary in order to begin at all. And then each day's sitting down is still rather tense, though the tension goes away as the novel progresses, and when the end is even distantly in sight, the strain becomes small, though it's always there. So alcohol in moderate amounts and at a fairly leisurely speed is valuable to me—at least I think so. It could be that I could have written better without it . . . but it could also be true that I'd have written far less without it.

—*Kingsley Amis*

LSD? Nothing much happened, but I did get the distinct impression that some birds were trying to communicate with me.

—*W. H. Auden*

Actually, there's no secret. One simply pulls the cork out of the bottle, waits three minutes, and two thousand or more years of Scottish craftsmanship does the rest.   —*J. G. Ballard*

The hallucinogens produce visionary states, sort of, but morphine and its derivatives decrease awareness of inner processes, thoughts and feelings. They are pain killers, pure and simple. They are absolutely contraindicated for creative work, and I include in the lot alcohol, morphine, barbiturates, tranquilizers—the whole spectrum of sedative drugs. As for visions and heroin, I had a hallucinatory period at the very beginning of addiction, for instance, a sense of moving at high speed through space, but as soon as addiction was established, I had no visions—vision—at all and very few dreams.

—*William Burroughs*

It is very useful to have some depressant, perhaps. Extreme fatigue can serve. Filming "Beauty and the Beast" on the Loire in 1945 immediately at the end of the war, I was very ill. Everything went wrong. Electricity failures nearly every day; planes passing over just at the moment of a scene. Jean Marais's horses made difficulties, and

ON ARTIFICIAL STIMULANTS

he persisted in vaulting onto them himself out of second floor windows, refusing a double, and risking his bones. And the sunlight changes every minute on the Loire. All these things contributed to the virtue of the film. And in "The Blood of a Poet" Man Ray's wife played a rôle; she had never acted. Her exhaustion and fear paralyzed her and she passed before the cameras so stunned she remembered nothing afterwards. In the rushes we saw she was splendid; with the outer part suppressed, she had been let perform.   —*Jean Cocteau*

One of the reasons why Hart, and many writers, turn into alcoholics is that early in their lives they find that getting drunk is part of the creative process, that it opens up visions. It's a terrible sort of creative device, because three out of four who involve themselves in it become alcoholics. But it does open up doors in the beginning. Hart Crane would even make a first draft when he was drunk; he'd come out and read it, and say, "Isn't this the greatest poem *ever* written?" It wasn't. But then he would work over it patiently, dead sober, for several weeks, and it would amount to something. Not the greatest poem ever written, but still extraordinary.   —*Malcolm Cowley*

I drink very strong coffee and very weak tea. Scenery can be a violent stimulant. Wordsworth, I think, was thinking of that. I love it. But rather like Wordsworth, I think too much of it isn't good for you. And I'm so susceptible to horror that reading the newspaper is enough for me; when I actually see the news on television it makes me feel terrible for days.   —*Margaret Drabble*

One thing that Hemingway wrote that greatly impressed me was that writing for him was like boxing. He took care of his health and his well-being. Faulkner had a reputation of being a drunkard, but in every interview that he gave he said that it was impossible to write one line when drunk. Hemingway said this too. Bad readers have asked me if I was drugged when I wrote some of my works. But that illustrates that they don't know anything about literature or drugs.

To be a good writer you have to be absolutely lucid at every moment of writing and in good health. I'm very much against the romantic concept of writing which maintains that the act of writing is a sacrifice and that the worse the economic conditions or the emotional state, the better the writing. I think you have to be in a very good emotional and physical state. Literary creation for me requires good health, and the Lost Generation understood this. They were people who loved life.   —*Gabriel García Márquez*

What I do get is, say if I was in an apartment high on mescaline, I felt as if the apartment and myself were not merely on East Fifth Street but were in the middle of all space time. If I close my eyes on hallucinogens I get a vision of great scaly dragons in outer space, they're winding slowly and eating their own tails. Sometimes my skin and all the room seem sparkling with scales, and it's all made out of serpent stuff. And as if the whole illusion of life were made of reptile dream.   —*Allen Ginsberg*

I had two trips on the Mexican mushroom back in 1954 or so. None since. And never on LSD. First of all it's dangerous, and secondly ergot, from which LSD is made, is the enemy of mankind. Ergot is a minute black fungus that grows on rye, or did in the Middle Ages, and people who ate rye bread got manic visions, especially Germans. They now say that ergot affects the genes and might disorder the next generation. It occurs to me that this may explain the phenomenon of Nazism, a form of mass hysteria. Germans were rye-eaters, as opposed to wheat-eaters like the English. LSD reminds me of the minks that escape from mink-farms and breed in the forest and become dangerous and destructive. It has escaped from the drug factory and gets made in college laboratories.   —*Robert Graves*

I don't think there is any generalization one can make on this. Experience has shown that there's an enormous variation in the way people respond to lysergic acid. Some people probably could get direct aesthetic inspiration for painting or poetry out of it. Others I don't think could. For most people it's an extremely significant experience, and I suppose in an indirect way it could help the creative process. But I don't think one can sit down and say, "I want to write a magnificent poem, and so I'm going to take lysergic acid." I don't think it's by any means certain that you would get the result you wanted—you might get almost any result. —*Aldous Huxley*

They [Hemingway and Faulkner] should have gotten better as they got older; *I've* gotten better. We're not professional athletes; it's reasonable to assume that we'll get better as we mature—at least, until we start getting senile. Of course, some writers who write their best books early simply lose interest in writing; or they lose their concentration—probably because they want to do other things. But Hemingway and Fitzgerald really lived to write; their bodies and their brains betrayed them. I'm such an incapable drinker, I'm lucky. If I drink half a bottle of red wine with my dinner, I forget who I had dinner with—not to mention everything that I or anybody else said. If I drink more than half a bottle, I fall instantly asleep. But just think of what novelists do: fiction writing requires a kind of memory, a vigorous, invented memory. If I can forget who I had dinner with, what might I forget about my novel-in-progess? The irony is that drinking is especially dangerous to novelists; memory is vital to us. I'm not so down on drinking for writers from a moral point of view; but booze is clearly not good for writing *or* for driving cars. You know what Lawrence said: "The novel is the highest example of subtle interrelatedness that man has discovered." I agree! And just consider for one second what drinking does to "subtle interrelatedness." Forget the "subtle"; "interrelatedness" is what makes novels work—without it, you have no narrative momentum; you have incoherent rambling. Drunks ramble; so do books by drunks. —*John Irving*

When I was under, I noticed that the nice English psychiatrist had a scar on his neck—from a mastoid operation perhaps. His face went green and the scar started gaping as a wound and for some reason I thought, "Now at last the Gestapo have got me." Or was it the KGB? It was one of the two. The psychiatrist had a standard lamp and the base of it suddenly developed bird's claws. Then I flipped for a moment into normality and told myself, "You are hallucinating, that's all—if you touch the claws they'll go away." So I touched them. But they didn't go away. Not only a visual but also a tactile hallucination. It was very frightening. So when you ask me what madness is—it is when your perceptions are dramatically deviating from reality. That is not a scientific definition, however. When I came back from this experience of induced schizophrenia, the aftereffects lasted for several months. Timothy Leary went round the bend, of course. I came to the opposite view to Huxley's. These things have no particular spiritual value but they might have clinical value. For example, I think every psychiatrist should have a session with mescaline or LSD in order to know what a psychosis is like, what hallucinations are like. It should be part of the psychiatrist's curriculum.   —*Arthur Koestler*

Liquor, in my parents' world, was always your reward at the end of a hard day—or an easy day, for that matter—and I like to observe that old family tradition. But I've never drunk for inspiration. Quite the contrary—it's like the wet sponge on the blackboard. I do now and then take a puff of grass, or a crumb of Alice Toklas fudge, when I've reached the last drafts of a poem. That's when you need X-ray eyes to see what you've done, and the grass helps. Some nice touches can fall into place.   —*James Merrill*

I happened to collide with Ken Kesey; he lived just a couple of streets away. That whole scene was just ready to take off. And I thought I knew all about peyote and drugs and such. It didn't bother me to experiment. Kesey had a job as an orderly in the Veteran's Hospital and he was involved in the first experiments that were being conducted in psychedelic drugs. He was a volunteer. They were doing all these crazy drugs on an experimental basis. Some of them worked, some of them did not. I can remember really off-the-wall things called IT290s; they didn't even have names they were so arcane. Whatever IT290 was, I remember walking through the woods and suddenly encountering this huge locomotive, a green locomotive with gold trim, a very detailed hallucination which I remember particularly well. —*Robert Stone*

Allen [Ginsberg] once gave me one he said was a little bit like LSD but something new. It was a white drug and I became very ill after. It was very strange. I took this drug when I was staying at the Chelsea Hotel; Allen gave me this drug and went away. I spent most of the day in a blackout. But I later had to get up and go read in Town Hall. I was a little high. I thought, "People will think I am drunk." I was in a strange mood. For the first time in my life I forgot my lines, and didn't know why I was there. But when I saw the audience and after Robert Lowell (I think) introduced me, my old reflexes began working again. I was like a reading machine. It was very difficult for me to come on to the music of poetry because of this drug experience. I read the first poem by instinct; the second poem was hard but then it got better and better as the poetry took over and the drug went away. And I forgot about the drug. One doctor told me that it was very good; I was destroyed after the reading; I was not longing for more drugs. Drugs don't help poetry. When you try to write on pot, you think it's very good, but you are false because you have no real feelings. You think it is very good, but later when you read it, it's bullshit. —*Andrei Voznesensky*

Different
Forms

ON BIOGRAPHY

Read no history: nothing but biography, for that is life without theory.   —*Benjamin Disraeli*

I was day and night with Lincoln for years. I couldn't have picked a better companion.   —*Carl Sandburg*

Just how difficult it is to write biography can be reckoned by anybody who sits down and considers just how many people know the truth about his or her love affairs.   —*Rebecca West*

The difference between a novelist and a biographer resides in the biographer's having to master a narrative of inquiry. Biography has to explain and examine the evidence. The story is told brushstroke by brushstroke like a painter, and the biographer often has to say he simply doesn't know—he cannot fill in the gaps. There's so much that can never be known, whereas the omniscient novelist can be— well, omniscient, something impossible in biography.   —*Leon Edel*

Biography cannot be fiction. I have said a novelist is free to do anything—the novel is as much a work of the imagination as the writer wants to make of it. The novelist creates the characters, supplies their background. Turgenev used to give each character a lengthy dossier as if the person had a police record. The biographer doesn't have that freedom. The characters are real. The dossiers have to be real. Lytton Strachey once gave Queen Elizabeth a jewel to wear at a great occasion, but when asked, he admitted he put the jewel there to add a touch to his picture. That was a piece of fictional "property" imported into the story. George Kennan once admitted that in one of his histories he put a goat into the landscape between Russia and Finland when he was describing the departure of some important diplomat or personage from Russia to Finland. This was historic license. But he did add that he had usually seen goats in that landscape even though he didn't know whether there was one there on that particular day. These of course are small details but they define the difference between fiction and history.

· · ·

Biography is a scrofulous cottage industry, done mostly by academics who get grants and have a good time going all over the place interviewing. How seldom it is that one has ever heard of the person writing the biography. What are the models, what are the qualifications? And it is not only the full-scale computer printout that these things are, but the books brought forth by lovers, friends from youth, cousins, whatever. I remember how horrified Dickens was when he met, in later life, the model for Dora in *David Copperfield*. Now Dora would hire a hack and write about Dickens.

—*Elizabeth Hardwick*

ON CHILDREN'S
BOOKS

To talk to a child, to fascinate him, is much more difficult than to
win an electoral victory. But it is also more rewarding.

—*Colette*

Don't set your wit against a child.

—*Jonathan Swift*

When I sat down to write *Mary Poppins* or any of the other books,
I did not know children would read them. I'm sure there must be a
field of "children's literature"—I hear about it so often—but sometimes I wonder if it isn't a label created by publishers and booksellers
who also have the impossible presumption to put on books such notes
as "from five to seven" or "from nine to twelve." How can they
know when a book will appeal to such and such an age?

If you look at other so-called children's authors, you'll see they
never wrote directly for children. Though Lewis Carroll dedicated
his book to Alice, I feel it was an afterthought once the whole was
already committed to paper. Beatrix Potter declared "I write to please
myself!" And I think the same can be said of Milne or Tolkien or
Laura Ingalls Wilder.

I certainly had no specific child in mind when I wrote *Mary Poppins*.
How could I? If I were writing for the Japanese child who reads it
in a land without staircases, how could I have written of a nanny
that slides up the bannister? If I were writing for the African child
who reads the book in Swahili, how could I have written of umbrellas
for a child who has never seen or used one?

But I suppose if there is something in my books that appeals to
children, it is the result of my not having to go *back* to my childhood;

I can, as it were, turn *aside* and consult it (James Joyce once wrote, "My childhood bends beside me"). If we're completely honest, not sentimental or nostalgic, we have no idea where childhood ends and maturity begins. It is one unending thread, not a life chopped up into sections out of touch with one another.

Once, when Maurice Sendak was being interviewed on televison a little after the success of *Where the Wild Things Are,* he was asked the usual questions: Do you have children? Do you like children? After a pause, he said with simple dignity: "I was a child." That says it all.

But don't let me leave you with the impression that I am ungrateful to children. They have stolen much of the world's treasure and magic in the literature they have appropriated for themselves. Think, for example, of the myths or Grimm's fairy tales—none of which were written especially for them—this ancestral literature handed down by the folk. And so despite publishers' labels and my own protestations about not writing especially for them, I am grateful that children have included my books in their treasure trove.   —*P. L. Travers*

Anybody who shifts gears when he writes for children is likely to wind up stripping his gears. But I don't want to evade your question. There *is* a difference between writing for children and for adults. I am lucky, though, as I seldom seem to have my audience in mind when I am at work. It is as though they didn't exist.

Anyone who writes *down* to children is simply wasting his time. You have to write up, not down. Children are demanding. They are the most attentive, curious, eager, observant, sensitive, quick, and generally congenial readers on earth. They accept, almost without question, anything you present them with, as long as it is presented honestly, fearlessly, and clearly. I handed them, against the advice of experts, a mouse-boy, and they accepted it without a quiver. In *Charlotte's Web,* I gave them a literate spider, and they took that.

Some writers for children deliberately avoid using words they think a child doesn't know. This emasculates the prose and, I suspect, bores the reader. Children are game for anything. I throw them hard words, and they backhand them over the net. They love words that give them a hard time, provided they are in a context that absorbs their attention. I'm lucky again: my own vocabulary is small, compared to most writers, and I tend to use the short words. So it's no problem for me to write for children. We have a lot in common.

—*E. B. White*

ON CRITICISM

There's more ado to interpret interpretations than to interpret things, and more books upon books than any other subject.
                                        —*Michel de Montaigne*

This is not a novel to be tossed aside lightly. It should be thrown with great force.   —*Dorothy Parker*

Do not remove a fly from your friend's forehead with a hatchet.
                                        —*Chinese proverb*

Unless one is a regular reviewer, or one is reviewing a book of reference where the facts are wrong—then it's one's duty to inform the public, as one would warn them of watered milk. Writing nasty reviews can be fun, but I don't think the practice is very good for the character.   —*W. H. Auden*

When somebody told me to write a review of a certain *History of Literature*, I found there were so many howlers and blunders, and as I greatly admire the author as a poet, I said: "No, I don't want to write about it, because if I write about it I shall write against it." I don't like to attack people, especially now—when I was a young man, yes, I was very fond of it—but as time goes on, one finds that it is no good. When people write in favor or against anybody that hardly helps or hurts them. I think that a man can be helped, well, the man can be done or undone by his *own* writing, not by what other people say of him, so that even if you brag a lot and people say that you are a genius—well, you'll be found out.

—*Jorge Luis Borges*

Criticism, analysis, reflection is a natural response to the existence in the world of works of art. It is an honorable and even an exalted endeavor. Without it, works of art would appear in a vacuum, as if they had no relation to the minds experiencing them. It would be a dismal, unthinkable world with these shooting stars arousing no comment, leaving no trace. But it is the mind of the critic, somehow, the establishment of his own thought and values, that counts; and that establishment is the authority of the voice, whether it comes from creative work in the arts or creative work in criticsm. When I read a review, a mere short review, I am more interested at first in who is doing the reviewing than in the work under discussion. The name, what is attached to it by previous work, by serious thought, tells me whether it is likely to have any meaning or value for me. It is not a question of right or wrong specific opinions, but of the quality of the mind.

—*Elizabeth Hardwick*

I write only favorable reviews. A writer of fiction whose own fiction comes first is just too subjective a reader to allow himself to write a negative review. And there are already plenty of professional reviewers eager to be negative. If I get a book to review and I don't like it, I return it; I only review the book if I love it. Hence I've written very few reviews, and those are really just songs of praise or rather long, retrospective reviews of all the writer's works: of John Cheever, Kurt Vonnegut, and Günter Grass, for example. And then there is the occasional "younger" writer whom I introduce to readers, such as Jayne Anne Phillips and Craig Nova. Another thing about not writing negative reviews: grown-ups shouldn't finish books they're not enjoying. When you're no longer a child, and you no longer live at home, you don't have to finish everything on your plate. One reward of leaving school is that you don't have to finish books you don't like. You know, if I were a critic, I'd be angry and vicious, too; it *makes* poor critics angry and vicious—to have to *finish* all those books they're not enjoying. What a silly job criticism is! What unnatural work it is! It is certainly not work for a grown-up.   —*John Irving*

I find [reviewing] extremely stimulating. I get two really pretty serious books a month—and I must say they're extremely good at trying to give me something that I like—and I really think it's rather good for you to have to review, say, a book about the organization of the Roman Army in the first half of the month and then the life of Christina Rossetti in the second. So far from being bad for you, I think it's very *educative* and it really makes your mind work. In fact, as I said before, I'm really rather lost now if I *don't* have something like that that I've got to do. . . . But of course there *are* demoralizing forms of literary journalism, and I've done my stint of reviewing five novels in a column and so on. You know how it is: your friends say, "Are you mad saying this terrible book is quite good?" But you can't week in, week out keep saying this is all absolute rubbish.
                                                    —*Anthony Powell*

When I was a critic—on my local paper in Bristol and later for a magazine in London—I floundered between pronouncing what I hoped were magisterial judgments and merely declaring my own taste. If I might quote myself from a previous interview—"I was not a good critic because I never had the moral character to pan a friend. I'll rephrase that—I had the moral character never to pan a friend."   —*Tom Stoppard*

I do it (a) when some author, like Spark or Borges, excites me and I want to share the good news (b) when I want to write an essay, as on romantic love, or Barth's theology (c) when I feel ignorant of something, like modern French fiction, and accepting a review assignment will compel me to read and learn.   —*John Updike*

ON CRITICISM

On this matter of criticism, something that appalls me is the idea going around now that the practice of criticism is opposed to the literary impulse. Is *necessarily* opposed to it. Sure, it *may* be a trap, it may destroy the creative impulse, but so may drink or money or respectability. But criticism is a perfectly natural human activity and somehow the dullest, most technical criticism may be associated with full creativity. Elizabethan criticism is all, or nearly all, technical—meter, how to hang a line together—kitchen criticism, how to make the cake. People deeply interested in an art are interested in the "how." Now I don't mean to say that this is the only kind of valuable criticism. Any kind is good that gives a deeper insight into the nature of the thing—a Marxist analysis, a Freudian study, the relation to a literary or social tradition, the history of a theme. But we have to remember that there is no *one, single, correct* kind of criticism, no *complete* criticism. You only have different kinds of perspectives, giving, when successful, different kinds of insights. And at one historical moment one kind of insight may be more needed than another.

—*Robert Penn Warren*

I think the general state of reviewing in England is contemptible— both slovenly and ostentatious. I used to have a rule when I reviewed books as a young man never to give an unfavorable notice to a book I hadn't read. I find even this simple rule is flagrantly broken now.

—*Evelyn Waugh*

ON FILMS

You can fake all the sincerity in Hollywood, place it in the navel of a fruit fly and still have room enough for three caraway seeds and a producer's heart. —*Fred Allen*

A film is a petrified fountain of thought. —*Jean Cocteau*

Why only twelve? Go out and get thousands!
—*Samuel Goldwyn,*
on restaging the Last Supper

I didn't last long. I went out [to Hollywood] for a thousand a week, and I worked Monday, and I got fired Wednesday. The guy that hired me was out of town Tuesday. —*Nelson Algren*

In the old days in Hollywood you couldn't be a writer unless you could dictate your story to a secretary, and I never could dictate to anybody. So I had to go home at night to write where nobody could see me. I used to write in secret.

. . .

It [*Tobacco Road*] had good actors, good actresses, a good screen writer, and John Ford directing. It had everything in its favor. But then Darryl Zanuck came along and wanted a happy ending. So the characters go off to the poorhouse singing a folk song.
—*Erskine Caldwell*

I went to Hollywood to make money. It's very simple. The people are friendly and the food is good, but I've never been happy there, perhaps because I only went there to pick up a check. I do have the deepest respect for a dozen or so directors whose affairs are centered there and who, in spite of the overwhelming problems of financing films, continue to turn out brilliant and original films. But my principal feeling about Hollywood is suicide. If I could get out of bed and into the shower, I was all right. Since I never paid the bills, I'd reach for the phone and order the most elaborate breakfast I could think of, and then I'd try to make it to the shower before I hanged myself. This is no reflection on Hollywood, but it's just that I seemed to have a suicide complex there. I don't like the freeways, for one thing. Also, the pools are too hot . . . 85 degrees, and when I was last there, in late January, in the stores they were selling yarmulkes for dogs— my God! I went to a dinner and across the room a woman lost her balance and fell down. Her husband shouted over to her, "When I told you to bring your crutches, you wouldn't listen to me." That line couldn't be better! —*John Cheever*

I had just completed a contract at MGM and was about to return home. The director I had worked with said, "If you would like another job here, just let me know and I will speak to the studio about a new contract." I thanked him and came home. About six months later I wired my director friend that I would like another job. Shortly after that I received a letter from my Hollywood agent enclosing my first week's paycheck. I was surprised because I had expected first to get an official notice or recall and a contract from the studio. I thought to myself the contract is delayed and will arrive in the next mail. Instead, a week later I got another letter from the agent, enclosing my second week's paycheck. That began in November 1932 and continued until May 1933. Then I received a telegram from the studio. It said: *William Faulkner, Oxford, Miss. Where are you? MGM Studio.*

I wrote out a telegram: *MGM Studio, Culver City, California. William Faulkner.*

The young lady operator said, "Where is the message, Mr. Faulkner?" I said, "That's it." She said, "The rule book says that I can't send it without a message, you have to say something." So we went through her samples and selected I forget which one—one of the canned anniversary greeting messages. I sent that. Next was a long-distance telephone call from the studio directing me to get on the first airplane, go to New Orleans, and report to Director Browning. I could have got on a train in Oxford and been in New Orleans eight hours later. But I obeyed the studio and went to Memphis, where an airplane did occasionally go to New Orleans. Three days later one did.

I arrived at Mr. Browning's hotel about six p.m. and reported to him. A party was going on. He told me to get a good night's sleep and be ready for an early start in the morning. I asked him about the story. He said, "Oh, yes. Go to room so-and-so. That's the continuity writer. He'll tell you what the story is."

I went to the room as directed. The continuity writer was sitting in there alone. I told him who I was and asked him about the story. He said, "When you have written the dialogue I'll let you see the story." I went back to Browning's room and told him what had happened. "Go back," he said, "and tell that so-and-so—never mind, you get a good night's sleep so we can get an early start in the morning."

So the next morning in a very smart rented launch all of us except the continuity writer sailed down to Grand Isle, about a hundred miles away, where the picture was to be shot, reaching there just in time to eat lunch and have time to run the hundred miles back to New Orleans before dark.

That went on for three weeks. Now and then I would worry a little about the story, but Browning always said, "Stop worrying. Get a good night's sleep so we can get an early start tomorrow morning."

One evening on our return I had barely entered my room when the telephone rang. It was Browning. He told me to come to his room at once. I did so. He had a telegram. It said: *Faulkner is fired. MGM Studio.* "Don't worry," Browning said. "I'll call that so-and-so up this minute and not only make him put you back on the payroll but send you a written apology." There was a knock on the door. It was a page with another telegram. This one said: *Browning is fired. MGM Studio.* So I came back home. I presume Browning went somewhere too. I imagine that continuity writer is still sitting in a room somewhere with his weekly salary check clutched tightly in his hand. They never did finish the film. But they did build a shrimp village— a long platform on piles in the water with sheds built on it something like a wharf. The studio could have bought dozens of them for forty or fifty dollars apiece. Instead, they built one of their own, a false one. That is, a platform with a single wall on it, so that when you opened the door and stepped through it, you stepped right on off to the ocean itself. As they built it, on the first day, the Cajun fisherman paddled up in his narrow tricky pirogue made out of a hollow log. He would sit in it all day long in the broiling sun watching the strange white folks building this strange imitation platform. The next day he was back in the pirogue with his whole family, his wife nursing the baby, the other childen, and the mother-in-law, all to sit all that day in the broiling sun to watch this foolish and incomprehensible activity. I was in New Orleans two or three years later and heard that the Cajun people were still coming in for miles to look at that imitation shrimp platform which a lot of white people had rushed in and built and then abandoned. —*William Faulkner*

The reason that writers get submerged in the film business is simply a result of ordinary human greed. There's nothing literary about it— it's just greed. Why should I blame Warner Brothers for my own greed? Faulkner always presented himself as this martyr to Hollywood. Well, bullshit. His family evolved such a high nut that he had to keep doing it, because he was supporting seventeen people—his brother's children, retainers, aunts, uncles, an alcoholic wife—and whether old Billy wanted to go to L.A. or not they stuck that sucker on the train and shot him out there to make some more money.

—*Jim Harrison*

When I first went out to Hollywood one heard talk from writers about whoring. But you are not tempted to whore unless you want to be a whore. ——*Lillian Hellman*

Well, movies, movies, movies—they are our enemy, of course. Movies are the enemy of the novel because they are replacing novels. Novelists shouldn't write for the movies, unless, of course, they discover they're no good at writing novels. I like people who make movies, and I'm glad some of them, who are terribly smart, are not writing novels. There are enough people writing novels, God knows. Anyway, the main thing I learned by writing a screenplay of *Setting Free the Bears* was that screenwriting isn't really writing; it's carpentry. There's no language in it, and the writer is not in control of the pace of the story, or of the tone of the narration, and what else is there to be in control of? Tony Richardson told me that there *are* no screenwriters, so there is at least one director who agrees with me. It could be that it was the most valuable thing I ever did—to have my shot at writing a movie when I was so young, right after my first novel was published—because I was never tempted to do it again. ——*John Irving*

Screen writing made me rethink the role of a lot of the mnemonic things that most novelists leave in their books. The worst about these things is probably Faulkner, who frequently had his shit detector dialed down to zero. We all read Faulkner in a similar way: we move through these muddy bogs until we hit these wonderful streaks, and then we're back in the bogs again, right? Everyone agrees that Faulkner produced the greatest streaks in American literature from 1929 until 1935 but, depending on how you feel about this, you either admit that there's a lot of dead air in his works or you don't. After you've written screenplays for a while, you're not as willing to leave these warm-ups in there, those pencil sharpenings and refillings of the whiskey glasses and those sorts of trivialities. You're more conscious of dead time. Playwrights are even tougher on themselves in this regard. Twenty mediocre pages hardly hurt even a short novel but ten dead minutes will insure that a play won't get out of New Haven. Movies are like that: people just can't sit there, elbow-to-elbow with each other and stand ten boring minutes in a movie. Oh, they will to a degree if they're prepared enough about the historical moment, if they're watching *Gandhi* or something, but not usually. At any rate, I think I go more for blood now, scene by scene in my writing, than maybe I would if I had never had that movie training. But basically it would be more appropriate to ask me if having to do my own grocery shopping has affected my writing. According to reviewers, I've spent the last ten years of my life in Hollywood, but to tell the truth I have logged less than thirty days in Los Angeles. Total. I do have one level of interest in movies, and that's that I like to read screenplays. They're little books. If I hear there's a wonderful new movie out and I can get my hands on the screenplay, I'll read that rather than go to see the movie itself. I enjoy shooting the movie in my mind. I love to read plays for the same reason.

—*Thomas McGuane*

It's the people. Like the director who put his finger in Scott Fitzgerald's face and complained, "Pay *you*. Why, you ought to pay us." It was terrible about Scott; if you'd seen him you'd have been sick. When he died no one went to the funeral, not a single soul came, or even sent a flower. I said, "Poor son of a bitch," a quote right out of *The Great Gatsby,* and everyone thought it was another wisecrack. But it was said in dead seriousness. Sickening about Scott. And it wasn't only the people, but also the indignity to which your ability was put. There was a picture in which Mr. Benchley had a part. In it Monty Woolley had a scene in which he had to enter a room through a door on which was balanced a bucket of water. He came into the room covered with water and muttered to Mr. Benchley, who had a part in the scene, "Benchley? Benchley of *Harvard*?" "Yes," mumbled Mr. Benchley and he asked, "Woolley? Woolley of *Yale*?"

· · ·

Hollywood money isn't money. It's congealed snow, melts in your hand, and there you are. I can't talk about Hollywood. It was a horror to me when I was there and it's a horror to look back on. I can't imagine how I did it. When I got away from it I couldn't even refer to the place by name. "Out there," I called it. You want to know what "out there" means to me? Once I was coming down a street in Beverly Hills and I saw a Cadillac about a block long, and out of the side window was a wonderfully slinky mink, and an arm, and at the end of the arm a hand in a white suede glove wrinkled around the wrist, and in the hand was a bagel with a bite out of it.

—*Dorothy Parker*

I worked there sporadically from 1931 to 1942, and I can say in all sincerity that I would have spent my time to better advantage on Tristan da Cunha. The mere mention of Hollywood induces a condition in me like breakbone fever. It was a hideous and untenable place when I dwelt there, populated with few exceptions by Yahoos, and now that it has become the chief citadel of television, it's unspeakable. The closest analogy I can draw to describe the place is that it strikingly resembled the Sargasso Sea—an immense, turgidly revolving whirlpool in which literary hulks encrusted with verdigris moldered until they sank. It was really quite startling, at those buffet dinners in Beverly Hills, to encounter some dramatist or short-story writer out of your boyhood, or some one-shot lady novelist who'd had a flash success, who was now grinding out screenplays about the Cisco Kid for Sol Wurtzel. I remember, one day on the back lot at MGM, that a pallid wraith of a man erupted from a row of ramshackle dressing rooms and embraced me as though we had encountered each other in the Empty Quarter of Arabia. He was a geezer I'd known twelve years before on *Judge* magazine, a fellow who ran some inconsequential column full of Prohibition jokes. When I asked him what he was doing, he replied that he had been writing a screenplay of "Edwin Drood" for the past two years. He confessed quite candidly that he hadn't been able as yet to devise a finish, which, of course, wasn't too surprising inasmuch as Charles Dickens couldn't do so either.   —*S. J. Perelman*

You get an interesting technical exercise there—writing in hand-cuffs—which might one day be of considerable use in your own things.   —*Irwin Shaw*

In the 1940s I had a glorious time in Hollywood because I was fired almost at once from the project I was working on and they had to continue to pay me. That was in my contract. For six months they had to pay me $250 a week. This was in 1943, when $250 was equivalent to about $1000 now, I would guess. They had to pay me whether I had an assignment or not.

First they put me on *Marriage Is a Private Affair* for Lana Turner. Well, they expressed great delight with my dialogue, and I think it was good. But they said, "You give Miss Turner too many multisyllable words!" So I said, "Well, some words *do* contain more than one syllable!" And Pandro Berman, who loved me very much—Lana Turner just happened to be his girlfriend at the time—he said to me, "Tennessee, Lana can tackle two syllables, but I'm afraid if you go into three you're taxing her vocabulary!"

Then they asked me if I'd like to write a screenplay for a child star, one named Margaret O'Brien. I said, "I'd sooner shoot myself!" By that time I knew I'd get the $250 regardless.

So I lived out in Santa Monica and had a ball until the money ran out.   —*Tennessee Williams*

ON JOURNALISM

Literature is the art of writing something that will be read twice;
journalism what will be grasped at once.   —*Cyril Connolly*

Journalism is concerned with events, poetry with feelings. Journalism is concerned with the look of the world, poetry with the feel
of the world.   —*Archibald MacLeish*

The difference between journalism and literature is that journalism
is unreadable and literature is not read.   —*Oscar Wilde*

It's influenced my writing immeasurably more than I could possibly
define. When I was a boy, my father was a newspaperman, my two
brothers were newspapermen, my mother was intensely interested in
newspaper work, and I heard newspaper talk at every meal. In a
newspaper family you learn not only all the news that's fit to print,
but all the news that is *not* fit to print and you acquire an insight
into human nature and the essence of a community which is very
hard to acquire, I think, in any other way. I was the editor of a
newspaper for twenty years. During that time I had to deal with not
only the recorded news, but the news I knew about which might be
supportive of the recorded news but some of which could not possibly
be printed because it was so extraordinarily damaging and often
wounding. You find out what people are like, and how they live, and
what they're up to at night, and what goes on behind the lace curtains.
The world you report is rarely more than half the world you
know.   —*Robertson Davies*

ON JOURNALISM

I don't think there is any difference. The sources are the same, the material is the same, the resources and the language are the same. *The Journal of the Plague Year* by Daniel Defoe is a great novel and [John Hersey's] *Hiroshima* is a great work of journalism. In journalism just one fact that is false prejudices the entire work. In contrast, in fiction one single fact that is true gives legitimacy to the entire work. That's the only difference and it lies in the commitment of the writer. A novelist can do anything he wants so long as he makes people believe in it.

• • •

The writer's very attempt to portray reality often leads him to a distorted view of it. In trying to transpose reality he can end up losing contact with it, in an ivory tower, as they say. Journalism is a very good guard against that. That's why I have always tried to keep on doing journalism because it keeps me in contact with the real world, particularly political journalism and politics.

—*Gabriel García Márquez*

On the [Kansas City] *Star,* you were forced to learn to write a simple declarative sentence. This is useful to anyone. Newspaper work will not harm a young writer and could help him if he gets out of it in time. This is one of the dustiest clichés there is and I apologize for it. But when you ask someone old tired questions you are apt to receive old tired answers. —*Ernest Hemingway*

Journalism allows its readers to witness history; fiction gives its readers the opportunity to live it. —*John Hersey*

I think that journalism is a healthier occupation for a writer than teaching, especially if he teaches literature. By teaching literature, the writer gets accustomed to analyze literature all the time. One man, a critic, said to me, "I could never write anything because the moment I write the first line I am already writing an essay about it. I am already criticizing my own writing."

It's not good when the writer is both a critic and a writer. It doesn't matter if he writes a review once in a while or even an essay about criticism. But if this kind of analyzing goes on all the time and it becomes his daily bread, it may one day become a part of his writing: it is very bad when the writer is half-writer and half-critic. He writes essays about his heroes instead of telling a story.

—*Isaac Bashevis Singer*

It's a different kind of recording. Journalism is too immediate, too monotonous and superficial. A chronicler is alone in his room and writes. A journalist is rarely alone. He writes about other people, and the essential is always missed. I was a journalist long enough to know. You write only of the fleeting moment—the most dramatic, the most visible, not the underlying reasons.   —*Elie Wiesel*

ON POTBOILERS

Commissions suit me. They set limits. Jean Marais dared me to write a play in which he would not speak in the first act, would weep for joy in the second and in the last would fall backwards down a flight of stairs.
                                                      —*Jean Cocteau*

A cow is very good in a field, but we turn her out of a garden.
                                                      —*Samuel Johnson*

I've always been interested in these less respectable forms of writing—the adventure story, the thriller, science-fiction and so on—and this is why I've produced one or two examples myself. I read somewhere recently somebody saying: "When I want to read a book, I write one." I think that's very good. It puts its finger on it, because there are never enough books of the kind one likes: one adds to the stock for one's own entertainment.   —*Kingsley Amis*

I was asked to do an interview with Sophia Loren by the *Saturday Evening Post*. I did. I got to kiss her. I've had other offers but nothing as good.   —*John Cheever*

I've done hundreds and thousands of words of feature articles, all buried in remote periodicals. Some under my own name, some under initials. In Cairo I ran a comic column. And then I've written millions of words of Foreign Office dispatches—a much harder job than any foreign correspondent's because I was the buffer state between, say, four and four hundred correspondents in a situation where a statement of policy was expected on a split-second basis and so water-tight that it wouldn't fall apart under analysis. Of course, to make that kind of statement you have to have a policy, and in most of the places where I worked we didn't. In fact, I was selling a pig in a poke most of the time, living on my wits. Or, as Sir Henry Wotton said, "lying abroad for my country." But I mean it's an incomparable training, and by rubbing shoulders with a vast variety of journalists I learned most of the tricks of the trade—most of them rather shabby tricks, mind you, and magpie tricks and easy to learn. But one of the lessons, writing as you do under pressure in the journalistic world, is that you learn concision, which is invaluable, and you also learn to work for a deadline. Whenever the deadline is you've got to do it and you've got to have the will to do it. Well, you do it. Of course, the element of luck is very great. I might have written all my things and not had a publisher, or I might not have written them well enough to sell them. . . . I have to admit in my heart of hearts that I could have written books twice as good as the quartet and not have sold three hundred copies. The element of luck is absolutely mixed up with the whole thing.

· · ·

I have had to do a lot of potboiling in my career. Let me say this: if one stays absolutely sincere and honest towards a form—even when I'm writing this Antrobus nonsense, I'm writing it with a reverence to P. G. Wodehouse. I mean every form thoroughly exploited and honestly dealt with is not shameful. So that potboiling as an idea of someone writing with a typewriter in his cheek or something—I can't say I do that. I mean I put as much hard work into a dull Antrobus story, which may or may not come off, as I put into the next chapter of the book I have to get on with.

—*Lawrence Durrell*

It's impossible for a novelist not to look out for other media nowadays. It isn't that everything has been done in fiction—truly nothing has been done as yet, save Fielding, and he only started it all. It is simply that the novelist is a communicator and must therefore be interested in any form of communication. You don't dictate to a girl now, you use a recording apparatus; no one faints anymore, they have blackouts; in Geneva you don't kill someone by cutting his throat, you blow a poisoned dart through a tube and *zing,* you've got him. Media change. We don't have to paint chapels like Cocteau, but at the same time we must all be ever on the lookout for the new ways.

—*Henry Green*

I once started a detective story to make money—but I couldn't get the murder to take place! At the end of three chapters I was still describing the characters and the milieu, so I thought, this is not going to work. No corpse!   —*Mary McCarthy*

I was never too good a hand at writing for the magazines. I once did a satirical article for *Vogue,* I think it was. On a painter whom I did not admire. They thought I had got just the right tone and then Verhaeren died and they asked me to do a note on Verhaeren. And I went down and said, "You want a nice bright snappy obituary notice of the gloomiest man in Europe."

"What, gloomy cuss, was he?"

"Yes," I said. "He wrote about peasants."

"Peasants or pheasants?"

"Peasants."

"Oh, I don't think we ought to touch it."

That is the way I crippled my earning capacity by not knowing enough to keep quiet.   —*Ezra Pound*

ON SHORT
STORIES

Not that the story need be long, but it will take a long while to
make it short.   —*Henry David Thoreau*

The length worries me. There are two things which feel uncomfortable and awkward to me . . . like a wooden leg. One is the short
story of about four thousand words, and the other is the feature for
the *Times*. I could easily give them five thousand words or eight
thousand words, but I'm damned if I can do anything under one
thousand. So what I have to do is overwrite, give them eight thousand,
and let them cut it down to their required size. As for the short
story, I've done, as I say, several, but I've never felt happy in the
form. Either I've felt it should be another forty pages, in which case
it becomes a junior novel, a concertina novel, or else I've felt it should
be two pages . . . O. Henry and finish, you know. I admire the form,
but it doesn't come easily to me.   —*Lawrence Durrell*

The short story is the nearest thing I know to lyric poetry—I wrote
lyric poetry for a long time, then discovered that God had not intended
me to be a lyric poet, and the nearest thing to that is the short story.
A novel actually requires far more logic and far more knowledge of
circumstances, whereas a short story can have the sort of detachment
from circumstances that lyric poetry has. . . . My own experience
with the novel is that it was always too difficult for me to do. At
least to do a novel like *Pride and Prejudice* requires something more
than to be a failed B. A. or a failed poet or a failed short-story writer,
or a failed anything else. Creating in the novel a sense of continuing

262

life is the thing. We don't have that problem in the short story, where you merely suggest continuing life.

. . .

Short stories and plays go together in my mind. You take a point in time and develop it from there; there is no room for development backwards. In a novel I also take a point in time, but feel every room for development backwards. All fiction for me is a kind of magic and trickery—a confidence trick, trying to make people believe something is true that isn't. And the novelist, in particular, is trying to convince the reader that he is seeing society as a whole. . . . You can't do this sort of thing with short stories. They have a kind of immediate ethical text. Many of mine have punning titles. I take a platitude—"the wrong set," for example: the point is that no one knows what the wrong set is, and one person's wrong set is another's right set. And you get the pay-off, which is something I like. A play is rather like this, but has more depth. And plays and short stories are similar in that both start when all but the action has finished.

—*Frank O'Connor*

I always write a story in one sitting. I started "Flowering Judas" at seven p.m. and at one-thirty I was standing on a snowy windy corner putting it in the mailbox. And when I wrote my short novels, two of them, I just simply took the manuscript, packed a suitcase and departed to an inn in Georgetown, Pennsylvania, without leaving any forwarding address! Fourteen days later I had finished *Old Mortality* and *Noon Wine*.　　　　　　　　　—*Katherine Anne Porter*

The form of the short story is so free as to escape restriction to any theory. Theories just don't seem to hold up. I had a theory when I began and I know I haven't been able to follow it out. I wanted to write stories in each one of which the style and shape would be dictated, as far as possible, not by me but by the material itself. That is, I wanted to make the attempt to cut the umbilical cord between the creator and the character. The Promethean writer would be the one who sounded like a Russian artillery officer when he was writing "The Cossacks," a Dublin lush when he was writing "Counterparts," and a German professor when he was writing "Disorder and Early Sorrow." I know it's impossible, but some damned interesting writing might come out of the attempt.　　　　　　　*—Irwin Shaw*

I think it is the art of the glimpse. If the novel is like an intricate Renaissance painting, the short story is an Impressionist painting. It *should* be an explosion of truth. Its strength lies in what it leaves out just as much as what it puts in, if not more. It is concerned with the total exclusion of meaninglessness. Life, on the other hand, is meaningless most of the time. The novel imitates life, where the short story is bony, and cannot wander. It is essential art.

. . .

Stories begin in all kinds of ways. With a remembered schoolteacher, or someone who might later have had something to do with your life, or some unimportant occurrence. You begin to write and in the process of writing it is often the case that whatever it was that started you off gets lost. On other occasions, stories simply come out of nowhere: you never discover the source. I remember being on a train and I was perhaps walking down to the bar when I noticed a woman and a boy traveling together. He was in his school uniform and she was clearly in charge of him. I can remember now the fatigue on her face. Afterwards—probably years afterwards—I wrote a story called *Going Home.*　　　　　　　　　　　　　*—William Trevor*

I think I'd sooner write short stories than novels. I feel really happy with a short story. I like the sense of completing something. The only trouble is that if I do get a good idea, I rather want to work it into a novel. I mean, I'm rather wasting a novel if I write a short story.　　　　　　　　　　　　　　　*—P. G. Wodehouse*

ON THEATER

Be patient. Our playwright may show in some fifth act what this
wild drama means.   —*Alfred, Lord Tennyson*

Some writers take to drink, others take to audiences.

                                                              —*Gore Vidal*

There is all the difference in the world between writing a play for
an audience and writing a poem, in which you're writing primarily
for yourself—although obviously you wouldn't be satisfied if the poem
didn't mean something to other people afterward. With a poem you
can say, "I got my feeling into words for myself. I now have the
equivalent in words for that much of what I have felt." Also in a
poem you're writing for your own voice, which is very important.
You're thinking in terms of your own voice, whereas in a play from
the beginning you have to realize that you're preparing something
which is going into the hands of other people, unknown at the time
you're writing it. Of course I won't say there aren't moments in a
play when the two approaches may not converge, when I think ideally
they should. Very often in Shakespeare they do, when he is writing
a poem and thinking in terms of the theater and the actors and the
audience all at once. And the two things are one. That's wonderful
when you can get that. With me it only happens at odd moments.

                                                              —*T. S. Eliot*

There shouldn't be any difference between writing for the theater
and writing for anything else. Only that one has to know the theater.
Know it. To publish a novel or a poem one doesn't have to know

print types or the publishing world. But to do a play, no matter how much one wishes to stay away from it, one has to *know* the theater. Playwrights have tried to stay away, including Shaw and Chekhov, but in the end, they were involved. Chekhov used to send letters of instructions and angry notes. A play is not only on paper. It is there to share with actors, directors, scene designers, electricians.

—*Lillian Hellman*

The theater chose me. As I said, I started with poetry, and I also wrote criticism and dialogue. But I realized that I was most successful at dialogue. Perhaps I abandoned criticism because I am full of contradictions, and when you write an essay you are not supposed to contradict yourself. But in the theater, by inventing various characters, you can. My characters are contradictory not only in their language, but in their behavior as well.

—*Eugène Ionesco*

Young novelists come a dime a dozen, but the playwright must be older, more experienced and in more complete control of his craft. The scope of the novel is such that mistakes can be made, even serious mistakes, without impairing the value of the work. But the theater audience is hyper-critical, and the form of the play is extremely exacting and one mistake and you're through. I've had a hard time with the theater. I've always been anxious to write plays. I read all kinds of plays and books on the theater and books about how to write plays but all I learned was that playwriting is something nobody can teach you.

—*Irwin Shaw*

I've never much enjoyed going to plays myself; they always seem one act too long, and I often can't hear. The last play I went to, I remember, was "A Delicate Balance"; I sat next to the wall and trucks kept shifting gears on the other side of it and I missed most of the dialogue. The unreality of painted people standing on a platform saying things they've said to each other for months is more than I can overlook. Also, I think the theater is a quicksand of money and people with push. Harold Brodkey, a splendid writer my age, disappeared for five years into a play that was never produced. From Twain and James to Faulkner and Bellow, the history of novelists as playwrights is a sad one. A novelist is no more prepared to write for the stage than a good distance runner is equipped for ballet. A play is verbal ballet, and I mean to include in that equation some strong reservations about ballet. Less than perfectly done, it's very tiresome. A play's capacity for mimesis is a fraction of a novel's. Shakespeare, and to a lesser extent Shaw, wrote their plays as "turns" and exercises for actors they knew—without Will Kempe, no Falstaff. Without this kind of intimacy, the chances of life creeping into a play are slight. On both sides of the footlights, I think the present American theater mainly an excuse for being sociable.   —*John Updike*

A dramatist is one who believes that the pure event, an action involving human beings, is more arresting than any comment that can be made upon it. On the stage it is always *now*; the personages are standing on that razor-edge, between the past and the future, which is the essential character of conscious being; the words are rising to their lips in immediate spontaneity. A novel is what *took place*; no self-effacement on the part of the narrator can hide the fact that we hear his voice recounting, recalling events that are past and over, and which he has selected—from uncountable others—to lay before us from his presiding intelligence. Even the most objective novels are cradled in the authors' emotions and the authors' assumptions about life and mind and the passions. Now the paradox lies not so much in the fact that you and I know that the dramatist equally has selected what he exhibits and what the characters will say—such an operation is inherent in any work of art—but that all the greatest dramatists, except the very greatest *one*, have precisely employed the stage to convey a moral or religious point of view concerning the action. The theater is supremely fitted to say: "Behold! These things are." Yet most dramatists employ it to say: "This moral truth can be learned from beholding this action."

The Greek tragic poets wrote for edification, admonition, and even for our political education. The comic tradition in the theater carries the intention of exposing folly and curbing excess. Only in Shakespeare are we free of hearing axes ground . . . I regard the theater as the greatest of all art forms, the most immediate way in which a human being can share with another the sense of what it is to be a human being. This supremacy of the theater derives from the fact that it is always "now" on the stage. It is enough that generations have been riveted by the sight of Clytemnestra luring Agamemnon to the fatal bath, and Oedipus searching out the truth which will ruin him; those circumambient tags about "Don't get prideful" and "Don't call anybody happy until he's dead" are incidental concomitants. The theater *is* so vast and fascinating a realm that there is room in it for preachers and moralists and pamphleteers. But as to the highest function of the theater, I rest my case with Shakespeare — *Twelfth Night* as well as *Macbeth*.

• • •

All excellence is equally difficult, but, considering sheer métier, I would always advise any young writer for the theater to do everything—to adapt plays, to translate plays, to hang around theaters, to paint scenery, to become an actor, if possible. Writing for TV or radio or the movies is all part of it. There's a bottomless pit in the acquisition of how to tell an imagined story to listeners and viewers.   —*Thornton Wilder*

The Writer's Life

ON SOCIAL LIFE: WRITERS' COLONIES, SALONS, LITERARY COMMUNITIES, ETC.

Writing is a dog's life, but the only life worth living.
—*Gustave Flaubert*

I've told people I'm a medieval historian, when asked what I do. It freezes conversation. If one tells them one's a poet, one gets these odd looks which seem to say, "Well, what's he living off?" In the old days a man was proud to have in his passport, Occupation: Gentleman. Lord Antrim's passport simply said, Occupation: Peer—which I felt was correct. I've had a lucky life, I had a happy home, and my parents provided me with a good education. And my father was both a physician and a scholar, so I never got the idea that art and science were opposing cultures—both were entertained equally in my home. I cannot complain. I've never had to do anything I really disliked. Certainly I've had to do various jobs I would not have taken on if I'd had the money; but I've always considered myself a worker, not a laborer. So many people have jobs they don't like at all. I haven't, and I'm grateful for that.   —*W. H. Auden*

I went to Yaddo [the writers' colony] twice, once in the summer for two weeks, and for several months the winter before I went to Brazil. I didn't like it in the summer because of the incessant coming and going, but the winter was rather different. There were only six of us and just by luck we all liked each other and had a very good time. I wrote one poem, I think, in that whole stretch. The first time I liked the horse races, I'm afraid. In the summer—I think this still

271

goes on—you can walk through the Whitney estate to the tracks. A friend and I used to walk there early in the morning and sit at the track and have coffee and blueberry muffins while they exercised the horses. I loved that. We went to a sale of yearlings in August and that was beautiful. The sale was in a big tent. The grooms had brass dustpans and brooms with brass handles and they'd go around after the little colts and sweep up the manure. That's what I remember best about Yaddo.

—*Elizabeth Bishop*

I was never aware of wanting to become part of a community, no. I wanted to meet them. I suppose I simply felt that I was taking pot shots at clay pipes. Pop! Down goes Gertrude, down goes Jean Cocteau, down goes André Gide. I made a point of those things—meeting Manuel de Falla, for example—for no reason at all. I went to Granada, found his door, knocked, went in, and spent the afternoon. He had no idea who I was. Why I did that, I don't know. Apparently I thought such encounters were important or I wouldn't have bothered, because it involved a lot of work and sometimes a sacrifice of something I cared about. But exactly how I felt I can't remember, because it wasn't an intellectual thing. It was "unthought," and it's hard for me to recall the reason for it. Of course, I've never been a thinking person. A lot seems to happen without my conscious knowledge.

—*Paul Bowles*

My closest friends are theater people. Painters were once closest to me. For some years I lived among painters. But that changed. Now it's either performers or directors. I love theater people, they give me a great deal. I don't particularly like writers, and I am not prone to talk about writing. Since they're solitary workers, writers tend to *act out* in public, I believe. They seem to carry more hostility, maybe because they are responsible to more people (their characters), to a whole world—like God—than painters or actors. Maybe it's because writers are caught in the English language, which sometimes seems like a sticky web you can't pull your antennae out of, like insects

I've watched in webs, and are, in public and when they're with other people, still thrashing about in an invisible web. It is *enraging* to work in words, sometimes; no wonder writers are often nervous and crazy: paint seems to be a more benevolent, a more soothing and serene-making medium.

Musicians always want to play for you, which is wonderful and wordless; painters seem to want to talk only about sex or point out to you the hidden genital configurations in their canvas! Since the writer is truly a seminal person (he spits out his own web, as Yeats said, and then, as I just said, gets caught in it), the truly creative writer, I mean, he's full of the fear and the pride that a maker of *new* things feels. —*William Goyen*

Here's a major point of tension in most writers' lives: How can we rub enough with the world to nourish our writing, while keeping the world enough at bay to safeguard our creative energies? I like living where I do, in southern New England, because I can better control my impulsive, innate gregariousness. It's easier to resist temptations here and yet I can get into New York in two and a half hours, a few times a month, to sample that week's *Zeitgeist*. In a similar manner, teaching offers me a form of human contact which I find deeply satisfying yet less draining than most other social engagements. Listening to students' problems, inciting them to read Plato or Colette, the heatedness and fun of class discussions—that's one of the most nourishing and inspiring things I know. And the sheer boredom of most other traditional social contacts, the literary party circuit in the Hamptons or the Vineyard for instance, could lead me to the loony bin in the space of a weekend. The vapid tiddlywinks conversation, and the tedium of the endless cocktail hours! Cocktails is one American custom I continue to find loathsome; I can't abide dining with anyone who'll make me wait more than twenty-five minutes for dinner. There's a lot of the pedant in me; my idea of a good time is to sit under a tree with some close friends over a picnic of bread and cheese and wine and talk about Ficino's influence on Titian's concept of love, or chew over some new insights into William James. Now that's the *greatest* fun. So teaching is something born into me which I love deeply, and it's the form of fraternizing which I find least draining, most inspiring and nourishing. ———*Francine du Plessix Gray*

I don't think writers are comfortable in each other's presence. We can talk, of course, for five minutes or so, but I don't think we want to socialize. There's always an acute status consciousness relating to how high or low a writer exists in the opinion of the person he's talking to. I've noticed that the opening gambit in conversation between two writers—and I'm always very uncomfortable hearing it—is, "I like your work." I've heard it so often. It's so condescending. What if the person had not done any work?: he would not be spoken to at all. This sort of relationship is peculiar to writers—after all, our status is never challenged by anyone else, one's jeweler, or a dress-manufacturer. No, I don't think two novelists who have enjoyed a high measure of success can exist into their middle years living close to each other if both continue writing—I don't believe human nature can accept such a situation. ———*Joseph Heller*

I don't believe there is an ideal occupation for the writer. He could write under almost any circumstance, even in complete isolation. Why, look at Balzac: locked up in a secret room in Paris, hiding from his creditors, and producing the *Comédie Humaine*. Or think of Proust in his cork-lined room (although of course he had plenty of visitors). I suppose the best occupation is just meeting a great many different kinds of people and seeing what interests them. That's one of the disadvantages of getting older; you're inclined to make intimate contacts with fewer people. ———*Aldous Huxley*

The Collège was an enterprise dedicated to nihilism and irony, which in my view corresponded to Zen. Its chief occupation was to devise commissions, whose job it was to create subcommissions, which in turn did nothing. There was one commission which was preparing a thesis on the history of latrines from the beginning of civilization to our time. The members were students of Dr. Faustrol, who was an invented character and the prophet of Alfred Jarry. So the purpose of the Collège was the demolition of culture, even of Surrealism, which they considered too organized. But make no mistake, these people were graduates of the École Normale Supérieure and highly cultured. Their method was based on puns and practical jokes—*le canular*. There is a great tradition of puns in Anglo-Saxon literature— Shakespeare, *Alice in Wonderland*—but not in French. So they adopted it. They believed that the science of sciences is the *pataphysique* and its dogma, *le canular*. The Collège was organized with great precision: there was a hierarchy, grades, a pastiche of Freemasonry. Anybody could join, and the first grade was that of *Auditeur Amphitéote*. After that, you became a *Regent*, and finally a *Satrap*. The satrap was entitled to be addressed as *Votre Transcendence*, and when you left his presence you had to walk backwards. Our principal activity was to write pamphlets and to make absurd statements, such as "Jean Paulhan does not exist!" Our meetings took place in a little café-restaurant in the Latin Quarter, and we discussed nothing, because we believed— and I still do—that there is no reason for anything, that everything is meaningless. Our God was Alfred Jarry, and, apart from our meet- ings, we made pilgrimages to his grave near Paris. As you know, Jarry had written *Ubu Roi*, which was a parody of *Macbeth*. Much later I wrote a play based on *Macbeth* too. Anyway, the Collège gave dec- orations, the most important of which was *La Gidouille*, which was a large turd to be pinned on your lapel. At the premiere of *The Bald Soprano*, twenty to thirty of them turned up wearing their *gidouilles* on their lapels. The audience was shocked at the sight of so many big turds, and thought they were members of a secret cult.

• • •

Literary salons don't exist any longer in Paris, but in those days there were two. The first was the salon of Madame Dézenas—a rich lady who liked literature and the arts. All sorts of celebrities came there: Stravinsky, Etiemble, young Michel Butor, Henri Michaux. . . .

The second salon was La Vicomtesse de Noailles's. I went there once and met Jean-Louis Barrault. I remember how a ripple of excitement, a *frisson,* ran through the gathering when Aragon and Elsa Triolet were announced. "Here come the Communists!" they all said. Aragon was in a dinner jacket and Elsa was covered in jewelry. But *I* went there to drink whiskey and to meet friends, not out of worldliness.

—*Eugène Ionesco*

I'm somewhat withdrawn from what you call "the contemporary literary community," for two reasons: in the first place, I don't write for a living, and so don't have to keep in touch with literary editors and publishers and television people in order to earn money; and in the second, I don't live in London. Given that, my relations with it are quite amicable.

. . .

I've never been to America, nor to anywhere else, for that matter. Does that sound very snubbing? It isn't meant to. I suppose I'm pretty unadventurous by nature, partly that isn't the way I earn my living— reading and lecturing and taking classes and so on. I should hate it.

And of course I'm so deaf now that I shouldn't dare. Someone would say, What about Ashbery, and I'd say, I'd prefer strawberry, that kind of thing. I suppose everyone has his own dream of America. A writer once said to me, If you ever go to America, go either to the East Coast or the West Coast: the rest is a desert full of bigots. That's what I think I'd like: where if you help a girl trim the Christmas tree you're regarded as engaged, and her brothers start oiling their shotguns if you don't call on the minister. A version of pastoral.

—*Philip Larkin*

From any point of view, the decade of the twenties was a terrible decade: it was self-indulgent, it was fat, it was rich, it was full of the most loathsome kinds of open and flagrant money-making. All the worst aspects of the French came out as the franc dropped. And yet that decade in Paris was perfect. I suppose it was the right period for *us*. Because of the war, I was a lot older than I should have been to do what I was doing—trying to learn an art. But I was trying to do it alone, which is the best way to try to do it, and I was living in a city where you could *be* alone without ever being lonely, and I had Ada with me. She—I don't need to tell *you*—was a singer. A lovely singer with a beautiful, clear, high voice, and a superb musician. She was going great guns singing new songs for Stravinsky and Poulenc and Copland. So we were right in the middle of the most exciting period in almost a century of music. Also, the people who drifted along—Ernest, Dos, Scott, Gerald Murphy, above all, the Murphys—were people of extraordinary interest who were also—or became, most of them—close friends. I can see why this still interests *me*—I love to go back to it in my mind—but why anybody else forty, fifty, sixty years younger should be interested in it, I just don't understand. I can only answer for myself—what *I* saw and heard. Everyone was aware, I think, that work was being produced in Paris which was magnificent by any standard. This was true of all the arts—the arts generally—the arts as practiced by artists of many nationalities: French, Spanish, Russian, Irish, German, Greek, Austrian. We knew we belonged to a great, a greatly creative, generation—that we lived in a generative time. Everything seemed possible—*was* possible. To be young in a time like that was incredible luck—to be young and in Paris. That much is certain: the witnesses are innumerable. But when you narrow the circle to the American the answers are not so easy. American letters at the turn of the century had reached something which looked to my generation like rock bottom, and the achievements of Eliot and Pound during and after the First World War, though they had raised our hearts, had not wholly persuaded us that *we* belonged in this great resurgence of all the arts which was evident in Paris—this world resurgence of great art. So our excitement, real enough, was a little hesitant, a little tentative. Hemingway's *In Our Time* was the first solid American proof to appear on the Seine—proof that a master of English prose had established himself and that this master was indubitably American, American not only by blood but by eye and ear. But *In Our Time* was a collection of short stories. Would there be a great novel? A great *American* novel? We didn't know in Paris in the twenties. We only knew anything was possible.

I met Hemingway a year or so after we got to Paris and Gerald Murphy about the same time . . . Dos, Estlin Cummings, Bishop, Scott . . . but there was no "community" in the sense in which you, I think, are using the word. No Americans-in-Paris community. That notion is a myth concocted after the event by critics with fish to fry. There was the literary-tourist world of the Dôme and the Rotonde but no work came out of that. The real "community" was, of course, Paris—the Paris of Valéry and Fargue and Larbaud—the world center of art which had drawn Picasso from abroad, and Juan Gris and Stravinsky and all the rest of that great international generation including, first and foremost, Joyce. The world center of poetry which held Alexis Léger down at the Quai d'Orsay in his anonymity as St.-J. Perse. That community—real community—drew and sustained the young Americans who lived in Paris in those years, but they didn't belong to it nor did they communicate with it, except to watch and wonder like the rest of the world. I knew Fargue and Larbaud, and Jules Romains through Adrienne Monnier. Alexis Léger became a close friend many years afterward, when all this was gone and Paris was a Nazi slum. I knew Joyce and marveled at him. But I was not part of *that* Paris nor were any Americans I knew, with the possible exceptions of Tom Eliot and Ezra Pound, who sometimes appeared. In a touching letter toward the end of his life, Scott speaks of "the last American season" in Paris. If there ever was an "American season" in Paris in the twenties, Paris was not aware of it. Nor, I think, was anyone else.

—*Archibald MacLeish*

Mine has been a happy marriage—thanks mainly to my wife. Who would want to live with a novelist? A man underfoot in the house all day? A man, moreover, subject to solitary funks and strange elations. If I were a woman, I'd prefer a traveling salesman. There is no secret, or rather the secrets are buried in platitudes. That is to say, it has something to do with love, commitment and family. As to the institution, it is something like Churchill's description of democracy: vicissitudinous yes, but look at the alternatives.

· · ·

Novelists don't talk much about each other. Maybe this is because novelists secrete a certain B.O. which only other novelists detect, like certain buzzards who emit a repellent pheromone detectable only by other buzzards, which is to say that only a novelist can know how neurotic, devious, underhanded a novelist can be.

—*Walker Percy*

I recently heard the critic George Steiner, on English television, denouncing contemporary Western literature as utterly worthless and without quality, and claiming that the great documents of the human soul, the masterpieces, could only arise from souls being crushed by regimes like those in Czechoslovakia. I wonder then why all the writers I know in Czechoslovakia loathe the regime and passionately wish that it would disappear from the face of the earth. Don't they understand, as Steiner does, that this is their chance to be great? Sometimes one or two writers with colossal brute strength do manage, miraculously, to survive and, taking the system as their subject, to make art of a very high order out of their persecution. But most of them who remain sealed up inside totalitarian states are, as writers, destroyed by the system. That system doesn't make masterpieces; it makes coronaries, ulcers, and asthma, it makes alcoholics, it makes depressives, it makes bitterness and desperation and insanity. The writers are intellectually disfigured, spiritually demoralized, physically sickened, and culturally bored. Frequently they are silenced completely. Nine-tenths of the best of them will never do their best work just because of the system. The writers nourished by this system are the party hacks. When such a system prevails for two or three generations, relentlessly grinding away at a community of writers for twenty, thirty, or forty years, the obsessions become fixed, the language grows stale, the readership slowly dies out from starvation, and the existence of a national literature of originality, variety, vibrancy (which is very different from the brute survival of a single powerful voice) is nearly impossible. A literature that has the misfortune of remaining isolated underground for too long will inevitably become provincial, backwards, even naïve, despite the fund of dark experience that may inspire it. By contrast, our work here hasn't been deprived of authenticity because as writers we haven't been stomped on by a totalitarian government. I don't know of any Western writer, aside from George Steiner, who is so grandiosely and sentimentally deluded about human suffering—and "masterpieces"—that he's come back from behind the Iron Curtain thinking himself devalued because he hasn't had to contend with such a wretched intellectual and literary environment.   —*Philip Roth*

I don't like writers. I don't like seeing writers. I'm not good at it. It upsets me. It's been too hard a struggle. I'm very competitive, and that side comes out. I'm uncomfortable with writers. I love painters and sculptors.   —*May Sarton*

When I lived in Poland, I used to hang out at the writers' club. I'd be there every day. But there is nothing quite like that in America. I know practically no other writers. Once in a while I meet some writers at a cocktail party, and I like them: they are very fine people. But somehow it never goes beyond a superficial meeting. I am sorry about this. I would like to be friendly with more writers.

                                            —*Isaac Bashevis Singer*

I don't know that those marriages work out well ... whether it's two literary people or two movie actors, maybe even two school superintendents. My husband, Max, is not a literary person. If he were a terribly literary person who wanted to look at everything I wrote, I might not be able to stomach it. I cannot stomach it even when my editor shows tendencies in that direction. There are examples. Virginia Woolf had a literary husband and they worked together in the Hogarth Press. But then you have someone like Scott Fitzgerald and Zelda where there was such competition. So it's worked out for me. Max reads an occasional novel, but mostly ones that I say, "Hey, you're going to miss something if you don't read this." He reads books about schoolwork, about farming, investments. I think maybe if he had a different wife, he might never have bought anything but a practical book.

—Jessamyn West

I think it [being single] made it possible for me to practice my profession as a writer. You know what happened to poor Norman Mailer. One wife after another, and all that alimony. I've been spared all that. I give people money, yes. But I couldn't have afforded alimony, not to all those wives. I would've had to behead them!

—Tennessee Williams

Ethel has always been wonderful in that way. You've got to be alone quite a bit when you're writing. She doesn't mind that at all. I've always had great luck with the things that really matter in life. I should imagine an unhappy marriage would simply kill a man.

—P. G. Wodehouse

ON SECURITY:
GRANTS, PRIZES,
HONORS, ETC.

Anythin' for the quiet life, as the man said wen he took the sitivia-
tion at the lighthouse.   —*Charles Dickens*

The Nobel is a ticket to one's own funeral. No one has ever done
anything after he got it.   —*T. S. Eliot, on winning it*

One of the things which makes me happier today is that I will
never be a Nobel Prize candidate again.
                   —*Gabriel García Márquez, on winning the Nobel Prize*

There's no money in poetry, but then there's no poetry in money.
                                                      —*Robert Graves*

I know at last what distinguishes man from animals: financial
worry.   —*Jules Renard*

A writer who takes political, social, or literary positions must act
only with the means that are his. These means are the writer's
words.   —*Jean-Paul Sartre,
                                                  on refusing the Nobel Prize*

I turned down the National Institute of Arts and Letters when I
was elected to it in 1976 on the grounds that I was already in the
Diner's Club.   —*Gore Vidal*

I don't expect you'll hear me writing any poems to the greater
glory of Ronald and Nancy Reagan.
                  —*Robert Penn Warren, on being named poet laureate*

I would love to be the poet laureate of Coney Island.
                                                   —*Thornton Wilder*

ON SECURITY

We lived on top of a mountain peak [in Brazil]—really way up in the air. I was alone in the house with Maria, the cook. A friend had gone to market. The telephone rang. It was a newsman from the American Embassy and he asked me who it was in English and of course it was very rare to hear someone speak in English. He said, "Do you know you've won the Pulitzer Prize?" Well, I thought it was a joke. I said, "Oh, come on." And he said, "Don't you hear me?" The telephone connection was very bad and he was shrieking. And I said, "Oh, it can't be." But he said it wasn't a joke. I couldn't make an impression on Maria with this news, but I felt I had to share it, so I hurried down the mountain a half-mile or so to the next house but no one was at home. I thought I should do something to celebrate, have a glass of wine or something. But all I could find in that house, a friend's, were some cookies from America, some awful chocolate cookies—Oreos, I think—so I ended up eating two of those. And that's how I celebrated winning the Pulitzer Prize.

The next day there was a picture in the afternoon paper—they take such things very seriously in Brazil—and the day after that my Brazilian friend went to market again. There was a big covered market with stalls for every kind of comestible, and there was one vegetable man we always went to. He said, "Wasn't that Doña Elizabetchy's picture in the paper yesterday?" She said, "Yes, it was. She won a prize." And he said, "You know, it's amazing! Last week Señora (Somebody) took a chance on a bicycle and *she* won! My customers are so lucky!"   —*Elizabeth Bishop*

I don't think artists can compete—except as to money and prizes, and, of course, status. Which may be temporary. But not on the page. Or the canvas or the stone. Or the musical score. All you can hope to be is worthy of the company you respect.   —*Hortense Calisher*

My dear sir, in the Belle Epoque space-writers were paid one sou a line in the papers and an Apollinaire had to wait months and years before he could sign his articles and count on steady employment with regular pay. That was why he published pornography, to earn his bread. You can't imagine how solidly closed all doors were to us. I have the impression that today you're much better received, I run into young writers everywhere, on the papers, the radio, in the picture studios. Before 1914 those who wanted a job stood in line at the door, or at an employment window that never opened. The others contented themselves with playing the buffoon, the wild bull, in the streets. To hell with a job and a decent living. We laughed. The Paris girls were pretty.

—*Blaise Cendrars*

The writer doesn't need economic freedom. All he needs is a pencil and some paper. I've never known anything good in writing to come from having accepted any free gift of money. The good writer never applies to a foundation. He's too busy writing something. If he isn't first rate he fools himself by saying he hasn't got time or economic freedom. Good art can come out of thieves, bootleggers, or horse swipes. People really are afraid to find out just how much hardship and poverty they can stand. They are afraid to find out how tough they are. Nothing can destroy the good writer. The only thing that can alter the good writer is death. Good ones don't have time to bother with success or getting rich. Success is feminine and like a woman; if you cringe before her, she will override you. So the way to treat her is to show her the back of your hand. Then maybe she will do the crawling.

—*William Faulkner*

I'm reminded of Eugenio Montale's great piece on the encouragement of poetry, particularly by the state—National Endowments and things like that. He was very skeptical about the utility of encouraging poetry on a grand scale. Is encouragement what a poet needs? Open question. Maybe he needs *dis*couragement. In fact, quite a few of them need more discouragement, the most discouragement possible.

—*Robert Fitzgerald*

Well, I almost think that if I'd gotten the Nobel Prize when *The Recognitions* was published I wouldn't have been terribly surprised. I mean that's the grand intoxication of youth, or what's a heaven for. And so the book's reception was a sobering experience, quite a humbling one. When finally help did come along, recognition as you say, a Rockefeller Foundation grant, a Guggenheim Fellowship, the National Endowment for the Arts, they came in difficult times and allowed and encouraged me to keep on with the second book and start the third. Without them, I wonder if I might not just have dropped the whole damned business, though God knows what else I might have done, too late even to be any of the things I never wanted to be. There's always the talk about feeding at the public trough, disdaining grants because you've never been given one. I mean we'd all wish to come out with the fierce integrity of Samuel Butler, say, who never wrote simply to publish or published everything he wrote—*The Way of All Flesh* was posthumous after all—and that has been the luxury of the MacArthur. But then I never was a fellow to rush into print.   —*William Gaddis*

Well, I'm not a Buddha in the sense of I can sit under a tree for a thousand years. Who can? The climate doesn't allow for it, anyway. So we need money. We need money for houses and for comfort. To relax.   —*David Ignatow*

I was brought up to think you had to have a job, and write in your spare time, like Trollope. Then, when you started earning enough money by writing, you phase the job out. But in fact I was over fifty before I could have "lived by my writing"—and then only because I had edited a big anthology—and by that time you think, Well, I might as well get my pension, since I've gone so far.

•   •   •

Poetry and sovereignty are very primitive things. I like to think of their being united in this way, in England. On the other hand, it's not clear what the Laureate is, or does. Deliberately so, in a way: it isn't a job, there are no duties, no salary, and yet it isn't quite an honor, either, or not just an honor. I'm sure the worst thing about it, especially today, is the publicity it brings, the pressure to be involved publicly with poetry, which must be pretty inimical to any real writing.

Of course, the days when Tennyson would publish a sonnet telling Gladstone what to do about foreign policy are over. It's funny that Kipling, who is what most people think of as a poet as national spokesman, never was Laureate. He should have had it when Bridges was appointed, but it's typical that he didn't—the post isn't thought of in that way. It really is a genuine attempt to honor someone. But the publicity having anything to do with the Palace is so fierce these days, it must be really more of an ordeal than an honor.

—*Philip Larkin*

I have never written anything in order to make money. A story comes to me, is given me, as it were, and I write it. But perhaps the need to earn a living and my need to write coincided. I know that I would still write if tomorrow I was given a huge legacy, and I will always be profligate.

—*Edna O'Brien*

Now, that's something I can't understand about America. It's a big, generous country, but so many students of mine seemed to think they couldn't let anyone else support them. A student of mine had this thing about you mustn't live on your father and I argued with him. I explained that a European writer would live on anybody, would live on a prostitute if he had to—it didn't matter—the great thing was to get the job done. But he didn't believe in this, so he rang up his father and told him he'd had a story refused by *The New Yorker*, and his father said, "I can keep you for the next forty years, don't you think you can get a story in *The New Yorker* in forty years?" Now, I felt the father was a man I understood and sympathized with, a decent man. But the boy felt he mustn't be supported by his father, so he came down to New York and started selling office furniture.

—*Frank O'Connor*

Being in a garret doesn't do you any good unless you're some sort of a Keats. The people who lived and wrote well in the twenties were comfortable and easy-living. They were able to find stories and novels, and good ones, in conflicts that came out of two million dollars a year, not a garret. As for me, I'd like to have money. And I'd like to be a good writer. These two can come together, and I hope they will, but if that's too adorable, I'd rather have money. I hate almost all rich people, but I think I'd be darling at it. At the moment, however, I like to think of Maurice Baring's remark: "If you would know what the Lord God thinks of money, you have only to look at those to whom he gives it." I realize that's not much help when the wolf comes scratching at the door, but it's a comfort.

• • •

The art of the country so immeasurably adds to its prestige that if you want the country to have writers and artists—persons who live precariously in our country—the state must help. I do not think that any kind of artist thrives under charity, by which I mean one person or organization giving him money. Here and there, this and that—that's no good. The difference between the state giving and the individual patron is that one is charity and the other isn't. Charity is murder and you know it. But I do think that if the government supports its artists, they need have no feeling of gratitude—the meanest and most sniveling attribute in the world—or baskets being brought to them, or apple-polishing. Working for the state—for Christ's sake, are you grateful to your employers? Let the state see what its artists are trying to do—like France with the Académie Française. The artists are a part of their country and their country should recognize this, so both it and the artists can take pride in their efforts.   —*Dorothy Parker*

Even Saint Teresa said, "I can pray better when I'm comfortable," and she refused to wear her haircloth shirt or starve herself. I don't think living in cellars and starving is any better for an artist than it is for anybody else; the only thing is that sometimes the artist has to take it, because it is the only possible way of salvation, if you'll forgive that old-fashioned word. So I took it rather instinctively. I was inexperienced in the world, and likewise I hadn't been trained to do anything, you know, so I took all kinds of laborious jobs. But, you know, I think I could probably have written better if I'd been a little more comfortable.   —*Katherine Anne Porter*

Recently, the first American novelist to receive a special Congressional Gold Medal for his "contribution to the nation" was Louis L'Amour. It was presented to him at the White House by the President. The only other country in the world where such a writer would receive his government's highest award is the Soviet Union. In a totalitarian state, however, *all* culture is dictated by the regime; fortunately we in America live in Reagan's and not Plato's Republic, and aside from their stupid medal, culture is almost entirely ignored. And that is preferable by far. As long as those on top keep giving the honors to Louis L'Amour and couldn't care less about anything else, everything will be just fine.   —*Philip Roth*

I should from the beginning tell you quite bluntly—if I can say it in English—that the Nobel Prize is an accident, no more than an accident. It's not an appointment. And I have no feeling that I have been appointed to any sort of function. It is just an accident which one has to try and forget as soon as possible. Otherwise, if you are overdazzled by that sort of thing, you get lost and founder. At the time I won the prize, there was a sort of—how can I put it in English?—a sort of Cassandra-like critic who wrote that Seferis should be very careful because he's going to be completely dried up as far as his work is concerned and even die from various illnesses since that sort of thing happens to people who have that kind of success. He was just exaggerating the one side of it, without considering, after all, what showed in the way I reacted to the prize. For example, I said in Stockholm to my judges (or whatever they are): "Gentlemen,

ON SECURITY

I thank you"—this at the end of a sort of lecture I gave there—
"for allowing me, after a long effort, to be *nobody,* to be unnoticed,
as Homer says of Ulysses." And I was quite sincere. After all, I don't
recognize the right of anybody to take you by the back of your neck
and throw you into a sort of ocean of empty responsibilities. Why,
that's scandalous after all.   —*George Seferis*

When I started out, in the early 1930s, there were a great many
magazines that published short stories. And writers of fiction, when
they begin, are more likely to try the short form. At that time there
was a great market for it, greater interest in the short story, and the
young writer had a chance to practice his craft, to get criticism and
meet with editors. Since that time, unfortunately, the short-story
market has dwindled to almost nothing, and that form of expression
has become almost obsolete for all writers in America except those
who are willing to publish in small magazines or those writers who
have enough of a reputation that they can use the limited space in
two or three magazines throughout the country. However, from the
point of view of finances, getting started as a writer has become more
feasible. Although the number of newspapers has dwindled—and that
used to be a field where a lot of beginning writers could serve their
apprenticeship—there are many other forms that are lucrative. The
chief one is television, which devours huge amounts of the written
word, as does advertising and industry. The demand for quality in
the writing in magazines like *Time*, *Newsweek*, et cetera, is attractive
to bright young people of talent, and the proliferation of special-
interests magazines offers a multitude of opportunities for financial
security. However, those are dangerous places for writers to start in
with, because the money is good and the writing quickly falls into a
routine and people who had started out as serious are very likely to
find themselves in a financial as well as an artistic bind, since working
in those mediums is an all-day, all-week job. And they are liable to
find themselves artistically exhausted when they want to work on
something of their own. On the other hand, in my experience I've

found that if you're young enough, *any* kind of writing you do for a short period of time—up to two years, perhaps—is a marvelous apprenticeship. I told my son, who wanted to be a writer, that his newspaper experience—he was lucky enough to get four years of newspaper experience under demanding editors on the U.P.I. and *The Washington Post*—could only help him. But you must avoid giving hostages to fortune, like getting an expensive wife, an expensive house, and a style of living that never lets you afford the time to take the chance to write what you wish. So that, while writers in general can make a living much more easily than when I first started in the 1930s, the serious writer who doesn't want to compromise at all finds it much more difficult. Still, we're fortunate enough. The other day I got a contract from a magazine in Budapest. To reprint a short story of mine they agreed to pay me fifty dollars, out of which there would be deducted a thirty percent tax, a ten percent agent's fee, and furthermore I was required to send at my own expense two books to some bureaucratic organization of the Hungarian government. You can imagine how well writers are doing in Budapest.

—*Irwin Shaw*

The Dutch have kindly elected me to their Academy, the Erasmus Institute for the Arts and Letters. Unlike its French counterpart it includes a substantial prize, half of which one has to donate to a charity. I gave mine to the World Wildlife Organization. They protested at first, saying that the Institute was for the promotion of the Arts and Letters, not lions and birds! But I said that I would have to refuse the prize unless I could make my gift, and they accepted. How sincere are the Green and Ecology parties, and how much of it is political posturing, I simply do not know. But something has to be done before it is too late. It is almost too late already, with the acid rain destroying Europe's forests and the defoliation of the tropical forests in South America. —*Marguerite Yourcenar*

ON READINGS:
SEMINARS,
CONFERENCES, ETC.

It's a sad fact about our culture that a poet can earn much more
money writing or talking about his art than he can by practicing it.
> —*W. H. Auden*

"The time has come," the Walrus said,
"To talk of many things:"
> —*Lewis Carroll*

The Wedding-Guest sat on a stone:
He cannot choose but hear.
> —*Samuel Taylor Coleridge*

I'm not very fond of poetry readings. I'd much rather read the book.
I know I'm wrong. I've only been to a few poetry readings I could
bear. Of course, you're too young to have gone through the Dylan
Thomas craze. . . .

When it was somebody like Cal Lowell or Marianne Moore, it's
as if they were my children. I'd get terribly upset. I went to hear
Marianne several times and finally I just couldn't go because I'd sit
there with tears running down my face. I don't know, it's sort of
embarrassing. You're so afraid they'll do something wrong.

Cal thought that the most important thing about readings was the
remarks poets made in between the poems. The first time I heard
him read was years ago at the New School for Social Research in a
small, grey auditorium. It was with Allen Tate and Louise Bogan. Cal
was very much younger than anybody else and had published just
two books. He read a long, endless poem—I've forgotten its title*—

---

*"Mother Marie Therese" in *The Mills of the Kavanaughs.*

about a Canadian nun in New Brunswick. I've forgotten what the point of the poem is, but it's very, very long and it's quite beautiful, particularly in the beginning. Well, he started, and he read very badly. He kind of droned and everybody was trying to get it. He had gotten about two-thirds of the way through when somebody yelled, "Fire!" There was a small fire in the lobby, nothing much, that was put out in about five minutes and everybody went back to their seats. Poor Cal said, "I think I'd better begin over again," so he read the whole thing all over again! But his reading got much, much better in later years. —*Elizabeth Bishop*

It sure killed off poor Dylan Thomas. He didn't write even *one* poem in the last six years of his life. Everybody adored him, paid him a lot of money; why should he write another book of *poems,* and maybe give the critics a shot at him that would lower his reading fee? Everybody *loved* him; he was screwing all the coeds in America, drinking all the whiskey, and he'd get up there and read his poems, and then he'd go on and read them somewhere else. He got a lot of dough for it. I mean, what incentive for him to write *was* there? To survive, a poet has to find some way of maintaining his original enthusiasm for *poetry,* not for the by-products of poetry, not for the fringe benefits of poetry, but for *it.* —*James Dickey*

I do remember saying once that maybe the greatest female novelist in English was Constance Garnett. Sometimes I try to lighten the gloom of discussions but I notice that no one laughs. Instead you see a few people writing down the name. —*Elizabeth Hardwick*

I don't give readings, no, although I have recorded three of my collections, just to show how *I* should read them. Hearing a poem, as opposed to reading it on the page, means you miss so much—the shape, the punctuation, the italics, even knowing how far you are from the end. Reading it on the page means you can go your own pace, taking it in properly; hearing it means you're dragged along at the speaker's own rate, missing things, not taking it in, confusing "there" and "their" and things like that. And the speaker may interpose his own personality between you and the poem, for better or worse. For that matter, so may the audience. I don't like hearing things in public, even music. In fact, I think poetry readings grew up on a false analogy with music: the text is the "score" that doesn't "come to life" until it's "performed." It's false because people can read words, whereas they can't read music. When you write a poem, you put everything into it that's needed: the reader should "hear" it just as clearly as if you were in the room saying it to him. And of course this fashion for poetry readings has led to a kind of poetry that you *can* understand first go: easy rhythms, easy emotions, easy syntax. I don't think it stands up on the page.   —*Philip Larkin*

Eliot told someone that when he gave a poetry reading he always felt it was a kind of indecent exposure.   —*James Laughlin*

Oh, Germany last year, my God! That was the most disastrous trip. It was at some academic institution in Germany. I said to them, "Look, I want to do what I always do. I'll read the story and then I'll take questions." They said, the way they always do, "Oh, you can't expect the Germans to ask questions." I said, "Look, just let me handle this, because I know how." Anyway, what happened was typical in Germany: we met at four o'clock in order to discuss the meeting that was going to take place at eight. They cannot stand any ambiguity or disorder—no, no! Can't bear it. I said, "Look, just leave it." The auditorium was very large and I read a story in English and it went down very well, perfectly okay. I said, "I will now take questions." Then this bank of four bloody professors started to put questions to me, these immensely long academic questions of such tedium that finally the audience started to get up and drift out. A young man, a student sprawled on the gangway—as a professor finished something immensely long—called out, "BLAH, BLAH, BLAH, BLAH, BLAH." So with total lack of concern for the professors' feelings I said, "Look, I will take questions in English from the audience." So they all came back and sat down, and it went well . . . perfectly lively questions! The professors were absolutely furious. So that was Germany. Germany's the worst, it really is; the end.   —*Doris Lessing*

During the French program at Mount Holyoke one afternoon Wallace Stevens had a discourse, the one about Goethe dancing, on a packet-boat in black wool stockings. My mother and I were there; and I gave a reading with commentary. Henry Church had an astoundingly beautiful Panama hat—a sort of pork-pie with a wide brim, a little like Bernard Berenson's hats. I have never seen as fine a weave, and he had a pepper-and-salt shawl which he draped about himself. This lecture was on the lawn.

Wallace Stevens was extremely friendly. We should have had a tape recorder on that occasion, for at lunch they seated us all at a kind of refectory table and a girl kept asking him questions such as, "Mr. Stevens have you read the—*Four*—*Quartets?*"

"Of course, but I can't read much of Eliot or I wouldn't have any individuality of my own."   —*Marianne Moore*

I remember that Federico García Lorca was always asking me to read my lines, my poetry, and yet in the middle of my reading, he would say, "Stop, stop! Don't go on, lest you influence me!"
                                                                                                      —*Pablo Neruda*

One day the head of Administration House asked me if I would give a talk to the Indians. And I said, "How could I talk to them, these ancient people? It is they who could tell me things." He said, "Try." So they came into what I suppose was a clubhouse, a big place with a stage, and I stood on the stage and the place was full of Indians. I told them about England, because she was at war then, and all that was happening. I said that for me England was the place "Where the Sun Rises" because, you see, England is east of where I was. I said, "Over large water." And I told them about the children who were being evacuated from the cities and some of the experiences of the children. I put it as mythologically as I could, just very simple sayings.

At the end there was dead silence. I turned to the man who had introduced me and said, "I'm sorry. I failed. I haven't got across." And he said, "You wait. You don't know them as well as I do." And every Indian in that big hall came up and took me silently by the hand, one after another. That was their way of expressing feeling with me. —*P. L. Travers*

It was at the Guggenheim. I was staying at the Chelsea Hotel, and that day I felt I needed a haircut, so, foolishly, I went around the corner and sat down. The barber took the electric razor and gave me one of the wildest haircuts I think I've ever had. It infuriated me, but you can't put your hair back on. I even thought of wearing a hat. But I went on anyway, my head looked like hell. I had gotten some distance into the reading—I was reading "A Far Cry from Africa"—when suddenly there was the sound of applause from the auditorium. Now I had never heard applause at a poetry reading before. I don't think I'd ever given a formal poetry reading, and I thought for some reason that the applause was saying it was time to stop, that they thought it was over. So I walked off the stage. I felt in a state of shock. I actually walked off feeling the clapping was their way of saying, "Well, thank you, it's been nice." Someone in charge asked me to go back and finish the reading, but I said no. I must have sounded extremely arrogant, but I felt that if I went back out there it would have been conceited. I went back to Trinidad.

—*Derek Walcott*

Every now and then there are certain people to whom I show poems, and who show poems to me: Bill Meredith, Bill Smith, John Brinnin, and Cal Lowell, when he's around—we aren't in the same place at present. But that's just one-on-one. The last time I found myself involved in anything groupy was about seven years ago when Stephen Spender was staying at Wesleyan and certain people on the Wesleyan faculty were interested in reading poems to each other. Stephen, with his usual generosity—of course this wasn't part of any deal he'd signed on to do—joined the group. I suppose there were five or six meetings. We'd go around in a circle and everybody would read at least one poem.

One evening Stephen invited I. A. Richards to come, and Richards had not understood the character of the invitation. He hadn't realized he was going to have to listen to a lot of people read poems, one after the other, and then discuss them. And as soon as that became clear, he did the most glorious thing. He simply stood up and said, "Oh no, no, no. I'm sorry, no, I'm sorry, I can't. Good night! Good night!" and out he went. He didn't have any evidence that any particular, horrible poem was going to be read, but he thought the chances were pretty good and he didn't see why, at his age, he had to sit and listen to it.   —*Richard Wilbur*

ON POLITICS

King Louis Philippe once said to me that he attributed the great success of the British nation in political life to their talking politics after dinner. —*Benjamin Disraeli*

Nothing is more dangerous to the state than persons who try to govern kingdoms according to maxims drawn from books.
—*Richelieu*

For a country to have a great writer is like having a second government. That is why no regime has ever loved great writers, only minor writers. —*Alexander Solzhenitsyn*

If you ask me what I have come to do in the world, I who am an artist, I will reply: "I am here to live aloud." —*Émile Zola*

I have had very little contact with [politicians]. I knew some undergraduates, of course, while I was at Oxford, who eventually made it—Hugh Gaitskell, Crossman, and so forth. I think we should do very well without politicians. Our leaders should be elected by lot. The people could vote their conscience, and the computers could take care of the rest. Writers seldom make good leaders. They're self-employed, for one thing, and they have very little contact with their customers. It's very easy for a writer to be unrealistic. I have not lost my interest in politics, but I have come to realise that, in cases of social or political injustice, only two things are effective: political action and straight journalistic reportage of the facts. The arts can do nothing. The social and political history of Europe would be what it has been if Dante, Shakespeare, Michelangelo, Mozart, et al., had never lived. A poet, *qua* poet, has only one political duty, namely, in his own writing to set an example of the correct use of his mother tongue which is always being corrupted. When words lose their meaning, physical force takes over. By all means, let a poet, if he wants to, write what is now called an *"engagé"* poem, so long as he realizes that it is mainly himself who will benefit from it. It will enhance his literary reputation among those who feel the same as he does. —*W. H. Auden*

I don't think that as a group we'd be any better at running the world than the people who are botching it up. Poetry makes nothing happen. Politically committed artists like Gabriel García Márquez give honest voice to their political passion at no great cost to the quality control of their art. But do they really change the world? I doubt it, I doubt it, Abraham Lincoln's remark to Harriet Beecher Stowe notwithstanding: "So you're the little woman who wrote the book that made this great war!" Well, she didn't. No: without sounding too terribly decadent about it, I much prefer the late Vladimir Nabokov's remark about what he wanted from his novels: "aesthetic bliss." Well, that *does* sound too decadent. Let me change masters for a moment and say that I prefer Henry James' remark that the first obligation of the writer—which I would also regard as his last obligation—is to be interesting, *to be interesting.* To be interesting in one beautiful sentence after another. To be interesting, not to change the world.
—*John Barth*

Hemingway was never deeply committed, so he thinks that what is eternal in literature is what isn't dated, isn't committed. I don't agree. In the case of many writers, it's also their political stand which makes me like or dislike them. There aren't many writers of former times whose work was really committed. And although one reads Rousseau's *Social Contract* as eagerly as one reads his *Confessions,* one no longer reads *The New Héloïse.* —*Simone de Beauvoir*

ON POLITICS

A poet is only a professional sensibility. His opinion in politics is no better than anyone else's ninety-nine percent of the time. But they're always being interviewed and always being asked their political opinion: what should we do with the military, what should we do with the economy, with government spending, et cetera. Poets don't know anything about that. If they did, they wouldn't be poets. This is not to say that they are precluded from knowing anything about it at *all;* it is to say, however, that just because they are poets their opinions should not be paid any more attention to than anybody else's. It does not give them any privilege or any insight or any clairvoyance as to the political and economic and military future of America.

• • •

Poetry *can* speak on topical things eloquently. Look at Yeats on the riots of 1916, for example. But we should not be led into the corner of assuming that poetry is no good which does not speak on news items. If a man wants to write about the circle that's made in the water when a fish jumps, he should be able to write about that and should not be charged off as irrelevant because he's not writing about the Vietnam riots. You should have the whole gamut: political action, the jump of the fish, or the space program. You should have anything you want. —*James Dickey*

Recently, I've been calling my novels contemporary chronicles, which seems to fit them rather better. They have a strong political bent because after all—although it isn't the only thing—politics in our time has pushed people around more than anything else. I don't see why dealing with politics should harm a writer at all. Despite what he said about politics in the novel being "the pistol shot at the opera," Stendhal also wrote contemporary chronicles. Or look at Thucydides. I don't think his history was at all damaged by the fact that he was a political writer. A lot of very good writing has been more or less involved in politics, although it's always a dangerous territory. It's better for some people to keep out unless they're willing to learn how to observe. It is the occupation of a special kind of writer. His investigation—using blocks of raw experience—must be balanced. Sartre in his straight, plain reporting was wonderful. I can't read him now. A writer in this field should be both engaged and disengaged. He must have passion and concern and anger—but he must keep his emotions at arm's length in his work. If he doesn't, he's simply a propagandist and what he offers is a "preachment."

—*John Dos Passos*

We have to do more things in our culture than American writers do in theirs. They can have more time for themselves and for their writing, whereas we have social demands. Pablo Neruda used to say that every Latin American writer goes around dragging a heavy body, the body of his people, of his past, of his national history. We have to assimilate the enormous weight of our past so we will not forget what gives us life. If you forget your past, you die. You fulfill certain functions for the collectivity because they are obligations you have as a citizen, not as a writer. Despite that, you reserve your esthetic freedom and your esthetic privileges. This creates a tension, but I think it is better to have the tension than to have no tension at all, as sometimes happens in the United States.   —*Carlos Fuentes*

Everyone has his own conscience, and there should be no rules about how a conscience should function. All you can be sure about in a political-minded writer is that if his work should last you will have to skip the politics when you read it. Many of the so-called politically enlisted writers change their politics frequently. This is very exciting to them and to their political-literary reviews. Sometimes they even have to rewrite their viewpoints . . . and in a hurry. Perhaps it can be respected as a form of the pursuit of happiness.

—*Ernest Hemingway*

What I would never advise [young poets] to do is to begin with political poetry. Political poetry is more profoundly emotional than any other—at least as much as love poetry—and cannot be forced because it then becomes vulgar and unacceptable. It is necessary first to pass through all other poetry in order to become a political poet. The political poet must also be prepared to accept the censure which is thrown at him—betraying poetry, or betraying literature. Then, too, political poetry has to arm itself with such content and substance and intellectual and emotional richness that it is able to scorn everything else. This is rarely achieved.　　　　　　*—Pablo Neruda*

I don't like people who try to express world views in writing poetry. I remember once I had a reading in Thessalonik, and a philosopher stood up and asked: "But what, after all, Mr. Seferis, is your world view?" And I said: "My dear friend, I'm sorry to say that I have no world view. I have to make this public confession to you that I am writing without having any world view. I don't know, perhaps you find that scandalous, sir, but may I ask you to tell me what Homer's world view is?" And I didn't get an answer.　　　　*—George Seferis*

Always at the beginning of a war there is a demand from editors that poets should write war poetry. This comes from a recognition that, in a situation in which patriotic feelings are required, poetry may stimulate those feelings. I imagine the sonnets of Rupert Brooke at the beginning of the First World War probably did make some people join up to fight the Germans. During the Spanish Civil War, the poetry that was written probably helped the International Brigade. Then in a much wider sense poetry can be politically effective as well. Surely one can trace the sources of the movement for Italian unity to the fact that Dante decided to write *The Divine Comedy* in idiomatic Italian and not in Latin, which would have been the correct thing for him to have done. And Goethe, who created, really all by himself, modern German literature, also contributed greatly to the idea of German unity through doing this. He created a German culture and taught Germans that they could respect themselves in relation to France, especially, and other countries.

But I think it is wrong to believe that poetry is really very effective in politics. And politics can certainly be very bad for poetry. I was discussing this with Denise Levertov when she was here. She read a political poem, which was based on her visiting Hanoi and being taken 'round by the North Vietnamese to see damage done to hospitals by American aircraft. Of course she had extremely strong feelings about this, and I don't want to call it just a propaganda operation on the part of the North Vietnamese, but somehow to enter almost as a tourist into that kind of suffering and to make propaganda out of it is not what a poet should be doing. For a journalist it's all right, but a poet has to go in for an act of the imagination, which is on a deeper level. I mean, if you penetrate to the depths of the suffering, you see that it is not just inflicted by one side; it's something that human beings do to one another. Also if you write what one has to call propaganda poetry, you lay yourself open to a kind of argument which is all right in politics but which oughtn't to occur in poetry. Someone will say, "Well, if the North Vietnamese had had airplanes, they'd have done the same thing," which you can't really dispute. I don't think that poets ought to get themselves into that kind of argument.

There are, of course, political situations so absolutely unspeakable that they become quite literally unimaginable. It would be impertinent, for example, to imagine what was happening in the concentration camps during the 1930s and 1940s. The only way to know that suffering was to be a part of it, but if you became a part of it, you were destroyed. As a matter of fact, at the end of the concentration camp era, when various poets, particularly in Poland, emerged from the camps, they hated poetry. They regarded poetry as the greatest betrayal because it always in some way offers pleasure. It would therefore have to extract some kind of comfort, something pleasurable, from all these horrors. And so they started writing what they called anti-poetry. —*Stephen Spender*

It seems to me that only a great satirist can tackle the world problems and articulate them. Most writers write simply out of some strong interior need, and that I think is the answer. A great writer, writing out of this need, will give substance to and perhaps even explain all the problems of the world without even knowing it, until a scholar comes along a hundred years after he's dead and digs up some symbols. The purpose of a young writer is to write, and he shouldn't think too much. He shouldn't think that after he's written one book he's God Almighty and air all his immature opinions in pompous interviews. —*William Styron*

ON TEACHING:
ADVICE, WRITING
COURSES, ETC.

You shouldn't pay very much attention to anything writers say.
They don't know why they do what they do. They're like good
tennis players or good painters, who are just full of nonsense,
pompous and embarrassing, or merely mistaken, when they open
their mouths.   —*John Barth*

The wise may be instructed by a fool.   —*Rabelais*

Everyone who does not *need* to be a writer, who thinks he can do
something else, ought to do something else.   —*Georges Simenon*

Agassiz *does* recommend authors to eat fish, because the phosphorus
in it makes brains. But I cannot help you to a decision about the
amount you need to eat. Perhaps a couple of whales would be
enough.   —*Mark Twain*

I try to avoid the well-known cliché that you learn from your students.
Neither do I believe that there's something ennobling for a writer to
teach, that it's narcissistic to spend time wallowing in your writing
when you could be out helping in the world's work. Writers should
write, and poets especially spend altogether too much time at other
tasks such as teaching. However, since so many of us have to do it,
there are certain things to be said for it. You are forced to bring a
critical attention into play when you are reading students' work that
you would not use otherwise, and that can help when you return to
your own writing. And being immersed in a group of young unproven
writers who are fiercely serious about what they are doing can have
a chastening effect sometimes on us blasé oldsters. Besides, they may
be writing great poetry, only nobody knows it because nobody has

ON TEACHING

seen it yet. I sometimes think that the "greatness" my friends and I used to see in each other's poetry when we were very young had a lot to do with the fact that it was unknown. It could turn out to be anything; the possibilities were limitless, more so than when we were at last discovered and identified and pinned down in our books.

—*John Ashbery*

If I had to "teach poetry," which, thank God, I don't, I would concentrate on prosody, rhetoric, philology, and learning poems by heart. I may be quite wrong, but I don't see what can be learned except purely technical things—what a sonnet is, something about prosody. If you did have a poetic academy, the subjects should be quite different—natural history, history, theology, all kinds of other things. When I've been at colleges, I've always insisted on giving ordinary academic courses—on the 18th Century, or Romanticism. True, it's wonderful what the colleges have done as patrons of the artists. But the artists should agree not to have anything to do with contemporary literature. If they take academic positions, they should do academic work, and the further they get away from the kind of thing that directly affects what they're writing, the better. They should teach the 18th Century, or something that won't interfere with their work and yet earn them a living. To teach Creative Writing—I think that's dangerous. The only possibility I can conceive of is an apprentice system like those they had in the Renaissance—where a poet who was very busy got students to finish his poems for him. Then you'd *really* be teaching, and you'd be responsible, of course, since the results would go out under the poet's name. —*W. H. Auden*

If you are going to be a writer there is nothing I can say to stop you; if you're not going to be a writer nothing I can say will help you. What you really need at the beginning is somebody to let you know that the effort is real. —*James Baldwin*

A lifetime's experience urges me to utter a warning cry: do anything else, take someone's golden retriever for a walk, run away with a saxophone player. Perhaps what's wrong with being a writer is that one can't even say "good luck"—luck plays no part in the writing of a novel. No happy accidents as with the paint pot or chisel. I don't think you can say anything, really. I've always wanted to juggle and ride a unicycle, but I dare say if I ever asked the advice of an acrobat he would say, "All you do is get on and start pedaling. . . ."   —*J. G. Ballard*

I happen to think there's some justification for having courses in so-called creative writing. I know from happy experience with young writers that the muses make no distinction between undergraduates and graduate students. The muses know only expert writers and less expert writers. A beginner—such as I was when, with the swamp still on my shoes, I came into Johns Hopkins as an undergraduate— needs to be taught that literature is there; here are some examples of it, and here's how the great writers do it. That's teaching. In time, a writer, or any artist, stops making mistakes on a crude, first level, and begins making mistakes on the next, more elevated level. And then finally you begin to make your mistakes on the highest level— let's say the upper slopes of slippery Parnassus—and it's at that point you need coaching. Now sometimes coaching means advising the skier to come down off the advanced slope and back to the bunny hill for a while, back to the snowplow. One must be gentle about it. To shift metaphors violently, one must understand that the house of fiction has many windows; you don't want to defenestrate your young apprentices. But sometimes such a simple thing as suggesting to a student that perhaps realism instead of fantasy may be a more sympathetic genre, or humor instead of the opposite, or the novel rather than the short story—sometimes a simple suggestion like that can be the one that makes things click. It doesn't always.

. . .

As an undergraduate I had a couple of tutors in writing who were not themselves writers. They were simply good coaches. I've thought of that in a chastened way since. Dealing with my own students, many of whom are very skillful, advanced apprentice writers, I often wonder whether it's a good idea for them to have, at the other end of the table, somebody who's already working at a certain level of success and notoriety. Is that not perhaps intimidating? I just don't know, but I suspect the trade-off is fair enough. I might have learned some things faster had I been working with an established writer rather than a very sympathetic coach.

—*John Barth*

I've just read an article that strongly implies that teaching writing is a dismal racket, an impoverishing fraud, and maybe it is as practiced in some venues, but I'd hate this to be taken as generally true. At City College, where I teach a graduate workshop, the writing students are fully the equals in seriousness and accomplishment of the other graduate students. Maybe writing can't be taught, but editing *can* be taught—prayer, fasting and self-mutilation. Notions of the lousy can be taught. Ethics.

All of this is new in universities, didn't exist when I was in school, but it's hardly a racket. —*Donald Barthelme*

It depends on the kind of teaching you do. If you teach creative writing, you get absolutely nothing out of it. Or English—what are you teaching? People you read twenty years ago. Maybe you pick up a little if you keep on preparing, but very few people keep on preparing. Everybody is lazy, and poets, in addition to being lazy, have another activity which is very demanding, so they tend to slight their teaching. But I give courses in the history of civilization, and when I first began teaching here I nearly went crazy. I was teaching Christian origins and the Middle Ages, and I had certain weak spots. I was O.K. with *The Divine Comedy* and certain other things, but I had an awful time of it. I worked it out once, and it took me nine hours to prepare a fifty-minute lecture. I have learned much more from giving these lecture courses than I ever learned at Columbia or Cambridge. It has forced me out into areas where I wouldn't otherwise have been, and since I am a scholar, these things are connected. I make myself acquainted with the scholarship. Suppose I'm lecturing on Augustine. My Latin is very rusty, but I'll pay a certain amount of attention to the Latin text in the Loeb edition, with the English across the page. Then I'll visit the library and consult five or six old and recent works on St. Augustine, who is a particular interest of mine, anyway. Now all that becomes part of your equipment for poetry, even for lyric poetry. The Bradstreet poem is a very learned poem. There is a lot of theology in it, there is a lot of theology in *The Dream Songs*. Anything is useful to a poet. Take observation of nature, of which I have absolutely none. It makes possible a world of moral observation for Frost, or Hopkins. So scholarship and teaching are directly useful to my activity as a writer.   —*John Berryman*

If I had to give a young writer some advice I would say to write about something that has happened to him; it's always easy to tell whether a writer is writing about something that has happened to him or something he has read or been told. Pablo Neruda has a line in a poem that says "God help me from inventing when I sing." It always amuses me that the biggest praise for my work comes for the imagination while the truth is that there's not a single line in all my work that does not have a basis in reality. The problem is that Caribbean reality resembles the wildest imagination.

—*Gabriel García Márquez*

When you teach creative writing, you discover a great deal. For instance, if a student's story is really wonderful, but thin, you have to analyze to figure out why it's thin; how you could beef it up. Every discovery of that kind is important. When you're reading only classical and medieval literature, all the bad stuff has been filtered out. There are no bad works in either Greek or Anglo-Saxon. Even the ones that are minor are the very best of the minor, because everything else has been lost or burned or thrown away. When you read this kind of literature, you never really learn how a piece can go wrong, but when you teach creative writing, you see a thousand ways that a piece can go wrong. So it's helpful to me. The other thing that's helpful when you're teaching creative writing is that there are an awful lot of people who at the age of seventeen or eighteen can write as well as you do. That's a frightening discovery. So you ask yourself, what am I doing? Here I've decided that what I'm going to be in life is to be this literary artist, at best; I'm going to stand with Tolstóy, Melville and all the boys. And there's this kid, nineteen, who's writing just as well. The characters are vividly perceived, the rhythm in the story is wonderful. What have I got that he hasn't got? You begin to think harder and harder about what makes great fiction. That can lead you to straining and over-blowing your own fiction, which I've done sometimes, but it's useful to think about.

• • •

I hate nihilistic, cynical writing. I hate it. It bothers me and worse yet bores me. But if I have a student who writes with morbid delight about murder, what I'll have to do (though of course I'll tell him I don't like this kind of writing, that it's immoral, stupid and bad for civilization), is say what is successful about the work and what is not. I have to swallow every bit of my moral feelings to help the writer write his way, his truth. It may be that the most moral writing of all is writing which shows us how a murderer feels, how it happens. It may be it will protect us from murderers someday.

• • •

Working with intelligent undergraduate and graduate students— and working alongside intelligent teachers—I have a clear idea of my audience, or anyway of a hypothetical audience. I don't think a writer can write well without some such notions. One may claim one writes for oneself, but it's a paltry claim. One more word on all this, I'm obviously convinced that my scholarly career has made me a better writer than I would have been without it, but I'm no longer concerned—as I was in my tempestuous, ego-maddened youth— with proving myself the greatest writer of all time. What I notice now is that all around me there are first-rate writers, and in nearly every case it seems to me that what makes them first-rate is their similar involvement in teaching and scholarship. There are exceptions—maybe William Gaddis, I'm not sure. (A brilliant writer, though I disapprove of him.) Perhaps the most important exception is John Updike, who, unlike John Hawkes, Bill Gass, Stanley Elkin and Saul Bellow and so on, is not a teacher. But the exception means nothing, because, teacher or not, he's the most academic of all.

—*John Gardner*

I resent spending a lot of time on lousy stuff. If somebody is reading a bad paper in a seminar, it is nevertheless on Plato, and it is Plato we can talk about. Whereas if somebody is writing about their hunting trip—well—where can one go for salvation or relief? Creative-writing teachers, poor souls, must immerse themselves in slop and even take it seriously. Since I can't bear it, resent it, I shouldn't teach it. It is probably impossible to teach anyone to be a good writer. You can teach people how to read, possibly.

I am also aware of how little I can tolerate other people telling me how to write. So why should I do it to my students? I do not invite or accept this sort of personal criticism. I usually have poor to absent relations with editors because they have a habit of desiring changes and I resist changes. So why should I tell students to make changes? I also remember how bad I was. I wrote far worse stuff than I see from students. What can I fairly say to them?

—*William Gass*

Teaching writing is draining too, of course. Especially the way I do it. You see, I believe that everybody can write. And in believing and teaching this, what happens, of course, is enormous productivity on the part of many students. One's students produce so much that he is followed down the street by the mass of stuff he's encouraged! I mean, he's overtaken by it. And there's that much more work to do and more conferences to hold, and it's a depleting and exhausting thing. Just as exhausting as editing. —*William Goyen*

Let's say that he [an apprentice] should go out and hang himself because he finds that writing well is impossibly difficult. Then he should be cut down without mercy and forced by his own self to write as well as he can for the rest of his life. At least he will have the story of the hanging to commence with. —*Ernest Hemingway*

There's long been argument among writers about whether they should let themselves be captured by the academic world, whether they don't stultify there, and so on. I have always had the view that it really doesn't matter what a writer does; the argument that you should go out and meet raw life, work on the crew of a freighter, take part in revolutions and what not, doesn't seem to me valid. What matters is how a writer responds to the life around him. When I arrived in Pierson that first term, I had thought of the university [Yale] as an ivory tower, and had been afraid that if I was incarcerated there I would stagnate. But in the very first term we had every human manifestation that I could think of except for murder. And we almost had that, from time to time. We did have violent death, and suicide, and rape, and everything in degrees up to those traumas. So the life is around you wherever you are, whatever you do, and it's a matter of how keenly and sensitively you respond to what's happening.
—*John Hersey*

You can teach the *writing* of verse—like prose, an instrument—and the *recognition* of true poetry. The rest, writers must teach themselves. Before there were any creative writing courses, people set their own exercises. Look at Keats' or Blake's juvenilia, for example—exercises in verse forms, in order to discover their own private relationships with form, scheme and mythology. Now that self-help has been discouraged by the culture as a whole, I try to teach writers how to teach themselves. But not workshops—wasn't it Kingsley Amis who said that most of the terrible things that had happened to the world since 1945 had come out of a workshop?   —*John Hollander*

I was not necessarily "taught" anything there [Iowa Writers Workshop] as a student, although I was certainly encouraged and helped— and the advice of Vance Bourjaily, Kurt Vonnegut, and José Donoso clearly saved me some valuable time; that is, they told me things about my writing and about writing in general that I would probably have figured out for myself, but time is precious for a young writer. I always say that this is what I can "teach" a young writer: something he'll know for himself in a little while longer; but why wait to know these things? I am talking about technical things, the only things you can presume to teach, anyway.   —*John Irving*

Most of the desultory courses that I've taken in literature have had a peculiar snobbism about them. An adulation of certain writers is inculcated in the student by the instructor (who is probably a frustrated writer anyway), to the point where the student finds himself asking whether he has anything to say that Tolstoy or James hasn't already said better. Moreover, most of the instruction seems to be concerned with writings rather than with how to write, which is impossible to teach anyway.   —*James Jones*

In Puerto Rico, where he was teaching, I met Saul Bellow over a period of a semester. It was very important. I took his criticism very seriously and he was very helpful. He would explain to me that my writing was "fatty." I was saying everything twice and I had too many adjectives. He said it was also occasionally "clotty"—a kind of imprecision that he was talking about, an effort to use a word that wasn't quite precise enough and so just screwed up the clause or sentence. When he would point that out to me, I would go back through the whole book and slash—it turned me into a real fiction editor of my own copy, and it later helped when *I* became a teacher. If I was that ruthless with my own stuff, why shouldn't I be with everybody else's? Bellow also talked about being prodigal. He said that a writer shouldn't be parsimonious with his work, but "prodigal, like nature." He said, just think of nature and how many billions of sperm are used when only one is needed for creating life. And that principle was, it seemed, at the heart of *Augie March*. I mean, he just exploded with language and ideas. I never became that kind of writer, exactly, but I think the effusion, the principle, was important, and I was never afraid of writing too much or thinking that just because you've written a sentence it means something or that it's a good sentence just because you've written it. —*William Kennedy*

The academic world has worked all right for me, but then, I'm not a teacher. I couldn't be. I should think that chewing over other people's work, writing I mean, must be terribly stultifying. Quite sickens you with the whole business of literature. But then, I haven't got that kind of mind, conceptual or ratiocinative or whatever it is. It would be death to me to have to think about literature as such, to say why one poem was "better" than another, and so on.

—*Philip Larkin*

Steer clear of the writing departments of universities. Steer clear of English. Learn foreign, preferably dead languages, but learn them properly. Do not be a wastrel, don't just hang about the world. Poetry is about life. The quality of your poetry will be the quality of your life. And you can't regulate that by a knob. Read. Get or get near a very good library. Take more notice of Randall Jarrell than you do of any academic critic. Don't spend time attacking other writers. Dig to the bottom of your mind, and don't give two damns about publications.

Writing is like breathing or it ought to be. One's got to write poems. Like one has to go to church. Not out of social duty, or because there's any pressure on one to do so. Not even out of reaction to people who say one shouldn't do so. But just because of some decent, natural good behavior. One might as well go on with it.

—*Peter Levi*

[John Berryman] liked me a lot personally, and he worked very hard with me. He seemed to feel I had something genuine, but that I wasn't doing enough with it, wasn't demanding enough from my work. He kept directing me to poetry that would raise my standards. He knew an enormous body of poetry, and he wanted me to open myself to it. He was very sure of himself, very confident, and I think I caught some of that confidence and some of the confidence he had in me. Another very nice thing: when the semester ended, he said to me, "I'll let you send me some poems, four or five poems. I'll read them and comment on them and send them back. And that'll be that." So about a year and a half later I sent him four poems. He made his comments, and once again he let me know this was the last time. He was right, absolutely right. Out of the nest, into the world.

• • • •

By not going to Paris to study at the foot of Gertrude Stein or going to Harvard to study with Harry Levin or Walter Jackson Bate or Archibald MacLeish, I stayed at home and studied with my equals, people of my own age, which may have been right for me. I was better off with my equals. What was I going to write about Gertrude Stein?

I met a woman once who lived in a house here in New York with Emma Goldman, with whom she was in tutelage. I asked her what Emma was like. She said, "Well, first thing, she never taught me anything because she didn't like women, so she never really talked to me." I said, "She didn't like women?" She said, "No, she didn't think women were serious." She said, "My main remembrance of her was that in the morning she had a little glass bell; when she awakened she rang it. And we would bring her breakfast up to her." I thought, my God, this great freedom fighter for anarchism and the rights of

women and workers and everything else! Isn't it marvelous. Who
would have guessed?   —*Philip Levine*

I'd wanted to be a football player very much, and got my letter but
didn't make the team. Well, that was satisfying but crushing too. I
read a good deal, but had never written. So this was a recoil from
that. Then I had some luck in that Richard Eberhart was teaching
there.

He was a young man about thirty. I never had him in class, but
I used to go to him. He'd read aloud and we'd talk, he was very
pleasant that way. He'd smoke honey-scented tobacco, and read Bau-
delaire and Shakespeare and Hopkins—it made the thing living—
and he'd read his own poems. I wrote very badly at first, but he was
encouraging and enthusiastic. That probably was decisive, that there
was someone there whom I admired who was engaged in writing
poetry.

· · ·

Almost all the poets of my generation, all the best ones, teach. I
only know one, Elizabeth Bishop, who doesn't. They do it for a
livelihood, but they also do it because you can't write poetry all the
time. They do it to extend themselves, and I think it's undoubtedly
been a gain to them. Now the question is whether something else
might be more of a gain. Certainly the danger of teaching is that it's
much too close to what you're doing—close and not close. You can
get expert at teaching and be crude in practice. The revision, the
consciousness that tinkers with the poem—that has something to do
with teaching and criticism. But the impulse that starts a poem and
makes it of any importance is distinct from teaching.

I think you have to tear it apart from that. Teaching may make
the poetry even more different, less academic than it would be otherwise.

· · ·

I'm sure that writing isn't a craft, that is, something for which you
learn the skills and go on turning out. It must come from some deep

impulse, deep inspiration. That can't be taught, it can't be what you use in teaching. And you may go further afield looking for that than you would if you didn't teach. I don't know, really; the teaching probably makes you more cautious, more self-conscious, makes you write less. It may make you bolder when you do write.

—*Robert Lowell*

Take chances. "Dare to do," Eudora Welty says. She's right. One drags around a bag of fears he has to throw to the winds every so often if he expects to take off in his writing. I'm glad Virginia Woolf did *Orlando,* though it isn't my favorite of her books, and in essence she was avoiding a subject. Still, you don't have to tell everything you know. I like Updike's *Centaur,* Bellow's *Henderson.* Genius, after it has got itself together, may give out with a *Ulysses* or *Remembrance of Things Past.* One doesn't have to imitate the devices of Joyce or Proust, but if you're not a genius imitate the daring. If you are a genius assert yourself, in art and humanity.   —*Bernard Malamud*

I expect you can be taught to write a clean, decent sentence.

—*William Maxwell*

My method of teaching precluded genuine contact with my students. At best, they regurgitated a few bits of my brain during examinations. Every lecture I delivered had been carefully, lovingly handwritten and typed out, and I leisurely read it out in class, sometimes stopping to rewrite a sentence and sometimes repeating a paragraph—a mnemonic prod, which, however, seldom provoked any change in the rhythm of wrists taking it down. I welcomed the few shorthand experts in my audience, hoping they would communicate the information they stored to their less fortunate comrades. Vainly I tried to replace my appearances at the lectern by taped records to be played over the college radio. On the other hand, I deeply enjoyed the chuckle of appreciation in this or that warm spot of the lecture hall at this or that point of my lecture. My best reward comes from those

former students of mine who ten or fifteen years later write to me
to say that they now understand what I wanted of them when I
taught them to visualize Emma Bovary's mistranslated hairdo or the
arrangement of rooms in the Samsa household of the two homosexuals
in *Anna Karenina*. I do not know if I learned anything from teaching
but I know I amassed an invaluable amount of exciting information
in analyzing a dozen novels for my students. My salary as you happen
to know was not exactly a princely one.

• • •

A first-rate college library with a comfortable campus around it is
a fine milieu for a writer. There is of course the problem of fellow
readers. I remember how once, between terms, not at Cornell, a
student brought a transistor set with him into the reading room. He
managed to state that 1) he was playing "classical" music; that 2) he
was doing it "softly"; and that 3) "there were not many readers
around in summer." I was there, a one-man multitude.

—*Vladimir Nabokov*

I was taking a course with Lionel Trilling and wrote a paper for him
with an opening sentence that contained a parenthesis. He returned
the paper with a wounding reprimand: "Never, never begin an essay
with a parenthesis in the first sentence." Ever since then, I've made
a point of starting out with a parenthesis in the first sentence. Years
later, Trilling was cordial and very kind to me, and I felt redeemed,
though it took two decades to earn his approval.

• • •

When I've taught those classes, I always say, "Forget about 'Write
about what you know.' Write about what you don't know." The
point is that the self is limiting. The self—subjectivity—is narrow
and bound to be repetitive. We are, after all, a species. When you
write about what you don't know, this means you begin to think
about the world at large. You begin to think beyond the home-
thoughts. You enter dream and imagination.   —*Cynthia Ozick*

I went to London because I thought Yeats knew more about poetry than anybody else. I made my life in London by going to see Ford in the afternoons and Yeats in the evenings. By mentioning one to the other one could always start a discussion. That was the exercise. I went to study with Yeats and found that Ford disagreed with him. So then I kept on disagreeing with *them* for twenty years.

—*Ezra Pound*

He [Robert Lowell] was formal in a rather awkward New England sense. His voice was soft and slow as he read the students' poems. At first I felt the impatient desire to interrupt his slow, line by line readings. He would read the first line, stop, and then discuss it at length. I wanted to go through the whole poem quickly and then go back. I couldn't see any merit in dragging through it until you almost hated the damned thing, even your own poems, especially your own. At that point, I wrote to Snodgrass about my impatience, and his reply went this way, "Frankly, I used to nod my head at his every statement, and he taught me more than a whole gang of scholars could." So I kept my mouth shut, and Snodgrass was right. Robert Lowell's method of teaching is intuitive and open. After he had read a student's poem, he would read another evoked by it. Comparison was often painful. He worked with a cold chisel, with no more mercy than a dentist. He got out the decay, but if he was never kind to the poem, he was kind to the poet.   —*Anne Sexton*

I've never encouraged *anybody* to do that [to adopt writing as a way of life]. I think it's not only presumptuous, it's dangerous. When I first started teaching, I encouraged a few students in a couple of cases. But you can change the whole course of their career—a terrible responsibility. I wouldn't do it now. But if I ran across a talented student, I'd encourage him or her as much as I could. I used to try to direct those writing students to a job or a profession. I had a student at Davis who was very good, who said to me one day, "I'm going to go to the Academy of the Merchant Marine and be a ship's captain." I said, "Gee, that's wonderful! That'll be terrific for your poetry." Well, he went and he's still a captain of a ship somewhere. I haven't seen any more poetry from him. That still may be better than hanging around the academy all one's life.   —*Karl Shapiro*

A creative writing class can at least be good for morale. When I teach writing, I do things like take classes to bars and race tracks to listen to dialogue. But that kind of thing has limited usefulness. There's no body of technology to impart. But that doesn't mean classes can't help. The idea that young writers ought to be out slinging hash or covering the fights or whatever is bullshit. There's a point where a class can do a lot of good. You know, you throw the rock and you get the splash.   —*Robert Stone*

This business of taking novels apart in order to show bored children how they were put together—there's a madness to it. Only a literary critic would benefit, and there are never more than ten good critics in the United States at any given moment. So what is the point to these desultory autopsies performed according to that little set of instructions at the end of each text? Have you seen one? What symbols to look for? What does the author mean by the word "white"? I look at the notes appended to my own pieces in anthologies and know despair.   —*Gore Vidal*

In a creative writing class of twenty people anywhere in this country, six students will be startlingly talented. Two of those might actually publish something by and by.

They will have something other than literature itself on their minds. They will probably be hustlers, too. I mean that they won't want to wait passively for somebody to discover them. They will insist on being read.   —*Kurt Vonnegut*

A lady had decided she'd write a novel and got along fine till she came to the love scene. "So," she told my friend, "I thought, there's

William Faulkner, sitting right up there in Oxford. Why not send it to William Faulkner and ask him?" So she sent it to him, and time went by, and she didn't ever hear from him, and so she called him up. Because there he was. She said, "Mr. Faulkner, did you ever get that love scene I sent you?" He said yes, he had got it. And she said, "Well, what did you think of it?" And he said, "Well, honey, it's not the way I'd do it—but you go *right ahead*." Now, wasn't that gentle of him?

—*Eudora Welty*

I never taught creative writing courses. I believe in creative reading. That's what I am trying to teach—creative reading. I'd assign the Scripture and Midrash, Ovid and Kafka, Thomas Mann and Camus, Plato and André Schwarz-Bart. A writer must first know how to read. You can see whether a person is a writer by the way he reads a text, by the way he diciphers a text. I'd also say to a young writer, if you can choose not to write, don't. Nothing is as painful. From the outside, people think it's good; it's easy; it's romantic. Not at all. It's much easier not to write than to write. Except if you are a writer. Then you have no choice.

—*Elie Wiesel*

About the same way golf can be taught. A pro can point out obvious flaws in your swing. I did that well, I think, at the University of Iowa for two years. Gail Godwin and John Irving and Jonathan Penner and Bruce Dobler and John Casey and Jane Casey were all students of mine out there. They've all published wonderful stuff since then. I taught creative writing badly at Harvard—because my marriage was breaking up, and because I was commuting every week to Cambridge from New York. I taught even worse at City College a couple of years ago. I had too many other projects going on at the same time. I don't have the will to teach any more. I only know the theory.

It was stated by Paul Engle—the founder of the Writers Workshop at Iowa. He told me that, if the Workshop ever got a building of its own, these words should be inscribed over the entrance: "Don't take it all so seriously."

. . .

I think the best part of teaching from the point of view of the teacher-writer, writer-teacher, is that it makes you read a good deal and makes you be articulate about what you read. You can't read passively because you have to be prepared to move other people to recognitions and acts of analysis. I know a few writers who don't teach and who, in consequence, do very little reading. This doesn't mean that they are bad writers, but in some cases I think they might be better writers if they read more. As for the experience of the classroom, I enjoy it; I am very depressed by classes which don't work, and rather elated by classes which do. I like to see if I can express myself clearly enough to stick an idea in somebody's head. Of course there are also disadvantages, one of which is that the time one spends teaching could be spent writing. Another involves this very articulateness of which I've been speaking. It uses the same gray cells, pretty much, that writing does, and so one can come to the job of writing with too little of a sense of rediscovery of the language. That is one reason I like to live out here in the country and lead a fairly physical life—play a lot of tennis, raise a lot of vegetables, go on a lot of long walks. I do things which are non-verbal so that I can return to language with excitement and move toward language from kinds of strong awareness for which I haven't instantly found facile words. It is good for a writer to move into words out of the silence, as much as he can.   —*Richard Wilbur*

I think all are unfavorable to the writer. If by day you handle the English language either in the conventional forms which are journalism and advertising, or in the anaylsis which is teaching English in school or college, you will have a double, a quadruple difficulty in finding *your* English language at night and on Sundays. It is proverbial that every newspaper reporter has a half-finished novel in his bureau drawer. Reporting—which can be admirable in itself—is poles apart from shaping concepts into imagined actions and requires a totally different ordering of mind and language. When I had to earn my living for many years, I taught French. I should have taught mathematics. By teaching math or biology or physics, you come refreshed to writing.   —*Thornton Wilder*

ON PEERS: PORTRAITS

Writers seldom wish other writers well.　　　　　—*Saul Bellow*

"Sir," said Mr. Tupman, "you're a fellow." "Sir," said Mr. Pick-
wick, "you're another!"　　　　　　　　　　—*Charles Dickens*

There is no denying the fact that writers should be read but not
seen. Rarely are they a winsome sight.　　　　　—*Edna Ferber*

DJUNA BARNES

We were planning a special hardbound edition of *Nightwood*. Barnes
insisted she had to have paper that would last a thousand years. We
asked the paper dealers, and they said, "No, it's impossible. You can't
unless you go to an Italian or French handmade paper, which would
be exorbitant. We cannot *produce* a paper that we will guarantee for
more than five hundred years." So we finally printed the book on
Curtis Rag, which the manufacturer guaranteed for five hundred years,
but Djuna was never happy about it.　　　　　—*James Laughlin*

BRENDAN BEHAN

Behan always wore his shirt open to the navel; he never had shoelaces
and the tongues of his shoes would always hang out. You could see
his bare ankles and the heels of his shoes were always so worn away
that his ankles leaned over and he waddled around. Every year or so
he'd buy himself a new suit, and as soon as he walked into the pub
and someone would say, "Behan, you've got a new suit!" He'd say,

"Oh, you think it's new," and he'd immediately get off the bar stool, walk outside, and roll up and down in the gutter, then he'd come back in. If someone said, "Well, Behan, jeez, you've washed your hair!" he'd take his pint of Guinness and pour it over his head.

—*J. P. Donleavy*

MAXWELL BODENHEIM

He was a fascinating talker, in spite of the stammer, and he knew everybody. He was a great friend of Bill Williams. You must have heard the story of his broken arm? He called up Williams at Rutherford and said, "I've broken my arm. Can I come and stay with you till it heals?" Bill said, "Certainly." About a month or two went by and Max did nothing about having the cast examined or changed, so finally Bill insisted on looking at it and discovered that there had never been any broken arm.

—*Conrad Aiken*

LOUIS-FERDINAND CÉLINE

Céline I met. I once went out to see him when he was living in Meudon, an industrial suburb of Paris near the Renault plant. He had a small house, and outside it there was a high barbed-wire fence. He had two very fierce dogs that barked at me when I rang the gate bell. He had to come out and tie up the dogs. This was because Denoël, his publisher, had been murdered on a street in Paris. Denoël had been a collaborator, too. Céline was rather paranoid, but he was friendly to me. I had had contact with his wife, who was a ballet dancer. While they were in exile in Denmark during the war, she couldn't get ballet shoes for her practice. So she used to write to me and I'd go down to Capezio in New York to buy her ballet shoes and air-mail them over to her.

—*James Laughlin*

E. E. CUMMINGS

I was in doubt that I could make something of myself as a writer until I met two people who were very important to me: one was Gaston Lachaise and the other was E. E. Cummings. Cummings I loved, and I love his memory. He did a wonderful imitation of a woodburning locomotive going from Tiflis to Minsk. He could hear a pin falling in soft dirt at the distance of three miles. Do you remember the story of Cummings's death? It was September, hot, and Cummings was cutting kindling in the back of his house in New Hampshire. He was sixty-six or -seven or something like that. Marion, his wife, leaned out the window and asked, "Cummings, isn't it frightfully hot to be chopping wood?" He said, "I'm going to stop now, but I'm going to sharpen the ax before I put it up, dear." Those were the last words he spoke. At his funeral Marianne Moore gave the eulogy. Marion Cummings had enormous eyes. You could make a place in a book with them. She smoked cigarettes as though they were heavy, and she wore a dark dress with a cigarette hole in it. And Lachaise? I'm not sure what to say about him. I thought him an outstanding artist and I found him a contented man. He used to go to the Metropolitan—where he was not represented—and embrace the statues he loved.   —*John Cheever*

T. S. ELIOT

Eliot and I must have met at the end of my freshman year, when I was elected to the *Harvard Advocate.* We saw a great deal of each other, in spite of the fact that we were a year apart, and remained very close.

Of course, at the beginning, on the *Advocate,* we talked chiefly about poetry, or literature in general. But as the friendship, or kinship, developed—for in a way I became his younger brother—it widened to take in everything. And we met on very, very many quite frivolous occasions. Sports, comics, everything. We developed a shorthand language of our own which we fell into for the rest of our lives whenever we met, no holds barred—all a matter of past reference, a common language, but basically *affection,* along with humor, and appreciation of each other's minds, and of Krazy Kat. Faced with England, and the New World, and Freud and all, we always managed to *relax,* and go back to the kidding, and bad punning, and drinking, to the end. It really was marvelous. When he paid his infrequent visits here, we invariably met to get drunk together. There was a splendid occasion when he and I and our wives dined at "The Greeks' " after he'd received a silver bowl from the Signet Society; he was wearing a cowboy hat, and we all got plastered. We went on to the Red Lion Grill, after many drinks at the Silver Dollar Bar, the two toughest and *queerest* joints in Boston. He couldn't walk, for his ankles were crossed, so Valerie *lifted* him into the taxi.   —*Conrad Aiken*

I got to know him earlier, when I was in England in '31–'32. Vachel Lindsay had written to him, and he wrote me at Cambridge to invite me, saying, "Do drop in." You know, at Faber and Faber. I did. I went to see him and we talked about Cambridge, where I was working in philosophy. He was familiar with the people at Cambridge who were then my teachers or lecturers, C. D. Broad and G. E. Moore. This, of course, was a continuing interest in his life. He had, after all, done his dissertation on Bradley. Had he gone on in that direction, he was going to be a philosopher in the philosophy department here at Harvard. I think on the second or third of my visits I had the courage to hand him a poem. He looked at the poem for a long time. Great silence. He studied it, then he looked up and said, "Is this the best you can do?" *Whoo!* Quite a thing to say! I didn't realize then what I realized later—that it was an editor's question: "Shall I publish this or shall I wait until he does something that shows more confidence?" What I thought at the time, and there was also this about it, was that it was fraternal. Just talking to me as one craftsman to another. A compliment, really.   —*Robert Fitzgerald*

Once I was in the Faber offices—the old ones, "24, Russell Square," that magic address!—talking to Charles Monteith, and he said, "Have you ever met Eliot?" I said no, and to my astonishment he stepped out and reappeared with Eliot, who must have been in the next room. We shook hands, and he explained that he was expecting someone to tea and couldn't stay. There was a pause, and he said, "I'm glad to see you in this office." The significance of that was that I wasn't a Faber author—it must have been before 1964, when they published *The Whitsun Weddings*—and I took it as a great compliment. But it was a shattering few minutes: I hardly remember what I thought. I met Auden once at Stephen Spender's house, which was very kind of Spender, and in a sense he was more frightening than Eliot. I remember he said, Do you like living in Hull? and I said, I don't suppose I'm unhappier there than I should be anywhere else. To which he replied, Naughty, naughty. I thought that was very funny.

But this business of meeting famous writers is agonizing: I had a dreadful few minutes with Forster. My fault, not his. Dylan Thomas came to Oxford to speak to a club I belong to, and we had a drink the following morning. He wasn't frightening. In fact, and I know it sounds absurd to say so, but I should say I had more in common with Dylan Thomas than with any other "famous writer," in this sort of context. *—Philip Larkin*

Eliot was a very kind man. In those days I smoked and liked French cigarettes, and people used to give him French cigarettes, which he no longer smoked. So whenever I went to see him he would open a drawer and hand me a whole bunch. That was a big thing in London in the early fifties, and I was touched that he remembered. We used to sit and reminisce about America. There was a side of Eliot that was very homesick for the States, and I was feeling homesick in London, too. We had several wonderful conversations—about the Ohio River and about his family out on the Mississippi in St. Louis and about the riverboats. It's very strange to think of him having any connection with that world. He talked about the *Delta Queen,* that steamboat that went up and down the river until a few years ago. He really wanted to take a trip on that. I wanted to write verse plays in those days, when I was in my early twenties. But, after a while, I came to feel that the plays weren't going very well and that the verse certainly wasn't helping them. As long as I had this fixation about verse plays, I wasn't learning anything about writing plays. I talked to him about that. I said I was thinking of abandoning writing them in verse altogether and trying to write them in prose. "Well," he said, "I've thought of doing that, too, but if I were to write my plays in prose, there are so many other people who could do it better."

—*W. S. Merwin*

I didn't like him a bit. He was a poseur. He was married to this woman who was very pretty. My husband and I were asked to see them, and my husband roamed around the flat and there were endless photographs of T. S. Eliot and bits of his poetry done in embroidery by pious American ladies, and only one picture of his wife, and that was when she was getting married. Henry pointed it out to me and said, "I don't think I like that man."　　　　—*Rebecca West*

WILLIAM FAULKNER

Sometimes, of a Sunday morning, he used to stroll by a house I occupied in Beverly Hills. I noticed him only because the sight of anybody walking in that environment stamped him as an eccentric, and indeed, it eventually got him into trouble. A prowl car picked him up and he had a rather sticky time of it. The police were convinced he was a finger man for some jewelry mob planning to knock over one of the fancy residences.　　　　—*S. J. Perelman*

FORD MADOX FORD

Ford was a character; he was a liar, not for his own profit, but just because he had a very faint hold on actuality. He told beautiful stories of English literary life, in which he knew everybody, had a hand in everything, and his hand grew larger as he told the story. He had a roving eye for younger women, whom he especially liked to fascinate. He came to this country after the breakup of his marriage to Stella Bowen. I can remember on one occasion he came up to Robber Rocks—a place back in the woods near the New York–Connecticut line which was the country headquarters for Allen Tate, Hart Crane, and others—where a lot of young wives were around at the party. They would be fondled by Ford, and then escape him up the stairs. Ford, heavy and wheezing by that time, would follow them to the head of the narrow stairs, and the door would close in his face. He would wheeze back down, and a while later he'd follow another young woman until she took refuge behind a locked door.

—Malcolm Cowley

ROBERT FROST

I don't care much for Robert Frost, and have never been able to understand his reputation. He says a good thing now and then, but with a strange way of averting his eyes while saying it which may be profound and may be poppycock. If it were thought that anything I wrote was influenced by Robert Frost, I would take that particular work of mine, shred it, and flush it down the toilet, hoping not to clog the pipes.

—James Dickey

I met him only two or three times. He had a number of sides to his nature, as we know, including a very black one. He showed me his vain side. I had to give a dinner party for him, and had someone bellow in his ear the names of all the other people and had all their place names written out very large so he could see them at the table. He sat next to E. M. Forster, and asked, "And what magazine do you write for?" He just didn't take these people seriously, and didn't bother to find out who they were.

—Stephen Spender

ALLEN GINSBERG

Allen Ginsberg asked me when he was nineteen years old, should I change my name to Allen Renard? You change your name to Allen Renard I'll kick you right in the balls! Stick to Ginsberg . . . and he did. That's one thing I like about Allen. Allen *Renard!!!*

—*Jack Kerouac*

Yes, I like his "Howl." I love "Howl" and "Kaddish." He [Ginsberg] came to see me in the Soviet Union, and people thought he was mad. He went to Mayakovsky's grave and fell down crying and weeping and praying to him. He is very interesting. I feel he is a type of guru. We had a very good reading together on a ferryboat in New York. I read my poems and he read translations. But I'm very sad that at another reading, somebody I don't know personally said, "Please don't ask Allen to come to the stage, because so-and-so will be upset, they don't approve of him." I was upset and I repeated this to Allen who said, "Oh, Andrei, don't start anything please. I'll be here in the hall, in the auditorium. I'll be happy." But I like to read together with him, because he is a great performer. We read in a church once, for Bangladesh.

—*Andrei Voznesensky*

FRANK HARRIS

I can remember calling on Frank Harris—he was about seventy then—when I was on the Chicago *Tribune*'s edition in Nice. In his house he had three portraits on the wall—Mark Twain, Frank Harris, and I think it was Hawthorne. Harris was in the middle. Harris would point up to them and say, "Those three are the best American writers. The one in the middle is the best." Harris really thought he was wonderful. Once he told me he was going to live to be a hundred. When I asked him what the formula was, he told me it was very simple. He said: "I've bought myself a stomach pump and one half hour after dinner I pump myself out." Can you imagine that? Well, it didn't work. It's a wonder it didn't kill him sooner.

—*James Thurber*

A. E. HOUSMAN

Yes, and later I knew him quite well. He [Housman] told me a very funny story about Clarence Darrow. It seems that Darrow had written him a very laudatory letter, claiming to have saved several clients from the Chair with quotes from Housman's poetry. Shortly afterwards, Housman had a chance to meet Darrow. They had a very nice meeting, and Darrow produced the trial transcripts he had alluded to. "Sure enough," Housman told me, "there were two of my poems—both misquoted!" These are the minor headaches a writer must live with. My pet peeve is people who send for autographs but omit putting in stamps.

—*W. H. Auden*

CHRISTOPHER ISHERWOOD

I met him in the forties in California. At the time he was into Vedanta, an Eastern religious thing. He was living in a monastery. They had periods of silence and meditation, you know. The night I met him, through a letter from Lincoln Kirstein, I arrived during one of these silent periods. The monk who opened the door handed me a pencil and paper to write what my business was and who I'd come to see. I wrote, "Christopher Isherwood," and they regarded me with considerable suspicion from that point on.

In this big room in the monastery, everyone was sitting in . . . what do they call it? The lotus position? Including Christopher. All strictly observing the vow of silence. I didn't dig the scene.

I suddenly made some reference out loud about the Krishna. I didn't know who the hell he was, I was only trying to break the silence. Christopher got up, and wrote on a piece of paper, "I'll call you tomorrow." He was very polite, and he took me to the door.

—*Tennessee Williams*

JAMES JOYCE

An extraordinarily handsome man! He gave the impression of being a great surgeon but not a writer at all. And he was a surgeon, he was not a writer. He used to wear white surgeon's coats all the time and that increased the impression and he had this queer, ax-like face with this enormous jaw, the biggest jaw I have ever seen on a human being. I once did a talk on Joyce in which I mentioned that he had the biggest chin I had ever seen on a human being and T. S. Eliot wrote a letter saying that he had often seen chins as big as that on other Irishmen. Well, I didn't know how to reply to that.

—*Frank O'Connor*

D. H. LAWRENCE

We saw the Lawrences often during those last four years; they stayed with us in Paris, then we were together in Switzerland, and we visited them at the Villa Mirenda near Florence. My wife typed out the manuscript of *Lady Chatterley's Lover* for him, even though she was a bad typist and had no patience with English spelling—she was a Belgian, you know. Then she didn't always appreciate the nuances of the language she was typing. When she started using some of those four-letter words in conversation, Lawrence was profoundly shocked.

—*Aldous Huxley*

SINCLAIR LEWIS

It was in 1930, in Rome. He'd already been widely discussed in Italy, where he was trailing about with a squadron of jolly New York girls who were causing a scandal. One fine day he landed in Rome, where

I was making a movie. He let me know that he urgently wanted to meet me. I asked him to come to the studio, but he answered that he had a cold, he didn't like movies, and anyway he didn't have the time because he was leaving Rome the next morning for Stockholm to collect the Nobel Prize. So I went to his hotel, where I found half a dozen American girls completely drunk, making a gigantic cocktail in a soup tureen full of whipped cream, into which—while quarreling with each other about how much to put in—they were pouring two, three liters of vermouth. I didn't think I could join this scene of madwomen right away—one of them held out some scissors to me and dared me to cut her hair—so I thought I'd take a little stroll. But I changed my mind and decided to search the apartment for the master of the séance whom I hadn't seen yet. The door of the bathroom was half open, and boiling water was coming out. I went in. The bathtub was overflowing and the faucets were wide open. Two feet, dressed in polished dancing pumps, hung out of the tub, and at the bottom a man in a tuxedo was drowning. It was my Sinclair Lewis. I pulled him out of his unfortunate position, and that was how I saved his life so he could take the train the next morning for Stockholm and his prize.

The next day I put him on the train—he didn't even buy me a drink. It's true he had a hangover and probably didn't want to drink, or maybe he'd sworn never to drink again. But a drunk's oaths don't hold, you know.   —*Blaise Cendrars*

ROBERT LOWELL

It's a long story, part of it very funny. Allen Tate had called me from Chicago, and said, "Cal is not himself at all," and that he and Caroline Gordon had just put him on a train! Well, of course I was furious— Allen had no business putting him on a train. But I also knew that Allen had a great dramatic sense and I thought he must be exaggerating. I didn't think it was true when he said that Cal was beside himself, behaved strangely, frightened a child at the station, and that he had picked up Allen and carried him down the platform. True, Allen was very small! Anyhow, Allen said I was to meet Cal with the police at the railroad station! Anyway, as soon as Cal stepped off the train I could see he was out of his head. He wasn't the Lowell I knew. He was dirty and disheveled. So I took him to the faculty club and put him up there instead of taking him home. We had a new baby and I told him the baby was not well. But while we were having dinner in this place he began to sniff, and said, "Do you smell that?" I said no, and he said, "I know what it is, it's brimstone. He's over there behind the fern." I took him to his room, and went to my house. But a few minutes later I was called by the people at the club. They said he had come out of his room and run through the kitchen terrorizing the cooks, and then rushed out into the streets. I spent the early part of the night searching for him, going through the streets calling, "Lowell, Lowell," at the top of my voice. In the meantime he'd gone up to a movie house and stolen a roll of tickets—just reached in and grabbed the tickets and run off down the street! By now the police were looking for him too. We were all running around the town—Bloomington is not a big town!—and finally he knocked on a door that happened to be a policeman's house, and they took him in. For me the most traumatic part of it all was the next morning. I was just beside myself because we had been the closest friends— roommates and all—and I thought it was the end. I never thought he would be sane again. So the next morning I went down there to the jail, and he was in a block of cells, and there was nobody there with him. They let me in and locked the gate, and I went into the cell with him. I was scared to death. Finally I said, "Cal, let's pray," and he said, "Let's get down here and pray together to get out of this place." And I said—because I was scared—"Cal, I never could pray in the same room with anybody." So I went into the next cell, and we got down on our knees and prayed in adjoining cells. But then time went by and they changed guards. The new guard hadn't been told I wasn't also an inmate! I was in there four hours with him. I would call for them to let me out, and Cal would say, "That's not Christian. You call for them to let me out and I'll call for them to let you out!"

—*Peter Taylor*

Lowell and Elizabeth Hardwick were on a tour going to Brazil and they stopped off in Trinidad. I remember meeting them at Queen's Park Hotel and being so flustered that I called Elizabeth Hardwick Edna St. Vincent Millay. She said, "I'm not that old yet." I was just flabbergasted. And then we became very friendly. My wife, Margaret, and I took them up to the beach. Their daughter, Harriet, was there. I remember being up at this beach house with Lowell. His daughter and his wife, I think, must have gone to bed. We had gas lanterns. *Imitations* had just come out and I remember that he showed me his imitations of Hugo and Rilke and asked me what I thought about them. I asked him if two of the stanzas were from Rilke, and he said, "No, these are mine." It was a very flattering and warm feeling to have this fine man with this great reputation really asking me what I thought. He did that with a lot of people, very honestly, humbly, and directly. I cherish that memory a lot. When we went back to New York, Cal and Lizzy had a big party for us with a lot of people there, and we became very close. Cal was a big man in bulk but an extremely gentle, poignant person, and very funny. I don't think any of the biographies have caught the sort of gentle, amused, benign beauty of him when he was calm. He kept a picture of Peter, my son, and Harriet for a long time in his wallet, and he'd take it out and show it to me. He was sweetly impulsive. Once I went to visit him and he said, "Let's call up Allen Ginsberg and ask him to come over." That's so cherishable that it's a very hard thing for me to think of him as not being around. In a way, I can't separate my affection for Lowell from his influence on me. I think of his character and gentleness, the immediacy that was part of knowing him. I loved his openness to receive influences. He was not a poet who said, "I'm an American poet, I'm going to be peculiar, and I'm going to have my own voice which is going to be different from anybody's voice." He was a poet who said, "I'm going to take in everything." He had a kind of multifaceted imagination; he was not embarrassed to admit that he was influenced even in his middle-age by William Carlos Williams, or by François Villon, or by Boris Pasternak, all at the same time. That was wonderful. —*Derek Walcott*

CARSON McCULLERS

I had first known her in this nest that Linscott had up there for these little birdlings of writers. Carson had great vitality and she was quite beautiful in that already decaying way. She was like a fairy. She had the most delicate kind of tinkling, dazzling little way about her . . . like a little star. Like a Christmas, she was like an ornament of a kind. She had no mind and she could make no philosophical statements about anything; she didn't need to. She said far-out, wonderfully mad things, that were totally disarming and for a while people would say, "I'll go wherever you go." She'd knock them straight out the window. She had a devastating crush on Elizabeth Bowen. She actually got to Bowen's Court: she shambled over there to England and spent a fortnight. I heard from Elizabeth that Carson appeared at dinner the first night in her shorts, tennis shorts; that poor body, you know, in tennis shorts and she came down the stairs; that was her debut. It didn't last long. But that was Carson.

—*William Goyen*

SOMERSET MAUGHAM

He couldn't write for toffee, bless his heart. He wrote conventional short stories, much inferior to the work of other people. But they were much better than his plays, which were too frightful. He was an extremely interesting man though, not a bit clever or cold or cynical. I know of many affectionate things he did. He had a great capacity for falling in love with the wrong people. His taste seemed to give way under him so extraordinarily sometimes. He fascinated me by his appearance; he was so neatly made, like a swordstick that fits just so. Occasionally his conversation was beautifully funny and quite unmalicious. I object strongly to pictures of Maugham as if he were a second-rate Hollywood producer in the lavish age. His house was very pleasant and quiet and agreeable.   —*Rebecca West*

We got along on just sort of "how do you do" terms. I remember walking back from a cricket match at Lords in London, and Maugham came along on the other side. He looked at me and I looked at him, and we were thinking the same thing: Oh, my God, shall we have to stop and talk? Fortunately, we didn't.   —*P. G. Wodehouse*

THOMAS MERTON

He was so nice, so jolly. He wasn't a dour monk at all. He was a kind friend and interested in everything. I often went down to visit him at the monastery in Kentucky. The Abbot would give him a day off, and I'd rent a car. Tom would get an old bishop's suit out of the storeroom and start out in that. Then we would stop in the woods and he'd change into his farmworker's blue jeans and a beret to hide his tonsure. Then we'd hit the bars across Kentucky. He loved his beer, and he loved that smoked ham they have down there. He was a wonderful person. He wanted to read contemporary writers, but the books were often confiscated, so we had a secret system. I sent the books he wanted to the monastery psychiatrist in Louisville, who would get them to Merton. I sent him everyone he wanted to read: Sartre and Camus, Rexroth and Pound, Henry Miller and many more. We talked a great deal about the Oriental religions. He was very ecumenical. We talked about his situation and why he stuck it out in the monastery. Once I asked, "Tom, why do you stay here? You could get out and be a tremendous success in the world." He answered that the monastery was where God wanted him to be. He would have been misplaced if he hadn't been so determined to get what he wanted in the monastery—his own hermitage among the hills. He couldn't stand the "social life" in the monastery with all the monks talking sign language, having to go to church six times a day, going to chapter, and making cheese. He finally did persuade the Abbot to build him a hermitage. Tom was a shrewd operator. He got out of sleeping in the communal dormitory by learning how to snore so loudly that the other monks got together at chapter and said, "Father Louis has got to leave the dormitory." So Tom was allowed to use one of the old bishop's rooms. He believed that the old monastic tradition was so strict that it could no longer foster true spirituality.   —*James Laughlin*

EZRA POUND

I went to see him a couple of times, but I was a little uneasy with him. Pound always had some new discovery or enthusiasm; he was always finding the lowdown on something. On one of my visits to his little apartment, he announced loudly, "I've got the lowdown on the Elizabethan drama! It was all cribbed from these books," and he carried out two huge volumes of the Venetian State Papers. Well, it *was* a real discovery: the plots of several Elizabethan plays *did* come out of the Venetian State Papers.   —*Malcolm Cowley*

[I met Pound] through Frank Flint. The early Imagist and translator. He was a friend of Pound and belonged in that little group there. He met me in a book store, said, "American?" And I said, "Yes. How'd you know?" He said, "Shoes." It was the Poetry Book Shop, Harold Monroe's, just being organized. He said, "Poetry?" And I said, "I accept the omen." Then he said, "You should know your fellow-countryman, Ezra Pound." And I said, "I've never heard of him." And I hadn't. I'd been skipping literary magazines—I don't ever read them very much—and the gossip, you know, I never paid much attention to. So he said, "I'm going to tell him you're here." And I had a card from Pound afterwards. I didn't use it for two or three months after that. Just said, "At home, sometimes." Just like Pound. So I didn't feel that that was a very warm invitation. Then one day walking past Church Walk in Kensington, I took his card out and went in to look for him. And I found him there, a little put out that I hadn't come sooner, in his Poundian way. And then he said, "Flint tells me you have a book." And I said, "Well, I ought to have." He said, "You haven't seen it?" And I said, "No." He said, "What do you say we go and get a copy?" He was eager about being the first one to talk. That's one of the best things you can say about Pound: he wanted to be the first to jump. Didn't call people up on the telephone to see how they were going to jump. He was all silent with eagerness. We walked over to my publisher; he got the book. Didn't show it to me—put it in his pocket. We went back to his room. He said, "You don't mind our liking this?" in his British accent, slightly. And I said, "Oh, go ahead and like it." Pretty soon he laughed at something, and I said I knew where that was in the book, what Pound would laugh at. And then pretty soon he said, "You better run along home, I'm going to review it." And I never touched it. I went home without my book and he kept it. I'd barely seen it in his hands.

• • •

He admired at that time, when I first met him, Robinson and de La Mare. He got over admiring de La Mare anyway, and I think he threw out Robinson too. We'd just bring up a couple of little poems. I was around with him quite a little for a few weeks. I was charmed with his ways. He cultivated a certain rudeness to people that he didn't like, just like Willy Whistler. I thought he'd come under the influence of Whistler. They cultivated the French style of boxing. They used to kick you in the teeth. You know the song, the nasty song: "They fight with their feet—" Among other things, what Pound did was show me Bohemia. He'd take me to restaurants and things. Showed me ju jitsu in a restaurant. Threw me over his head. Wasn't ready for him at all. I was just as strong as he was. He said, "I'll show you, I'll show you. Stand up." So I stood up, gave him my hand. He grabbed my wrist, tipped over backwards and threw me over his head. Everybody in the restaurant stood up. He used to talk about himself as a tennis player. I never played tennis with him. And then he'd show you all these places with these people that specialized in poets that dropped their aitches and things like that. Not like the "beatniks," quite. I remember one occasion they had a poet in who had a poem in *The English Review* on Aphrodite, how he met Aphrodite at Leatherhead.* He was coming in and he was a navvy. I don't remember his name, never heard of him again—may have gone on and had books. But he was a real navvy. Came in with his bicycle clips on. Tea party. Everybody horrified in a delighted way, you know. Horror, social horror. Rednecked, thick, heavy-built fellow, strong fellow, you know, like John L. Lewis or somebody. But he was a poet. And then I saw poets made out of whole cloth by Ezra. Ezra thought he did that. Take a fellow that had never written anything and think he could make a poet out of him. We won't go into that.   —*Robert Frost*

I went up to Paris, lived in a tiny room in an insurance office which I rented for seven dollars a month, and after a while, I wrote to Ezra, not expecting a reply, really, just asking if I could come down to Rapallo to see him . . . and to my astonishment he sent me a telegram: "Visibility high." So I went down then to Rapallo. Ezra and I hit it off immediately. He found me an eager student, and certainly he was the thwarted professor. He found a room for me in the flat of an old German lady and I was enrolled in what he called the "Ezuversity." No tuition.

The Ezuversity instruction was mostly a monologue about the mail he'd received that morning. His mornings were devoted to his cor-

---

Frost is thinking of a poet named John Helston, author of "Aphrodite at Leatherhead," which took up fourteen pages of The English Review *for March 1913. Frost's recollection gives a special flavor, if one is needed, to the note appended to the poem by the editors of the magazine: "Without presuming to 'present' Mr. Helston after the manner of fashionable actors, we think it will interest the public to know that he was for years a working mechanic—turner, fitter, etc.—in electrical, locomotive, motor-car, and other workshops."*

respondence. He used to say that postage was his highest living expense. Then we'd have lunch in the dining room of the Albergo Rapallo, and then after the snooze he'd take, we would go swimming or play tennis. One of the wonderful things about those monologues was his mimetic ability. He could imitate Joyce, how he talked, or how Yeats talked. His stories were endless, and very funny, and what I remember about them—over all those years—was that I never heard him tell an off-color story.

Oh, you could never predict what he was going to do—even from the very first. I remember that one summer we drove up to Salzburg— Ezra, Olga Rudge, and my Harvard classmate John Slocum— to the *Festspielhaus,* where Toscanini was conducting Beethoven's *Fidelio.* Ezra didn't think much of Beethoven. After about twenty minutes into the opera, Ezra rose up and said in a very clear voice, "No wonder! The man had syphilis!" He started out, and all of us, of course, felt we had to file out with him. Toscanini was absolutely unfazed. He continued to conduct. —*James Laughlin*

I was staying with friends in Washington, at Easter vacation, when I went over to see Pound. He received me in this open ward, with people wandering around, flushing imaginary toilets. He sat in a deep chair and held forth. I was eighteen—I didn't have much to say to Pound—and he told me all about how, when the Hundredth Canto was finished, the whole thing was all going to fall into place and so on. It would be like putting the keystone in the arch, or the lintel on the doorposts. He was also wonderfully generous and wrote me post cards afterwards. "Read seeds, not twigs E.P.," he wrote. And he gave me a bit of advice about translating, about taking translating seriously as a kind of practice, about learning languages and trying to get as close as possible to the sense and the form of the original. I didn't know what he meant about a lot of those things until I had been practicing for a while, until I had been trying to do it.

—*W. S. Merwin*

MARCEL PROUST

Marcel combatted those things in his own way. He would circle among his victims collecting his "black honey," his *miel noir,* and then he wrote, "I beg of you, Jean, since you live in the rue d'Anjou in the same building with Mme. de Chevigné, of whom I've made the Duchess de Guermantes; I entreat you to get her to read my book. She won't read me; and she says she stubs her foot in my sentences. I beg you—" I told him that was as if he asked an ant to read Fabre. You don't ask an insect to read entomology.   —*Jean Cocteau*

GERTRUDE STEIN

Miss Stein arrived in America and said that there were two people that she wanted to meet. They were both in California at that minute—Chaplin and Dash [Dashiell Hammett]. And we were invited to dinner at the house of a friend of Miss Stein; Charlie Chaplin, Dash and myself, Paulette Goddard, Miss Toklas, our host and hostess and another man. There was this magnificent china and lace tablecloth. Chaplin turned over his coffee cup, nowhere near Stein, just all over this beautiful cloth, and the first thing Miss Stein said was, "Don't worry, it didn't get on me." She was miles away from him. She said it perfectly seriously. Then she told Dash he was the only American writer who wrote well about women. He was very pleased.
        —*Lillian Hellman*

She was going on her famous lecture tour through America, and somebody had suggested that in each city where she was scheduled she should hand out a press release explaining what she was going to be talking about. That was my job—to take these lectures and produce a one-page presentation for each. It was not easy at all. The *Lectures in America* are philosophical and dense. To try to identify their central themes and translate them from Steinese into American news-paperese was quite a task. I would try, carrying my attempts to her, and she would say, "No, no, you've missed the entire point. Go back and try again." That's why I stayed there a month. It took me that long to get these releases done to her satisfaction. The two of us sat out on the terrace in the mornings, working. Then in the afternoon we'd tour the countryside in her little Ford with Gertrude, who drove, sitting in the front seat with Alice B. Toklas, while I sat in the back with those two awful dogs—Basket, who was a white poodle, and Pepe, who was a nasty little black Mexican nipper. Trying to control the pair of them back there, I saw very little of the Savoie countryside. That part of the Savoie is a favorite place for hikers. They'd lose nails out of their hiking boots, and almost invariably the little Ford's tires would get a puncture. Gertrude would pull off to the side of the road and she and Alice B. Toklas would take out their picnic things from the car and find a nice cozy spot to overlook it all. They'd sit and chat and eat while I would change the tire, harassed, as you can imagine, by Basket and Pepe.

Gertrude had great natural charm, tremendous charisma. Marvelous head. Those wonderful flashing eyes. A deep, firm voice. So I couldn't help but be very much impressed by her at times, except that often she'd erupt with crazy ideas. She thought Hitler was a great man . . . this *before* the war, of course, but how a Jewess could be attracted to such a notion at *any* time is difficult to understand. She was certainly a woman of strong opinions—indeed to the point of megalomania. She felt she had influenced everyone. We had a big fight one day when I mentioned I was reading Proust. She said, "How can you read junk like that? Don't you know, J., that Proust and Joyce both copied their work from *The Making of Americans?*" She finally cooled on me. I simply didn't accept everything she said. That was disrespectful.

• • •

You know how Gertrude and Bill [Williams] broke up? One evening at her place in Paris she took out a big stack of her manuscripts and asked Bill what to do with them. Bill replied in his "Billyums" way, "I'd pick out the best one and throw the rest away." This was an impossible thing to tell Gertrude, who believed her every word was Great Art. Alice B. Toklas showed the Williamses to the door.

—*James Laughlin*

IGOR STRAVINSKY

I always think of Stravinsky in a very physical way. He was physically adorable; he was cuddly—he was so little, and you wanted to protect him. He was very demonstrative, a person who—I suppose it was his Russianness—was full of kisses and embraces. He had great warmth. He could be fearfully hostile and snub people and attack his critics and so forth, but personally, he was a person of immense joy and warmth. The first time I came to his house, he said to me: "Would you like to hear my Mass before we get drunk?" He was always saying things like that. He seemed to me to have a wonderful appreciation for all the arts. He spoke English fluently, but it astonished me what an appreciation he had of writing in the English language, although he was really more at home in German or French—after Russian. When I was seeing a great deal of him, I was usually drinking a great deal, too, because he had these wonderful drinks. I recall a fatal, beautiful liquid called Marc—Marc de Bourgogne—made out of grape pits, colorless but powerful beyond belief. I used to think to myself, Goddamit, I'm drunk again, and here's Igor saying these marvelous things, and I won't remember one of them in the morning. When I think of those days, I really seem to have behaved very oddly. I remember once I'd actually passed out on the floor, and, looking up, I saw at an immense altitude above me, Aldous Huxley, who was very tall, standing up and talking French to Stravinsky, who never seemed to get overcome, however much he drank. And Aldous, who I think was very fond of me, was looking at me rather curiously, as much as to say, "Aren't you going a little far?" It's not like me to behave like that, or so I imagine. Perhaps it is. But I suddenly realized how relaxed I felt, how completely at home.

It didn't matter if I blotted my copy book. The Stravinskys projected the most astonishing coziness. Because Vera Stravinsky was a part of it, she had enormous charm and style, and she's very amusing. Going out with them was always an experience. We drove up once to the sequoia forest, and I remember Stravinsky, so tiny, looking up at this enormous giant sequoia and standing there for a long time in meditation and then turning to me and saying: "That's serious."

—*Christopher Isherwood*

DYLAN THOMAS

It was difficult, because he always wanted to drink. I went on one bender with him in London which lasted for two days and three nights. We ended up sleeping on the floor of some lady's apartment and neither of us knew who she was. He always wanted to drink, but I'm not such a great drinker. When he came to New York he'd come in the office at ten o'clock in the morning and say, "Let's go to the White Horse Tavern." I'd say, "Dylan, I've got work to do." So he'd go off to the White Horse and meet various cronies and sycophants. Sometimes I'd join him late in the evening. He was a sad case, Dylan; he was basically a nice person, and when he started boozing he was very amusing, but he would never stop; he'd go on and on. It's very hard to get close to a drinker. There was always that thing between us, the boozing. He was a great talker, too; he was a wonderful talker, but I had work to do. When Dylan drank he wanted people to be with him, to listen to him. It was a method of attracting people. But he was very indiscriminate about whom he would attract. He had a bunch of hangers-on in New York, such as that jerk Oscar Williams, who were crumbs. That was a barrier, because he'd be with such crummy characters. You couldn't really have a conversation with Dylan when he was drinking. It wore me down. John Davenport had a good name for Dylan. He called him "Old Messy." He was. He was messy because of the drinking. You couldn't count on him. If you wanted to do something you couldn't count on his turning up sober or on time.   —*James Laughlin*

VIRGINIA WOOLF

I had left my first book of poems at her door, with some flowers, and the darling maid opened the door just then and said, "Oh, won't you come up?" I said, "Oh, no, I wouldn't think of it." I just left the book.

Elizabeth Bowen knew that I wanted to meet Virginia Woolf desperately, so she invited the two of us and a couple of other people to dinner. That was when I first met her. She walked in, in a "robe de style," a lovely, rather eighteenth-century-looking, long dress with a wide collar, and she came into the room like a dazzled deer and walked right across—this was a beautiful house on Regent's Park— to the long windows and stood there looking out. My memory is that she was not even introduced at that point, that she just walked across, very shyly, and stood there looking absolutely beautiful. She was much more beautiful than any of the photographs show. And then she discovered that I was the person who had left the poems.

She was very canny . . . she answered my gift of that book with a lovely note, which is now in the Berg collection, just saying: "Thank you so much, and the flowers came just as someone had given me a vase, and were perfect, and I shall look forward to reading the poems." In other words, never put yourself in a position of having to judge. So she never said a word about the poems. But she was delighted to find out that I was the person who had left them.

Then, later, we talked—Elizabeth and Virginia Woolf and I. The gentlemen were having their brandy and cigars in the other room. We talked about hairdressers. It was like something in *The Waves*! We all talked like characters in a Virginia Woolf novel. She had a great sense of humor. Very malicious. She liked to tease people, in a charming way, but she was a great tease.

But she put me at ease and I saw her quite often after that. Every time I was in England I would have tea with her, which was a two-hour talk. She would absolutely ply me with questions. That was the novelist. I always felt the novelist at work. Where did I buy my clothes? Whom was I seeing? Whom was I in love with? Everything. So it was enrapturing to a young woman to be that *interesting* to Virginia Woolf. But I think it was her way of living, in a sense. Vicariously. Through people.

She was never warm. That's true. There was no warmth. It was partly physical, I think. She was a physically unwarm person. I can't imagine kissing her, for instance, I mean on the cheek. But she was delightful, and zany, full of humor and laughter. Never did you feel a person on the brink of madness. That has distorted the image, because she was so in control.   —*May Sarton*

W. B. YEATS

I remember the taxi ride over. The taxi was left over from the First World War, and when we arrived in Pall Mall—we could see the Atheneum—the driver said he didn't feel he could get in. Finally I decided to abandon ship and take off on my own. So I went in and asked for Mr. Yeats. Very much like asking, "Is Mr. Ben Jonson here?" And he came down. He was much taller than I expected, and haggard. Big, though, big head, rather wonderful looking in a sort of a blunt, patrician kind of way, but there was something shrunken also. He told me he was just recovering from an illness. He was very courteous, and we went in to tea. At a certain point, I had a cigarette, and I asked him if he would like one. To my great surprise he said yes. So I gave him a Craven-A and then lit it for him, and I thought, Immortality is mine! From now on it's just a question of reaping the fruits of my effort. He did most of the talking. I asked him a few questions. He did not ask me any questions about myself, although he was extremely courteous and very kind. At one point he said, "I have reached the age when my daughter can beat me at croquet," and I thought, Hurrah, he's human! I made notes of the interview afterwards, which I have probably lost. One comment in particular I remember. He said, "I never revise now"—you know how much he revised his stuff—"but in the interest of a more passionate syntax." Now that struck me as a very good remark. I have no idea what it meant and still don't know, but the longer I think about it, the better I like it.

—*John Berryman*

• • •

Mostly reading aloud to him. Doughty's *Dawn in Britain,* and so on. And wrangling, you see. The Irish like contradiction. He tried to learn fencing at forty-five, which was amusing. He would thrash around with the foils like a whale. He sometimes gave the impression of being even a worse idiot than I am.

—*Ezra Pound*

I met Yeats, I think probably in 1935 or 1936, at Lady Ottoline Morrell's. Ottoline asked me to tea alone with Yeats. He was very blind and—I don't know whether he was deaf, but he was very sort of remote, he seemed tremendously old. He was only about the age I am now, but he seemed tremendously old and remote. He looked at me and then he said, "Young man, what do you think of the Sayers?" I hadn't the faintest idea what he was talking about—I thought perhaps he meant Dorothy Sayers' crime stories or something—I became flustered. What he meant was a group of young ladies who chanted poems in chorus. Ottoline got very alarmed and rushed out of the room and telephoned to Virginia Woolf, who was just around the corner, and asked her to come save the situation. Virginia arrived in about ten minutes' time, tremendously amused, and Yeats was very pleased to meet her because he'd just been reading *The Waves.* He also read quite a lot of science—I think he read Eddington and Rutherford and all those kinds of things—and so he told her that *The Waves* was a marvelous novel, that it was entirely up to date in scientific theory because light moved in waves, and time, and so on. Of course Virginia, who hadn't thought of all this, was terribly pleased and flattered. And then I remember he started telling her a story in which he said, "And as I went down the stairs there was a marble statue of a baby and it started talking in Greek to me"—that sort of thing. Virginia adored it all of course . . . I remember his telling the story of his trip to Rapallo to show the manuscript of *The Tower* to Ezra Pound. He stayed at the hotel and then went around and left the manuscript in a packet for Pound, accompanied by a letter saying I am an old man, this may be the last poetry I'll ever write, it is very different from my other work—all that kind of thing—and what do you think of it? Next day he received a post card from Ezra Pound with on it the one word "putrid." Yeats was rather amused by that. Apparently Pound had a tremendous collection of cats, and Yeats used to say that Pound couldn't possibly be a nasty man because he fed all the cats of Rapallo. I once asked him how he came to be a modern poet, and he told me that it took him thirty years to modernize his style. He said he didn't really like the modern poetry of Eliot and Pound. He thought it was static, that it didn't have any movement, and for him poetry had always to have the romantic movement. He said, "For me poetry always means 'For we'll go no more a-roving / By the light o' the moon.'" So the problem was how to keep the movement of the Byron lines but at the same time enlarge it so that it could include the kind of material that he was interested in, which was to do with everyday life— politics, quarrels between people, sexual love, and not just the frustrated love he had with Maud Gonne.   —*Stephen Spender*

He wasn't a bit impressive and he wasn't my sort of person at all. He boomed at you like a foghorn. He was there one time when Philip Guedella and two or three of us were all very young and were talking nonsense about murderers in Shakespeare and whether a third murderer ever became a first murderer by working hard or were they, sort of, hereditary slots? Were they like Japanese specialists and one did one kind of murder, another did another? It was really awfully funny. Philip was very funny to be with. Then we started talking about something on the Western Isles but Yeats wouldn't join in, until we fussed round and were nice to him. But we were all wrong; what he liked was solemnity and, if you were big enough, heavy enough and strong enough, he loved you. He loved great big women. He would have been mad about Vanessa Redgrave.

—*Rebecca West*

ON THE FUTURE

Light tomorrow with today.   —*Elizabeth Barrett Browning*

It is a mistake to think that books have come to stay. The human race did without them for thousands of years and may decide to do without them again.   —*E. M. Forster*

I have a tiny little secret hope that, after a decent period of silence and prose, I will find myself in some almost impossible life situation and will respond to this with outcries of rage, rage and love, such as the world has never heard before. Like Yeats's great outburst at the end of his life. This comes out of a feeling that endowment is a very small part of achievement. I would rate it about fifteen or twenty percent. Then you have historical luck, personal luck, health, things like that, then you have hard work, sweat. And you have ambition. The incredible difference between the achievement of A and the achievement of B is that B *wanted* it, so he made all kinds of sacrifices. A could have had it, but he didn't give a damn. The idea that everybody wants to be President of the United States or have a million dollars is simply not the case. Most people want to go down to the corner and have a glass of beer. They're very happy. In *Henderson the Rain King,* the hero keeps on saying, "I want. I want." Well, I'm that kind of character. I don't know whether that is exhausted in me or not. I can't tell.

But what I was going on to say is that I do strongly feel that among the greatest pieces of luck for high achievement is ordeal. Certain great artists can make out without it, Titian and others, but mostly you need ordeal. My idea is this: The artist is extremely lucky who is presented with the worst possible ordeal which will not actually kill him. At that point, he's in business. Beethoven's deafness, Goya's

351

deafness, Milton's blindness, that kind of thing. And I think that what happens in my poetic work in the future will probably largely depend not on my sitting calmly on my ass as I think, "Hmm, hmm, a long poem again? Hmm," but on being knocked in the face, and thrown flat, and given cancer, and all kinds of other things short of senile dementia. At that point, I'm out, but short of that, I don't know. I hope to be nearly crucified. I'm scared, but I'm willing. I'm sure this is a preposterous attitude, but I'm not ashamed of it.*

—*John Berryman*

I think that words are an around-the-world, ox-cart way of doing things, awkward instruments, and they will be laid aside eventually, probably sooner than we think.　　　　　　—*William Burroughs*

I was talking a few months ago in Mexico with one of the great film makers of our time, Luis Buñuel. He was eighty years old, and I was asking how he looked back on his career and on the destiny of the film. He said, "I think films are perishable, because they depend too much on technology, which advances too quickly and the films become old-fashioned, antiques. What I hope for is that technology advances to the point that films in the future will depend on a little pill which you take; then you sit in the dark, and from your eyes you project the film you want to see on a blank wall."　　　　—*Carlos Fuentes*

I realize from time to time that certain poems were written for the wrong reasons, and feel obliged to remove them; they give me a sick feeling. Only the few necessary poems should be kept. There's no mystery about them: if one is a poet, one eventually learns which they are. Though of course a perfect poem is impossible. Once it had been written, the world would end.　　　　　—*Robert Graves*

Reading novels—serious novels, anyhow—is an experience limited to a very small percentage of the so-called enlightened public. In-

*Delusion.—J. B., March 1971

creasingly, it's going to be a pursuit for those who seek unusual experiences, moral fetishists perhaps, people of heightened imagination, the troubled pursuers of the ambiguous self.

Today, people are absorbed in the most common denominator, the *visual*. It requires no education to watch TV. It knows no age limit. Your infant child can watch the same program you do. Witness its role in the homes of the old and incurably sick. Television is everywhere. It has the immediacy which the evocative medium of language doesn't. Language requires some inner triggering; television doesn't. The image is ultimately accessible, i.e., extremely attractive. And, I think, ultimately deadly, because it turns the viewer into a bystander. Of course, that's a situation we have always dreamt of . . . the ultimate hope of religion was that it would release us from trauma. Television actually does so. It "proves" that you can always be an observer of the tragedies of others. The fact that one day you will die in front of the live show is irrelevant— you are reminded about it no more than you are reminded about real weather existing outside the TV weather program. You're not told to open your window and take a look; television will never say that. It says, instead, "The weather today is . . ." and so forth. The weatherman never says, "If you don't believe me, go find out."

From way back, our major development as a race of frightened beings has been towards how to avoid facing the discomfort of our existence, primarily the possibility of an accident, immediate death, ugliness, and the ultimate departure. In terms of all this, television is a very pleasing medium: one is always the observer. The life of discomfort is always accorded to others, and even *this* is disqualified, since one program immediately disqualifies the preceding one. Literature does not have this ability to soothe. You have to evoke, and by evoking, you yourself have to provide your own inner setting. When you read about a man who dies, part of you dies with him because you have to recreate his dying inside your head.

—*Jerzy Kosinski*

People have been saying the novel is dead for as far back as I can remember. The novel will never die, but it will keep changing and evolving and taking different shapes. Storytelling, which is the basis of the novel, has always existed and always will. Nowadays, there are too many books and not enough good ones. Something will have to happen, but I don't think it will come from Britain or America. Things have gone too far in sophisticated countries; the intensity of emotion, the moral conflicts, all that was the basis of great novels has gone. The change will come from somewhere quite unexpected. But it will happen—human beings have infinite resources of renewal.

—*Rosamond Lehmann*

I'm not saying it [the novel] will disappear, just entertaining the idea. Assume it does; then someday a talented writer writes himself a long heartfelt letter and the form reappears. The human race needs the novel. We need all the experience we can get. Those who say the novel is dead can't write them. —*Bernard Malamud*

Even the great characters that have survived in novels are found now more in handbooks and histories, as though in a museum. As living creatures they get worn out, and they grow feeble. Sometimes we even see them die. Madame Bovary seems to me to be in poorer health than she used to be. . . . Yes, and even Anna Karenina, even the Karamazovs. First, because they need readers in order to live and the new generations are less and less capable of providing them with the air they need to breathe. —*François Mauriac*

These are more careless times. Literature is no longer sacred, it is a business. There is an invisible umbilical cord between the writer and his potential reader, and I fear that the time has gone when readers could sink into a book the way they did in the past, for the *pace* of life is fast and frenetic. The world is cynical: the dwelling on emotions, the perfection of style, the intensity of a Flaubert is wasted on modern sensibility. I have a feeling that there is a *dying,* if not a *death,* of great literature. Some blame the television for it. Perhaps. There is hardly any distinction between a writer and a journalist—indeed, most writers *are* journalists. Nothing wrong with journalism any more than with dentistry, but they are worlds apart! Whenever I read the English Sunday papers I notice that the standard of literacy is high—all very clever and hollow—but no dues to literature. They care about their own egos. They synopsize the book, tell the plot. Well, fuck the plot! That is for precocious schoolboys. What matters is the imaginative *truth,* and the perfection and care with which it has been rendered. After all, you don't say of a ballet dancer, "He jumped in the air, then he twirled around, etc. . . ." You are just *carried away* by his dancing. The nicest readers are—and I know by the letters I receive—youngish people who are still eager and un-contaminated, who approach a book without hostility. But when I read Anita Brookner's novel *Look at Me,* I feel I am in the grip of a most wonderful, imaginative writer. The same is true of Margaret Atwood. Also, great literature is dying because young people, although they don't talk about it much, feel and fear a holocaust.

• • •

As you know, the future itself is perilous. But as regards books, there is first the financial aspect of publishing. Already books are very expensive, so that a first novel of quality will have less of a chance of being picked up. Say a new Djuna Barnes, or indeed Nathalie Sarraute, might not get published. If Woolf's *The Waves* were to be published today it would have pitiful sales. Of course, "how-to" books, spy stories, thrillers, and science-fiction all sell by the millions. What would be wonderful—what we *need* just now—is some astonishing fairy tale. I read somewhere the other day that the cavemen did not paint what they saw, but what they *wished* they had seen. We need that, in these lonely, lunatic times.   —*Edna O'Brien*

INDEX

Addison, Joseph, on humor, 219
Ade, George, on publication, 144
Aiken, Conrad: on Bodenheim, 324;
    on drugs and alcohol, 229; on
    Eliot, 325–26; on revising, 125;
    on typewriters, 176–77; on
    writing exercises, 48
Albee, Edward: on the creative pro-
    cess, 100–102; on critics, 157–
    158; on curtain lines, 167; on
    names, 170; on work habits, 49
alcohol, *see* artificial stimulants
Algren, Nelson: on his film-writing
    career, 248; on plot, 187; on
    style, 177
Allen, Fred, on films, 248
Allen, Hervey, 121
Amis, Kingsley: on admired writers,
    3; on alcohol, 229–30; on
    character, 194, 208; on dia-
    logue, 208; on humor, 219; on
    motivation, 28; on potboilers,
    259; on sex, 212; on work-
    shops, 311–12
Apollinaire, Guillaume, 52–53
Aristophanes, on humor, 219
artificial stimulants: Aiken on, 229;
    Amis on, 229–30; Auden on,

230; Ballard on, 230; Burroughs on, 230; Cocteau on,
230–31; Cowley on, 231; de la
Mare on, 63; Drabble on, 231;
Faulkner on, 56; García Márquez on, 231–32; Ginsberg on,
232; Graves on, 232; Heywood
on, 229; Huxley on, 232–33;
Irving on, 233; Johnson on,
229; Koestler on, 233–34;
Merrill on, 234; Stone on,
234–35; Thurber on, 229; Voznesensky on, 235; Wilder on,
66; T. Williams on, 66–67
Ashbery, John: on endings, 168; on
    revising, 125–26; on teaching,
    304–5
Auden, W. H., 40, 87; on the audi-
    ence, 90; on childhood favor-
    ites, 3–4; on Housman, 331; on
    indifference, 146; Larkin on,
    327; on LSD, 230; on noticing,
    37; on politics, 297–98; on
    readings, 291; Spender on, 162;
    on success, 144–45; on teach-
    ing, 305; on telephones, 48; on
    writing as occupation, 271; on
    writing reviews, 244

357

120; Steinbeck on, 169; Stoppard on, 169

Behan, Brendan, Donleavy on, 323–324

Bell, Clive, 73

Bellow, Saul, 38–39, 155; on the act of writing, vii; on the audience, 90–91; on being taken seriously, 90; on bestsellers, 145; Goyen on, 225; Kennedy on, 312–13; on writers, 323

Benchley, Robert, 97, 139, 253

Berryman, John: on fame, 145–46; on genius, 146–47; Levine on, 314; on ordeal, 351–52; on reviews, 146; on teaching, 307–8; on Yeats, 347–48

biography: Disraeli on, 239; Edel on, 71–72, 107, 239; Hardwick on, 239–40; Huxley on, 36; Sandburg on, 239; R. West on, 239

Bishop, Elizabeth: on being in a writer's colony, 272; on poetry readings, 291–92; on winning the Pulitzer Prize, 283

Blake, William, 87

Bodenheim, Maxwell, Aiken on, 324

Böll, Heinrich: on the audience, 91; on humor, 220; on names, 171; on plot, 187; on titles, 171; on writer's block, 224

Borges, Jorge Luis: on the audience, 91; on destroying one's work, 127–28; on encyclopedias, 4–5; on names, 171; on reading his own works, 91; on reviews,

244–45; on style, 177–79; on Twain, 178

Boswell, James, 94

Bowen, Elizabeth, 336, 346

Bowles, Paul: on meeting other writers, 272; on work habits, 50

Boyle, Kay, 54

Bradley, Wendell P., E. B. White on, 17–18

Brautigan, Richard, on endings, 167

Brodkey, Harold, Updike on, 267

Brodsky, Joseph, on the audience, 91

Brontë, Charlotte, 152

Brontë, Emily, 152–53

Brooke, Rupert, Spender on, 301

Browning, Elizabeth Barrett, 351

Buechner, Frederick, 116

Buñuel, Luis, 352

Bunyan, John, G. B. Shaw on, 178

Burgess, Anthony: on the anxiety of writing, 50; on the audience, 91; on sex, 212–13

Burroughs, William: on drugs and alcohol, 230; Kerouac on, 78; on words, 352

Burton, Robert: on humor, 219; on sex, 212

Butler, Samuel: Gaddis on, 285; on titles, 170

Byron, George Gordon, Lord, 167

Caldwell, Erskine: on character, 194; on Hollywood, 248; on quitting poetry, 135; on readers vs.

374
```

INDEX

151; Mailer on, 151; Mauriac

O'Brien on, 152–53, 355;

O'Connor on, 153; Ozick on,

153; I. Shaw on, 153–54, 289;

Steinbeck on, 227; Stoppard

Travers on, 155; Updike on,

155; West on, 155–56; E. B.

White on, 26–27

Puig, Manuel, McGuane on, 209

Rabelais, François, 304

Racine, Jean, Mauriac on, 152

Radiguet, Raymond, 145

Barth on, 4; Borges on, 4–5;

Caldwell on, 5; Capote on, 5;

Cendrars on, 5–6; Cheever on,

6; Cortázar on, 6; Davies on, 7;

Didion on, 7–8; Dos Passos on,

8; Edel on, 8–9; García Már-

Goyen on, 9–11; Green on, 11;

Hardwick on, 11; Hemingway

Johnson on, 3; Kosinski on,

352–53; Mailer on, 12–13; Mal-

Merrill on, 13–14; A. Miller

15; Porter on, 15–16; Steele

E. B. White on, 18; T. Wil-

291–92; Carroll on, 291; Cole-

Hardwick on, 292; Larkin on,

292–93; Laughlin on, 293;

Lessing on, 293–94; Moore on,

294; Neruda on, 294; Travers

Wilbur on, 295–96

Renard, Jules, on money, 282

125–26; Baldwin on, 126;

Borges on, 126–27; Capote on,

52; Carver on, 127; Cowley on,

231; Dos Passos on, 127; Dur-

Faulkner on, 72, 128; F. S.

Fitzgerald on, 128, 132; Forster

Hardwick on, 111; Horace on,

125; Irving on, 60; Isherwood

Japanese proverb on, 125;

Johnson on, 125; Jonson on,

125; Kennedy on, 129; Kosinski

Leish on, 115, 130; Malamud

Moore on, 130–31; O'Connor
```